The Hollow of His Hand

Pamela Goodrode Symonds

Pamela_goodrode@hotmail.com

PublishAmerica
Baltimore

ISBN: 1-4137-7974-3
PUBLISHED BY PUBLISHAMERICA, LLLP
www.publishamerica.com
Baltimore

Printed in the United States of America

The Hollow of His Hand

Pamela Symonds

11-08

Isaiah 40:12

Dedication

This book is dedicated
to three very important
people, whom I love
very much.
My Dad
Alfred Goodrode
who gave me the heart to dream.
My Mom
Anna Pearl Brown
who gave me the courage to dream.
My "sister" and very dear friend
Gwen Morgan
who helped give me a childhood
that dreams are made of.

Chapter One

Dear God,

I'm not exactly sure what happened tonight.

I didn't know what to expect when Margie invited me over to meet her friends from church. God, when I heard the happiness in their voices and saw the friendship they shared, I wanted so much to be a part of that, to have what they have. As You already know, Margie said I needed to accept Your Son into my life and then she prayed with me. Now I'm a Christian, Your child. Margie says You gave Your Son's life for me. I think about my son. God, would you check and see how he's doing?

Thank You. Amen.

Eddie slumped forward as the car thumped to a halt, his seat belt kept his head from resting on the dashboard. A low moan escaped his lips but he made no attempt to right himself. Windy Bilmon sat behind the wheel, a frown covering her oval, slightly freckled face. Wavy brown hair touched her shoulders and spattered across her forehead. Frown lines appeared on her brow.

"Eddie, Eddie wake up. I think we have a flat tire." Windy shook her husband, receiving a loud, odorous belch in response. "Oh, Eddie, please wake up." She shook him again and this time he answered her with a smack across her arm. "Shup..." he mumbled.

Windy turned off the car, pulled the key from the ignition and stepped into the soft moonlight that smiled on the first snow of the season. Her appreciation of the beauty quickly died as the bitter wind slapped her hair about her face. She checked first the front tire of the rusty brown compact, then the back and found the culprit. Last week she had mentioned that tire to Eddie.

"Yup, looks pretty bare," he had agreed. "Guess I better get it changed."

Now at 2 AM, miles from town, Windy stood in three inches of snow, with a passed-out husband and a flat tire.

"Could be worse, Windy," she said with all the positive thinking she could muster. "He could be awake and cussing.

As she walked to the rear of the car, her small frame hunched forward against the cold, Windy chided herself for forgetting her gloves.

"You won't need 'em, Babe. We'll either be in the car or in the store." Eddie had replied when she wanted to run back up to their apartment to get them. Now her cold fingers could hardly find the key she needed. She managed to open the trunk and locate the tire iron, jack and spare tire before jumping back into the car and restarting the engine. She placed her fingers under the dash soaking up the warmth of the heater. At least she could stay warm; she noted the gauge registered three quarters of a tank. Rummaging around on the floor Windy found one brown jersey glove under Eddie's feet, soaked from his wet boots. She placed it next to the heater and ventured out into the cold again.

The freezing air sapped her strength as it filled her lungs. She managed to wrestle the items she needed from the trunk and drop them to the ground before returning once more to warm her hands.

"It may be a slow process," she informed her sleeping husband, "but I guess we're not in a hurry to go anywhere, are we?" She turned the glove over. Looking at her husband, she shook her head and frowned. "Thanks for the lovely evening, Eddie."

In truth the evening had been enjoyable. Eddie usually worked six days a week and had always reserved Saturday evening for his wife. This afternoon Windy had Eddie's clean clothes waiting for him when he arrived home. She anticipated a night that started with 'dinner' at a fast food place then moved to the local mall. Windy loved Christmas shopping with her husband.

He was like a child in his enthusiasm to buy just the right thing for those on their Christmas list. Later, they rented a romantic movie to take home and finish their special evening.

How Windy wished they had gone straight home, but Eddie ran into a couple of his young buddies at the video shop. They wanted to have a party and promised Eddie 'a few' if he'd buy beer for them. He shrugged off Windy's reminder of what happened the last time he agreed. She could still hear the judge's warnings.

"That wasn't last time, Babe, that was just the last time we got caught," Eddie laughed.

They followed his young friends to a house in the country where his 'few' turned into many and Windy had to almost carry her husband to the car. With warm fingers Windy pulled her coat closer around her bare neck and slipped outside.

Using her feet, clad only in tennis shoes, she pushed the snow and gravel under the car into a level area then placed the car jack on the spot and attempted to lift it to the bumper. The freezing metal stuck to her fingers threatening to tear the skin from them.

Again she returned to the warmth of the car, checking the glove that remained damp. "Better'n nothing," she told the sleeping form in the passenger seat. Then she went back to her task.

Once Windy had the car far enough off the ground to take the weight of the tire she again warmed herself then quickly returned to her chore. Locating the lug nuts in the moonlight, Windy found herself grateful that Eddie had not gotten around to putting the hub caps back on the wheels. For several minutes she tried to loosen the tire but found the lug nuts weren't about to budge. She pulled and twisted, kicked and even jumped on the tire iron to no avail.

Back in the car Windy studied her husband's face. His dark complexion and black wavy hair had initially drawn Windy to him. She remembered the tears that fell from those deep, dark, puppy dog eyes when she told him her dad had found work on the east coast.

After dating Eddie all through her senior year Windy knew she wanted to marry him. Two years older than she, he had quit school shortly after his 16th birthday and quickly became an established mechanic with a large equipment company. His straight jaw reflected the determination in his character that resulted in the young girl repeating wedding vows as soon as she finished high school.

Her parents liked Eddie, but never quite approved of him for a son-in-law.

"He's a nice boy, Windy," her mother had said. "But his family is...well, you could do so much better."

Windy, the complacent child, finally rebelled. "I don't believe in one person being better than another. It's wrong to put people in classes."

Dad allowed the marriage but never tried to disguise his disappointment. He hated to see his little girl give up her scholarship to the fine university they'd chosen out east. Windy could still see clearly the concern in her dad's eyes as he and her mom drove away, heading for their new life, while Windy began hers. His words were just as clear, 'if you change your mind I'll come back for you at a moment's notice, anytime.'

Windy and Eddie shared a year of wonder and bliss. His youthfulness and love for life shone in everything he did. Windy found being a wife took little effort. She need only be there to enjoy her husband. They laughed and played and loved.

Returning to the cold, Windy searched the trunk of the car for anything that might help loosen the tire. She found an empty can of WD-40. As she threw the can back into the trunk she wondered if she could swallow her pride and go east to her parents. Did she really want to give up on her marriage without first giving it every effort she had?

Again she tried her might against the lug nuts only to lose her balance and fall into the cold snow. About to give up, Windy heard a car engine. A short distance in front of her, car lights pulled onto the road and headed away.

She quickly searched the darkness to see where the car had come from and saw a lighted house. Thinking if she got there in time someone who could help her might still be awake, Windy quickly set off across the field to the beckoning lights.

Walking through the snow, she remembered the discussion she and Eddie had about buying winter boots. He said it wasn't practical to buy her boots when she never went out into the snow. So by not buying her any they could spend more money on his and get good ones that would keep him warm in the huge cold garage or out on runs with the wrecker. Windy couldn't deny his logic, but right now she certainly envied his boots.

Windy recalled when Eddie used to put her first, when he thought of her needs before his. Was that so long ago? Last winter she didn't have boots, but neither did he. Last winter Eddie wore broken shoes so she could have this warm coat. Last year things were different. Last spring things were different. When they celebrated their first anniversary in June, Eddie used what little he had saved to buy her the small diamond ring he couldn't afford the year before.

When had it all changed? What had she done to lose the man she loved so much?

The yard around the lighted house was strewn with snow covered motorcycle pieces. Windy recognized tires, handlebars, several gas tanks, and what appeared to be a couple engines. An outside workbench sprouted an assortment of rusty tools.

Windy stepped to the door and hesitated, not accustomed to asking a stranger for assistance in the wee hours of the morning. She debated returning to the car and trying the tire again. Maybe Eddie would wake up if she persisted. The thought of Eddie trying to change a tire in his drunken state was enough to make Windy tap on the stranger's door. She heard a muffled voice and a moment later the door opened. The dim lights behind the form in front of her revealed several people, most of them sitting on the floor. The air exploded with hard rock music and Windy smelled the too familiar odor of beer.

"Hey.," the word came long and drawn out, a bearded face surrounded by long unruly hair bobbed slightly in front of her.

"Can you…" Windy's eyes, adjusting to the different light, settled on the man and she suddenly realized he wore only his beard.

"Uh…" Windy exhaled, her mind racing. How could she possibly ask a naked man to help her change a tire? He'd freeze! Should she ask to use a telephone? Did she dare step inside this room? If she did, who would she call? "Uh…" she repeated locking her eyes on the door frame.

"Hey…you gotta be cold…c'mon in…join the party."

The bizarre scene shook the young woman who still blushed at the sight of her husband's flesh. Reason flew from her mind and fear quickly made its bid for power.

"No. Thank you." She tried to find a reason to decline the invitation. After all, she was the one who knocked on this man's door. "My husband," She motioned over her shoulder. "He's calling me. Must have it fixed. Thanks anyway, bye!" Windy turned and ran for the car. "I'm coming, Honey," she called for the benefit of the bearded stranger.

The girl's heart pounded in her chest. She felt blood rushing through her veins, feeding her fear and giving her energy to run. Her lungs felt as though they would burst from the cold air she forced into them.

The powdery snow wasn't deep enough to hinder her flight but her frozen feet sent a shock of pain up her legs each time they hit the hard ground.

Finally, Windy reached the car and jumped inside. She revved the engine and a moment later turned off her lights hoping to give the impression that she had pulled away.

She placed her frozen feet under the dash, shaking violently with cold and fear. As warmth returned to her body, reason returned to her thoughts and she laughed at herself.

"This is one night I won't easily forget," she told her sleeping husband. "Are you still in there?" Windy reached over and placed a shivering hand next to Eddie's face, feeling his breath on her fingers. "Yup, I guess so. Well, now what, my hero? If you wake up in this car in the morning, I'll never hear the end of it. Tell you what, Eddie, you rest, don't trouble yourself. I'm just gonna thaw my feet and then I'll go back out in the cold and change that tire. Okay with you?"

The sleeping form grunted at the voice that threatened his rest. Windy leaned her head back against the seat and closed her eyes, promising herself a little luxury before returning to her task.

Chapter Two

Dear God, I don't know you very well yet, but I understand You've known me for a long time. I'm new at this prayer business and I'm going to need a lot of help, but Margie tells me I should pray to You everyday. Thank You for sending Your Son to die for me. Speaking of sons, will You be with mine? If he doesn't know You lead him and his family to You. Please. Amen

"Don't expect this much excitement everyday," Officer Joe Kozininski warned his cub. "I've been on the force for 15 years and I've participated in three of these chases."

They had attempted to make a stop inside the city limits, when the driver refused to pull over and headed out into the county. Joe radioed the station who then alerted the State Police. Joe stayed with the offending car even after the boys in blue took over, making certain back up was available if needed. Once the car had been pulled over and everything was under control, Joe headed back towards the city.

Rick Notts looked in awe at his senior partner who sat behind the wheel. They met just hours ago and already Rick knew this man would influence his life greatly. Joe's short brown hair was streaked at the temples. His square face held slightly wrinkled eyes and a nose that Rick's dad would have described as a 'Roman nose'.

Although Joe stood not much taller than Rick's own five feet seven inches, Rick had been surprised at the amount of muscle Joe possessed and the ease with which he used it.

"Chief said you just got out of the service. Which branch?" Joe asked.

"Army, for three years," Rick replied. "Dad advised me to go in. He said I could practically get my police training there."

"So you were an MP."

"No, that's what they promised. I wound up in supply. But when my time was about up they offered some courses in various civilian work. I took law enforcement."

"You intend to stay on a city force, or is school in your future?"

"School. I admit I'd like to work for the state. Better benefits, you know, and a chance to move around, maybe find an area I like better. We always took our vacations up north. I like it there. You ever consider working for the state?"

"Too old now. I thought about it years ago, but my wife didn't like the idea of being moved around. She was especially afraid of being sent to the 'waste lands' of the Upper Peninsula. She wanted to stay here, in civilization. Then she decided she didn't have what it took to be a cop's wife, whatever that is. You remember that when you start looking. Make sure the girl you pick knows what she's getting into."

"I don't have to worry about that for a long time," Rick smiled, shaking his head. "At least four years of college, money in the bank and maybe even my own place."

"Dream on, son. That's what we all say. Things never happen according to plan."

"Maybe not, but I don't see it any other way. I'm old fashioned enough to believe a man should provide for his family. I don't want to start what I can't care for."

"Ho! What do we have here?" Joe slowed down at the sight of a car parked beside the road. He noted the jack lifting the car up and the exhaust still coming from the tailpipe. "They should have their lights on. Not too bright, these people." He eased the patrol car to a stop behind the still vehicle. "Grab your flashlight, Rick, and check out the passenger side."

In one swift movement Joe had his hat on, his coat zipped and stood outside the car while Rick fumbled with his own hat.

Joe waited until his partner emerged and together they walked toward the car. Their lights revealed two sleeping figures inside. Joe tapped lightly on the driver's window, trying to awaken the woman, neither occupant stirred and he tapped again. When the third tap proved fruitless he tried the door which opened with a creak.

The startled woman grabbed the door handle and tried to pull it closed again. She was no match for Officer Joe Kozininski. When she couldn't close the door, she swung her arm out in defense.

"Get out of here! Go away!" She yelled.

"Miss, settle down," Joe gripped her arm avoiding what could have been a sound hit. "We're police officers; we're here to help you."

"Police?" She repeated, trying to see around his glaring flashlight.

"Yes," Joe turned the offending light away. "Just sit back and take it easy." When the woman relaxed he continued. "You appear to have tire problems. Do you need help?" She nodded. "Are either of you hurt?" He glanced at her passenger who hadn't moved in all the commotion.

"No," she shook her head. "The tire just went flat."

"That your husband?"

"Yes," she whispered.

"What's wrong with him?"

"He's a heavy sleeper?" She ducked her head and looked at the officer, eyes questioning.

"Yeah." Joe replied with understanding. He studied the man, visible in the glow from Rick's flashlight, then stood. "Rick, you want to see what you can do with that tire?"

"Sure." Rick slid his light into his belt and turned his attention to the rear of the car.

"The lug nuts are too tight, I couldn't get them off," the woman explained.

"Would you step out of the car, please?"

She complied, closing the door quietly behind her.

"Have you been drinking, ma'am?"

"No sir, I don't drink."

"Where are you headed?"

"Home, town."

"At a party were you?"

15

"If you want to call it that."

"May I see your driver's license, please?"

"It's in my purse," she hesitated. "In the car."

"Would you get it, please?" Noting her reluctance he added, "I really don't think he'll wake up."

"No, I guess he won't."

Windy carefully opened the door. She certainly didn't want Eddie to wake up now. He'd be angry at her for not getting the tire changed, even angrier that the police had stopped. She pulled her purse from between the bucket seats and quickly closed the door.

It took a few minutes to make her cold fingers pull the license from its plastic envelope.

"Windy Bilmon," the officer read. "Bilmon…I know that name. What's your husband's first name?"

"Eddie."

"Eddie Bil…Eddie Ray Bilmon," he nodded in recognition. "Do you have your registration and proof of insurance?"

"In the glove compartment," Windy answered.

The officer shined his light into the car. Eddie's knees rested against the dash. Windy wouldn't be able to open the compartment without disturbing him.

"I believe you," the officer said. "You can get back in the car; we'll have the tire changed in a few minutes."

He handed Windy her license and watched as she returned to her seat and closed the door.

She glanced in her rear view mirror, looking to see if the other officer had made any progress with the lug nuts. She felt the car slowly sink to the ground. The trunk being closed rocked the car slightly and a moment later the other officer appeared at her window.

"Did you give up already? I can help if you like…"

"It's finished, Ma'am, the tire is changed. Be sure to get that one fixed, you don't want to be without a spare."

Windy nodded. "Thank you," she said before rolling the window back up. She wondered how long she'd been sleeping. Curious, she glanced at the house across the field, light still shone through the windows. A shiver ran down her spine, thankful that she'd be out of here in a few minutes.

Then her eyes caught movement on the passenger side of the car and she saw Eddie's door opening.

The first officer looked in. "I'm sorry, Mrs. Bilmon, but we'll have to take Eddie with us."

"Because he's drunk?" Windy asked in disbelief.

"No, because we have a bench warrant on him."

"A what?"

"It appears he didn't show up for his last court date. Eddie," he addressed the sleeping form. "Eddie, wake up. This is Officer Kozininski, Eddie. You have to come with us."

"He went to court," Windy informed the officer. "I went with him."

"Last week?"

"No…no, more like a month ago."

"Well, he had another date last week that he missed. We have to take him to jail tonight. You can either bail him out in the morning or wait until the arraignment on Monday."

"He works on Monday."

"Then you'll probably want to get him tomorrow. He'll be housed at the city jail. Eddie, wake up." The officer shook him gently, patted one cheek, then the other.

"Shup…" Eddie stirred.

"C'mon, Eddie…"

"Shu up!!" Eddie declared, pushing the officer's hand away. "Stop it, Windy."

"It's Officer Kozininski. Eddie, you have to come with me." After a short scuffle, the two officers managed to handcuff Eddie and maneuver him into their back seat. The officer told Windy they would follow her home to be sure she made it. Now as she pulled into her driveway and watched the police car continue past, she thought ahead to morning when she would have to bail Eddie out of jail. Their check book held just enough money for the rent and a few groceries. They had depleted what was left of their savings when Eddie started drinking. Windy sighed as she turned off the ignition and pulled her tired body from the car. She would worry about that tomorrow, for now she just wanted her warm bed and a couple hours of sleep.

Chapter Three

Dear God, I've had a very discouraging week. I know I Should pray everyday like Margie said. Sometimes I forget, sometimes I just don't take the time. I'm sorry, Margie also says You forgive, please forgive me, help me to pray more And please be with my son, and whoever You've chosen for him. Encourage them both. Speak to them the way You spoke to me. Thank You. Amen.

"Open this door, boy!" Banging fists and a demanding voice jarred Eddie out of a sound sleep. He opened an eye and peered into the darkness at the clock which assured him he still had an hour before he needed to rise. Sachel, Windy's black cat, who lay at her feet, lifted his head and laid his ears back.

"Eddie Ray, open this door!" came the voice again.

'*No*,' thought Eddie as he recognized the voice. '*NO, NO, NO! Not him*', he silently pleaded. Eddie thought he had heard that voice for the last time more than five years ago. Now it bellowed at his front door insisting it be allowed back into Eddie's life.

"Who is it, Hon?" Windy peeked out from under the sheet. The street light shone softly on her innocent face. Eddie frowned at his wife. He didn't want to subject her to this tyrant who ruled his childhood and haunted his dreams.

"I think it's my ole man," he answered. "Go back to sleep, I'll try to get rid of him."

"Your dad? I thought he lived out west somewhere?"

"Iowa."

Windy nodded, "Well, that's west of here."

Eddie shook his head, indicating he hadn't heard her comment over the pounding on the door. He slid from beneath the covers and retrieved his jeans from the floor as Sachel disappeared under the bed.

Eddie's stomach churned as he opened the door to his dad. The older man stood no taller than Eddie, but his frame held at least a hundred more pounds. A stained blue work shirt barely covered the man's protruding stomach. A soiled jacket stretched over his shoulders. Several days growth of beard scattered across the scarred face, a cigarette hung from his mouth. Eddie noticed less hair topped the man's head and much of it was now a dirty gray. Eddie's two brothers and one sister stood behind their imposing father.

The young man felt like a little boy again; fear raising from within and threatening to make him sick to his stomach.

"What cha want?" he asked, hoping his voice didn't reveal the dread he felt.

"What do I want? What do you think I want, boy? Ain't seen my son in five years and I come fer a visit. Ain't you glad to see yer own daddy?"

"Just didn't expect you, that's all."

"Wanted to surprise ya. Guess we did just that, huh? We been traveling all day, got some grub?"

"Daddy, we're sleeping. Can't you come back in the morning?"

"We'd like to be sleepin too, boy, but we didn't bring no beds. Thought you might have a spare one."

"No, Daddy, we ain't. We got no room for you."

"I kin understand that comin from yer uppity Aunt Darla, but who you think you are telling yer ole man you got no room for 'im? Thought I taught you better manners'n that."

So they'd already been to Aunt Darla's and she wouldn't have them? Eddie wished it would be that easy for him. He marveled at how two people born of the same parents and raised in the same home could be so very different. Aunt Darla was the sweetest person you could meet, but her brother…

"You taught me a lot, but never manners." He tried to hold the contempt from his voice. He knew better than push his daddy too far. He knew the consequences of crossing the old man.

And then he felt them as the older Bilmon slapped Eddie hard enough to knock him to the floor.

"Don't sass me, boy, you know what happens when you sass me."

Eddie jumped back up, anger raising above the fear. "I'm a grown man, now, a married man, with a good job and my own place. I don't have to take this from you anymore. I'm not gonna let you push me around like when I was a kid."

The man sneered. "You got no choice, boy," he walked past Eddie into the kitchen and opened the refrigerator door. "I said I'm hungry, what you got to eat?"

"If I feed you, will you leave?"

The man glared at him. Eddie swallowed.

"I'll make you some bacon and eggs. Will that be enough?"

"We'll see."

Eddie reached into the fridge and pulled out a carton of eggs.

"Wait a minute, boy. You said you was married."

Eddie looked at his dad without replying. His thoughts turned to Windy. What would this man do to her? How could he possibly protect her?

"I ain't never watched a Bilmon cook whilst his wife laid in bed," his Dad continued. "Fetch yer woman and make her do this woman's work."

"No, you leave her out of this. She has nothing to do with you."

"She's my kin."

"She's no kin to the likes of you."

The old man raised his fist to strike his son once more.

"Here let me take that, Hon," Windy stepped from the bedroom, wearing sweats and a sweat shirt. "You guys sit at the table and I'll make some breakfast." Eddie looked into his wife's eyes, seeing the sheer terror in them. He tried to convey reassurance but knew she saw the fear in his eyes as well.

"Git that beer in the fridge, for it gits warm," Mr. Bilmon addressed one of the young men still standing in the doorway. The rest of Eddie's family entered the small apartment. Eddie watched as his sister took the eggs from Windy.

"I'll help," she volunteered, not looking at her brother. Eddie thought of the last time he'd seen her, she was about 10, a scared, skinny little thing who badly needed the mama who had run out on them. He could only imagine the abuse she had suffered at her father's hands.

For the next two hours Windy cooked and served the hungry men. She watched Eddie slip into the bedroom, knowing he would call his boss and take the day off work. Windy knew they couldn't afford it, but she was thankful not to be left here alone with these people.

Late in the morning Windy picked up Sachel and quietly slipped down to Cora's apartment. She feared the older Bilmon might easily find sport with her helpless pet and wanted a safe place for him. She found her landlady kneading bread dough. A smile spread over the little lady's plump face. She wore an apron dusted with flour and her white hair was pulled into a bun at the back of her neck. Windy still felt the urge to look for a little yellow tweedy bird every time she saw Cora.

"Sounds like you have company."

Windy nodded, trying to act nonchalant. "Eddie's family is visiting. I'm sorry if they woke you up when they arrived this morning."

"I was able to go right back to sleep, don't you worry. I'll have some fresh bread for supper," she peered over her glasses at Windy, "will they still be here?"

"I really don't know, they didn't say. If so, I'll come down and get a loaf, thank you. Cora, could Sachel stay here for a while, it's a little crowded upstairs, I...I wouldn't want him to get stepped on."

"Of course, dear, Sachel's always welcome here."

Windy set the cat on the floor and he quickly escaped into the living room. "I guess I should go back up," Windy hesitated, dreading the thought, but not wanting to leave Eddie to fend for himself.

She smiled at Cora. "Thanks, I'll see you later."

The day wore on. Mr. Bilmon and his sons, ate, drank and napped between poker games. Windy felt as though she and her husband were under siege, prisoners in their own home. She watched Eddie's fearful eyes and did her best not to let him see her own panic. This man obviously held a lot of power over his children. The girl, Aggie May, waited on her dad and brothers, eating only when Windy insisted she do so. When questioned, Aggie answered in short sentences. Windy found out she was 16 and still attended school, when her daddy couldn't find anything else for her to do. Aggie whispered her answers to Windy's questions about the others, her information sketchy at best. Windy determined Aggie to be the youngest with Eddie between the two boys. Mr. Bilmon's wrath focused on Eddie, the only child who questioned his father's actions and authority. But even Eddie soon submitted to the old man's demands and drank a beer.

Windy watched with dread as Eddie opened the can. He stared an apology at his wife before taking the first drink and Windy's heart sank. She had been so proud of him. The last drink he'd taken was over two months ago with his underage friends. After Windy used the rent money to bail him out of jail that cold November Sunday he promised her he would go on the wagon. He admitted he really didn't want that kind of life and couldn't explain what had tempted him into it in the first place. Eddie had been able to plea bargain, and the court, not wanting to spend the taxpayer's money, gave him an extension on his probation. Windy's hopes in their marriage were revived and they had shared a time similar to their first year.

Now she watched as her husband finished the beer and accepted the next one his dad held out to him.

By late afternoon the beer supply ran out and one of the boys used Windy's car to get more. She placed their last roast in the oven along with half of their small bag of potatoes and a couple carrots knowing this meager fare would not satisfy the men's appetites.

Eddie's brother returned with the beer, displaying a couple 'girlie' movies he'd found at the corner video store. Windy gave silent thanks for the wall that divided her from the laughing and rude remarks in the living room. She thought of Cora, knowing some of their laughter and remarks would be heard by the older lady's sensitive ears.

As Windy and Aggie washed the supper dishes, they listened to the disgusting sounds coming from the television. All the men had forsaken their card playing to watch movies. Knowing Eddie had joined them, watching whatever matched those sounds, caused the bile to rise in Windy's throat. Eddie had never watched that type of stuff; he even denounced his friends that did. Now he joined in, his laughter and comments just as loud as the other's.

A loud belch preceded Mr. Bilmon into the kitchen. "I gotta go like a penned up mule," he announced as he walked past the girls into the bathroom. He relieved himself, not bothering to close the door.

"Aggie!!" The girl jumped as her father's voice slapped her ears. "Git me another beer, ya lazy, good fer nothin brat."

Aggie placed the bowl and drying towel on the counter.

"Right now, girl!" The man stood beside his daughter, staring at her through drunken eyes.

"Yes, Daddy."

Before she could open the refrigerator the man pushed her aside, knocking her against the counter and the bowl she had left there. The bowl flipped and crashed to the floor, breaking into several pieces.

"Now look what ya done! Is this how ya repay yer sister-in-law's hospitality, by breaking her dishes?"

Aggie shook her head, cowering before the angry man. He raised his hand to strike her.

"Mr. Bilmon," Windy interrupted. "It wasn't her fault."

The man looked at Windy, a smirk on his face.

"I suppose you gonna say it was yer own fault."

"Well, no, I'm not," Windy answered, lifting her head and staring into the man's glazed eyes.

"Whose fault was it then?" he asked, his voice low and menacing.

Windy swallowed, studying the angry face before her. "Yours." She quietly replied.

His eyes narrowed. "What'd you say?"

"I said 'yours'."

For several minutes the man looked at her, evil pouring from his eyes. Windy's heart thumped within her so loud she knew he must hear it, but she held his gaze, unwilling to give in to this monster.

"Eddie?!" the monster bellowed. But he needn't have, all three of his sons had witnessed Windy's defiance from the living room doorway. None appeared impressed.

"Eddie!!" It yelled again.

"What?" Eddie replied quietly.

"Yer woman sassed me."

"I heard."

"What you gonna do about it?"

"What do you want me to do?"

"I never heard a Bilmon sassed by a woman. It ain't gonna start now. You gonna punish her or am I?"

Windy looked at her husband, her eyes daring him to 'punish' her, yet pleading at the same time.

Eddie shook his head. "Leave her be."

"Can't. You don't take her in hand now, you'll regret it. You don't punish her, I will."

"She's my wife. I'll settle this with her later."

"This happens to be Eddie's house, not yours, Mr. Bilmon." Windy found her tongue and her courage. She had had enough of this man and his meanness.

"He's capable of taking care of his own unfinished business. I think it's time you leave." Windy walked to the door and opened it. "I'm sorry. I had hoped to welcome you as family, but you're no longer welcome here."

"That was a big mistake, little lady." Mr. Bilmon stepped closer to her, his intent obvious on his angry face. "No woman tells me to git out. Never."

Before the Monster could reach her, Eddie slipped between them and in a surprise move, turned his beer can upside down over Windy's head. The sour smelling brew drenched her hair and poured down onto her shoulders, causing the male onlookers to laugh with delight. Windy's eyes teared as the offensive liquid ran into them before flowing down her face and dripping off her chin.

"Git me another beer, Aggie," Eddie told his sister. "Mine seems to be empty." He turned away from his wife and grinned at his dad.

"Now that's my boy!" The monster slapped his son on the back and reached out to pass him the can Aggie offered. "See girl, if you'd done as yer daddy asked in the first place yer sister wouldn't be drippin wet and Eddie wouldn't a wasted his beer. Hand me one, girl." Aggie quickly complied and watched as the laughing horde returned to the living room.

The girl grabbed a towel and handed it to Windy. "I'm sorry," she repeated over and over.

"It's not your fault, Aggie, don't worry about it."

"Eddie really saved you," the girl whispered.

"Saved me? He humiliated me!"

"Daddy'd done worse."

"I don't believe this," Windy shook her head and began to cry. "This is madness, what's happening here?"

"That's just how they is," Aggie explained.

The siege lasted for three days. Eddie never left the apartment, and after the second day Windy suspected he no longer minded. Windy avoided any contact with her husband and especially his 'daddy'. She and Aggie managed to get a few hours sleep in the bedroom each night while the men passed out in the living room or at the kitchen table. She tried to talk to Aggie, offer her some comfort and maybe a way out of this horrid life. Aggie assured Windy that when they returned to Iowa she would run off with her boyfriend. She admitted she was afraid of what her daddy would do if he found her, but anything was better than the way she lived now. Windy tried to talk to the girl about school or college, telling her that running away with a boy was no way to live, but Aggie had obviously been making plans in her mind for some time and would not listen to what Windy had to say.

Occasionally Windy slipped downstairs where life suddenly appeared normal again, but if she stayed too long she could hear the noise upstairs of Eddie or his daddy looking for her.

The men stayed drunk the whole time by depleting what was left of Windy's bill money, kept in the desk drawer. Her grocery money fed them for the three days and when all the available funds ran out the troop departed as suddenly as they appeared. Left in their wake were two angry, broken people and a marriage that could never be restored.

Chapter Four

Dear God, It's me again. Thank You for this day, for the sunshine and all. Help me to be the person You want me to be. Margie told me a nice verse, something about all things working out for good. Help me understand the Bible so I can be closer to You and Your will in my life. And please be with my son and his family. Does he have a family, God? Is he even married? Thank You. Amen.

"Rick, my boy, how about some fishing this week? This is the last Saturday in April, trout season opens today and I'm anxious to get started."

Rick had put off Joe's invitation to go ice fishing too many times, and knew the cold would no longer serve as a good excuse. He loved being outside, he just wasn't a hunter or fisherman. At 14 he'd watched his dad bring down a buck and the scene imbedded itself in his memory. Rick watched the deer change from a graceful, living creature to a thrashing dying one. He lost his desire for the hunt before it even began. As for fishing, he'd gone a couple times, more for the companionship than the sport.

"When do you want to go?" After four months of days, Rick and Joe had returned to midnights for the remainder of Rick's six month training period which was almost over.

"We have Wednesday and Thursday off, which day is best for you?"

Rick shook his head. "You tell me, I'm open both days."

"How about Wednesday morning as soon as we get off work?"

"Why so early?"

"Fish bite better then, besides if I let you go home and to bed, you'll forget all about fishing."

Rick knew that to be true. He'd much rather sleep than fish when coming off a shift of midnights.

"Remember that little trout stream we saw last November when we backed up the State boys?" Joe asked.

Rick searched his memory, recalling the chase that ended on a dirt road out in the country. Being his first night and given all the excitement, he'd not taken time to notice his surroundings.

"North of town?"

"Yeah, that's the place. Well, I found out who owns the property, I went to see him and he's more than happy to let us fish it." Rick decided a day out of the city would suit him. A walk in the woods and a few hours next to a quiet creek might be just the thing.

But when Wednesday morning arrived he opened his duffle bag in the back room of the police station and looked at the clothes he should change into. His eyes drooped and he yawned.

"I'd rather go home and put on my pajamas," he remarked to Joe as he pulled out a pair of jeans.

"I know that's how you feel now." Joe answered. "But wait till we're sitting beside the stream, the sun shining on our faces and fish begging for a place in our basket. You'll be singing a different tune then."

"I doubt I'll be singing any tunes." Rick unbuttoned his uniform shirt and carefully hung it over the pants draped on the hanger. He pulled a wrinkled flannel shirt from his bag and worked his arms into it.

Dr. Stephan Michaels looked in the mirror and noticed the gray hair at his temples. *'When did this happen?'* He wondered. *'When did I lose my youth? Yesterday I was an intern, today I'm middle aged.'*

'Middle age' as defined by the doctor happened on his fortieth birthday. Though his hair grayed around his ears, he still possessed plenty of it, brown on the rest of his head to match his deep handsome eyes. A few lone wrinkles guarded those eyes. Standing nearly six foot tall he wore his 190 pounds quite well. But today he saw a single, 40 year old doctor, the last in the line of prominent Michaels.

"You need a wife," the man in the mirror informed him.

"Now why didn't I think of that?" he replied. "Guess I better find one." He pulled the toothpaste from the medicine cabinet and brushed for exactly 60 seconds starting on the upper left outside and ending on the lower left inside. After rinsing his mouth and replacing his brushing utensils he took a cloth from inside a lower cabinet door and cleaned any water splashes on the counter.

Stephan flicked off the light and walked into the bedroom, his bare feet sinking into the carpet. Pulling the shade down to block out the morning sun, he looked at the clock. It was exactly 7:46, the time he always crawled into bed after a shift of midnights.

"If you had a wife, old man," he mused. "This bed wouldn't be so cold and lonely."

Scrunching his pillow to fit his head he looked quickly back at the last two decades. Years full of medical school, internship, a struggling practice and finally, much deserved recognition as one of the best internists in the state. He'd just been too busy to consider marriage. Even now, his willingness to work hours other established doctors refused, kept him busy. Where would he ever find the time to meet, court and marry a woman? Where would he find one young enough to give him an heir for the Michaels name who would marry an old man like himself? Despite the questions the doctor fell asleep almost immediately. As in all of his life, he never worried; he simply made a decision and planned to follow it. Anyone who knew the doctor would have laid odds he'd be married by fall.

Joe turned down a gravel road, his truck tires jumping their way over the chatter bumps. "Look familiar?" he questioned his passenger.

"Joe, it was dark, my first night, my first chase…"

"Yeah, I suppose. Up here on the left is Mr. Packard's house. He owns a couple hundred acres bordering on this road and around the corner." Rick noted the house Joe pointed out, an older, two story house with a freshly plowed garden taking up most of the side yard and children's toys dotting the front.

Joe passed the house and turned left down a narrow dirt road. "This other place belongs to him, too, guess his wife's grandfather left it all to them when he died." Joe indicated a small two story house that sat back from the road on a little hill. A creek ran parallel with the road and Joe pulled into the driveway crossing a narrow wooden bridge that groaned under the weight of his truck.

Large aspen trees sheltered the drive leading to the house and a handmade 'For Sale' sign lay on the ground where the wind and rain must have downed it.

As soon as the truck stopped Rick jumped from the cab and walked over to the sign. "This place is for sale?"

Joe shrugged. "I don't know how long the sign's been there. I guess it's possible."

Rick quickly scanned the area noting the beauty and serenity of it. He walked toward the house, drawn it seemed, his eyes never leaving the structure. The drive veered to the left and ran into a small garage, with weathered siding the same natural wood as the house. To the left of the garage stood a sturdy, old barn once painted red. But Rick's eyes returned to the house. He heard Joe come up beside him.

"The best fishing is behind the house Packard said. Supposed to be another bridge over the steam, leading into the back acreage. I've got the poles."

Joe walked past the garage while Rick continued on his own journey. He mounted the wooden steps of the house and walked across the porch placing his hand on the screen door. It opened with a squeak but the inside door resisted his push.

He closed the screen door and followed the porch around the building looking in the windows as he went. By the time he reached the back steps he had his plans made. The down payment could come from the money he saved during his service time. If Mr. Packard wouldn't consider a land contract he would apply at the bank. Since he'd only been on the police force for five months they would probably turn him down in which case he would ask his dad. He couldn't wait for him to see this place. He knew his dad would be as drawn to it as he. Rick's position gave him a clear view of the back yard. The house appeared to sit on a little peninsula; he could see the stream winding its way beside and behind the house. Joe had found the bridge he spoke of and was sitting on it, baiting a hook when Rick joined him.

As they fished, Rick unfolded his plan to Joe who said little but nodded a lot. He then assured Rick they would stop at the Packard home when they left.

"You know, I been thinking," Joe said. "Your probation time is almost over. You'll be put on afternoons, cause you're the newest officer and no one else wants that shift. I'll be put back on days, which I hate, cause days is all PR and politics. You and I work well together—what say we tell the chief we'll partner on afternoons?"

Rick looked at his friend and nodded. His respect and admiration for this man reflected in his eyes. Rick considered it an honor that Joe wanted to work with him.

"I would really like to continue working with you. You've already taught me a lot and I know there's still much more for me to learn but I thought you'd be glad to get rid of your 'tag-a-long.'"

Joe shrugged. "Anything's better'n days, even you." But his smile belied his fondness for the young man.

Rick yawned as he looked at his watch. "Quarter to eleven, Joe, time to go home yet?" Rick simply couldn't concentrate on fishing, he wanted to meet Mr. Packard and inquire about the house.

Joe pulled his line out of the water and dropped another trout into the basket to keep the others company. "Getting sleepy?" he teased a wide-eyed Rick. "I figure Packard should stop home for lunch in another hour."

"An hour?" Rick echoed. He stood and stretched. "I'm going to take a little walk; my legs are a bit cramped."

"Might as well," Joe answered. "You sure can't catch any fish today."

Rick followed the path back to the barn, opened a walk-through door and entered. The barn had not been used for some time, and even then Rick doubted the land had been farmed. He had not seen open fields large enough for planting. A stack of used lumber rested in one corner while dried sunflowers, years old, hung from a cross beam. Another corner held a small, enclosed stall, the only part of the barn with a cement floor. Large double doors filled in both ends of the structure.

He exited the same way he entered, carefully pulling the door closed behind him and wandered toward the garage.

Again, he found the walk-through door unlocked. He opened it but did not enter. From where he stood he viewed the workbench, shelves, and enough space for one car. He secured the door and turned toward the house. Its rough wood siding gave it the impression of belonging to nature. Rick bounded up the back steps and opened the screen door, glad to find the door locked just as the front had been. Mr. Packard cared enough to protect the house from vandals.

All the window curtains were tied open though, and Rick had a clear view of the ground floor lay-out. The house was almost square, but longer then it was wide. There were basically three rooms downstairs. On the left of the front door was a dining room with kitchen behind it, the stairway open to the dining room. To the right was a long living room complete with fireplace half way down on the outside wall. The bathroom appeared to be behind the living room with the entrance off the kitchen. He liked what he saw. After Rick had seen all he could, he wandered out into the yard, noting the neglected flower beds. Daffodils now shared the same space as dandelions.

A battered pick-up pulled into the drive stopping behind Joe's. A man of medium height and build with thinning brown hair stepped out. "You must be Officer Joe's friend," he held out his hand.

Rick grasped it. "Rick Notts, sir. Are you Mr. Packard?"

"Call me Wil, son. You a gardener?" He nodded to the flower bed Rick had been studying.

"No," Rick smiled and shook his head. "But I am interested in this place. Is it for sale?"

"It is. My wife's grandad lived here. He died almost two years ago. We put the sign on the ground there, knowing that if anyone came this far in, they'd truly be interested."

"How much acreage is there?"

"How much you want? I got 200 hundred acres, be willing to part with 20 or so."

Rick could hardly imagine himself lucky enough to own this house much less 20 acres of prime wooded land. "I doubt I could afford that much, probably just the acre the house and buildings are on."

"Tell you what, you and Officer Joe come home and meet Missy, we can discuss it over lunch."

Rick left the Packard home a short time later. The only hope the friendly couple had given him was their promise to 'pray over it' and let him know in a day or two.

Chapter Five

Dear Lord, I don't understand why some things happen. Margie says we aren't supposed to understand everything because then we wouldn't need You. Well I know I need You and I would still like to understand but I am willing to trust that You know best. For instance, my son; there's so much I don't understand, but I am trusting You to be in his life and take him. Help him to understand that he needs to trust You too. Thank You. Amen.

John Garvey, EMT, checked the girl's vital signs as the ambulance sped through the darkened streets. His large, thick hands moved deftly from one instrument to another.

Brown hair framed the girl's pallid face. She moved her head slightly and moaned. Her eyes fluttered open.

"Hello, Windy," he used the name given by her neighbor. "I'm John. You're on your way to Community General." He spoke in a soft, clear voice. "You've got quite a bump on your head. Do you remember how you got it?"

"Yes," she whispered. "I fell." She closed her eyes and retreated to the blackness of her lie.

John touched the swollen eye and bleeding lip and shook his head. He'd seen it before, the battered, fearful wife. John thought of his own wife's youthful face, her soft blonde hair and shining eyes. He couldn't imagine touching her in any way but love.

"How's she doin'?" Tony Dionne called from the driver's seat.

"Says she fell."

"Yeah, we've heard that before haven't we?" He said in his best Cheech Marin voice.

"Too many times." John shook his head. "These women become their own worst enemy. They think they're protecting themselves but they're only making their situation worse."

"Hey, Man, what they gonna do? Call a cop? You know how easy it is for a guy to walk on those kinds of charges."

"There's got to be some one who can protect them."

"Like who? The shrinks say they stay cause they like it. And the courts call it a 'civil matter'."

"I know. Hey! Why don't we invite a few judges and lawyers and so called professionals to spend a day with us? Let them help clean up after the scum this society labeled abusive husbands. Let them see the fear, the pain, the blood. Then see if they still say these women asked for it?"

"Spend a whole shift with people like that? No thanks! Spendin' it with you is bad enough." Tony grinned at his partner in the rear view mirror.

John smiled back, but his smile faded when his attention returned to Windy. Tony was right. No wonder this girl preferred her husband's wrath to those meant to protect her.

Tony stopped the ambulance in front of the emergency entrance and ran to the back of the vehicle where he opened the double doors. Together the men lifted their patient out and wheeled her into the building.

Nurse Bernice Laswell inserted a key into the supply cabinet. She opened the door and placed a few articles on the shelf. She considered quiet nights in the ER a blessing. Some of the nurses actually looked forward to their week on ER duty, saying it broke the monotony. But Nurse Laswell preferred the mundane to the fear she felt while waiting for that next emergency.

Banging doors intruded on her quiet night. She watched John and Tony wheel the stretcher in. The look on their faces told her this was another hard one.

"Evening, Bernie," John greeted her.

"Accident victim?" she asked, noting Windy's face as she reached John.

"Yeah," Tony answered. "She fell."

Nurse Laswell caught his meaning and shook her head.

"Who's on duty tonight?" John asked.

"Dr. Michaels."

"Good," he said with a smile.

Windy groaned as Nurse Laswell lifted her eyelids and checked for pupil reaction.

"What's the story, boys?" Mrs. Laswell asked as they lifted the girl from stretcher to emergency room table.

"Pretty sketchy. Downstairs neighbor heard 'a noise', she found Windy on the kitchen floor and called us."

"Was there any one else in the apartment?"

"The neighbor said the husband just left. She wasn't talking, but I think we can assume what happened."

"Well, you've done a good job stabilizing her, as usual." She smiled at John. His large frame nearly filled the small cubicle. Nurse Laswell knew his gentleness matched his size. She placed a warm blanket over Windy's shivering body. "When's that new baby expected?"

John grinned. "Sally's due tomorrow, but she says the doc's wrong, that it won't be till next week."

"Heed what she says. There are some things even doctors don't know."

Dr. Stephan Michaels entered the cubical. "Fill me in." John repeated what he knew, adding what they had done for her in the ambulance.

Dr. Michaels quickly, but thoroughly, examined the young woman then sent her down to x-ray. Her injuries were only superficial and he worried about her drifting in and out of consciousness. He analyzed the x-rays himself but could find nothing wrong. By this time Windy rested in a small, empty ward. Dr. Michaels opened the door to her room and found John sitting beside the quiet girl.

"You're not off duty yet, are you John?"

"No, but it's been a quiet night except for Windy here. Tony said he'd beep me if we got a call."

"Has she stirred any?" the doctor asked lifting Windy's wrist between his thumb and forefinger. Her heartbeat remained strong.

"A little. Not enough to be coherent."

"That bothers me. I find no reason for her unconscious state. Admissions isn't happy either. Admitting someone without an insurance number always makes them nervous."

"I'm a bit nervous, myself. Did the x-rays show anything?"

"Nothing. No concussion. All injuries are superficial."

"That's what I thought. Guess she's turned it all off, huh?

Dr. Michaels touched one of the bruises on her arm. "Many of these are days old. I wonder how long she's endured this treatment. What did you notice about the house?"

"The usual in a case like this, a cold meal on the table, several empty beer cans, one spilled on the floor, a couple chairs knocked over. We're just EMT's, you know. We didn't have a search warrant."

"But you did inform the proper authorities?"

"As soon as we arrived."

The doctor nodded, catching the light on his silver temples. He noted the time and updated her chart. "Well, young man, this place is quiet too, and I'm here for the duration. Would you mind getting us some coffee? I happen to know there's a fresh pot in the lounge."

"Sure, Doc."

After John closed the door, Dr. Michaels looked closely at Windy. He judged her to be about 20, too young to be at the mercy of a madman. *'But young enough'* he thought, studying the tanned face and strong shoulders, *'to start over'*.

Chapter Six

Dear Lord, I've memorized that verse Margie told me about. I even know where to find it. Romans 8:28. When I feel sad about my son I think of that verse. I know you are Lord over everything, please help me remember that. Please be with my son, lead him to You. And lead him to the girl You choose for him. Thank You. Amen.

Cora Davis peeked through the curtain before timidly opening the front door. Two uniformed men stood on her porch, the soft glow from the outside light reflected on their badges.

"Yes, officer?" she asked over the securing chain. "Ma'am, I'm Officer Joe Kozininski." Cora could see little gray hairs peeking out from under the policeman's hat. "This is Officer Rick Notts." He indicated the young man standing beside him. "We're responding to a call of an unconscious woman here."

"You just missed them. The ambulance came and took Windy to the hospital."

"We're aware of that, Ma'am. Do you know the woman?"

"Yes, of course, poor, poor girl."

"Would you be able to answer a few questions for us?"

Cora tightened the belt on her robe, then slipped the chain off the door. "Come in, I'll tell you what I know. That's the least I can do for Windy."

The officers followed the little lady into a small entryway that contained a flight of steps. A door on their right opened into a small, cozy kitchen that immediately took Rick back a few years to his grandmother's home. He sat in the chair Cora indicated, his mouth watering as she lifted the cover on a tin and pulled out fresh cinnamon rolls. He shot a grin to his partner, who nodded his appreciation while the tea kettle began to whistle.

As they savored the pastries Cora told them about her upstairs tenants, the frequent arguments and terrible noise that woke her earlier that night. When their cups were empty Cora handed a key to Joe.

"I watched him leave, but I would feel safer if you checked the apartment. I'm quite the coward since I lost my Clifton three years ago."

"I don't know if I can agree with that, Mrs. Davis, I think you're a brave little lady." He smiled as she blushed at his compliment. "One more thing," he added. "Have you ever seen Mr. Bilmon, tonight or ever, strike his wife, or mistreat her in any way?"

"Seen it? Why, no. I've only seen the results."

"Thank you, Ma'am." Joe turned and led the way up the stairs. Once through the door they began a routine search. Nothing they found surprised them.

The small apartment was tidy and clean except for the kitchen. In the only bedroom a worn spread covered the bed. Women's clothes hung neatly in the closet on one side, the other side held a few men's shirts. One of the two chest of drawers gaped at them, its contents spilling from it.

The living room held sparse furniture. Turning on the table lamp Rick noticed a picture of a young couple. He picked it up and studied the girl, guessing her to be about 18 in the picture, a little thing, maybe 5'2". A timid smile graced her lips. Though Rick wouldn't call her beautiful, something about her expression, the innocence, the trust, caught his attention.

"What you got there?" Joe asked. The younger man lifted the picture so his partner could see it, reluctantly letting go.

"Yeah, that's Eddie all right."

"You know him?" Rick remembered the name Mrs. Davis had given them.

"I've arrested him a time or two. He was your first arrest. You changed his tire. This must be his wife, fearful little thing if I remember." He set the picture back on the table, looked around the room then left.

Rick reached for the light but found himself grasping the picture instead. Again he studied the girl. Then he frowned. He remembered the night Joe spoke of. This was the girl who drove that car, the girl not strong enough to loosen the lug nuts. This was the girl they followed home; the same girl who lay in a hospital bed tonight. He felt his stomach tighten, his head spin slightly.

"This is what it's all about, get used to it," he warned himself as he set the picture back on the table and turned off the light. His foot rolled slightly at the first step. Bending down he retrieved a broken pencil from the floor.

WINDY JORDAN CLASS OF The year had disappeared along with the missing end. He held the pencil for several minutes, reading it over and over.

"We've got just enough time to get back and make out our report before midnight," Joe called. "You ready?" Rick slipped the pencil into his pocket and joined his partner in the kitchen.

"Shouldn't we interview Mrs. Bilmon?" Rick asked as they trooped down the stairs.

"No, I'll turn it over to one of the day guys for follow up."

"Hey, Stephan, have a cigar." Dr. Porter greeted Stephan just outside his newest patient's room. The band on the offensive brown cylinder proclaimed "IT'S A BOY!"

"Why, George, you sly old fox, I didn't know Cynthia was pregnant."

His colleague laughed. "Not Cynthia, our daughter-in- law. Gerald and Vickie made me a grandfather!"

Stephan stared at his friend. George was hardly older than himself. A year maybe two and here he was, a grandfather before Stephan had even thought of becoming a father.

"Say, Stephan, isn't it about time you started thinking about a family? Be a shame if you weren't around to play with your grandchildren. Marilyn, have a cigar." Dr. Porter reached out to a passing nurse, then walked down the hall with her leaving Stephan to chew on his last remark.

"A little late for visitors, isn't it, Mrs. Bilmon?"

Windy, propped up with pillows, sat in the hospital bed, her hair flowed softly around her shoulders. Tender brown eyes thinned almost into two lines when her pouty mouth smiled at the newcomer.

"Hi, Dr. Michaels. John's not a visitor, he's a rescuer. Didn't you know that?"

"Doc, you sure this is the same girl I brought in here less than 24 hours ago? The one who only knew English as a second language?"

"The same. But she is no longer a lady of mystery. She woke up singing like a bird this afternoon, even made admissions happy with her insurance information."

"For what good it does," Windy shook her head. "I don't think the insurance is active any longer."

"You let admissions worry about that," the doctor said. "You concentrate on getting well."

"I'm not really sick, and I could concentrate just as well in my own bed."

"I'll be the judge of that."

John's beeper interrupted. "Well, folks, it's time for that rescuing thing I do so well."

Doctor and patient bid him good-bye.

When the door closed Windy's attention was drawn to the doctor. She judged him to be almost twice her age. His tall frame easily carried broad shoulders. His stout torso revealed a man who took care of himself. The skin around his eyes wrinkled when he smiled. His competent hands impressed Windy most. She felt a man's hands revealed much about his character. *'Eddie's hands were strong'*, she thought. *'Except when they were wrapped around a beer can.'*

"You're still here?" she asked the doctor.

"I'm on night ER duty this week."

"But you were here this morning and afternoon."

"I can't ignore my other patients."

"How does Mrs. Michaels feel about being ignored?"

"If there were a Mrs. Michaels, she would understand."

He inspected Windy's injuries then picked up her chart. "I see they have 'OC' written on here under medications. What kind do you take?"

Windy hesitated, trying to remember what she could have told the nurse that would have resulted in her writing that. The only pills she took were birth control pills, but wouldn't that be BC?

"OC, oral contraceptive. Do you know what type and milligram?"

Relieved, she answered. "I don't remember. They asked me that, too."

"Do you have any with you?"

"I didn't pack before I left."

"How long have you been taking them?"

"Two years, I started when we got married."

"Any break from them?"

"I stopped for about a month last summer, thought I might be pregnant, but it was a false alarm."

"Do you have any children?"

"No." He wrote something on her chart.

"You were asleep until after noon. How did you know I was here this morning?"

"I read my chart."

"Entirely against the rules, you know. Anyone well enough to break the rules should be well enough to be discharged. Tell me. Were you able to decipher my writing?"

"Quite easily, really. I know you're Dr. Steven Michaels..."

"Stephan," he corrected. "It's a family name derived from the Biblical Stephanas."

"Oh."

"Continue."

"I forgot where I was."

"Well, I haven't. You're the patient, I'm the doctor. You rest, I'll read the charts. I assume you have other things to concern yourself with. What's the situation on the home front?" Dr. Michaels pulled up a chair and sat next to the bed.

Windy studied the man before her wondering why she should tell him anything about her home situation. Cora had called and said the police came by last night after Eddie left. Windy remembered the judge's warning last week. 'Your bargaining days are over son.' She assumed Eddie believed it this time. Last night after several beers Eddie began telling Windy what a witch she was and how if she were worth coming home to he wouldn't want to go out with the guys. Then he threatened to leave and Windy said she wished he would. 'Wrong answer' she told herself.

She shrugged. "I'm sure everything will be fine."

"Do you have family here?"

"My folks moved out east right after I graduated. Dad had a job waiting for him there."

"And your father's business is?"

Windy hesitated, still wondering why this man showed so much interest in her personal life. It wasn't any of his business that her dad was presently an unemployed carpenter.

"Construction," she answered.

"Have you had any further education?"

"I had a full scholarship to an Eastern university. I thought about attending here, but decided to just be a wife for a while."

"No siblings?"

"An older brother who's a career marine, secret type stuff."

"I'm curious about your name."

Finally the girl smiled. Everyone was curious about her unusual name. "Windy," she nodded, "the name of a popular song when mom was carrying my brother."

"I remember it, '67, I believe."

Windy laughed, not surprised the older man remembered the song. "Yes, if he'd been a girl, I'd probably be Susan or Carol."

The doctor looked at her chart. "Windy E. What's your middle name?"

"Elaine, rather proper isn't it?"

"I would term it elegant."

Windy hesitated. "I suppose it is. It just doesn't fit me."

"It could. By the way, what name did your brother end up with?"

"Robert Drake Jordan, the third, better known as Robbie." Windy finally realized the doctor's curiosity was probably because of her being unconscious for a while. He was obviously checking her mental capabilities. "May I go home tonight?"

"No," he answered, standing. "I'll release you tomorrow, unless you break another rule."

Windy returned his smile. *'For an older man, he's actually quite handsome,'* she thought.

Few women caught the eye of Dr. Stephan Michaels. But he studied the young woman and liked what he saw. He noted the sparkle in her blackened eye and the smile on her bruised face. He mentally reviewed her answers; father in the construction industry, brother possibly in the secret service. Her intelligence had won her a full scholarship which she rejected for love. She was a typical woman, a typical YOUNG woman capable of bearing children. For a moment Dr. Michaels indulged himself in something he rarely did, he imagined. 'I wonder what her children might look like.'

Rick Notts, property owner, stepped into his house, papers in hand. Joe thought him crazy to spend the night here tonight, but Rick didn't care. He wanted to sleep in his new home. He turned on a lamp in the living room and sat in the old stuffed chair by the fireplace. The furnishings all belonged to Mrs. Packard's grandparents; most had been here as long as the couple themselves. The couch, chair and carpet showed signs of being old, but well made, as was the dining set in the other room. The kitchen came right out of a 1930's scene except the fridge which had been updated in the Fifty's. Rick loved it. This was exactly how he remembered his gramma's house, old and worn but clean and always welcoming. Some day, when he had that certain someone in his life, they would go through the house and make whatever changes she wanted; but not until. He wanted her approval, wanted her to be comfortable, to make this her home.

Mrs. Packard had removed a couple items that held special memories for her, but since the family had no need for the furniture they included it in the deal. And what a deal! Wil Packard had insisted Rick needed some property to get started. He named a more than fair price for the house and 10 acres. He accepted Rick's down payment and shook hands on a land contract. The papers Rick held, signed that day, were a formality insisted on by the state.

The Packard's claimed God's approval on their decision and though Rick knew little about God, he was thankful for His opinion in this matter.

Rick climbed the creaking stairs and looked into the two bedrooms, each occupying half of the upstairs floor except in the Northeast corner where a small bath sat directly over the one downstairs. He checked the linen closet in the small hallway and found plenty of musty smelling bedding. He settled for a not-too-offensive blanket and a fairly new pillow. These he took into the smaller bedroom having already decided not to use the master bedroom until he could share it with someone. Removing his uniform, Rick settled onto the creaky bed and into a contented sleep.

Chapter Seven

Dear Lord, I decided to get up a little earlier so I can start my day with You. My, what a beautiful sky! I forgot what this time of day could look like. Margie invited me to Bible study tonight. I don't know what to expect but I'm looking forward to going. Please be with me today And with my son. Is he married? Engaged? Has he even met the girl You have for him? Am I a gramma? Thank You. Amen.

"Thank you for bringing me home. I never expected such treatment from my doctor." Windy surveyed the inside of the sedan, noting the car fit Dr. Stephan Michaels, sensible but not boring. "But I did expect a doctor's car to be a Caddy or something impressive."

"You don't approve of my choice of cars?"

"Actually, I do."

Everything about this man spoke of class. But he wore his money well, looking more like a tennis pro in his polo shirt and jeans than a well-to -do doctor.

"I think I should see you safely in your home."

"Thank you, but I'm sure I'll be fine." Windy declined, hesitant to invite a strange man into her apartment. She opened the door but Dr. Michaels touched her arm.

"At least let me see you to the door."

She nodded her agreement and waited for him to help her from the car.

Cora suddenly appeared on the steps and trotted down the sidewalk, moving faster than Windy had ever seen her move. "I'm so glad you're home," she managed to say between breaths.

"See here, if you're not careful, I'll have two patients instead of one," Dr. Michaels smiled at the little lady.

Windy introduced Cora who promptly invited the doctor in. Windy wondered if that slight look of victory on his face was her imagination.

"You look much better than you did the other night," Cora remarked. "Dr. Michaels must have taken good care of you."

Windy agreed that he had, then asked hesitantly, "Has anyone been around?"

The woman shook her head. "No dear, he hasn't been back. Most of his things are gone along with your car. But it's small payment for your life."

"Oh, Cora, it wasn't that bad," Windy corrected her, quickly looking at the doctor. He knew how she'd gotten hurt, had said as much, but she'd not yet admitted it to him. 'Why should I?' she asked herself.

Cora suggested tea and fresh baked banana bread, but Dr. Michaels advised rest for Windy. "Oh, my yes," the little lady agreed, eyes glistening behind her glasses. "You take her right upstairs, and I'll bring her some lunch in a little while."

"I can see myself upstairs," Windy insisted but the doctor interrupted.

"I believe the consensus is against you, come along."

Windy finally gave in, knowing she wouldn't get any peace until she did and led the way upstairs. Dr. Michael's gaze took in the small kitchen including the wooden table and chairs laden with many coats of paint.

"Early attic," Windy explained the decor. "My parents gave us some of the furniture when they moved."

"It has a homey feeling. Would the word quaint be too corny?"

"Not to me."

"I'm a little thirsty; may I have a glass of water?"

Again Windy hesitated but quickly rebuked herself. The man was just concerned for her health, why did she insist on being so rude. She smiled.

"How about a cherry cola, I haven't had one in days?"

"I don't touch the stuff, water is fine."

Windy turned on the tap and let the water run while she looked in the fridge for a can of pop. She filled a glass with water and one with cherry cola then motioned to the table. "Have a seat," she invited.

The conversation flowed easily enough surprising Windy. Before long Dr. Michaels reluctantly admitted he must return to the hospital.

"Will you join me for lunch tomorrow?" he asked.

Windy looked at him in surprise. "I...well I don't think so. I thought I was supposed to be resting."

"Exactly; fixing lunch might prove a strain for you. Besides, I need to see you again tomorrow for observation purposes and it may as well be at Chester's as opposed to the hospital."

"But what if something's still wrong with me? Wouldn't we be better off at the hospital?"

"Chester's is just down the street. I could get you medical attention in minutes. Better say yes, I could always have you readmitted for disobeying doctors' orders."

Windy smiled. "I don't think it would be proper but I do appreciate it."

"Then I'll see you next week in my office, call and make an appointment through the hospital. And the name is Stephan, remember?"

"Yes, a form of Stephanas. I remember." When he left she sat down at the table and tried to sort out the events of the past few days. A knock interrupted her thoughts and Cora opened the door cautiously.

"I brought you some soup and warm bread, oh and I found Sachel cowering under the bed yesterday morning." She passed the dishes to Windy as Sachel ran into the kitchen. "Just relax this afternoon, dear. I'll let you know when supper's ready."

"Cora, you don't have to..." The door closed on a smiling Windy. She pulled the cat close and rubbed his ears. "Oh, Eddie," she whispered into Sachel's soft fur.

Walking into the living room she picked up the picture from the end table and stared at the couple who smiled back at her. "Most people said we'd never make it and we said we'd prove them wrong. What have we proved?"

Windy allowed time and memories to wonder through her mind as her eyes moved over every familiar detail of her husband. Sitting wearily on the couch she placed Sachel beside her, he rolled over, daring her to rub his belly. When she did he grabbed her hand between his paws and pretended to fight her.

"Well, Sachel, let's see if we can find your Papa and try to get this mess straightened out. I don't know of any place he could have gone to accept his Dad's, of all places." She found the telephone book and looked to see if the

45

older Bilmon's number was written in the back. It was, in what was probably Aggie's handwriting. Below the number was an address in Iowa. Windy picked up the phone and started dialing. Nothing happened. She clicked the button trying to get a dial tone. Dropping the receiver in its cradle she frowned and let her head fall against the back of the couch. "I suppose he didn't pay the phone bill. He knew they were threatening to turn it off. I guess I'll write him instead, it might be better than talking to him right now."

Windy lifted a notepad from the table and looked for the pencil she kept there for messages. Unable to find it she went in search of another one. After ten minutes she gave up and flopped down on the bed. Stuffing a pillow under her head she sighed and let her tears spill. Sachel came in looking for his mistress and curled up beside her, purring loudly.

"Windy, do you go to church?" Stephan asked. She sat on a sterile examining table in the good doctor's office.

Windy frowned. "Church didn't quite fit Eddie's life style."

"Why is it when I ask about you, I hear about Eddie?"

"I don't know, because he's my husband, I guess. My life is half me, half Eddie. Isn't that how it's supposed to be?"

"Does Eddie share your feelings?"

"Sure. Of course." 'When we first married,' she added silently.

"Before Eddie, did you attend church?"

"I had a friend involved in a youth group. I used to go to special events with her, you know, parties and roller skating. But I always managed an excuse when it came to regular meetings. Why?"

"I attend church when my schedule allows. I think it's helped me be a better person. I know it's been a source of strength in the midst of the illness and death I face so often. Would you like to come with me this Sunday?"

"I, uh, I don't think so. I mean, you've been really nice to me and I'd like to return the favor, but…" she shook her head.

"How about a picnic that afternoon then?"

"Dr…Stephan, I'm okay now. I didn't pass out today or anything and I don't need anymore observing."

"I just thought an afternoon of relaxation would be good for you."

"Maybe it would. And if Eddie's back by then, I'll suggest we do just that." She noted the startled expression on his face. "I am married, remember?"

"But he left you."

"Oh," she laughed, "he'll be back."

"And you'll stay with him after all he's done to you?"

Windy refused to meet the doctor's gaze.

"Windy?" Stephan finally spoke up. She met his look, tears glistening in her eyes.

"I love him."

Chapter Eight

Dear Lord, Bible study has become the highlight of my week. I never knew there were so many wonderful thoughts in Your book. I know when I accepted Jesus as my Savior You took my sins away. But I've been remembering some of those sins lately. Please help me live with my past while I look to my future. And Lord, be with my boy and his girl. Thank You. Amen

Windy sifted through the mail a third time, searching for the familiar handwriting.

Cora opened her door. "Anything for me?"

Windy handed her the bundle. "All of it."

"Come in and have some tea, won't you?"

Windy followed her friend into the familiar room. She loved having tea in Cora's kitchen among the house plants and knick-knacks and the smell of home-made bread.

"Who's the lucky one today?" Windy asked peering under the towel stretched over three warm loaves.

"My niece's family. He's been out of work for three weeks now. You were fortunate to find your job so quickly."

"Dad always said a person could find a job if he wanted one bad enough." She sat down tracing the pattern of hearts on the print table cloth then quickly looked up. "Oh! I'm sorry, I didn't mean that your nephew," she shook her head, "niece's husband…" The last thing she wanted to do was offend Cora.

"Don't worry, dear," the kindly lady smiled. "Roger says the same thing. He goes out everyday, and soon he'll pester some one into giving him a job."

Cora took the place of the grandmother Windy never knew and the mother she missed. Many times they sat at this table discussing people or events in their lives. They came to treasure their time together.

Cora set two steaming cups on the table, pushing the honey over to her guest. "When did you last hear from your folks?"

"Just a couple days ago." She smiled at Cora's puzzled expression. "I hoped for a letter from Eddie. It's been almost two weeks since…since he left. I've written twice now, if he weren't there you'd think his dad would tell me."

Cora nodded. Windy hesitated to bring up Eddie's name. Cora always fell silent when the conversation turned to him. At least she never said anything bad about Windy's husband. They sipped their tea in silence.

"What did you tell your folks?"

"Nothing yet; there's no sense worrying them. Or giving them false hopes, they probably wouldn't be too disappointed if they knew Eddie was gone."

Cora nodded before asking, "How have you been feeling, dear? You're not overdoing with this new job are you?"

Windy smiled. "I'm just fine. My feet get a little tired from standing all day, but at least I get to walk around. I'm glad the store hired me as a stocker instead of a cashier. Six hours standing in one place sounds so boring."

The telephone interrupted them. Cora picked it up and greeted her caller cheerfully. She politely answered a couple questions then handed the phone to Windy.

"It's that nice young doctor."

Windy hesitated for a moment, not remembering any young doctors. "You know," Cora said, "Dr. Michaels."

Windy smiled. Of course Cora would consider Dr. Michaels young, even with his graying hair and wrinkled eyes.

She thanked Cora and spoke into the receiver.

"Well, my timing is good today, isn't it?" he said. "I haven't heard from you in a while and wondered how you're doing."

They talked for a few minutes, Windy told him about her job and he told her about John's new son.

"Sally was right," Stephan said. "John Jr.'s birth came one day before she predicted. Mother and baby are fine. I'm taking them to dinner tomorrow evening, I know it's short notice but, would you join us?"

Windy hesitated, thinking of Stephan's lunch request and picnic suggestion. Then she wondered if he would bring up church again. She remembered John from the hospital and enjoyed hearing him talk about his wife and expected child. She thought of Eddie's silence in answering her letters.

"John has mentioned you to Sally and she'd like to meet you. They're nice people." Stephan encouraged.

"Sure," Windy replied, chiding herself for questioning the good doctor's motive. "How thoughtful of you."

When she hung up, Windy told Cora about the dinner for John and his wife. Cora clapped her hands and giggled.

"I just know you'll have a wonderful time. I haven't met anyone as nice as Dr. Michaels since I met my Clifton."

The next evening when Stephan came to the front door, Cora answered it. She handed him a white bakery box tied with a string.

"I imagine you rarely taste good home-baked rolls," she explained. He thanked her warmly and headed up stairs.

Windy opened the door, purse in hand. She wore a print dress with a high lace collar. Her upswept hair held two sweetheart roses, matching the colors of her dress.

"Don't tell me you're ready?"

"You said six, didn't you?"

"Yes, but I thought etiquette requires a woman to keep her date waiting."

"I doubt that's polite. Besides this isn't a formal date. I'm just having dinner with some friends."

"Please, excuse me," he smiled. "Is it polite for me to tell you how beautiful you look?"

Windy blushed. "Thank you," she said.

Windy felt like a princess all night. She and Stephan met the other couple at a restaurant Windy had passed many times, never expecting to dine there.

John's remarks about her good looks made her uncomfortable, until she saw him look at his wife. Sally, though smaller than her husband stood a head taller than Windy. Blonde hair cascaded down her back. She clasped Windy's hand and held it warmly. With broad shoulders and large frame, Sally still carried some of the extra weight from just having a baby. Her blue eyes shone every time she looked at her husband or child. Johnny, as his parents lovingly called him, slept quietly in a carrier on a chair placed between Sally and Stephan.

Half-way through dinner Johnny awoke. Stephan, nearly finished with his meal, picked the baby up and cradled him in his arms. He ceased to cry.

"You're a natural, Doc!" John exclaimed. "Too bad you don't have a passel of kids yourself."

"It is too bad, isn't it?" he answered, looking directly at Windy. She stared at him for a moment, unable to believe the look in his eyes. Focusing her attention on her last bit of food she avoided his look for the remainder of dinner.

Stephan stopped the car in front of Windy's house. He turned and looked at her.

"I'm sorry if I embarrassed you tonight. I usually have better manners."

"Not embarrassed, just surprised."

"I don't know why I should have. Don't you realize how I feel about you?"

"About a married woman?"

"Which gives me all the more reason to admire you. You've been handed a raw deal, yet you won't compromise your standards. I would think less of you if you did."

"Stephan, you've been good to me and I appreciate it; but what about your standards? I mean, you're the one that goes to church, yet you're showing interest in a married woman."

"First of all, going to church doesn't make me a saint. Second, you may be married, but your husband is the scum of the earth. Any man who would beat his wife…"

"Eddie never beat me!" Windy protested loudly.

"Then who did?"

She looked away. Beat. The word conjured up pictures of horrid men with clubs and whips. She touched her face involuntarily. Eddie slapped her, even knock her down a time or two. But he never meant to hurt her. It was just when he drank that he raised a hand to her; and then only because she nagged him. Eddie was a good man. The man she loved and wanted as her husband and she'd not stand by and let this stranger accuse him.

"Thank you for a nice evening, Dr. Michaels. I enjoyed seeing John and his family. Goodnight."

She slipped out of the door and headed for the house. Stephan jumped from the car and caught her.

"Windy, I'm sorry, truly sorry. But when I saw you lying in the hospital like a throw away toy I felt such… concern for you. I didn't mean to belittle your husband. If you love him, he must have some redeeming qualities."

"That's it, Stephan. When some one says bad things about Eddie, they may as well say them about me. I love him, I chose to marry him. If he's so evil what does that make me that I would choose evil?"

"Innocent," he replied.

Innocent. The word echoed in Windy's mind. Could she truly be without fault in her marriage?

"Windy," Stephan broke into her thoughts. "I'll behave myself. I'll not say another word against your husband. Please, let's be friends."

"You'll not make any more…passes."

He smiled at the word. "No more."

"Okay. Friends," she held out her hand and he took it gently in his.

"Friends," he agreed. "Say, do you happen to have one of those cherry colas?"

"You never touch the stuff, remember?"

"Humble pie makes me thirsty."

Windy laughed and shook her head. "C'mon, friend."

Chapter Nine

Dear Lord, the pastor spoke about disappointment in his sermon. I guess my walk with You is new enough that I haven't had time to be disappointed. Please keep Your arms around me, keep me walking with you. And Lord help my son and his girl turn to You in their disappointments. Thank You.

Unsure of the handwriting but excited about the return address, Windy tore open the envelope and unfolded the letter.

Windy, I know this ain't none of my business but I think you aught to know. Eddie picked up a girl hitchhikin' on his way out here last month. Theys living here with us. Eddie reads yers letters to Daddy and the boys. They all laff at you, Aggie.

She read it several times before retreating upstairs. Pictures of her husband holding a stranger, paraded through her mind. She imagined his kisses, his caresses being given to someone else. In the living room she plopped down on the couch staring at the picture on the end table. Her Eddie, her husband. She put the letter on the table and laid down, closing her eyes. Sachel jumped on the couch and curled next to her soft hair. His purring brought Windy a desire to be comforted and she began to cry, silently at first, then with the sobs of one suffering from the cruelest of jokes. When her body began to shake and her breath came in gasps the cat jumped from the couch and found refuge in the farthest corner of the bedroom.

Windy searched the drawers in the kitchen a second time, then turned to count the coins lying on the table. Pay day wasn't till Friday, and she just couldn't wait that long. She had to talk to him now, before he drifted too far away. He loved her, she knew he did. He just needed to hear her voice again, if she could stir his memories, he'd realize he must come home.

She stuffed the change in one pocket and the paper with his dad's number in the other. Checking her face she hoped she didn't encounter Cora on the way out. Her friend would be suspicious of her puffy eyes.

Outside, the day lingered late into evening. Already eight-thirty and the sun still blazed above the tree tops. Windy quickly covered the half block to the pay phone. Watching the other people on the sidewalk, she wished for more privacy but picked up the phone and dialed the operator.

"Hello?" Eddie's voice sounded on the other end.

"Eddie? It's Windy. I…I miss you, Eddie."

"Yeah, I miss you, too, Babe," he said, using her pet name.

"Eddie, when are you coming home?" she asked hesitantly. "I've found a job, it doesn't pay much, but it'll get us by till you find something you like."

Windy heard muffled noises, as though Eddie held his hand over the receiver. She remembered Aggie's letter and wondered if he shared this conversation with the others.

"Eddie?"

"Yeah, Babe. Look, if I was to come back, things would be different, you know?"

Laughter, clear then muffled, as she heard Eddie shush the other voices.

"Different? Sure Eddie. I know I'm not a good wife. But I've been thinking about all the times I was wrong. And I'm sorry."

"Well now, that's what I needed to hear, Babe, that yer sorry."

"Oh, I am, really. Eddie, next week is our anniversary. You didn't forget, did you? June tenth."

"Naw, I didn't forget! Listen, I'll be back then and we'll celebrate. Okay?"

Windy closed her eyes, tears streaming down her face. He said he'd come home. He said it.

"Okay. I love you. See you soon."

"Bye." He hung up before she could say good-bye but not before she heard the laughter. She pictured them; him, his dad, his brothers and the faceless girl, laughing at her. Well, let them laugh. He was coming home, and she would show him how good marriage could be. She'd be a better wife and they'd never talk about this separation, though they would be closer because of it.

Wiping the remnants of tears from her face she glided back to the house. As she opened the door the smell of fresh cinnamon rolls greeted her and she wondered what delicacy Cora would bake for Eddie's homecoming.

Upstairs she took a quick inventory of the work to be done before Eddie returned. Today was Tuesday the third, she had one exactly one week. She marched into the living room and retrieved Aggie's letter, holding it above the kitchen sink, she put a match to it and watched the words slowly burn away.

Windy announced the good news to Cora the next morning. Cora smiled but didn't share Windy's enthusiasm. At work Windy hummed, and smiled and her co-workers commented on her changed attitude. Since she'd never told any of them about her situation, she just smiled and hummed louder. At home she spent every spare minute cleaning, and rearranging. 'We need a whole new start,' she told herself.

Anything not anchored to the floor found a new resting place. She even bought more lead wire and moved the television. Eddie always complained about the glare from the window.

By Tuesday morning, everything stood ready. Work dragged by, but finally five o'clock came and Windy hurried home. She showered quickly, sprayed on Eddie's favorite cologne, and fixed her hair the way he liked, pulled back and curly on the ends. Her best blouse and new jeans lay on the bed waiting for her. At 6:30 she popped the baked potatoes in the oven and set the table. She placed a card next to Eddie's plate, glad she'd resisted the small bouquet of flowers. He felt such things were nonsense.

Trying to calm her nerves, Windy sat on the couch and attempted to finish the magazine she'd borrowed from the library, an issue full of secrets to a happy husband.

Windy stared at the darkened street from the bedroom window. Every pair of headlights brought anticipation then disappointment. At eleven o'clock she placed the over-done potatoes in the refrigerator, glancing at the uncooked steaks. Cora's Dutch apple pie sat on the table. Windy covered it with plastic wrap and turned out the lights.

Just as she pulled the bed covers over her, someone banged on the door. Windy froze. Eddie was home. She remembered their last night together and touched her face, suddenly afraid to go to the door.

"Windy!" he yelled.

Quickly she ran into the kitchen and slid the bolt back, hoping Cora hadn't been awakened.

"Hey, babe," he said, pushing his way in. "Happy Anniversary." He pulled Windy close and kissed her hard. She tasted his last sour beer.

A young girl stood behind him. Her fearful look tugged at Windy's heart. "Crissy, meet my wife, Windy."

Mascara smudged under the girl's eyes and Windy wondered what kind of treatment she'd suffered at Eddie's hands.

"No place like home," Eddie mumbled, his eyes scanning the kitchen. "Hey, my favorite! Dutch apple pie. That ole lady bake this just for me?" Windy nodded. "So, you told her your long lost husband was returning? Be sure to thank her for me, will you?"

Windy stared at this intruder, her husband. He looked nothing like the young, happy man in the picture. He needed a haircut, a shave and from the looks of his eyes, less beer and more sleep. His face looked gaunt and he'd lost weight. Had he changed this much in one month? Or had he looked like this when he left? Sadly, Windy realized this Eddie had replaced the one in the picture months ago.

"Sit down," she motioned to Eddie and the girl. "Have you eaten? I can warm the potatoes…"

"Just give me a fork, don't want the old hag to think I ain't grateful." Eddie tore the plastic from the pie. "Sit down," he growled at the girl.

Windy retreated into the bedroom and pulled her robe around her, shivering despite the warmth of the night. Back in the kitchen, she poured Eddie a glass of milk and offered Crissy a can of pop.

Eddie ate half the pie then handed the wrap to Windy. "I'll take it with me, a midnight snack, you know." He looked at Crissy, "Go down to the car, I'll be out later. And take this with you." He handed her the pie.

Windy hoped the girl had enough sense to run while she had a chance, but not in the car. She just wanted Eddie to leave. She realized how foolish she'd been, thinking they could actually have a marriage in the midst of this insanity.

When the door closed Eddie turned his attention to Windy.

"You didn't tell me Happy Anniversary."

Windy remained silent, the card on the table forgotten.

"What's the matter, Babe? I thought you wanted your Eddie home, wanted him real bad. Well, I'm here. Let's celebrate!" Windy backed away from him, reaching for the counter behind her.

"Eddie, I'm sorry I asked you to come back. I can see you've found some one else. Are you happier now?"

"I never been unhappy." He closed the distance between them and put his arms around her. "But I been mad before. You ain't gonna make me mad tonight are you? I'd hate to have to hurt you on our anniversary."

She felt the familiar touch, not the one she'd dreamed about and longed for, but the one she feared. Her heart raced and her throat became dry.

"Umm, don't you smell nice? That's the perfume I bought for you, guess you've really been looking forward to seeing me. They say absence makes the heart grow fonder. Are you fonder of me, Babe?"

He began kissing her, hard and mean. When she struggled he tightened his arms around her. She pushed against him, but was no match for his strength. Angry, he grabbed her hair and pulled her head back.

"You forget who you're messing with, Babe. I'm your husband, remember? I've got the right to do whatever I want. You gave me that right and you can't take it away."

He ripped her robe and then her night gown exposing her soft flesh. Windy began to cry.

"No, Eddie, please don't do this, please.

Chapter Ten

Dear Lord, I read a verse about suffering today. Funny, I always thought suffering was bad, but in the Bible it sounds more like a privilege. Please be with my son, if he is suffering, let him know You're there, and his girl too. Maybe You could show them that same verse. Thank You. Amen

Windy awoke to the sunlight streaming in on her face. She moaned and rolled over, looking at the clock.

Nine-thirty, an hour and a half, before work started, she'd better get a shower. Jumping up, her head spun and she fell back on the bed. Noticing blood on her pillow, she touched her lips. They were hard and dry. She sat up and stared into the mirror atop the dresser, unprepared for what she saw. One eye was swollen shut, the other discolored. Scratches marked the left side of her face. Her hair hung in tangles, clumps of it lay on her shoulders. Several bruises dotted her bare chest.

Looking about, she noticed the bedcovers flowed onto the floor, her nightgown and robe lay in the doorway. Picking up the pink blanket she wrapped it around her went into the kitchen and bolted the door. A noise from the living caught her attention. Her breath stopped in her throat. Moving quietly through the kitchen she peeked around the corner. Sachel stretched on the couch.

"Come here, boy," she whispered.

The cat ran to her and rubbed her blanketed legs. She picked him up and held him tight.

"Are you okay?" she asked. He answered in a contented purr.

Windy ran some fresh water in his dish then entered the bathroom. Carefully she washed the blood from her face and lips, covering the wounds with medicated cream. Dropping the blanket, she quickly examined herself for other injuries. Red welts formed on her arms and several more bruises decorated her legs.

Returning to her room she pulled on a tee-shirt and pair of sweats. Tugging the sheets off the bed, she stuffed them into the hamper.

"I'd burn you," she threatened, "if I could afford new sheets."

Her head began to spin again so she sat on the bed. When it cleared she picked up her brush and started pulling at the tangles. Tears spilled from her eyes from the pain and the amount of hair she pulled out with each stroke.

Glancing at the clock she remembered work. She couldn't show up looking like this. But calling in sick, meant facing Cora. It had to be done, she couldn't afford to lose her job. But she would shower first and look as presentable as possible.

Cora showed more concern than surprise when she opened her door to Windy. She quickly ushered her into the welcome kitchen.

"Sit down, and I'll fix you a cup of raspberry tea."

She placed the kettle on the burner and reached for the phone.

"Hello, may I speak to the manager, please?" She smiled at Windy. "Hello? This is Cora Davis, Windy's landlady. Windy seems to have come down with a bad case of the flu. I doubt she'll be able to work the rest of the week. Yes, I'll do that. Thank you."

Windy stared wide-eyed at her friend. She'd never heard Cora lie before.

The woman shrugged. "What else could I tell them?" she asked.

"I should have done it. I don't like you lying on my account."

Cora smiled. "I'll seek forgiveness later."

Windy spooned a little honey into her tea and took a sip. It tasted good. She felt she should talk to Cora, explain her appearance, but she didn't know how to begin.

The older woman broke the awkward silence.

"We might as well talk about this, no sense trying to skirt the issue. I saw him and that young girl. They got out of the car as I pulled the kitchen shade for the night. I heard them go upstairs and a short while later the outside door banged and I saw the girl running down the street. Then I heard voices coming from your room." Cora's chin began to quiver and Windy feared she would start crying if Cora did. "Oh, Windy dear, I'm so sorry, I should have called the police. I shouldn't have let you go through that. But I was afraid. Forgive me," she cried.

Windy hugged the woman and they cried for each other. Soon Cora detached herself and pulled a Kleenex from her apron pocket. She wiped her nose, and handed Windy the box she always kept on the counter. "Now sit down and drink your tea before it gets cold. I know it's almost too late, but I'm calling the police now." Windy started to protest but Cora held her hand up. "This needs to be on record."

"Why?"

"For your safety, dear, in case he ever comes back."

"I don't think he will."

Cora spoke into the phone, explaining the situation to her listener. "Are you willing to go to the police station?" she asked Windy.

Windy answered by shaking her head.

"Can't you send someone here? What about those nice officers that came the last time? What's that?…yes, this has happened before…the officer's name?…let me see…no. No, I don't remember…it's on your report?…and you'll have them follow up? That's very good of you, thank you." She hung up and looked at Windy. "I know it'll be hard dear, but you really should see this through." Placing her empty cup in the sink, Windy nodded, admitting to herself that Cora was probably right.

Back in her apartment Windy stuffed the dirty sheets into the pillow case and threw the blanket over her bed. Memories of the night before flashed through her mind. Eddie's face leered at her while his voice taunted.

"I'm your husband," he reminded her. "I can do anything I please because it's my right. The right you gave me." Her voice answered him, pleading for him to stop. This was her husband, the man she married, the one to whom she willingly gave herself, completely. Now this stranger ruthlessly forced himself upon her. She searched for the man she once knew in the familiar body, in the face that used to smile lovingly at her. Where were the intimate looks they once shared? Where had her husband gone?

Windy tried to shake the memory from her mind. She felt betrayed. For two

60

years she did all she could to please this man, because she loved him. Now his actions mocked her love, denying its worth.

Windy curled up on the bed and held her pillow tightly, crying into it. Soon she drifted into a fitful sleep.

Windy carefully descended the stairs, laundry under one arm, a grocery bag in the other. If Cora insisted on cooking for her, at least she could supply some of the food. After all she'd stocked up this week thinking she'd be cooking for two. Cora insisted Windy use her washer and dryer, too, saying she simply couldn't go out to do her laundry.

Stephan greeted Windy as she opened Cora's door. Instinctively, she looked away, setting the bag on the table.

"I'm going to throw these in the washer," she told Cora as she left the kitchen. Windy felt their eyes on her as she walked through the living room and down the hall to the laundry room. She wanted to be angry at Cora, but couldn't find it in her.

She watched the water fill the tub and dilute the soap powder. Stuffing the sheets into the washer, she seriously thought of leaving through the back door and climbing the outside stairs to her apartment. She probably would have if the little door in the living room weren't locked.

Summoning her courage, she headed for the kitchen, ready for Stephan's 'I told you so'. She stopped in the bathroom and checked her eye glad to see the swelling had gone down considerably. She could even see out of it.

The conspirators sat at the table drinking tea. A third steaming cup sat opposite Stephan.

"Those are luscious looking steaks," Cora said. "Since they've not been frozen we should eat them tonight."

"Good idea." Windy sat down and spooned honey into her cup. She glanced up at Stephan. Rather than the triumphant look she expected, she saw concern in his eyes as he looked at her battered face. She looked away clenching her jaw tight, determined not to cry again. Stephan cleared his throat. After a moment he spoke. "I had some free time and thought how nice a hot buttered roll would taste. I dropped in on Cora unexpectedly."

Windy shot Cora a questioning look. The woman held her hands up defensively. "He's telling the truth. I didn't call him, if that's what you're thinking. I simply can't turn someone away when they come to my door."

Windy managed a slight smile, even though it hurt.

"As long as I'm here, I really should take a look at you."

Windy wanted to refuse, but knew she would be silly to do so. She nodded her consent. Stephan moved to her side of the table and pulled her to her feet.

"The lighting is brightest here, I believe."

She flinched, though he touched her gently. He examined every inch of her face and throat, commenting on the loose hair lying on her shoulders. Then he asked her to sit while he looked at her scalp.

"What about your arms and legs?" he asked, noting the long sleeves and pants, despite the hot kitchen.

"Just bruises," she replied, shaking her head. "My eye is what worried me, but it seems fine now."

"Well, I'm not an optometrist. You need to have it checked as soon as the swelling is gone."

Windy nodded, knowing she wouldn't. Optometrists cost money.

Cora made herself busy and when Stephan offered to help peel potatoes she actually let him, surprising Windy who was never allowed to help.

Windy heard the washer stop and excused herself. She dropped the sheets into a basket and went out the back door. A clothesline stretched the length of the small yard and Windy pinned the sheets to it. She loved the smell of clothes dried outside and hoped it would help her to sleep tonight. She checked the sun, still shining in the western sky, assured they would dry before the dew fell. The screen door shut behind her and Windy knew who it was before she turned.

"Cora suggested we sit out here for a while. Says she's not used to help in the kitchen," he said.

Windy nodded, unable to find an answer. She pulled a couple lawn chairs into the sun and sat down. Closing her eyes she laid her head back and let the warmth caress her face.

"You'll be wrinkled as badly as I am in a few years, if you're not careful," Stephan said, moving his chair into the shade and closer to hers.

Windy acknowledged him with a smile but said nothing.

Silence engulfed them as Stephan reached over and gently took her hand in his.

After supper Stephan helped with dishes, then left for the hospital. Cora invited Windy to spend the evening, but Windy politely declined and carried her laundry back upstairs.

She'd just finished making the bed when she heard a knock on the door. Holding her breath, she moved cautiously to the window and peered out. A police cruiser sat in front of the house. The knock sounded again as Windy turned and stared into the mirror. Slowly, she reached for the lamp on the night stand and turned it off. She closed the bedroom door and stood silently in the darkness listening to the officer call her name.

Chapter Eleven

Dear Lord, Why does my past keep surfacing? I know with my head that You've forgiven me, that You've taken away my sins Why God, why don't You take away the memories? What about my son's memories? Do they hurt him and his girl? Remind them they can be forgiven. Remind me too, please. Thank You, Amen.

Windy's 'flu' lasted until the end of that week. She returned to work on Monday morning, her eye puffy and an unsightly scab on her lip. No one asked any questions and she offered no explanations.

Days passed into weeks.

Stephan showed up often, but kept a respectable distance, never doing more than holding Windy's hand or guiding her by the elbow.

She resisted his invitations to church, saying she didn't feel 'right' about going. When he took her to see his house she simply refused to get out of the car, surprised at her own stubbornness. But the more stubborn she became, the more patient Stephan grew.

The people at work were friendly, but their lives were busy enough without including another person. Most of the kids Windy went to school with had moved away or started their own families, some were still in college. Windy realized how much she had alienated herself from others as Eddie's wife. Her world revolved around him. Now it tumbled down around her.

Fireworks exploded above their heads and landed in the small inland lake. While those around them ohhhed and ahhhed, Windy wished the show would quickly end. She admitted the were pretty but she found it difficult to enjoy herself. She didn't like July Fourth, but couldn't remember why. Slowly she reviewed the holiday through out her childhood. She remembered sparklers and firecrackers, the long drive to Lake Michigan where they sat on the beach watching the brilliant sparks rain down into the lake. Then she exclaimed about their beauty.

When had it changed for her? What did it hold last year? Eddie, getting drunk for the first time. Eddie and two new buddies shooting off M-80's and a myriad of other illegal fireworks. Eddie and his friends leaving about midnight. Windy shivered as his homecoming played through her mind like an horror movie. That was the first time he hit her. The attack began verbally. First he slandered her parents then raised questions about her virtue. When he ran out of words he allowed his fists to strike the blows. Windy winced at the thought of his hands on her, hitting her, pulling at her hair and clothing.

You're not cold, are you, Elaine?" Stephan asked. He sat beside her on the sand, wearing jean shorts and a tee-shirt. His deck shoes sat next to his bare feet. He'd started using her middle name as soon as he became a regular visitor. At first Windy resented it, but soon she came to like it. When Stephan said her name in his deep voice she felt like a woman rather than a little girl.

"I really don't feel well. Could we leave?"

"Of course." He stood and reached his hand out to help her up. Fireworks exploded behind him, placing her in his shadow, she shivered again.

He started the car and drove down the beach road, fireworks illuminated the darkened sky. "Would you like to talk about it?

Windy shook her head.

Stephan took a deep breath and continued. "If not to me, then someone else?"

Like who?"

"A counselor, a pastor, perhaps."

"Why?"

"Elaine, you're doing too well. Major changes in a person's life are stress factors. They include such things as a change of job or residence, loss of a family member through various ways, being a victim of a crime, the list goes on. Ignoring those changes and the stress they bring only makes the situation worse. Results can be physical, ulcers for instance, or emotional, but always harmful."

"You should have been a psychiatrist."

"It doesn't take a professional to know those things, just common sense. Besides, I constantly see the physical results in my patients." He decided to say no more, the next move must be hers.

Soon she began to speak, pouring out her hurt and frustration. As Stephan drove along the dark highway, Windy spoke of dreams gone sour and love betrayed.

She haltingly told of Eddie's last visit, of the fear and loneliness she felt in his presence. She relived the torment of that night, with surprisingly few tears.

When she fell silent Stephan searched for words of comfort. He'd seen heartache many times, in cancer patients, accidents victims, but had never been subjected to it personally. He simply didn't know how she felt.

"I have dealt with rape victims many times. It is a heinous crime. I know it's little consolation, but at least he was your husband, not a stranger."

"Not a stranger?" she repeated. "What comfort is there in that?"

"Well, It's not as though he had never…been with you before."

She sat quietly for a moment, then seemed to change the subject. "Has anyone ever filed a mal-practice suit against you?"

He looked surprised. "Yes," he answered. "Why? Are you thinking of filing one for giving bad advise? I said I'm not a professional counselor, remember."

"Who," she asked, ignoring his remark.

He shrugged. "A couple patients."

"Strangers?"

"Can any doctor call a patient a stranger?"

"But not close personal friends?"

"One was," he admitted quietly.

"How close?"

"Very. Our friendship began in college. He specialized in physical therapy." Windy hit a raw nerve, Stephan had never discussed the case with any one other than his lawyer.

"How long ago?"

"Five years."

"Are you still friends?"

"No."

"So, you went to college and med school together? He must have a practice here?" Stephan nodded. "You probably had dinner a time or two, golfing, tennis?" He nodded again. "He came to you with a medical need and you. served him as best you could, but it wasn't good enough. He sued you. Did he win?"

"We settled out of court," his voice barely audible.

"And the others, the strangers?"

"Other," he corrected. "I was simply in the wrong place at the wrong time."

"Settle that out of court, too?"

"Nothing to settle, he had no case."

"Did you ever have dinner with him," Stephan frowned and shook his head, "shared a tennis match, or a dream? Did you feel betrayed when he filed papers against you? Tell me, Stephan, which hurt worse?"

He pulled unto a side street and shut off the engine. Turning in his seat, he reached for her hand, but she pulled it back.

"Don't you see? Being in the wrong place at the wrong time, having someone harm you because you happen to be there, how can that compare? This wasn't just a physical violation. It went clear to my soul, it affected everything I am and have been for over three years. I wouldn't want some stranger touching me, but it would be impersonal, a random choice. This was my husband," Windy's voice faltered as tears escaped her eyes, "the man I gave everything to. The man I adored," she swallowed and wiped the tears from her cheeks, "who once adored me and loved me. Is this what my love did to him? Made him evil? What does that make me?"

Stephan moved over and pulled her into his arms where she wept unashamedly. He stoked her hair and whispered to her.

"You're a victim, Elaine, an innocent, trusting victim. You're not to blame. It wasn't your fault. Believe me, it wasn't your fault."

Chapter Twelve

Dear Lord,

I'm growing. It's been an interesting summer, full of learning and listening. Sometimes I feel excited about having You in my life. Sometimes that knowledge brings me such peace. I enjoy these morning times with You more and more. Lead me today in Your will. Lead my son in to Your will, too, Lord, and his girl. Open their hearts to You and show them Your wondrous love. In Your Sons name, amen.

Excuse me. Where can I find the razor blades?"

Windy looked up from the case of shampoo sitting on the floor in front of her. A young man of average height and build with light brown hair stood looking at her. She placed her marker on the shelf and stood up

"Razor blades," she repeated as she walked down the aisle. Reaching the display she added, "I hope you know what kind of razor you have. There's so many to choose from."

"Actually, I need…" his voice cracked and he cleared his throat. Windy then felt the man's nervousness. She turned to look at him, wondering what caused it. His cool gray eyes were on her and he seemed to be searching for words. His mouth moved but no sound came through.

Windy knew she should make some suggestions and although she'd priced the blades that morning, knew all the brand names and their cost, she couldn't recall any of them. All she saw were those eyes locked onto hers and she couldn't look away.

Her thoughts spun. She wondered what the others in the store thought of her and this stranger as they continued in the involuntary stare-down. She wondered what time it was, heard the ringing of the cash registers and voices of children arguing in the next aisle. Though her thoughts moved on, her eyes refused to budge.

The man swallowed, cleared his throat again and spoke. In the jumble of words that followed Windy recognized two. "...straight...razor..."

"Yes, we have that kind of blade." Her hand reached toward the display, but her eyes remained on the man.

The children from the next aisle suddenly rounded the corner, and connected with the back of Windy's knees. She slowly tumbled backward, her head missing the shelf by inches. The man instinctively reached for her and kept her from landing on the floor.

"We're sorry!" The two little boys yelled as they continued down the aisle.

"Are you alright?" The man asked, his arm still braced Windy's back.

"I'm fine," she answered, relieved the spell had been broken, though she would have preferred a less dramatic way. Regaining her composure she stepped away and pulled a package of razor blades from its hook. "I believe you wanted these?"

"Yes. Thank you, Miss...?" he looked at her name tag. "Windy." He sounded as though he were testing her name to see how well it came off his tongue. He obviously liked its sound for he repeated it as a child would take a second bite of candy that he'd desired for a long time.

"You're welcome, and thank you for, um, catching me."

He smiled and the cool eyes jumped to life. "My pleasure," he said, embarrassing Windy with the sincerity of his comment. "Yes, these are just what I wanted." He slapped the package of razor blades against his open hand, not bothering to even look at them. His gaze had returned to Windy and before history could repeat itself she quickly turned.

"Have a nice day, sir," she said over her shoulder.

Windy walked through the screen door, a smile on her face. She loved summer, loved the hot sun on her face and the warm breeze in her hair. Having met a nice looking young man at work helped make the day a little better, too.

She picked up the mail and quickly scanned through it. Cora evidently had taken hers already as everything bore the Bilmon name. Upstairs she placed the envelopes on the table and stared at them, knowing what they contained. She still owed the hospital for her stay in May. She was amazed at how quickly the expenses built up. Ambulance. Emergency Room. Hospital. Doctor. Consulting Doctor. Lab. Lab Technician. Add all those to the bills she and Eddie had accumulated in the last two years and Windy had no idea how she would pay them all.

"I don't believe in divorce," Windy stated. "I saw too many kids messed up because their parents split. My folks were a rock for me, and I promised myself I would never get a divorce."

"Elaine, you have no children to hurt."

"That doesn't change my standard"

"Then what do you intend to do? Invite him home again?"

She flashed Stephan a warning look as they sat in her apartment, dining on pork chops and fried potatoes.

"Why do I have to decide now?"

"Why put it off?"

Windy dropped her fork on the plate and massaged her temples with her fingertips. "You're the one who said too many changes, too quickly, causes stress."

"As does living in uncertainty."

"Can't we just have a nice quiet evening? Must we discuss this tonight? Heavens, listen to me! I'm starting to talk like you."

Reaching across the small table, he caressed her hand. "Elaine, I love you. I have loved you since the first night I saw you."

She looked hard at him trying to see past the longing in his eyes. She wanted to dig into his soul and see if this man could honestly love her. She'd seen it building since the night she opened her secret doors to him. What did he really feel for her? Pity? Wealthy, handsome men didn't just drop out of the sky and fall in love with poor little girls. This was the real world, not a fairy tale.

Windy pulled her hand away, picked up her plate and walked to the sink. She turned and looked at him.

"You don't even know me."

"I believe I know you well enough."

She shuddered slightly. "Well, I don't know you." Stephan was, without doubt, a good man, one of the most eligible men in this town. A hundred mothers would kill to call him son-in-law. But he was, in her sight, an old man. She just couldn't see herself calling him husband.

"I think it's best that we not see each other for a while. At least until I decide what to do about Eddie."

She heard Stephan rise from the table and stand behind her.

"I do not consider that an option."

Windy drew in a breath. She wasn't a confronter.

Rarely did she express her opinion, much less stand her ground. Every time she did, it brought pain. She remembered not backing down to Mr. Bilmon and the consequences that brought. She thought of spending a night in the hospital when she stood up to Eddie. If there was a time to stand up to Stephan this was it.

"It's the only option I will consider," she stated, cringing inside. She waited for his reaction, expecting words that would demand her obedience. But he stood silent behind her. After several minutes Windy surprised herself when her mouth opened and she her voice continued.

"Maybe you should leave now." As the last word left her mouth she braced herself for the onslaught. Instead she felt him walk away. She looked in time to see him stop at the door and turn, as if to say something, but he just shook his head and left.

Windy stared after him her heart pounded inside her chest. She could hardly believe that she still stood, mentally as well as physically. She heard the downstairs door open and close, heard a car pulling away.

Well, he's gone. Good. She told herself. I allowed this thing to go to far. I should have stopped it long ago. Should never have let it get started.

She washed the dishes, scouring the sinks and stove then rubbed her hands with lotion when she finished. In the living room, she popped the movie into the cheap VCR the one luxury she and Eddie had allowed themselves. As film credits rolled on the screen she opened her sewing basket and took out the small crocheted tablecloth. Stephan admired her handiwork on Cora's living room lamp table and she promised him one for his home, the home she refused to enter.

Her fingers skillfully pulled and looped the thin yarn while her mind tried to sort out what was happening. Eddie's picture laughed at her from the end table, his ring on her finger caught the light with each movement.

She wove a gift for one man while another mocked her. Who did Stephan think he was, coming into her life and demanding she make decisions? Who was Eddie, taking her love and giving pain in return? The questions bore into her, deeper and deeper. She tried to silence them with the noise of the movie, but they cried for answers. Answers she didn't have, didn't want.

Their words became louder, accusing, pleading, defending. Eddie couldn't help hurting you. He's sick. Everyone knows alcoholism is a disease. He suffered, too, more than you. If you divorce him, you'd be walking out on your responsibility as his wife. He needs you, now more than ever. Would you leave him if he had cancer?

Isn't his disease self-inflicted? Another question raised. He chooses to have it. He wants no cure. How can you help him? You trusted him and he betrayed you. You must never trust again. Trust brings hurt and pain. Haven't you had enough?

How could you not trust Stephan, when all he's ever done is help you? Another voice joined the silent conversation. You question their right to hurt you, but what gave you the right to hurt Stephan? Couldn't you see the pain in his eyes?

"Shut up," she warned. Sachel, curled up on the end of the couch, flicked his ear.

He offers you life again, happiness. And you punished him for someone else's misdeed.

"Shut up!" she yelled. Sachel raised his head in annoyance.

If some one like Eddie couldn't love you, what makes you think this fine man possibly could?

"I said shut up!" Windy threw the tablecloth on the floor, picked up Eddie's picture and smashed it with her fist. She tore the ring off with bloody fingers and hurled it across the room. "Leave me alone!" She cried, running through the apartment. She fell across the bed and pounded her anger into the pillow.

Moments later, the front door flew open. "You leave her alone, you monster," Cora yelled. "Windy? Windy, where are you?"

Windy emerged from the bedroom, staring at her friend. Cora stood in the open doorway, wrapped in a pink chenille bathrobe, iron skillet in hand. Her thin white hair hung in a long braid.

Windy took one wide-eyed look at her and began to laugh.

Cora stared back in disbelief.

"What are you doing?" Windy finally managed to ask.

"I'll not stand by and do nothing. No one will ever harm you again while I'm here. Not even him!"

"Who?"

"Dr. Michaels!"

"Stephan? Oh, Cora, you dear, dear lady. Stephan left some time ago. The only one harming me tonight is me." Cora looked around, suspiciously. "I promise," Windy said. "Sit down, it's my turn to offer you a calming cup of tea." She took the skillet from Cora and placed it on the table. Cora sat down, still shaking.

"You meant business, didn't you?" Windy asked, washing her hands, trying to conceal her bleeding fingers.

"I just decided I couldn't sit back and do nothing again."

"If I had been in danger, you would have been also." She filled the tea kettle and placed it on a hot burner.

"I don't care, there comes a time when you have to stand up and do what's right." Cora looked around the room. "Why did Dr. Michaels leave so early?" Noticing the look on Windy's face she continued, "you two didn't have a tiff did you?"

"No, not really. Oh, Cora," Windy sat down. "I'm so confused. Tonight he said he loves me."

"Wonderful!" Cora clasped her hands together.

"I told him we shouldn't see each other for a while."

Cora pondered that for a moment. "Good," she said. "You need to end one relationship before starting another. Now don't misunderstand me, I don't believe in divorce myself. Marriage calls for commitment, working through the hard times. My dear husband and I traveled many difficult roads. At times we both thought about walking away. But we didn't, because we believe in keeping a promise. Now I don't believe in murder either, but it was in my eyes when I came up those stairs. Remember your wedding vows?" Windy nodded. "Have you kept them?"

"Yes; as best as I could. I tried to honor and obey."

"Did Eddie keep his vows? Did he protect you, provide for you? Did he cherish you?"

They sat in silence as the tea kettle whistled. Finally, Windy removed it from the burner and poured the steaming water. She placed the cups on the table and opened the honey jar.

"Then you think I should get a divorce, too."

"Yes," Cora answered firmly. "I think you should get on with your life. Windy, your marriage was never destined to be. Teenagers jump into marriage, like they're going to a party, that doesn't mean they've done the right thing. Once they're in it, they have a responsibility to each other. That's where doing the right thing comes in, trying everything you can to make it work. I think you did that. I think you filled your promise. He treated you like a servant, not a wife. He used you. All those nights he stayed out until dawn, who do you think brought him home?"

"His drinking buddies."

"Yes and one in particular. She drove a little orange car. Deny you ever saw it. You innocent little child, you trusting little girl, it's time to grow up."

Stephan pulled into his driveway and hit the garage door opener. He looked at his darkened house; once again he would spend the night alone. He tried to rid his mind of Windy Elaine Bilmon.

Who does she think she is refusing my love as though I had offered her a cup of coffee? He asked himself. How dare she tell me what she will or will not consider? But I suppose it's a good thing this happened before I became too involved with her. Well, she's out of my mind now and none too soon.

Stephan parked the car and pulled the keys from the ignition, hitting the door control again. He walked into the connecting breezeway and then entered his kitchen. He drew hot water from the tap into a cup and placed it into the microwave.

"No," he told himself. "I need something stronger." He worked his way toward the front of the house and the small bar that stood in the parlor. After mixing a drink he sat on the couch and stared into the empty fireplace.

"I determined to be a doctor, and I became one," he told the gaping hole. "I worked my way through college and med school. I studied on lunch breaks and into the night. I managed to save this house and pull us out of debt during that same time. I have always accomplished what I have set out to do. Always. And now some little snip of a girl thinks she can call the shots. She will not run my life. She will not determine what Stephan Michaels can and can not do. I decide what is best for me. I always have and I always will. I have never offered my love to a woman and I will not be denied when I do." He lifted he glass in salute. "To you, Win-dee, you have not seen the last of me yet."

Chapter Thirteen

Dear Lord,
I really feel a burden for my son and his girl, my girl, today. Do they have decisions to make, are they considering opening their hearts to You? Are they ready to let go of their past and let You fill their future? Touch them this day. Guide and love them. In Your Son's name, amen.

Windy looked up from the box of hand lotion to see a young man walking toward her. He carried a long thin box tied with ribbon.

"Elaine Bilmon?" he asked.

"Yes," she answered, accepting the box. The young man retreated. Windy made for the break room where she quickly discovered a dozen red roses and a note from Stephan.

Just let me know when you're ready.

Windy smiled and shook her head. She left the box in the cooler and resumed her work, silently wondering if Gray Eyes would stop in today.

The flowers came on a regular basis, once a week, and soon Windy found herself looking forward to their arrival. A couple of the girls at work had teased her, but she refused to reveal her admirer's identity.

As the air turned cold and the leaves fell from the trees, Windy began to feel an emptiness in her heart. She longed for the warmth of a man's arms around her. Eddie hadn't been the best husband but he had been attentive, even quite romantic at times. She looked at the approaching winter, and loneliness engulfed her. At night she watched romantic movies, then cried herself to sleep. Finally, with Cora standing beside her, Windy called the good doctor's phone number and left a dinner invitation on his machine.

Windy paced the floor, looking at the clock. He said he'd be there by six. That passed an hour ago. Windy opened the oven door and checked the pot roast. Thankfully it remained tender and the oven still warm.

It was all too familiar, the waiting, checking the meal, the fear in the pit of her stomach. She thought that part of her life had ended.

Walking into the bathroom, she checked her hair again. The curls bounced and shone from the extra attention they'd received. She heard a knock on the door but stood still.

"Didn't he say it's proper to keep your date waiting?" she asked her reflection.

The knock came a second time.

Windy opened the door to a weary man with tired, red eyes. "An emergency, just as I prepared to leave," Stephan explained. She quickly led him into the living room where he collapsed on the couch, resting his head in his hands.

"Stephan, I'm sorry," Windy sat beside him, not knowing what to do she put her hand on his shoulder. She studied his face, having almost forgotten what it looked like in the weeks since she'd seen him. It seemed so natural to comfort him, to touch his hand, his face.

"A car accident, a little baby not strapped in. I couldn't save him," he stated matter-of-factly. Windy wanted to put her arms around him and hold him like a mother holds a wounded child, comforting, loving, but still she hesitated.

He looked at Windy. "I have learned to distance myself from such things. But this was a baby, an innocent child. Why do people do that? Why do they take the most precious gift they have and neglect it, abuse it?"

Windy had no words; she was struck dumb by this man's compassion. Suddenly, she saw him not as a strong, handsome, self-sufficient man who helped other people, but as a person who needed love and understanding. She felt sorry for the way she had treated him on his last visit. Now she wanted to love him, care for him; share his hurts, his dreams.

The moment had come as Windy knew it would. She sat next to Stephan, their heads almost touching. She was about to kiss 'the doctor', the older man who had helped her, who had looked at her in a way she refused to be looked at. His eyes told her what he expected and she suddenly wanted nothing more than to please him.

She hesitated but a moment, pushing aside fear, then repulsion. In the time it took to take a simple breath a dozen reasons issued forth as to why she shouldn't let this happen but with the next breath she pushed them all aside refusing them audience.

She allowed him to touch lips that had been reserved for Eddie. After months of romantic inactivity her mouth awoke to the soft pressure of Stephan's. His kiss brought no excitement; it was neither too dry nor too moist. His lips were soft, almost too soft. Windy listened to her heart, hoping to hear it miss a beat or jump with anticipation. Nothing happened.

She tightened her embrace trying to arouse her own passion and he responded with every fiber of his being.

"I love you, Elaine," he whispered. "I need you."

"I love you, Stephan." The words came automatically, the normal response to such a revelation. They kissed again, and though Windy still felt no tingle, she knew the gentleness of his touch. The ache in her heart lessened as it opened itself to the need of being loved.

Windy placed the cold washcloth on Stephan's tired eyes. "Now it's my turn to care for you," she said.

He still sat on the couch, with Sachel curled up beside him. "I would like that," he replied.

Windy moved Sachel and took his place. She propped a pillow behind Stephan and gently pushed him back on it.

"It's good to see you again. I guess I didn't realize how much I missed you till you came in tonight. How have you been?"

He breathed deeply. "Lonely," he replied.

"Are you ready to eat? We can talk later if you like." Windy studied his half hidden face, wanting to kiss him again. She loved kissing, enjoyed it more than anything else involved with intimacy. Stephan's kiss, though nothing special, tasted much nicer than Eddie's second-hand beer kisses. "Let me put the food on the table, I'll call you when it's all ready."

As she placed the steaming dish on the table Stephan called to her. Stepping into the living room, she saw him holding a handful of overdue bills. She'd forgotten and left them on desk earlier that day.

"Elaine, why didn't you let me know you needed help?"

"Why would I tell you, Stephan?"

He closed the gap between them and took her in his arms. "Because I am the man who loves you and wants to take care of you." He kissed her tenderly. "It bothers me to see you struggling when I can help."

For a moment Windy allowed herself the luxury of imaging her debts being paid. The bank now wanted to repossess a car she hadn't seen in months. She'd even contacted the bank and given them Eddie's address. But they weren't about to send for a car hundreds of miles away that probably sat in a junk heap. No, her name was on the loan, and they wanted cash. Her name also now belonged to several collection agencies, she tried to pay a little on everything each month, but the little she sent just wasn't enough. She seriously considered taking Cora's advise about getting a divorce, hoping there would be some way to force Eddie to help pay their bills, but she certainly had no money for a lawyer.

Windy looked at Stephan. "Let's eat while it's hot, we can talk later," she said, taking the bills from him and placing them inside the desk. With a little luck he'd forget about them.

"This is the movie we intended to watch when you were here last. I thought it appropriate to rent it tonight." Windy explained as she loaded a movie into the VCR.

The strains of the movie's theme set a romantic background for the couple as they nestled together on the couch. Windy savored the feeling of security she felt when Stephan slipped his arm around her and pulled her close.

They attempted to give their attention to the characters on the screen, but found each other much more interesting. Windy wanted to sit here in Stephan's arms, with no pressure, no expectation, forever.

She snuggled closer, pressing her nose against his collar. Beneath the sweat and antiseptic she caught the faint odor of his cologne. She couldn't identify it, but she liked it. Eddie smelled good when they first met. Then she came to recognize him by the sour smell of beer. How she hated that smell.

Stephan yearned for this moment for months; now that it finally happened he feared it would slip away from him. Maybe he was dreaming, again, and if he moved too suddenly he would wake up to the stark reality of his loneliness. He congratulated himself on his perseverance and victory. He nuzzled

Windy's head, her soft hair smelled fresh and clean. Oh, what he had missed all these years, dedicating himself to his career. Memories of women he had been with brushed through his mind. They had simply been part of his experience with life, he'd never considered marrying any of them. He had enjoyed their company for a short time, not allowing them to distract him for his more important goals. But now those goals had all been achieved and he knew it was time to concentrate on the next one—a wife and heirs.

His eyes focused on a scene being played out before him, and he chuckled at what he saw.

"I'm sorry," he said. "But that was cute."

Reluctantly, Windy pulled her face away from his collar and gazed at the couple on the television. They seemed the perfect pair, their good-natured bantering expressed confidence in their relationship. Windy resolved to have that openness between her and Stephan.

She peered up at his face, studying the wrinkles around his clear, blue eyes. *'I don't even know how old he is,'* she thought. *'At least 40 and I'm only 21.'* She pushed away the rising doubts and returned to her observations. A run-a-way lock of hair fell over his forehead. The graying at the temples added a touch of dignity. She noticed a small scar at the corner of his mouth; she'd never seen it before. Windy reached up and traced the straight line of his nose with her fingertip. He smiled, then kissed her gently.

Lost in a world of their making, they alternated between the romance on the screen and the one forming in their hearts.

Windy pulled a tissue from the box as Stephan turned the television off and hit the rewind button on the VCR. "Movies like that should come with a warning label," she sniffed.

Stephan returned to the couch, "Not going to kick me out tonight, are you?"

Windy laughed. "Never again."

"I take it you've had a change of heart?"

She pondered his statement for a moment. "Call it…a changing. Don't expect miracles overnight. I'm still me, young and scared and…"

"Innocent," he finished. "Just how I like you."

"I still don't believe in divorce, but I'm trying to come to grips with reality. Stephan, if my marriage to Eddie were salvageable, I wouldn't stop trying."

"A trait that benefits me, I would say."

"He's still in my heart and I don't know why, but I'm not sure I want that part of my heart to change. If you want me, you'll have to take me like I am."

"And live with Eddie all my life?"

She shook her head. "No, just the confusion. I won't blame you if you have sense enough to walk away. But I want an honest relationship and we might as well start now."

Stephan studied her thoughtfully. In time, after she experienced the love of a decent man she would see the reality of her infatuation. Very pleased with the outcome of the evening, nay, the whole summer he planted a kiss on her forehead.

Chapter Fourteen

Dear Lord,
Where are my kids today? Are they walking with you? My own walk
has been so weak lately. Is it the cooling temperature? Or is Your newness
wearing off? Margie says I'm not even a year old, 'a babe in Christ' she
calls me. But what of my baby? Where is he now? And my girl? Who is she,
God, what does she look like?

Six weeks later, Windy held her divorce papers in her hand, unable to believe it went through so quickly. But Stephan knew a 'good' lawyer who placed high priority on her case and never sent a bill.

Stephan wanted to take her to dinner that night, but she didn't feel like celebrating. She closed a door on an important part of her life, and she felt the loss. She decided to spend the evening alone.

After the first visit to the lawyer, Stephan began talking about marriage. Windy resisted. Jumping from one marriage to another seemed unwise. She remembered what he said about changes in a person's life, and wondered why those changes were harmful except when suggested by Stephan. But each time she silently questioned him, an inevitable rebuke followed. Windy felt at war with herself.

She crossed a bridge of no return; Eddie was no longer her husband. If she married Stephan, she would simply cross another bridge, with no more guaranties than last time. Another marriage was a big step and Windy preferred to walk slowly.

Stephan, however, was not easily put off. He allowed her the lone evening, but showed up early the next morning, bringing rolls for breakfast. When he dropped her off at the grocery store he asked how much longer she intended to work.

"Stephan, you're pushing too fast. I haven't even been single for 24 hours and already you're trying to change that."

"Elaine, I grow older by the day. I found you, I want to marry you and see no reason to wait any longer. We've spent most of our time together these last weeks, why not as husband and wife?"

Husband. Until yesterday that word meant Eddie. Suddenly, it was supposed to mean Stephan. Windy sighed.

"Don't tell me you want to enjoy your freedom, date a few guys…?"

"No, Stephan, it's not that." As Windy denied it the sight of Gray Eyes jumped into her mind. "I'm tired, in my brain. I need to rest, to think, to adjust."

"You've had months to do that. If it hasn't happened by now, a little more time won't make any difference. I want you to rest, in comfort, as my wife."

Windy closed the car door and walked into the store. She looked around at her co-workers. After five months she still didn't know them, their families, what they did in their off-time. She glanced back at Stephan. He waved as he pulled away. Suddenly, she wanted to run after him, to be his wife, his little girl, to let him take care of her. She didn't want to spend her hours with people she hardly knew, stocking items on shelves, or alone in her little apartment. Windy wanted to belong to someone, someone who loved her and whom she could love.

Gray Eyes happened into the store again and walked down Windy's aisle, looking straight ahead. She didn't understand why but her hands started to shake as soon as she saw him.

"I…I forgot where you found those razor blades," he said when he reached Windy. He didn't look at her so she didn't have to avoid his eyes. She was surprised to find herself disappointed.

"Right here," she said pointing, before hiding her shaking hands behind her back. This time she stared at him, waiting for him to return her gaze, hopefully afraid that he might.

"Must be blind," he commented. "So how are you, Windy?" Now his eyes looked straight into hers.

"Fine," she answered weakly. "How are you?"

"Fine."

An awkward silence hovered over them as Gray Eyes tried to speak. It was apparent to Windy that he wanted to say something, anything, but everything he thought of he rejected. She silently willed him to speak to her, wondering if he would show an interest in her. Would he even go so far as to ask her to dinner or a movie? Would she dare accept? Stephan's image hovered over her and the girl knew in her desperate heart this could be the last tie to her own life. Just one word of interest, that's all it would take to keep her from stepping into Stephan's arms.

"Thank you," he finally managed, holding up the package of razor blades. "Bye."

Windy watched him walk away, wanting to call out to him, but chiding herself for even considering it.

As she walked home that afternoon, Windy was tempted to pass the house, to walk right on by, into a world where there were no demands on her, no strangers, and no friends. Instead she turned up the familiar sidewalk and opened the front door for the hundredth time. She stopped and picked up her mail off the little table in the hall, then knocked on Cora's door before entering.

"Sachel, what are you doing here?" she asked the cat rubbing her legs.

Cora appeared down the hall by the laundry room. "You forgot to bring your trash down this morning. When I went up to get it, Sachel came with," she explained.

"I brought some fruit home, thought I'd make a salad for tonight. Sound okay?"

"Sounds good. I've got chicken in the oven. Run along, I'll let you know when it's ready."

"Come on, Moocher. After a day with Cora you'll turn your nose up to your food again."

Master and pet climbed the stairs together. Inside the apartment Windy set the groceries on the table, knocking something off when she did. On the floor lay a heart shaped key ring with four keys on it. Windy stiffened, her heart racing. Quietly she retrieved the keys and studied them. They weren't the ones she feared, the ones belonging to the car Eddie took. But whose were they? Something clicked; Sachel downstairs, mysterious keys on the table. Windy placed the perishables in the refrigerator and returned to the scene of the crime.

"Cora?" she called, accusingly.

The little lady stood at the sink, her back to Windy.

"Yes, dear?"

"Who's been in my apartment?"

"I told you I got your trash. It is Friday, you know, pick-up day."

"And who else?" Cora stayed busy at the sink, intently washing a glass. "Cora, I found some keys; do you know who they belong to?"

Cora turned, wearing a smile from ear to ear. "You! Look across the street."

Windy pulled the curtain away from the window. Opposite the house sat a small blue convertible.

"Dr. Michaels brought it by, said it's just been sitting in his garage and you might as well be using it." Cora's face beamed like a child's and although Windy's hands shook with sudden anticipation, she enjoyed Cora's reaction more.

Overwhelmed and more confused than ever, Windy sat down at the table and began to cry. Cora sat beside her, tears streaming down her cheeks, too. "I know, dear. Isn't it wonderful to be loved so?"

Later that evening Stephan showed up at Windy's door.

"I thought I'd accept my thank you in person," he explained.

"Why?" She uttered the one simple word.

"It's growing too cold for you to walk to work, and" he continued, holding up his hand to stop her comment, "you can not just keep using Cora's car when you need it."

Windy nodded. As usual he was right, though she hated to admit it.

They settled comfortably on the couch, the radio tuned to an 'oldies' station.

"Do you work tomorrow?" Stephan asked.

Windy nodded. "Afternoon shift."

"So you don't have to arise early, we have the whole night to ourselves." He enveloped her in his arms and she clung to him, savoring the security she felt. But Stephan's caresses soon revealed what he had in mind for their 'whole night'.

Windy pulled herself away. "No, Stephan."

"Why not?" he asked, his voice husky with desire.

"You know as well as I do. We're not married."

"A problem that can easily be corrected." He pulled back slightly, giving her the impression that her point had been accepted. "It is not wrong to love someone, to share and express that love," Stephan reasoned. "I will certainly make an honest woman of you. Is that what you fear, Elaine that I will leave?"

"No, of course not," she reassured him.

"It's not as if we are both ignorant of the joys of intimacy, we're two consenting adults, are we not?"

"I'm not sure about the consenting part," she replied.

Stephan pulled completely away and stared at the young woman. "I can not believe you would accuse me of forcing myself on you. You know me better than that Elaine." He walked to the doorway and leaned against the wall looking truly hurt. Windy felt a chill when his warmth left her side. She remembered his generosity in the little blue car parked in her driveway and felt ashamed.

"I'm sorry, Stephan, I didn't mean it to sound that way. I'm not accusing you of anything. I just think it's wrong to act married, when you're not."

"You think it's wrong for me to want to express my love for you? Elaine, a piece of paper makes no difference when two people love each other. The commitment is what counts and I want to give that commitment to you. For months I have denied the passion building in my heart, I have refrained from making any moves you might deem inappropriate. And now you imply that I would 'have my way with you'."

"Oh, Stephan, come sit down." She wanted his arms back around her, making her safe and warm. "You're edgy tonight, come, I'll rub your shoulders."

He obeyed sitting in front of her on the floor. She massaged his strong shoulders and tensed-up neck muscles.

"You work too hard," she told him. "You should relax more. Take life a little less seriously."

Stephan looked up into her face. "I need you to show me how," he said, sounding more like a little boy than a competent, mature doctor.

Moments later Stephan joined her on the couch and Windy sighed as she breathed in the masculine smell of cologne and antiseptic. She wanted to be loved, needed to be cared for and not by someone who would abuse her and run away. She needed a steadfast man, one she could depend on, one who would never let her down. She needed Stephan in her own way, and he needed her in his.

Hours later Windy said goodnight to Stephan. She walked into the bathroom and looked at herself in the mirror. She began to cry.

"Now you have to marry him," she told the reflection.

Chapter Fifteen

Dear Lord,
I've felt such unrest all day, today. Is it because I'm going with Margie
to the Women's Retreat tomorrow? I'm sure I'll have a good time. I hope
to break this rut I'm in and find a new awareness of You. Or is it my kids?
Oh, Lord, I leave them to you. Touch them in a special way. In Jesus'
name, amen.

"Mrs. Elaine Michaels. I like that." Stephan read the name from the paper
he held in his hand. "A new start, a new life and a new name."

"I don't think I'll ever be an Elaine."

"In time, and with a little effort, you can be."

They stood in the entry of the Community Church, waiting for Cora to put
her coat on. The little woman wiped her nose with a Kleenex. One hand found
its way through her sleeve, the other appeared lost forever.

Stephan held her coat up and found the missing hand, guiding it to the proper
opening.

"Thank you," she sniffed, turning her red eyes on Windy. "Whatever will
I do without you?"

"I'm only going across town," Windy replied, hugging the woman. "And I'll
visit you often."

"Are you ready to brave the cold?" Stephan opened the door and they rushed into the wind. He reached the sedan and held the door open as Cora slid into the back. Then he opened Windy's door for her. As he moved around the car, Cora tapped Windy on the shoulder.

"I hope you can get used to such treatment."

"I'll just grin and bear it, I guess." The women smiled at each other and Cora turned to admire the rich material of the seat.

After seeing Cora safely into her warm house, Stephan slid back into the car and pulled Windy close to him.

"I still wonder if I'm dreaming, Mrs. Michaels."

She kissed him lightly. "If you are, I hope you never wake up, Mr. Michaels."

"Any regrets?"

"I don't know. Give me a week."

"I mean about the small wedding."

"Oh, you mean the marriage ceremony we just participated in? What did you call it? A wedding?"

"You are sorry."

"No. I knew my parents couldn't make it back. Besides, Dad gave me away once, I wouldn't want to ask him to go through that again."

Shifting the car into drive he pointed it toward home.

Stephan slipped his arm around her. "I always frowned when I saw young couples sitting so close in a car. Now I understand a little better." He kissed her lightly. "But I had better concentrate on my driving; I do not want to delay our homecoming."

They drove through the grand old section of town. Many of the homes belonged to the original founders. Stephan pulled up in front of a stately Victorian house.

"Welcome home," he said, allowing Windy a long look before he drove up the drive and into the garage. "This used to be the stables until my Grandfather converted it."

"What do you know about the house?"

"Just about everything. I have an abstract on it, giving the names of all the owners and anything interesting that happened here. Such as the mad doctor who tried to create living beings in his basement laboratory."

"Any relation?"

"My great, great grandfather, I believe. He was the first Michaels to live here."

"And it's been passed from generation to generation?"

He nodded. "I am last in line, which is why it is imperative we have a son."

Stephan walked around to Windy's side of the car and opened the door for her. He led her through the attached breezeway, up a couple stairs and into the kitchen.

Noting Windy's curious looks he informed her, "Oh, no. You had your chance to explore this house months ago. Now you will just have to wait."

"Until when?"

"Until I go back to work," he said, pulling her into his arms.

"And when will that be?" she asked between kisses.

"Depends on you." He led Windy to a stairway.

"This is the back stairs," she protested. "I'm not coming into a house like this for the first time and going up the back stairs."

Reluctantly, Stephan led her out of the kitchen and through a large dining room. In the foyer Windy gasped at the divided staircase and balcony that ran around the top of the open room.

"I think from now on I shall call myself Princess Windy Elaine."

"Come, Princess Elaine, your Prince is waiting."

"Where are my things?"

"Your clothes are in the master bedroom. The rest will wait until later," he answered impatiently.

She frowned as he led her toward the stairs. "Gosh, it's only eight o'clock. I never turn in this early. Maybe there's a good romance on TV."

Stephan turned and swept her into his arms. "The only romance I'm interested in is happening live."

He carried her to the landing, turned right and ascended the remaining steps. She quickly glanced down at the impressive sight below her before they disappeared into a large bedroom. Windy looked around, hardly able to believe the beauty of the room. Windy imagined a real Princess choosing the solid oak furniture. When Stephan set her down, her feet sunk into plush carpeting.

"I feel like Cinderella," she whispered.

"Come, and I will make you feel like the Princess you truly are," Stephan closed his arms around her.

Officer Rick Notts laid the paper back on the Sergeant's desk. The blaring of the radio and the conversation in the back room were lost to him. He involuntarily patted the left front pocket of his trousers.

So the ex-Mrs. Eddie Bilmon was getting married? It said so right there in the County Clerk's report – marriage license granted to Dr. Stephan Michaels and Windy Jordon.

The good doctor hadn't wasted any time. Rick remembered his initial satisfaction upon hearing who would care for Windy. He had called the hospital that fateful night in May asking specifically for Nurse Laswell. Her friendly disposition and willingness to cooperate made her popular with the 'boys in blue'.

"Dr. Michaels states that she's in good condition." Bernie told him and he smiled his approval.

"Could snow tonight," Sergeant Mays informed the men.

"I've seen it, even this late in October," Joe confirmed the possibility.

Rick reached his left hand into his pocket and extracted a broken pencil, running his thumb over the gold lettering, WINDY JORDAN CLASS OF… He dropped it into the waste basket.

"You're dumb, Rick, dumb for carrying that thing around with you all this time," he muttered to himself.

"What say, Rick?" Joe walked around the corner in time to hear Rick's utterance.

"Nothing," the young man replied.

The older officer threw the squad car keys to him. "Here, you're driving tonight. Mays says it's gonna snow."

"No, I didn't, weather man said there's a chance."

Rick could have easily caught the key ring, but he felt it slip through his fingers and clatter into the trash can.

Joe shook his head. "Hope you keep a better grip on the wheel."

"Ah, Joe," Mays interjected. "You're lucky the kid still lets you join him on his shift. Nobody else will work with you."

Rick retrieved the keys, groping for the wooden cylinder he had thrown there a moment ago.

"You're dumb, Rick, dumb," he repeated as he slipped the broken pencil back into his pocket before following Joe into the cold night.

Windy opened her eyes to the darkness, and stiffened, aware of an arm laying over her. Her throat went dry and she feared she would cough. She held her breathe, afraid to wake Eddie, wondering how he'd gotten into her apartment. Her heart continued to beat, faster and louder each minute. She quickly rejected each plan for escape, grasping for another, one that wouldn't disturb her sleeping husband.

"Elaine?" murmured Stephan. "What's wrong?" Relief flooded over Windy as she realized the arm belonged to Stephan.

My husband, she thought. Rolling over she caressed his unseen face. He pulled her close, kissing her lightly, then with passion. Windy pushed away from him. But Stephan held tight. "Stephan, no!" she whispered, pushing away harder.

"Why not?" he asked, his voice husky with emotion.

"I...I just don't want to. Will you hold me? Just hold me?"

"Of course," he whispered, relaxing his arms. He touched her face, moving the hair away from her eyes and kissed her tenderly.

Windy relaxed. '*Maybe he really does love me*', she thought. '*How nice to be loved for myself and not for what I can give.*' She nuzzled close to his neck, smelling the scent she now recognized as Stephan.

"My husband," she whispered.

Chapter Sixteen

Dear Lord,
I'm sure new adventures await me today. Margie is confident the lull in my life will end with this retreat. Lord, what do You have in store for my son today? and my girl, bless her heart. I pray she has a good day. Lord, You'll let me meet her some day, won't You?

The following morning the hospital called. One of Stephen's patients had gone into cardiac arrest. He stabilized but Stephen felt it important to reassure him.

"Remember, I once told you if there were a Mrs. Michaels she would understand?" Stephen said when he told Windy.

"I remember and I understand."

"You're a sweetheart," he said kissing her.

"No, I just want time to explore the house!" she called as he disappeared into the bathroom. When she heard the shower running she jumped out of bed and opened what she hoped were the closet doors. She guessed right, and found a walk-in closet almost as big as her bedroom back at the apartment. Stephen's clothes filled the left half and her meager wardrobe sat in the middle of the right half like an island. The end wall had cubby holes for shoes or hats and hooks to hang belts and ties on. Her robe hung on a hook inside the door. Slipping it on she walked to the window and peered out at the other homes lining the block. I never dreamed I'd live here; she smiled and stepped away just as Stephen emerged from the bathroom rubbing his head with a towel.

"That's your dresser." He indicated a small version of the one he pulled his clothes from. "Your clothes are either in the closet or still in the boxes you packed. I'm sure you'll keep busy while I'm gone."

Windy nodded, happy to just listen to his voice. She walked up to him and watched as he slipped his t-shirt over his head.

With a wondering look on her face, she asked. "Are you mine?"

Stephen smiled and kissed her lightly. "Forever."

She studied him as he finished dressing and said good-bye. Then she pulled the curtain away from the window and watched him pull out of the driveway. He looked up and waved at her. A shiver of excitement ran down her spine and she hugged herself, letting tears of joy flow.

Windy showered and slipped into a comfortable pair of jeans and a sweatshirt. She quickly put away the few articles packed in boxes. She smiled as she placed her toothbrush next to Stephan's and her shampoo in the shower.

Then she ventured out into the hall. Afraid she might get lost in her new mansion she followed the route Stephen took last night and found the kitchen. She opened every cupboard and drawer, familiarizing herself with the location of the most important items. She poured herself a glass of milk and decided to check on the food reserve. Finding a paper and pencil in one of the drawers she started an inventory.

She found little food in the kitchen. A few steaks and TV dinners shared the freezer. A couple green carrots and the remains of a head of lettuce hid in the crisper. Other then the half-gallon of milk, a tub of butter and a carton of yogurt the refrigerator was bare.

In the bread box Windy found a partial loaf of bread and pulled out a slice to pop in the toaster. She looked the bread over carefully, then held it to her nose. It hadn't started growing anything yet, but the soil smelled ready.

Windy took another sip of milk and decided to check the date on the carton. October 30. Tomorrow. At least, she felt safe drinking that.

When Stephen got home she'd ask about his eating habits and what they needed to buy. She thought about going to the grocery store where she had worked and entering as Mrs. Michaels, the customer.

Windy returned to the cupboards. Testing her memory, she found the glasses on her first try. She inspected the plates, admiring Stephen's taste in dinnerware. One blue flower adorned the edge of the dish, pretty, but not too feminine for a man.

Everywhere Windy looked she found the kitchen to her liking.

She strolled into the dining hall. The long elegant table seated 20. Scroll backed antique chairs with red velvet seats waited for her first guests. Two candelabrums decorated the polished oak table.

A china cabinet held dishes Windy dared not touch, certain they belonged to the first Mrs. Michaels to entertain here. Both dining hall and kitchen were decorated in tans and browns.

The foyer held an antique coat tree. Windy remembered seeing one like it in the movie Mary Poppins. She traced the intricate wood work, and when she looked at her finger, found no dust.

Suddenly a thought occurred to the girl. As mistress of this fine house, she would be responsible for its upkeep. She looked around quickly at archways leading into adjoining rooms, at closed doors, holding their secrets and wondered how much time she would be able to spend with her husband and still keep the place dust-free.

In answer to her dilemma, the back door opened and Stephen came in.

She ran into the kitchen and took his hat and coat from him.

"Stephen, how will I ever keep this place clean?"

He frowned at her, and pulled her in for a kiss. "Do not worry about that, the maid comes twice a week."

"Maid?" Windy stared at him, trying to understand. "Then what am I supposed to do?"

"Just keep your husband happy. I don't want you to spend time cleaning house." She smiled and put his hat and coat on a chair in the kitchen.

"Have you been exploring?" he asked as he lifted the items from the chair and placed them in a small closet.

"Only familiar territory. I thought I might get lost. How's your patient?"

"Doing fine, I really wasn't needed but I'm glad I went. He's an older gentleman and wanted my assurance."

Windy beamed, realizing what a good man her husband was, and how others looked up to him. "It's almost noon. I thought I'd fix us lunch, but I couldn't find anything salvageable in the kitchen."

"Do you think for a minute I'd let my bride cook on her honeymoon?"

"What honeymoon?"

"The one we're taking in between patients."

"And how long are we supposed to live on love alone? Or do you have a cook, too?"

"No, no cooks. That will be your job. But for a few days we'll dine out."

"I hope you're not a three-meal-a-day person. We'd spend all our time either getting ready or going out."

He pointed to the sack on the counter. "We can dine out, in." He pulled two submarine sandwiches from the bag. "Just pop them in the microwave for a couple minutes and we have instant lunch."

Windy looked at the size of the sandwiches. "For the whole week," she added.

When they finished eating Stephen took his new bride into the dining where he pointed out pictures of the previous generations. Windy loved the history of the house and the family that occupied it, asking enough questions to raise Stephen's admiration for her.

"How I wish my family had something like this to pass along. All I have is a couple Christening gowns and a harmonica."

"We almost lost the house, once," he said, leading her back into foyer and to his left into a room directly under his bedroom. "This is the parlor; I spend most of my time here. Windy noted the plush out-dated surroundings.

"A fireplace!" She exclaimed. "I love an open fire!"

"And we'll have plenty," he touched the rough field stones. "Grandfather Michaels lost nearly all his wealth when the stock market crashed. He held on to the house by letting everything else go. He had to take a job as an errand boy." Stephan smiled. "Imagine a thirty-two year old errand boy. He learned the business and within five years worked his way up to vice-president. Father followed him through the ranks."

He took Windy's hand and led her across the foyer into a small sitting room, then beside that to his den.

"Do you remember your Grandfather?"

"Oh, yes, quite well. I remember walking this very same route with him. He always told me this house would someday belong to me. He made me promise to fill it with laughing little Michaels." Windy smiled into her husband's eyes.

"Is that the only reason you want a passel of kids?"

"Not at all," he assured her before continuing his tour. "Mother was somewhat of a spend-thrift. She came from a well-to-do family and never learned to manage money. Grandfather and Father died in a plane crash. Mother had no head for business. She followed some bad advice, sold the business for a fraction of it's worth. She invested the money unwisely and by the time I was ready for college, we were broke."

Through an archway under the left side of the stairway he lead her into the library. Windy's eyes popped open at the sight of all the books. A large desk sat near the back of the room.

"But you had the house?"

"Thankfully. I looked at our options—sell the house and pay our debts or mortgage it. I chose to mortgage. The bank was willing, after all, look what they had for collateral." He swept his arm out. "I sold many of the original furnishings, worked two jobs, and took out loans for college. Those eight years were the hardest of my life. But they were worth it. I learned the value of a dollar and of my own self-worth. I kept hearing that promise to Grandfather and I knew I had to keep this place, for him and for his descendants."

"Couldn't your mother's family help?"

"They, too, were in financial straits. I suppose Mother inherited her ignorance from her father."

The harsh word stunned Windy and she looked at Stephan. "Aren't you a little hard on your mother?"

"I'm sorry, that really wasn't the word I meant to use. Come." He took her back into the kitchen and showed her the bathroom and maid's room. They ascended a small enclosed stairway and ended up in a long hallway lighted by a window. "There's another bath here," he indicated a door to their right. "These are guest rooms," he passed three doors and stopped at a fourth. "This is the nursery." Stephan opened the door to reveal a large room. "Everything is here from my childhood." Windy noticed a crib in one corner and a small child's bed in another and numerous furnishings throughout.

He pulled her close. "Had enough history for one day? I have something very special for you." They walked out onto the balcony and he headed toward his bedroom.

"What's over there?" Windy asked pointing to a door on the other side of the balcony.

"That was mother's room. You can look at it another time.

They entered his room. "Sit down," he indicated the bed, as he opened an ornate wooden box that sat atop his dresser. He placed something in his hand then sat beside Windy. "You are the fifth Mrs. Michaels to wear this," he said reverently. He placed a double silver band upon Windy's finger. She studied the ring. The thick lower band contained several small green stones. The thinner top band held a large diamond in the center, the same green stones trickled down across the gold foundation.

Windy wasn't sure how Stephan wanted her to react, she didn't know if the ring was meant for her or not.

"The fifth?" She questioned. "And you said you'd never been married." Windy's smile vanished when she saw the solemn look on her husband's face.

"This is a very valuable piece of jewelry. It has been in my family for generations, you should be honored to have it placed on your finger."

"Oh, I am, Stephan, I just never expected to wear something so...so beautiful."

"It is lovely, isn't it?" He held her hand up, admiring his gift.

"It even fits, I'm surprised. I wear a smaller ring than most girls."

"Grandfather told me to look for a woman with dainty fingers."

"Thank heaven for my 'dainty' fingers," Windy whispered as her husband pulled her close.

Chapter Seventeen

Dear Lord,
Oh, thank You, God, for this beautiful day in this beautiful setting.
Thank you for the wonder of yesterday and please continue this miracle
in my heart today. Be with my kids, wherever they are. I pray that they're
attending church today, that they're hearing Your word. Lord, I pray for
their salvation. In Jesus' name, amen.

"Wake up, beautiful." Stephan kissed her and she pulled him close.

"It's my turn to say no," he said. "It is Sunday morning and we are going to church."

Windy watched her husband climb out of bed. She wondered if she could possibly wake up this happy every morning. She slid out from under the covers and retrieved her robe from the chair. While Stephan showered she studied her clothes. The only dress suitable for church was the print she'd worn when Stephan took the Garveys to dinner. It had also served as her wedding dress but it would have to do.

She found a run-free pair of nylons in her drawer along with a slip, graying from so many washings. She needed some new clothes but could not bring herself to ask Stephan for them.

Well, if I wear the print to church again next week, maybe Stephan will notice.

When Stephan vacated the bathroom she fought the steam and showered quickly. She blew her hair dry and pinned it up on her head then slipped her dress on.

They reached the church within minutes. Windy nervously held her husband's arm as he led her up the steps. Once inside they were greeted by two men, one handed her a piece of paper while the other took Windy's jacket. She watched as he hung it up next to the expensive wool coats. Her down jacket looked completely out of place. Stephan introduced the men as she shook their hands.

"Gentlemen, this is my wife, Elaine." After several more introductions Stephan guided her to a seat in the middle of the sanctuary. Windy studied the huge building. She remembered little of it from the ceremony, having only seen Stephan that night. She shivered with anticipation. They had started their marriage in this very room. She wondered what other marvelous things it held for her.

For the next hour they stood on cue, sang from the hymnals and listened attentively as the minister talked about the God of love. Disappointed, Windy saw the service as routine more than anything else.

As they were leaving Stephan greeted the minister and again thanked him for performing the ceremony on Friday evening.

"I'm certain the ladies would love to meet Mrs. Michaels. Maybe you could attend their Missionary Meeting on Tuesday night. I believe it's at Mrs. Dunkirk's home."

Windy looked at Stephan hoping he would provide an out for her.

"Possibly next time, Rev. Stockwell. Mrs. Michaels has not yet settled in properly."

"Of course, how thoughtless of me."

"We do, however, want to set up a time for Elaine to speak with you about joining the church."

"Of course, call me Tuesday morning at my office and we'll compare schedules." He turned to Windy and extended his hand. "It is such a pleasure to have you with us today."

"Thank you," she replied and followed Stephan out. As he escorted her through the parking lot she noticed the wind had risen in the last hour.

Once inside the car she turned to Stephan. "I must admit it wasn't as frightening as I thought it might be."

"Frightening? What were you expecting?"

"Oh, I don't know. Maybe something like those preachers who say you're going to hell if you don't do what they say, or that if I give them enough money I can buy my way to paradise."

"Well, you need not worry. I, myself, would never listen to such idiocy much less subject you to it."

"It wasn't as exciting as I'd hoped either."

"Exciting? Elaine we were in church, not at a circus."

"I wonder though…" her voice trailed off.

"Speak up, Elaine, I can not hear you."

"I…I wonder if I might understand the preacher better if I had read the Bible."

"I suppose it is possible. What did you not understand?"

"Everything. I mean the sermon was plain enough but it sounded as if God is rather, well, small and limited."

"Now I do not understand."

"Well, from what little I remember, I guess I always thought of God as someone who knew everything. But today he sounded more like a friendly little man who pats people on the head and says 'Have a nice day'."

"There are many conceptions of what God is like. I believe we all must find God in our own hearts to understand who he is and what he wants for us."

"Sounds nice, but I guess I hoped for someone with a little more authority."

"That does not surprise me at all."

"What do you mean?"

Stephan pulled into the driveway and stopped the car. "I have not time to explain it to you now; I need to go to the hospital for rounds."

"Oh, no. I wanted to curl up in front of the fireplace with you this afternoon."

"Sickness does not have Sundays, Elaine." He stepped from the car, circled it and opened Windy's door. Together they ran across the yard to the front door, the wind whipping through Windy's hair. She shivered waiting for Stephan to unlock the door and rushed inside.

"I tell you what," Stephan offered as he took his gloves off. "Why don't you take the blue car to the store, pick up some fresh bread and cheese?" He took his wallet from his pants and held out a five dollar bill. "That ought to get us through the day."

"As long as I'm there I may as well do the shopping."

"What else do we need?"

"Oh, Stephan, your cupboard is bare! We need everything."

"Bread and cheese will suffice for today. Tomorrow we will go to the store."

"Okay," she agreed, giving him a kiss and sending him on his way.

As soon as Windy saw Stephan's car pull into the drive she took the plate of cheese out of the fridge and cut several thick pieces of the homemade bread. She patted herself on the back for stopping at Cora's before going to the store. Cora's bread tasted much better than store-bought and now she had a little extra spending money, too.

A fire roared in the parlor fireplace, pillows lay in front of it. Windy placed their 'meal' on the coffee table and threw another log on the fire.

"Do you have a Bible, Stephan?" Windy asked as soon as they settled in.

"Why this sudden interest in a Bible?"

"I don't know, but as long as I'm going to attend church and become a member I might as well know what's going on."

"You realize my schedule will not permit us to attend regularly."

"I know you can't go every week, but I thought I would."

"By yourself?"

"Sure. Any objections?"

"I suppose not; although it is proper for us to attend together." When Windy looked surprised he added, "You live in a different world now, Elaine, a world where propriety reigns."

Windy nodded. She supposed Stephan's world would take some getting used to. Maybe she wouldn't care to be at his church alone anyway.

"Could we talk about what you mentioned earlier? I'm really curious about the comment you made."

Stephan sighed deeply. "I am not up to Theological or psychological discussions. I am tired. Those four hours at the hospital seemed more like four days. I would like to lay back and enjoy my wife for awhile."

Windy liked that idea and the rest of the day they spent sipping tea and eating bread and cheese. Sometimes they read, sometimes they talked, sometimes they just held each other. Most importantly, they were together without any interruptions from the outside world.

Monday morning dawned cold and clear.

Windy awoke and showered before Stephan. She wanted to go to the hospital with him and learn more about his world so she could fit in without embarrassing him. He consented reluctantly.

Once they arrived Stephan left Windy in the competent hands of Mrs. Laswell who enjoyed showing her around.

In the maternity ward Windy gazed at the beautiful little creatures bundled up in their blankets, wearing white knit hats.

"Doctor loves children," Mrs. Laswell commented. "But I guess you know that by now."

"Yes, I know."

"There's one baby who has no parents. Would you like to hold him?" She led Windy into the nursery and motioned for her to sit in the rocker. Then she handed Windy a tiny silent bundle. The baby slept fitfully, his little arms and legs twitching from time to time.

"Why doesn't he have parents?"

"He's a cocaine baby. The mother is a young girl from the streets. She gave birth last week and left."

"What will you do with him?"

"Keep him as long as we need, then he'll go into foster care. His future is very uncertain. We've no way of knowing how much damage the cocaine has done. The family who accepts this little guy is probably in for a difficult time."

Windy held the baby, whispering to him. Although he never cried he continued to twitch and his little arms and legs jerked occasionally.

"How long may I hold him?"

"As long as you want to. Like all hospitals in big cities we always have at least one parentless baby, whether it be from cocaine or alcohol and now AIDS. There are people who volunteer their time just to hold these little ones, giving them the love they can't receive from an overworked hospital staff."

"I wonder if Stephan would let me volunteer."

"I think you'd make him very proud if you did." Mrs. Laswell returned to her duties and left Windy with a promise to tell Stephan where to find her.

Two hours later he peeked into the nursery in time to see Windy change the baby's diaper. He stood by silently admiring the scene.

"Oh, Stephan, why don't we just take him home with us?" Windy asked when she saw her husband.

"It's tempting isn't it?"

She wrapped the baby back up in his blanket and held him close. "He doesn't twitch so much when I hold him."

Stephan put his arms around her, cradling the baby between them. "In time we'll have our own little boy."

Windy smiled up at him and he kissed her. "Now, I'm done with my duties. Are you ready to go shopping?"

"Can I come back sometime?"

"If you wish."

"Bernie said I could be a volunteer and hold the babies whenever I come in."

"We will see."

Windy placed the baby in his bassinet. "He doesn't even have a proper name. Good-bye, little Boy Evans."

Windy couldn't keep her mind on shopping; it kept going back to the motherless baby in the sterile white hospital crib.

Stephan grew more irritated each time he asked Windy what they needed. She just kept saying 'everything'. Finally he settled for the few things that somehow found their way into the basket and headed for the check out. Upon leaving he picked up the store sale bill and stuffed it into the bag.

When they arrived home Stephan placed the whole bag in the fridge then followed Windy upstairs.

He put his arms around his wife and smiled at her.

She looked up at him with tears in her eyes.

"Couldn't we bring him home, keep him until they find foster parents for him?"

"I'm anxious to start our family, but not that anxious."

"I don't mean adopt him. Just let him start his life like all babies should, with arms to hold him when he needs love, which is all the time right now."

"If I let you bring him home I'd never get him away from you again. No, Elaine. Soon enough he'll have a family that will care for him, properly." He lifted her face to his and kissed her tenderly. "I love you for caring about that baby, but for now I want my wife all to myself for, oh, at least nine months!"

"Only nine months?" She responded to his kiss. "That doesn't give us much time does it?"

Chapter Eighteen

Dear Lord,

Thank you for that marvelous week-end. Help me to keep my eyes on You as I return to everyday life. I know there are trials ahead, but I know You'll see me through them. See my kids through their trials, too; Lord protect them and guide them, please. In Jesus name, amen.

Windy accompanied Stephan to the hospital the next day, went straight to the maternity ward and checked in at the nurse's station. She found little Boy Evans and cuddled him close. Through-out the morning and into the afternoon she cared for the baby. She fed and changed him, introduced him to his room mates, then tried to sneak him out of the ward.

"I'm sorry, Mrs. Michaels, the babies can't leave the area." The nurse informed her, peering at Windy over her glasses.

Nurse Payne fit her name perfectly, Windy decided.

"Oh, it's alright, I'm just going to the cafeteria for a cola. I'll even bring it back here to drink."

"You're welcome to come and go as you wish. But the baby stays here." She reached out to take the precious bundle. Windy retreated.

"I'll do it."

The nurse watched as Windy put the baby back and headed for the elevator.

Windy hoped to find Stephan eating lunch. When she didn't see him she put her change in the pop machine and pushed the cherry cola button.

"Mrs. Michaels, what are you doing here?"

Windy turned and faced John Garvey. She reached out and grabbed his large hand.

"How good to see you, and it's Windy," she reminded him. "I came in with Stephan and while he's being the great doctor, I'm taking care of a baby in the maternity ward, an abandoned baby."

"The little cocaine baby born last week?"

"That's him. Nurse Laswell introduced us yesterday."

"I haven't seen him yet. How's he doing?"

"Not as good as a healthy baby, of course. But I'm sure he doesn't twitch and jerk so much when I hold him. What about you? What are you doing here?"

"Just brought in an accident victim and I thought I'd grab some lunch. Care to join me?"

Windy felt torn between her friend and little bundle upstairs. "For a few minutes, I guess."

John motioned to a table holding a well-stocked tray where Windy prompted John to talk about his own little bundle. Between bites he recounted Johnny's latest feats.

"So when are you and the doc going to start your family?"

"Give us time John, we haven't even been married a week. I suggested we take little boy Evans home."

"Oh, yeah? The doc would never go for that. But, you know, I did always wonder why he hadn't married when it's so apparent he loves and wants kids."

"It's that obvious?"

"Sure. He's the last of a prominent line, you know." Windy nodded in agreement and John continued. "This last year he's talked about his 'heirs' enough for anyone to know how important a son is to him. I hope you don't let him down," John teased.

"I'll do my best not to. But in the meantime, I'll practice being a mommy. Take care, John, and tell Sally hello for me." She stood to leave but stopped and looked at the big man. "What did you mean—Stephan would never 'go for that'?"

"Adopting a baby. Bloodlines, you know."

Windy shook her head. "I don't think I do."

"Doc could never give the Michaels name to a little cocaine baby," he said with a shrug of his shoulders.

"Oh." Windy nodded but her puzzled look remained.

Windy looked at the clock, glad for the extra time with the baby, but a little concerned. Stephan should have been up to get her fifteen minutes ago. She'd been waiting rather impatiently. John's remark bothered her and she alternated between asking Stephan what it meant and keeping quiet. The last year with Eddie showed her the virtues of silence.

"Bye, little Jordan." Windy whispered the name she secretly gave the baby. Stephan had said that should be the name of their first son. This precious baby was her heart's first born. "Mommy will see you tomorrow." She gave him one more kiss then laid him back in his crib.

She made her way to the first level, taking the stairs because elevators always made her shudder. She had tried to explain this to Stephan, suggesting all the 'shudderable things' she could remember. For many people it's chalk on a black board. For her mom it was cotton balls. Windy always got the job of opening any bottles containing the terrible stuff. For Windy elevators equaled shudders.

She ran down the three flights quickly enough and followed the yellow line on the wall to the emergency room. As she entered she smiled. This was where they'd met. Although she didn't remember it, she pictured their meeting many times. She imagined him looking at her and falling in love.

That's when he said it happened.

Stephan's voice guided Windy to a curtain pulled around one of the examining tables. Windy positioned herself so as not to deprive the patient of privacy. She only wanted to watch her husband at work.

He stood over the injured woman, commanding respect just by his presence. John Garvey, Tony Dione and Nurse Laswell stood there with him, watching his every move. In a soothing voice, Stephan asked pertinent questions. He smiled and the woman on the table relaxed, even tried to smile back.

Windy heard Stephan politely instruct Nurse Laswell, she quickly obeyed.

'*He treats everyone so well,*' Windy thought. '*His love for people shines bright in his every action.*' She studied his strong hands, looked up to the distinct profile. '*And he chose me. He opened the gates to his world and pulled me in. He's given me security and purpose. I should be forever grateful.*'

Stephan patted the woman's arm and spoke reassuringly.

'Those hands caress my cheek.' Windy thought.

Stephan watched with concern as the attendants wheeled her away.

'I don't mind the caring looks, for I know the ones he saves for me.'

His duty fulfilled, Stephan emerged from the curtain, seeing Windy. She longed to fold herself into his protective arms, but his eyes locked onto hers and she couldn't move. He closed the distance between them and guided Windy into an empty waiting room.

"Elaine," his voice fell softly. "You must never, never come in here and watch the treatment of a patient."

"I'm sorry," she bowed her head. "I just wanted to see you at your finest." Then she smiled and looked up at him. "Remember, I'm the one who breaks the rules."

"This is nothing to joke about." His eyes attested to the seriousness of his voice. "An injured person is entitled to privacy and respect. You have no right to take that from them."

"I didn't mean any harm."

"I am sure you didn't. I have called you innocent and so you are. Not innocent of wrong-doing, mind you, just innocent in your intent. Never do it again."

"I won't. I promise." She shifted her weight, moving slightly closer to Stephan, wishing he would put his arm around her, assure her of his forgiveness.

"Come along, little one. I am tired and hungry. We will just stop and pick up something to take home."

Wednesday morning Windy and Stephan entered the church office where Windy listened for half an hour to the Rev. Stockwell explain their doctrine. Windy didn't understand much of it. She did realize she was now the wife of a prominent doctor and must be socially acceptable. She signed a statement saying she would keep the rules of the church and adhere to it's doctrine. She agreed that if she should ever bring shame upon the church she would expect to be asked to leave and renounce her membership.

"Some honeymoon you're having." Nurse Laswell stood over Windy and watched as the girl tenderly changed Boy Evans diaper.

"I'm enjoying it. Really."

"Uh-huh. Every day you're both here, the doc to see his patients and you to see yours."

"Oh, Jor…the baby is hardly a patient anymore. See how much better he is? He rarely twitches, he eats more and he's gaining weight. Even his coloring is good."

Nurse Laswell lifted the sweet-smelling baby from the changing table. She hefted him a couple times and nodded her agreement about the weight. Pulling him close to her breast she cuddled the little guy, surprised when he responded.

"You've worked wonders with him." She commented to Windy before whispering little love words to the baby.

Windy stood by, very much the proud mom.

A couple days later Stephan started midnights. The next morning Windy decided to explore the room Stephan labeled as his mother's. The door stood straight across the open foyer from the master bedroom and Windy padded on thick carpeting along the balcony to reach it. Turning the handle she pushed on the door. Inside she saw a woman's room, decorated in pink and white with delicate eyelet curtains and matching bedspread. Its lay-out resembled the master bedroom in a slightly smaller version with a bathroom and walk-in closet in the corner on her right. But this room had a tub, an old deep, claw foot tub. Windy knew she would welcome any time she could spend in this room.

"Why can't I go to the hospital myself? You might sleep better if I'm not in the house anyway."

"There is no need for you to go."

"I want to see the baby."

"As I said, there is no need."

"Please, Stephan, I haven't seen him for three days, ever since you started the night shift."

"It's only a week long shift. When I go back on days you can go with me. Besides you spend too much time at the hospital. This past month you have been there more than you have been home."

"I've only gone when you do."

"I rest my case."

"Well, I'm not resting mine." She stood between her tired husband and his inviting bed. "You do want to get to sleep before the morning sun starts shining through that window, don't you?"

"Alright, have it your way." He handed her the keys to the convertible. "But I tell you this is not the way to make your husband happy."

When Windy reached the hospital she headed for the elevator. Much as she hated it, it was faster than climbing three flights of stairs. When the door opened she bolted down the hall, straight into the nursery and up to the baby's crib. It was empty, the name plate gone. Running back to the station she confronted the nurse.

"Where's the baby?"

"What baby?"

"Boy Evans!"

Nurse Payne picked up a chart and slowly scanned it.

"Social Services picked him up yesterday and took him to a foster home."

"But he wasn't ready, he still twitched! Will they know how to care for him? He's so young!"

The nurse peered over her glasses at Windy. "Mrs. Michaels, I assure you we wouldn't let the baby leave if it weren't ready and certainly not into incompetent hands!" She marched around Windy and down the hall.

Chapter Nineteen

Dear Lord,
Thank you for Margie. She's such a good friend if it hadn't been for
her I would never have met You. Lord, please, send a friend into my son's
life. One who will share Your word with him, as Margie did with me. And
send one to my girl, too. My girl. She's a part of me now, you know. I've
prayed for her every time I come to You. I wish I could say everyday. With
Your help, that's a goal I can attain.

"I feared this would happen." Stephan said when he awoke and found
Windy in the parlor, crying. "I should not have let you go there everyday."

"But I wanted to; it wasn't a question of you letting me. I knew he would
be put in foster care. I thought I could handle that. It just came so soon, and
I didn't even tell him good-bye."

"Elaine, what you did for that little guy, loving and caring for him, will make
a difference in his life. You just have to accept that and let him go."

"I wish I had a picture of him, just a picture. Or knew where he's been
taken. I called Social Services and they wouldn't even talk to me."

"Of course not. You have no right to know."

Windy's tears started again and Stephan pulled her into his arms. He
comforted her as she had comforted the baby, talking softly and kissing her.

"How about Italian tonight? Pizza, maybe?"

"I'm not hungry."

"Elaine," his voice grew deep. "I understand you are upset, but do not act like a child, I will not have it." He spoke as if to a child.

Surprised at his scolding, Windy pulled away and looked at him.

"You look like a puppy who just got swatted with a newspaper," he laughed.

"I feel like one."

"What do you want me to do? Allow you to sulk? You are a grown woman, such things are going to happen and you can not cry every time they do. Listen, this is the first Tuesday of December. There is a missionary meeting tonight. I will call the church office and ask where it is." Windy started to protest and Stephan held up his hand. "You will find out about hundreds of little babies all over the world and how you can help each one of them. Do it for me? Do it for Boy Evans?"

Windy managed a weak smile. "I don't know anyone."

"I will call Sally and ask if she is going."

"Sally Garvey? I didn't know they go to church."

He nodded and kissed her forehead. "Go wash your face. I'll make the phone calls."

When the still red-eyed Windy returned to the parlor Stephan had arranged everything.

"Pizza will be here in 20 minutes and Sally will pick you up at 6:30. She is delighted you have decided to go."

"You mean you decided I should go."

He studied her for a moment. "If you are that set against it, I will call her back," he said with disapproval.

"No, I'll enjoy seeing Sally if nothing else."

Sally arrived on time, with little Johnny strapped in his carrier in the back seat.

"I'm glad you're coming with. I know you'll enjoy yourself," she said as soon as Windy buckled her seatbelt.

"I've never been to a missionary meeting. What do you do there?"

"Well, let's see, where do I start?"

"At the beginning."

"Most denominations have missionaries all over the world. We have them in 27 countries. Our church alone helps to support three missionaries and their families. Each month the ladies take an offering which goes to our National

Office. At Christmas we send a package to each family we support. That's what those are for." She pointed to the brightly decorated gifts in the back seat.

"The rest of the year we send a package a month to one family. If they have a special need, they let us know, otherwise we just send things that are useful."

Windy stared at the gifts, dreading the meeting more each minute.

"I didn't know I was supposed to bring something."

"You weren't. This is your first time so you're a guest. Next time you should bring something."

Windy smiled at her friend, silently rejecting a 'next time'.

At the church Windy carried Johnny in while Sally ladened herself with presents. Once inside the fellowship hall, they were greeted by several ladies, all of whom were much older than Windy. She found a seat and released the baby from his chair. Johnny squealed with delight at being free. Windy noticed his thick legs and strong arms. He was definitely a John Junior.

"How old is the baby?" Windy looked up to see a large gray haired woman standing over her. Diamonds sparkled from the woman's ears. Her eyes hid behind big, jelly-like cheeks.

"Let's see," Windy began counting. "Just over five months. He's a healthy guy, isn't he?"

"And you're so little! Did you have a hard time?" Windy detected no real concern in the honey dipped words.

She stared at the woman for a moment before understanding the question. "Oh! He's not mine. This is John Garvey, Jr., Sally's baby."

"Oh yes, I see that now," the woman replied not even looking at the baby. "And who are you, dear?"

"Wi...Elaine Michaels." Windy remembered how Stephan had introduced her. She had hoped Stephan would keep that as a 'pet' name, but remembered he had introduced her at church that way.

"So you're the new bride? I'm pleased to meet you. Your wonderful Dr. Michaels always gives to the missionary fund, but now that you're here, maybe you can convince him to give a little more." Her remark startled Windy. "Oh, not that his contributions aren't generous, but we woman have a better understanding of need."

Windy smiled and nodded, wondering what this woman understood about need. Sally approached and greeted Windy's visitor.

"Mrs. Dunkirk, how nice to see you. Have you met Elaine Michaels?" Windy noted Sally's use of her name.

"We've already become conspirators!" Mrs. Dunkirk smiled at Windy then excused herself. Sally lifted Johnny out of his carrier and suggested she introduce Windy to some of the other ladies. In the next ten minutes, Windy met some of the most influential ladies in the city, including the mayor's wife. Then Sally showed her the package that would be sent to South America the next day.

"Ladies, ladies, it's time to start our meeting." Mrs. Dunkirk clapped her hands and motioned for them to sit in the big circle of chairs. Windy sat, gladly taking possession of Johnny. She quickly glanced around the circle, catching the eyes of a young woman she hadn't met. Plainly dressed and not much older than Windy, the woman looked somewhat out of place. She smiled and Windy felt a sudden warmth, then another young woman sat beside the first, obstructing Windy's view.

"Let's begin our meeting by having the newcomers tell us a little about themselves." Mrs. Dunkirk smiled at Windy. "Mrs. Michaels would you start?"

Windy hesitated. Sally took Johnny from her and whispered, "Go ahead, stand up."

Reluctantly, Windy stood. "I'm Wi…Elaine Michaels. Stephan and I were married just over a month ago." She looked around nervously then sat.

"Mrs. Michaels, what are some of your interests?"

Windy stared at Mrs. Dunkirk, then stood. "I like to sew and do all kinds of needlework." She sat again.

"Do you belong to any organizations?"

Windy shook her head at the woman.

"Well," Mrs. Dunkirk said in an irritated tone. She turned her attention further down the circle. "We have two other guests. Would you tell us your names and a little about yourselves?"

Both woman stood as though used to such interrogation.

"I'm Mary Ames," the first woman said. Her shoulder length dark brown hair emphasized her pale flawless skin. Soft brown eyes smiled at Windy.

"And I'm Jenny McCourt." Jenny's long blonde hair was pulled back into a low pony tail. Her bright blue eyes sparkled as she talked. "We're elementary school teachers and moved to your fair city in August to begin the school year. Mary and I went to college together and found we had many interests in common, such as working in the CPC on campus. We've already been to the one here and volunteered our services."

"We also grew up in the same denomination, but there's no sister church here so we're attending the different churches to see where we fit in." Mary added, both smiled and looked at Mrs. Dunkirk.

"What's a CPC?" one of the ladies questioned.

"Crisis Pregnancy Center," explained Jenny, obviously the spokesman for the two.

"What's it for?" Asked another. "It's an office where women of any age can be given a pregnancy test, then counseled on how to handle her situation," said Jenny.

"Do you do abortions?"

"No," Jenny replied. "CPC's are usually run by volunteer Christian lay-people, not doctors. We do not perform nor do we refer abortions. Hasn't anyone here ever worked in a CPC?"

"Thank you ladies," Mrs. Dunkirk interrupted, dismissing Mary and Jenny. "We are touching on a controversial topic and that's a no-no. Evelyn, would you open with prayer?

Windy made a mental note to speak to the young women at the end of the meeting then bowed her head.

Afterwards, Windy sought out Mary and Jenny. They stood near the door, putting on their coats. "Hi," Windy ventured. "Hello Mrs. Michaels," answered Jenny.

"Windy," she corrected. "I'm sorry Mrs. Dunkirk cut you short. I'd like to hear more about what you do."

Jenny opened her purse and handed Windy a card. Under the words 'Caring Pregnancy Center' was Jenny's handwritten name and phone number.

"That's our number at home. We're at school all day, of course, but you can call us in the evening."

"Where do you live?"

"We share an house on Maple Street." Jenny explained.

Windy took a piece of paper from her purse, scribbled her number on it and handed it to Jenny. "I'll be in touch."

She hurried out to the car where Sally already had Johnny strapped in and ready to go.

After starting the car Sally turned to Windy. "I noticed you spoke to the teachers. Elaine, be careful. They sound kind of radical to me."

"Radical?"

"There are those who do weird things in God's name, you know. Like blowing up abortion clinics or protesting in front of them. You might not want to get involved with them."

"They didn't look very violent to me."

"You don't have to be violent to inflict your opinions on others."

"Where do you stand on abortion?"

"I'm not really sure. I know that I'm glad to live in a country that offers so many liberties and I'm leery of what could happen if the government is allowed to limit our rights. I'm not on either side of the fence. I'd never get an abortion because I love and want children. But I'm not in a position to judge other women and their situations. What about you?"

"I've never really thought about it."

"You shouldn't have to. Why bother yourself with something that doesn't concern you? I have my family to care for, some day soon you will too. But for right now you need to focus all your attention on that new husband of yours."

"Yes, I think you're right."

"Of course I'm right. Elaine, the adjustments of the first year of marriage are hard enough. If you get friendly with those women they'll want you to work in their CPC and find all sorts of things for you do. There is plenty of church work to be done without getting involved in something like that. As I said, you'd be better off to stay away from them."

Chapter Twenty

Dear Lord,
Our first snow came today. It's so clean and white, it reminds me of the
cleansing that takes place when Christ begins to work in our lives. I pray
that my children will experience such a cleansing. I pray this day for their
salvation.

"Stephen, what's your opinion on abortion?" Windy lay next to her husband, staring at the scar on his lip and watching it's movement as he twisted his mouth.

"Unfortunately, that's a 'controversial' subject, and it should not be. The anti-abortion faction has dredged up a lot of self-righteous nonsense and started trouble where there should be none."

"You didn't answer my question."

"Elaine, I am an internist. I have studied how the body works and I have witnessed wonderful medical break-throughs. I also understand the devastating effects of back-alley abortions. I want the medical profession to be able to continue offering the best care and treatment to our patients. This is a democracy, not a socialist country. The government has no place in medicine."

Windy sighed and lifted herself to her elbow. "Are you saying abortion is okay?"

"I am saying individual rights must be protected. We as a society, can not force a woman to bear a child she does not want or can not care for. The world's population has grown at an alarming rate. Babies are being born for the sole purpose of living a degrading handicapped life. Children are abused, because they are unwanted. Children are becoming parents. Abortion is a means of controlling some of those terrible situations."

"Do you perform abortions?"

"No."

"Why not?"

"I am an internist; that is my area of expertise."

"You mean there are specialists for abortions?"

"You could say that."

Windy digested his words for a moment, resting her head back into the softness of her pillow. "What about the baby?"

"The fetus, you mean? Nature has used miscarriages since the beginning of time to eliminate imperfect fetuses. Abortion is just a form of unnatural miscarriage."

Windy unconsciously stiffened at that word; she didn't want the conversation going in a different direction.

"So abortions are only performed in early pregnancy?"

"In most cases. A woman usually knows right away whether she wants a child."

"What if Boy Evans' mother decided not to have him?"

"I do not doubt he would have been better off. He will spend his childhood in a succession of foster homes, some good, some not. Already in his short life, he has experienced a trauma most grown-ups find difficult to deal with. Insisting a baby be brought into this world, knowing what kind of future he's facing is, in itself, a form of child abuse."

Windy recalled Stephen's gentleness with Johnny and his agreeing with John about the 'passel' of kids. She remembered his sorrow when he couldn't save the baby in the accident.

"You love children, don't you?"

"Yes, that's why I believe they should be thought of first and not the wishes of a few fanatics." Windy snuggled close to her husband. If this gentle, loving man saw no harm in abortion, then there couldn't be any.

"Why the sudden interest?"

"There were a couple ladies at the meeting last night who work at a CPA."

"A what?"

"Crisis Pregnancy Center," she said slowly. "Sorry, I meant CPC."

"What were they doing at the meeting?"

"Looking for a church. They're teachers, just arrived here in August."

"I shall have a talk with Mrs. Dunkirk. She knows better than to allow such controversial subjects to be discussed at a missionary meeting."

"She was upset about it, Stephan, she said, no controversial subjects were allowed. Oh, please, don't say anything to her. I'd be so embarrassed."

"Trying to make a good impression are you? Don't worry, then, I will not cause any adverse attention."

Windy almost replied but thought better of it. She couldn't imagine Stephan thinking she wanted to impress Mrs. Dunkirk. The woman might be influential but Windy wasn't the least bit concerned what she thought of her. Better not to tell Stephan, though. He'd probably had dealings with Mr. Dunkirk and their relationship might be important.

"You are getting up now are you not? I would like to get some sleep today."

"Sure," Windy replied, crawling out of bed. She'd hoped for a little more affection this morning. Since Stephan started nights he had hardly even hugged her.

Pulling the shade down, Windy contemplated the long day ahead of her. She thought of going to the hospital to see Jordan only to remember he wasn't there. Maybe she could visit Cora and do some Christmas shopping. She and Stephan hadn't begun that, hadn't even talked about it.

Windy slipped over to the bed, sat down quietly and rubbed Stephan's shoulder.

"Stephan?" she whispered.

"Um?"

"Could I do a little shopping today?"

"What for?"

"Christmas. This is December, you know. The last couple years I've taken Cora Christmas shopping. It would be something for me to do while you sleep."

"Bring me my wallet." She did. After counting out fifty dollars he closed his wallet and placed it on the nightstand. "Do not spend it all."

Windy looked at the bills. "You mean, 'don't spend it all in one place'," she corrected.

"How could you possibly spend that much money?" He sat up and in the dim light Windy noticed a scowl on his face.

"Well, I'd like to get something to send to my parents, something for Cora, and for you, of course."

Stephan sighed heavily. "Buy for your parents and Cora. I do not need anything. Goodnight."

Windy gathered the clothes she'd left out the night before and exited the room. She looked at the money in her hand and remembered the fun she and Eddie had had Christmas shopping. They scoured the malls, looking for bargains to stretch their money as far as possible. But they'd always spent more than fifty dollars.

Windy opened the door of the pink room and threw her clothes on the bed. She checked the bathroom, but found no toiletries. All of hers were in the master bath.

Discouraged, she sat on the bed, checking the time.

7:30 AM.

"Guess I need a course of action," she muttered.

After dressing she went to the kitchen where her breakfast consisted of toast and coffee. She didn't like the stuff but Stephan drank a lot of it so she decided to try it again. She choked down half the cup and dumped the rest down the sink. She reached for the phone, knowing Cora would already be up and about. With Christmas nearing, her dear friend would be baking for the neighborhood.

Sachel rubbed Windy's legs before jumping into her lap. She scratched behind his ears then held his face to hers.

"I miss you, too. And if you weren't in such good hands I'd never dream of leaving you here."

"I suppose I should say it's a shame you can't take Sachel with you, but frankly," Cora stood at the counter easing a warm loaf of bread from its pan, "I'm glad for the company. Having him, keeps a part of you here."

"I thought Stephan liked animals the way Sachel took to him when he first appeared. It's probably a good thing I didn't know when we married that Stephan didn't allow any animals in the house. He gave Sachel permission to live in the garage but I just couldn't imagine exiling this loving guy to such a cold, dreary place."

Sachel purred as he curled up in Windy's lap. She had no doubt the cat was very happy with his present master, but Windy again felt that pang of loss she had when Stephan told her Sachel couldn't come with them.

Cora touched the first of many loaves lined up on the counter. She slipped it into a bag and twisted the tie securely.

"Baking for an army today?" Windy asked, counting the loaves. There were ten.

"Concern For The Aged always sees that their folks have fresh bread this time of year. I need to do my part now, so when I'm old someone will care for me. Then there's a new family down the block, moved in last week. They drive a beat up car, but I see them coming home every day after the factories let out. There's at least six children who walk past on their way to school. I'm sure a loaf or two of bread would be welcome."

"So now that I'm gone, you've found some one else to help?"

Cora smiled. "There's always some one." She placed the last loaf in its bag, then loaded the loaves into two brown shopping bags. "You don't mind if we drop these off do you?"

"Be glad to." Windy helped Cora on with her coat and gave Sachel another pat before picking up one of the bags. "You'll have to tell me where, though, I've never been to Concern For The Aged."

"Oh, it's right next to the mall."

"How convenient." Windy smiled, closing the door behind her.

Stephan was still sleeping when Windy carried her loot into the house. She'd done quite well on just fifty dollars and she even had change.

Upstairs she went into the late Mrs. Michaels room, the 'pink room' as she had dubbed it, and placed her packages on the bed. Quietly she emptied the bags. The small brown one she took into the bathroom, from it she extracted several small bottles. She placed the shampoo and conditioner on the counter along with a small bar of soap. The lotion, deodorant, toothbrush and paste she slipped into the medicine cabinet.

On the bed were several packages of aida clothe, two crosstitch books, a handful of floss and over a dozen skeins of yarn. The presents she'd looked at were fairly expensive and since Jordan no longer waited to be held at the hospital, Windy reasoned she'd have plenty of time to make her gifts.

She placed the goodies back in the bag along with a roll of wrapping paper and a package of tags. The bag she put in the closet. She retraced her steps to the bathroom where she quickly showered. She toweled her hair dry, slipped her shirt and panties back on and left the room. Quietly she opened the door to the master bedroom and slipped into it's darkness.

Stephan responded to her touch, pulling her under the covers beside him.

Chapter Twenty-One

Dear Lord,
Margie hurt my feelings today. I never expected that from her and I
don't know what to think. Her remark was cutting and intended. Help me
understand what lay behind her words. And Lord, if I've done something
to earn Margie's displeasure, help me seek her forgiveness. Amen. Oh,
Lord, my children. Please don't let me think so much of myself that I forget
my children. Please, be with them.

Wendy tossed Stephan's remark around in her mind, as she dried the last of the supper dishes and put them away. She remembered his statement about her cooking when they first married. 'No cooks. I like how you prepare a meal.'

Had that been just a month ago? How many times since then had Stephan commented negatively on the meal she'd prepared? Tonight he delivered the most surprising blow.

"Maybe you should look into cooking classes. I am sure they offer them at the college."

She'd been so stunned she hadn't replied.

"Elaine, I am talking to you."

"I know. I thought you liked the way I cook."

"It's fine for the two of us, but if we ever have guests over you will need to know what you are doing."

They finished the meal in silence, Windy finding something wrong with each bite. The pork chops were tough, the beans dry and the baked potatoes hard in the middle.

Putting the last clean pan in the cupboard Windy resolved to call the college tomorrow and find out if they offered classes. She'd not been a good wife to Eddie, and she refused to make the same mistake with Stephan.

She wanted him to be proud of her. She wanted everything about their marriage to be perfect and she was willing to change and work hard to see that happen.

Turning off the kitchen light she peeked into the parlor and saw Stephan reading a thick text book. Rather than disturb him she went up to the pink room and retrieved her treasures from the closet. She leafed through the cross stitch book till she found the picture she'd chosen for her parents. An angelic little girl sat on a clump of grass. Her wide eyes and sweet expression invited a hug. Soft pastels gave the picture a dreamy appearance. But what attracted Windy was the frog the little angel held in her hand. The pink dress covered all but the creatures head, his bulging eyes begged for release.

Wendy knew her mom and dad would be able to see their own little angel in the picture. The stitching would be difficult, requiring a lot of hard work, but Wendy knew if she started now she could finish this and the other two gifts in time.

She sorted through her old sewing bag picking out needles, scissors and an embroidery hoop. Gathering all she needed into her arms she went back down to the parlor and sat in the chair across from Stephan. She carefully looked over the instructions, noting little details and suggestions. Then she began.

About an hour later Stephan looked up from his book. "What are you doing?"

"Cross stitching a gift for my parents." She handed the book to Stephan, indicating her project.

"Looks like a lot of work."

"It will be."

"What else did you buy?"

"More of the same. I have plenty of time since I won't be going to the hospital and thought hand-made gifts would have more meaning."

Stephan smiled. "You are very resourceful. By the way, where is my change?"

"Change?"

"Yes, I told you not to spend the whole fifty dollars."

"It's in my purse. I thought if I needed something later, I'd be able to buy it."

"If you need something you can ask me."

Windy stood.

"Where are you going?"

"To get your change."

"Don't be silly…" relieved that he had been teasing her she smiled and sat down, "…you can give it to me when I go up to change clothes."

Her smile faded, but Windy resumed her work and Stephan returned to his book. Some time later he looked up at her and watched her for several minutes. "That's my good girl," he said.

"Did you call the college today?" Stephan asked Wendy as he entered the parlor. His eyes were still slightly puffy with sleep. Wendy looked at the clock. 2:30.

"No, I intended to but I forgot. I started working on this as soon as I got up." She laid her work aside, ready for a break, anyway.

"Don't bother," her husband said. "I will call."

Windy closed her eyes and stretched the muscles in her neck. She gently messaged her temples and rubbed her tired eyes. She covered a yawn as Stephan walked back into the room.

"Unfortunately, there will be no classes until next semester. But I signed you up."

"Thank you." She rose and walked over to Stephan putting her arms around him and laying her head on his chest.

"They will send the date and time to you. It cost seventy-five dollars, so make sure you do not miss any classes."

"Seventy-five dollars?" Wendy looked at him in astonishment. "For cooking classes?"

"They are not just simple cooking classes. Your instructor will be a chef and you will learn to prepare gourmet food, not pork chops and beans."

"But still, that's a lot of money."

"That's alright, dear, consider it your Christmas present."

The angel's face stared crookedly at Windy. Irritated, Windy counted the stitches again, finally finding the problem. She slid the needle under the last stitch and pulled. Then she pulled out another. The mistake lay three rows back and must be corrected or everything would be crooked.

Windy's initial anger at Stephan had subsided, replaced by remorse. She berated herself for the anger, reminding herself of her determination to be a better wife. If seventy-five dollar gourmet cooking classes would make Stephan happy and he was willing to pay for them, she should feel privileged to attend. Still the fifty dollars for Christmas presents and Stephan's change continued to bother her.

"Windy Michaels, you're an ungrateful brat," she scolded herself. What right do you have to question how Stephan spends his money? she continued silently. He works hard and deserves to make his own decisions.

Frustrated, Windy stood and dropped her handiwork on the chair. It was time to start supper and she knew if she left the stitching alone for a while she could come back and correct her mistake without much difficulty.

Once in the kitchen, she hesitated. The chicken she'd taken from the freezer that morning was thawed and ready for roasting. Wendy's confidence wavered. Eddie loved her roasted chicken. But would Stephan find something wrong with it?

"I rather hope so," she told herself. "If he does then I'll know how to prepare it next time."

She rolled up the sleeves of her blouse, noticing the frayed cuffs, washed her hands and dug in.

"Excellent meal, Elaine!" Stephan complimented as he placed his linen napkin on his plate. "You just might be able to give that college chef a few pointers."

Windy tingled inside, tears formed in her eyes. She wanted to please her husband, but she hadn't expected that kind of praise.

"How about if I start a fire in the parlor and we can cuddle until I go to work?"

Wendy smiled and nodded her agreement, too happy to speak. She quickly cleaned up and joined him.

The fire lit the cozy room. Wendy walked straight to Stephan and sat beside him, folding her frame next to his. He pulled her close and kissed her warmly.

"Oh, sweetheart, these nights just get harder all the time," he whispered into her hair, breathing in its fragrance. "Last night we had another accident. A young woman died."

Wendy savored his touch and the intimacy of this moment. Stephan rarely shared his work with her, unless it truly bothered him.

"What happened?" she whispered into his ear before kissing it.

"A drunk driver headed home after a night on the town hit a car head on. The woman driving it had no chance. She was in the right, all the way down to her fastened seatbelt. But her little car was just no match for his pick-up."

"Do you have to work these hours? Don't you have enough years in to be exempt from them?"

"Of course, I do." His hand reached for her buttons. "I have worked these hours not out of duty but from desire to serve in every capacity I am able to. However, I determined long ago that I would stop when I had a family to spend my evenings with."

Wendy pulled him closer, desiring to provide the answer to his midnight dilemma.

Chapter Twenty-Two

Dear Lord,
I thought having You in my life would make Christmas more bearable.
But the old loneliness is still there. I think of how different my life could
have been if only... Margie asked my forgiveness today and we talked for
a long time. She reminded me that she's very human and I must look only
to Jesus as my example, not to her. She's invited me over for Christmas
again this year. Lord, be with my children. Let the true meaning of
Christmas shine for them this year.

"Elaine!" Stephan yelled from the kitchen, anger sounded clearly in his
voice.

She jumped up from the couch, pulling the afghan around her body, and
rushed to her husband.

"Why are these dishes sitting on the counter?" He indicated the supper
dishes Windy had stacked there earlier.

"I thought I'd wait until you left to wash them."

"In this house we do not leave dirty dishes lying around to collect bugs.
Never leave the dishes again!"

"But I wanted to spend the evening with you. I intend to do them as soon
as you're gone."

"I repeat," he looked fiercely into her eyes. "Never do this again. I will not
have my house turned into a dump for a couple of leisurely hours. Is that clear?"

PAMELA GOODRODE SYMONDS

Windy nodded as Stephan stomped past her. She watched the door slam and heard the car pull out of the driveway. She tugged the scratchy afghan closer around her body feeling terribly naked and vulnerable beneath it.

Minutes ticked by as the girl stood staring toward the back door. Finally her jaw began to tremble and tears rolled down her cheeks. Her body shook as it slid to the floor. There she wept unhindered.

The clock showed 2 AM when Windy finally turned off the light and laid her head on the pillow. She closed her eyes but as exhausted as she was sleep didn't come.

Stephan's words resounded in her ears. MY HOUSE. MY HOUSE! Of course it's his house, dummy, she chided herself. It's his boyhood home passed down through generations. You're the visitor here, invited and welcome as long as you understand the rules.

Downstairs, the kitchen sparkled. Dirty dishes had been washed and put away. The sinks shone from the scrubbing they'd received as did the stove, fridge and floor. A myriad of emotions had cleaned that room. Fear started it, anger did its share, as did shame. A true desire to be 'good' gave it the final rinse.

Now Windy's tired puffy eyes closed in relief but her mind continued to rage. Anger returned with its friends. They kept the girl company for hours before finally departing and allowing her to fall into a sound, dreamless sleep.

Stephan walked through the hospital doors into the cold morning air. It sucked the breath right out of him and filled his lungs with ice. He ran to the car and without warming it he drove the several blocks home to his inviting bed.

He still shivered as he stepped through the back door. The clean kitchen screamed its silent witness of his anger from the night before. He stood for a moment, looking around. He suspected if he pulled out a white glove he'd not soil it in this room.

Upstairs he ran his hands under hot water until he imagined the warmed blood moving through his veins. Turning the faucet off, he picked a long brown hair out of the sink and dropped it into the waste basket. Then he walked to the bed and stared at his wife.

From the puffiness around her eyes, he guessed she'd cried herself to sleep. A lump formed in his throat. Here lay this little creature; rescued from a waste of humanity and completely dependant on him, Stephan Michaels, bachelor and sometimes idiot. He didn't doubt the hurt he caused her all because of a few dishes left so she could make love to him before sending him to work.

Coming home to someone in his bed enticed Stephan, it also bothered him. Since his college days he'd lived alone, never worked his schedule around anyone. Nothing dared move out of place in his home. Coats hung in the closet above a neat line of shoes. Dishes were kept cleaned, dried and in the cupboard. He detested seeing a drain board on the counter. Yet for over a month he'd noticed run-a-way shoes laughing at him, coats slung over a chair, hair in the bathroom sink.

He couldn't call Elaine messy. She always picked up after herself; eventually. But he insisted on working and living under spotless conditions. He knew marriage meant changes. But he thought they would all be good ones. He remembered Elaine telling him if her marriage to the scum was salvageable she wouldn't quit. Truly, she desired to make this relationship work. If he would just tell her, she'd listen and she would try harder. But that meant not insisting things be so perfect. Yes, he would have to give also. He must settle for something a little less than what he wanted. But surely, it would be worth it.

Stephan crawled in beside his wife and pulled her close. Her arms went around him as she laid her head on his chest.

"I'm sorry, Stephan. I'm so sorry."

"I know you are."

"I'll do better, I promise."

"Shhh, we'll talk about it later." He kissed the top of her head. '*Yes, it is worth it*', he thought. He touched her soft skin, smelled her delicate fragrance. He felt her cheek on his chest. Well worth it. He smiled and relaxed, letting the welcome sleep take over.

Windy looked at the package. The handwriting loped easily across the brown paper. But the name in the upper left hand corner drew Windy's attention; Mrs. Stephan Michaels, Sr., from New York.

Addressed to Dr. Stephan Michaels, Windy knew better than to open it. She placed it on the hall table, knowing Stephan would see it there with his other mail.

With dust cloth and spray bottle in hand she set about polishing anything that resembled wood, determined that when Stephan awoke he would believe her resolve to be a better wife.

When he descended the stairs Windy came out of the parlor, pushing the vacuum. She opened the closet door under the stairway and deposited the machine.

"Good morning." She embraced Stephan, lifting her head for a kiss. His lips lingered on hers as he held her close. Then he lead her into the room she'd just left and pulled her down beside him on the couch.

"You need not do the vacuuming, that is why I have Gretchen come in."

"I don't mind, really."

"Elaine, I may have been a bit harsh last night. I once told you Mrs. Michaels would understand. But I can not expect you to understand what you are not aware of. I have lived in this house all my life, and for the last twenty years, alone. It's going to take some getting used to having another person here."

"I know. I need to be more aware of your feelings. I asked myself today how I would feel if it were my home and you came here to live. It would be hard."

"This is your home, too, of course. Please do not feel as though it isn't. Just put up with me a bit, okay?"

"If you promise to have patience with me."

They sealed their bargain with a kiss.

The phone interrupted them and Stephan went into the hall to answer it.

"No, I am sorry, she's not available." Windy listened from the parlor surprised by Stephan's end of the conversation. "I don't believe I will relay your message." His voice was kind but firm. Windy stood up and joined him in the hall just as he hung up.

"Mary Ames," he answered her puzzled look. When she didn't appear to recognize the name he continued. "She is one of the women from the missions meeting. She wanted to invite you to lunch Saturday. Of course, you will not go."

"Why not?"

"I took the liberty of talking to Sally Garvey, trying to find out a little more about those women. Elaine, you do not need to get involved with politics, especially their kind."

Windy resented Stephan's actions. Why should he and Sally decide who she should or shouldn't see?

"Let me put it this way. I do not want you involved with them. I'm selfish. I want your undivided attention."

Still unconvinced she hesitated when he reached for her, but once inside his arms she felt secure.

He's doing it for your own good, she reminded herself, responding to him. Then she remembered the package and curiosity pulled her back.

"What's this?" she nodded at the brown box on the table. "Are you hiding a secret ex-wife somewhere?"

"No. That says senior. It is from my mother."

"You're mother? I thought she was...had, passed away."

"No."

"Aren't you going to open it?"

"No. It's just cookies and sugar things. Gretchen usually takes them home to her children."

"You get Christmas cookies from your mom and you give them away? Does she bake them herself?"

"I suppose. I have never eaten any."

"Do you send her anything?"

Stephan cast Windy a look that informed her he was tired of this conversation. "No," he answered, walking away.

Chapter Twenty-Three

Dear Lord,
This winter lingers, it's slowly pushing it's coldness into my heart.
Refresh me, Lord, renew me. How does the Psalmist put it? Oh, yes, revive
me. That's what I need, to be revived. Place a yearning in my heart for
Your word, a desire, a hunger, to replace this indifference. And please,
Lord, be with my children.

Christmas left Windy feeling empty. If it hadn't been for Cora asking Windy
to drive her around on Christmas Eve to deliver baked goods, Windy would
have wondered if there had even been a Christmas that year.

Cora loved the needlepoint Windy presented her and hung it over the
kitchen table. Stephan smiled when he opened his gift. He placed the framed
hand worked poem on the mantle then quietly reminded her that she wasn't to
get him anything.

Windy's parents sent her one hundred dollars. She wanted to go right out
and buy some new clothes but also wanted to keep it until needed. She did
however buy herself a pair of practical snow boots, tired of having cold, wet
feet for she still wore the same tennis shoes as last year.

Windy and Stephan settled into married life, minus scenes like the one over
the dishes. Whenever Windy felt Stephan's disapproval she jumped into action,
not always sure what upset him, but knowing he liked to see her busy.

Windy wasn't sure how to approach the subject of money with her new husband. She had managed finances for her and Eddie, though she rarely spent money on herself at least she always had a little. She assumed Stephan would allow her control over the food budget, but that wasn't the case. If she wanted something she put in on the grocery list. When they shopped Stephan always questioned the need of such an item. He never refused to purchase it but often made Windy sorry she even asked.

Sometimes she marveled that this same man paid her hospital and personal bills and let her use his car before they even married.

The car became another sore spot. Stephan said Windy could use it anytime she wanted. But he asked where she intended to go, why, and when she planned to be home. She didn't know where he kept the keys to his sedan and often he took the little convertible to work saying it saved gas.

Twice in January Stephan's schedule permitted them to attend church. Windy wore the same print dress and although Stephan never noticed, Mrs. Dunkirk did. Stephan heard the old woman's comment and the next day gave Windy twenty dollars for a new church dress. She went to a chain discount store where she'd always bought her clothes. The twenty dollars didn't cover the cost of the only dress she liked so she found it necessary to dig into the money from her folks. When she showed the dress to Stephan he admired it. Then she mentioned not seeing any of the ladies from church while shopping at the discount store. The comment went over his head and Windy decided a bargain dress was better than none at all.

She managed to avoid the Missions meetings by reminding Stephan the 'radicals' might be there. But in March he came home and announced he'd talked with Sally. Mary Ames and Jenny Mc Court hadn't been seen since the January meeting. Evidently, they hadn't found what they were looking for at the Community Church and were lobbying elsewhere.

Stephan breathed a sigh of relief while Windy began her search for another excuse.

She often asked if there were any new babies in the nursery that needed arms to hold them. Stephan didn't know, he made it a point not to find out.

Windy never mentioned Mrs. Stephan Michaels, Sr. in New York, but couldn't help wondering about the woman, her mother-in-law. Did she live alone or with relatives in New York? Just after Christmas Windy had questioned Gretchen about Mrs.Michaels but she either knew nothing or wasn't talking. She did bring Windy a sample of the baked goods from the package. Windy noticed many different kinds of cookies and pastries. Mrs. Michaels obviously went to a lot of trouble. Windy asked Gretchen if she remembered the return address. She didn't.

Each month Stephan kept a close eye on Windy's health and wore a disappointed look when she acknowledged that everything was functioning normally and on time.

During the cold winter days, Windy often wandered through the big house. Television never interested her but she gave it a try. The daytime soaps were ridiculous, she admitted but she quickly got caught up in them. After two weeks in front of the tube she decided she could do without their trash. The morning talk shows didn't last a week.

Once in a while she would look at the card in her purse with Jenny McCourt's number on it. She was tempted to call, but knew it would displease her husband.

Windy grew more restless each day. She often thought of Eddie and how life had never been boring with him.

'Painful,' she thought. *'But never boring.'*

In some ways she missed Eddie. She remembered those two years with longing. At times she desired to retrieve them. At such times she blamed her boredom on Stephan's hours or her difficulty in adjusting to such a fine way of life.

When Stephan worked midnights Windy slept in the pink room at his request. It enabled him to sleep longer and better. Windy could also sleep in a little too, rather than get up when he came to bed. At first Windy resented the move, then she began to look forward to it. This room was always warmer than Stephan's. He preferred his sleeping room cool, whereas Windy liked hers warm. She came to feel this was one little part of the house that actually belonged to her.

She placed her clothing in the drawers and closet, a few articles at a time. This kept her from waking Stephan when she forgot to lay them out the previous night. Before long the room contained most of her sparse wardrobe. Windy found if she showered in the guest bathroom she didn't have to worry about Stephan finding her long hairs in his sink. Besides, she loved the long hot soaks she took in the tub.

Because of the snow filled streets, Stephan hesitated to allow Windy use of the car. That left the girl with long lonely days and quiet evenings.

About twice a month Stephan relented and brought home a movie. When she reminded him of the many movies they'd watched before they married his reply cut to her heart.

"You've no idea how much that courtship cost me. I'm paying dearly for the time I took away from my studying. Elaine, new breakthroughs constantly occur in medicine. I'm just now catching up on what happened last summer."

So Stephan read while Windy knitted. He did supply her with plenty of pastel yarn and books on baby sweaters, booties and blankets. Unlike its mother, Windy's baby would never have to wear the same outfit twice.

A phone conversation with Cora became the highlight of her day. The older lady even kept up with Stephan's schedule so as not to interrupt the 'newlyweds'. Cora looked forward to those talks as much as Windy.

Windy's apartment was still empty and Cora hesitated to place ads in the newspaper. She feared who might want to rent the apartment and as an old woman living alone she wanted to choose her next tenant carefully. She also feared being taken to court if someone she didn't approve of wanted to rent it.

The cooking classes were attended and tolerated. Windy didn't care for the food she learned to prepare there. She preferred her pork chops and fried potatoes. The other ten members of the class were would-be chefs or cooks. On the first night they all identified themselves and their career ambitions. Windy was the sole housewife there to please her husband. She never missed a class, received an excellent grade and resented every minute of it.

Windy had always been a fairly good housekeeper but felt there were more important things in life. Stephan helped her see the error of her ways. Slowly, unknowingly, she began to resent the beautiful old house. Obviously, she existed for it, not it for her. She saw to its needs and if she performed properly the house rewarded her with its comfort.

Nightly a fire roared in the parlor and daily Windy emptied the ashes, setting the paper and kindling for the next one. A man brought a load of wood every week. Windy watched him from the kitchen window. He backed his pick up into the driveway and carefully stacked the wood against the far side of the garage. At first, if he noticed Windy, he waved. Now he appeared to look for her familiar face in the window. Windy thought of inviting him in for a cup of the ugly black stuff, but decided Stephan would probably object. Windy couldn't tell the age of the man beneath his worn red scarf and hat with the ear flaps pulled down. She guessed him to somewhere in his forties.

One Friday morning in early March Windy awoke to an empty bed and a blinding snow storm. She moved about the house performing the daily chores listed on a piece of paper kept on the kitchen memo board. Stephan gladly supplied this list when Windy asked him what she could do to make him happy.

Many of the items were obsolete. Windy learned to put things away as soon as she finished with them. She kept her handiwork in the pink room closet, out of Stephan's sight. She became as irritated at a run-a-way shoe as Stephan did. The house hardly had the opportunity to collect dust or dirt.

This morning when Windy heard the gears grinding in the driveway she took the coffee pot to the window and pulled back the curtain. The man looked up as soon as he stepped from the truck, smiled when he saw her, and nodded. Windy quickly put on her jacket, stuffing several packets of sugar in her pocket. She pulled two cups from the cupboard, filled them and headed outside.

The wind whipped hair into her face making her sorry she hadn't put on a hat. Awkwardly, she handed the cup to the workman. He motioned they walk to the side of the garage where they'd be somewhat protected.

"Much obliged," he said. His voice held a slight Southern accent. "It's mighty cold today and the old beast lost it's heater years ago. This here is just what I needed."

Windy smiled and pulled out the sugar.

"No, thanks. I like it strong and unhindered."

She tried to balance her cup and open a packet.

"Here let me help." The man took the cup from her and held it while she opened four packets and poured them into the ugly black stuff. "You ain't much of a coffee drinker?" Windy shook her head, blowing on the liquid. "I live on the stuff. It's my only vice, though. Guess the good Lord will forgive me for it." Windy smiled, not understanding why coffee required forgiveness.

The man continued talking between sips. He spoke to Windy of his wife and four 'youngins'. He'd lost his job the summer before when a major plant closed down but his wife's grandfather owned a couple hundred acres of land full of birch and maple trees. When the old gentleman died he left it to them. Until his job searching turned up something, he could at least feed his family.

He handed his empty cup to Windy and repeated his thanks saying he'd better 'git ta work'.

As Windy opened the kitchen door she heard the telephone ring. She ran to answer it and was rewarded with Cora's voice. As she listened to Cora's excited chatter she slipped her jacket and shoes off, placing them in the closet.

"Oh, Windy, it's the most wonderful thing! I have a new tenant. The sweetest little girl, reminds me of you, though she's not married. I met her at CFTA." Windy tried to remember, Concern For The Aged, oh yes. "She spends a couple evenings a week reading to those who can't anymore. And she reads from the Bible. Such a sweet girl, you've just got me meet her. She's moving in tomorrow and could use a little help I'm sure, if you've nothing else to do."

"I'm sure Stephan will let me have the car to do that. What time should I come?"

"Splendid! Oh, she's coming in now. I'll see you tomorrow. Bye dear!"

Windy smiled as she hung up; thankful that Cora's dilemma had ended. But deep inside she felt a little pang of jealousy. Cora had another 'granddaughter' to fuss over now. *'Maybe this is how she felt when I married Stephan and moved away from her,'* Windy thought.

Well, tomorrow she would meet this sweet rival and hopefully share Cora's enthusiasm.

Cora said the girl read from the Bible. It certainly would be nice to know a little on that subject for tomorrow's meeting. Windy passed through the foyer and into the small library. She'd checked this room out months ago and found dozens of text books that interested her even less than the classics Stephan's great-grandfather must have purchased hot of the press.

Having never taken literature in high school she hadn't acquired a taste for those kinds of books. Now she searched slowly and thoroughly. Certainly, there must be some kind of Bible in here.

The shelves held no such treasure and Windy turned to leave the room when she saw a huge book lying on a table in the corner. Of course, she'd dusted it enough times how could she have forgotten about it?

Carefully she opened the heavy leather cover imprinted with the words HOLY BIBLE. The pages were thick and slightly discolored, one held a list of births, the next marriages and another, deaths. Stephan's birth was the last one recorded. Had his father been an only son also? She found no evidence to the contrary. His father and grandfather's deaths appeared with the same date, 25 years earlier. Those entries along with Stephan's birth and the marriage of his parents were written in the same thin writing. The previous entrees bore a similar pattern.

Windy turned more pages and found Genesis. She congratulated herself on remembering it as the first book of the Bible. 'Let's see, Genesis, Exodus, Numbers, ummm…,' she recalled one started with a D but couldn't remember it. Then there's Matthew, Mark, Luke and John'. She thumbed through the pages, quickly finding, but unable to pronounce the D book. Finally she found the four men's names. Windy read the name "Jesus" at the beginning of Matthew. She looked down half the page at a long list of names, most of which she couldn't pronounce. But by the number 18 she read the words 'Now the birth of Jesus Christ…' Windy pulled up a small arm chair and continued to read, leaving the book on the table.

Stephan found her there when he arrived home, hours later.

Chapter Twenty-Four

Dear Lord,
I've been given my first duty at church! The pastor called today asking
if I would work on the benevolence committee. I'm excited about being a
servant to others, especially the sick. Use me, Lord, make me a blessing.
Make my kids blessings too.

"Windy! Meet Jenny Mc Court!" Cora bubbled before Windy could close
the door behind her. Windy stared wide-eyed at the woman, recognizing her
as one of the so- called radicals. So this was Cora's sweet little girl?

"I'm glad to meet you," she fumbled.

"I believe we've met," Jenny replied.

Windy listened to the tone, did it accuse? "Yes, yes we have," she
answered trying hard to regain her composure. She slipped her jacket off and
placed it on a familiar hook on the back of the door. "At a church meeting I
recall." She watched the girl intently. Had Mary told her about the phone call
and Stephan's refusal to let Windy talk? Did Jenny know she stood right there
during that conversation? A dozen thoughts whirled through Windy's mind.
The fact that Jenny was now Cora's tenant meant Windy must either accept
her or stop coming to see Cora. She looked at the precious little lady. Never.
Never would she turn away from Cora. She sat down, determined to make the
best of an awkward situation. It turned out to be anything but.

For the next hour the three talked. Cora told Jenny about Windy, often adding 'like I told you'. The first time she did so Windy felt a bit embarrassed, wondering how much Cora had already told Jenny about her. But she listened closely and heard only things she considered good, mostly about their relationship.

Jenny talked a little about herself, where she lived, meeting Mary and how they came here to teach.

Windy relaxed as she learned more about the girl, realizing she was just a young woman making a life for herself.

"Where is Mary now?" Windy ventured her first question.

"She'll be married April 1st." Jenny responded to Windy's smile. "It's really quite interesting how I came to be here." She looked at Cora. "Mind hearing the story again?"

"Not at all, it's a wonderful story."

"Mary and I rented an apartment close to the school knowing Mary would move out in the spring. She and Andrew, he teaches high school math, found a quaint little place that came available about the time they needed it. I advertised for a room mate beginning the same time. And I found one. By Christmas we had everything settled. Then last week it all changed. The owners of the quaint little house transferred, putting the house up for sale. Then my intended roommate called. Her parents were hurt in an accident and she moved back home. Suddenly we were left with one apartment and too many people. Then the Lord saw fit to deliver me safely into Cora's hands."

"And she already knew you," Cora added. "Jenny says the good Lord had it all planned; your meeting last fall, the house and roommate, meeting me, everything. What's that verse you told me?"

'Oh, oh, here it comes,' Windy thought. *'Glad I did some reading yesterday.'*

"And we know that God causes all things to work together for good."

"Jenny says God knows everything, has it all planned out even. Isn't that right Jenny?"

"Yes, Cora." Jenny smiled lovingly at the excited old woman. "He cares about everything that happens to us."

Windy felt uncomfortable with the direction of the conversation. In the few sermons she'd heard at church the minister never indicated any such knowledge. Stephan gave her the impression that God wasn't quite as big as

Jenny seemed to think and she couldn't recall Jenny's words from the ones she'd read the day before.

"Do you need any help moving, Jenny? I thought as long as I have the whole day free."

"Cora told me of your kind offer. As a matter of fact, I do. One of my fellow teachers lent me his pick up. Do you mind driving over to the apartment with me?"

"Not at all. That's why I'm here."

They pulled their coats on as Cora put the cups into the sink. Windy noticed Jenny's warm, pretty boots and looked at her own plain black ones. *'Maybe being the wife of a rich doctor isn't much different than being the wife of a poor mechanic,'* she thought.

"I'll have a nice hot lunch waiting for you." Cora promised.

When they arrived at Jenny's, Mary greeted them at the door. Windy remembered the smile that appeared so inviting the first time she saw her.

Mary grasped Windy's hand and gave it a firm shake.

"I'm just delighted to see you. When Jenny told me about Cora knowing you I hoped we would be able to get together."

Windy expected a rebuff from this young woman considering the one Stephan had dished out, yet Mary welcomed her with enthusiasm.

"I…I'm sorry I never got back with you. Settling into married life can be hectic, you know."

"I will very soon!"

"That's right; April first is just a couple weeks away." Windy breathed easier having said her apologies and gladly changed the subject.

The three chatted for a few minutes then set to work, Jenny didn't have much but what she had was scattered through out the apartment. She retrieved her items as Windy and Mary wrapped and boxed them for her. When they had a pickup load all three rode over to Cora's where they were welcomed and fed lunch.

It took the three women most of the afternoon to load Jenny's few items of furniture. Mary didn't accompany them on the second trip, and as she hugged Jenny good-bye Windy felt a little sad, though she didn't know why. Then Mary turned to her, smiled and said how glad she was to have seen Windy again. Involuntarily Windy stepped forward and lifted her arms, Mary responded with a willing embrace.

On the trip back to Cora's the girls made plans to get together that weekend. Windy felt safe in telling Stephan she'd be going to Cora's and looked forward their meeting. For the first time since losing little Jordan she smiled inside.

"I have not seen this in a while; to what do we owe the pleasure?" Stephan indicated Windy's smile when she met him at the door that afternoon.

"I spent the day helping Cora's new tenant move in. It was so good to see Cora again." She took her husband's coat and hung it in the closet.

"You talk to her every day."

"I know, but talking over the phone and enjoying a cup of tea in her kitchen are very different."

"Yes, I'm sure they are. Who is now occupying your old flat?"

"Her name is Jenny, she's a teacher and she's just as delightful as Cora said she is. She's part of the reason for the smile, I guess. I really like her; she's nice to be around."

"What's her last name?" Windy cringed. She hoped to avoid that question. She knew if Stephan found out Jenny's identity he wouldn't allow her to return to Cora's. She didn't want to lie, and worked hard not to.

"She didn't tell me. I made you a special supper." She handed Stephan a dish, complete with pot holders, and headed him back toward the dining room. She followed close behind, a casserole in hand. Stephan sat his dish on the table and lifted the lid. Steam rushed out at him and he took a deep breath, savoring the smell. Windy paused to light two candles on the table.

"Well, whoever your new friend is, I must approve. I have not had a meal like this since you finished your classes."

Windy listened to Stephan's praises for the next half hour, thankful he liked the meal and pleased to be complimented. But she felt a bit uneasy. She hadn't lied to Stephan, but she held something back. Her desire to see Jenny again, was strong, stronger than her desire to be completely honest with her husband. It saddened her that she had to sacrifice honesty for friendship and she determined that she would tell Stephan as soon as possible about Jenny.

The spring sun heralded the arrival of Saturday morning. Windy awoke before Stephan, but lay next to him, studying his features in the dim light. She longed to wake him and tell him about Jenny. To explain how good her heart felt this morning, knowing she would see her friend again. Her friend. After spending only one day with Jenny she accepted her into the small circle consisting of Stephan and Cora. Maybe Cora's excitement caused Windy to accept Jenny so quickly. Or maybe it was the warmth she felt from both Mary and Jenny. What ever it was she wanted more.

She longed to hear what Jenny had to say about God today. Earlier in the week Windy called Cora and heard Jenny's voice in the background.

"Ask Jenny where I can find that verse she quoted," Windy prompted. Cora asked, then relayed the information. As soon as their conversation ended, Windy ran into the parlor and started turning pages in the old Bible.

After much difficulty she found it. She read the verse, then the previous ones and the ones that followed. The words were awkward, the meaning unclear. Windy decided she would swallow her pride and ask Jenny what it all meant.

Stephan stirred and rolled over, a minute later the alarm sounded. He groaned as he reached up to silence the clock.

"I think I will stay home today," he said, rolling back toward Windy. "Would you like to spend the day in bed with me?"

Windy smiled, covering the dread in her heart.

"You mean doctors are allowed sick days and you never told me?"

"Yes, we are allowed sick days." Stephan scooped his wife into his arms and kissed her longingly. "But we must be dead to take them."

"You don't have to work tomorrow do you?"

"No, but tomorrow is Sunday."

"And you prefer padded pews to this lumpy mattress."

"Padded pews in the morning, lumpy mattress the rest of the day!" He gave her a kiss filled with promises then slid from the bed. Windy smiled as she watched him disappear into the bathroom. Today she'd see Jenny, tomorrow she'd have her husband all to herself and she could tell him the secret that disturbed her so.

Chapter Twenty-Five

Dear Lord,
I know when You saved me, You took away my sins. I wish You had
taken away the memories, too. Sometimes, I hurt so bad when my mind
relives those difficult days. Thank You for loving me even when I didn't
love You. Please help my kids with their memories.

Windy flipped the light switch off as she walked out of the bathroom. The movement came so naturally it startled her.

"What's wrong?" Jenny asked from where she sat at the table.

"I've done that a thousand times. It suddenly seems strange not to be doing it anymore."

"How long did you live here?"

"Over two years. I found the apartment just before we got married. It was our honeymoon hide-a-way."

Memories of Eddie came easily in this familiar place. Windy found herself telling Jenny things she'd never told anyone about her and Eddie, about their thoughts and dreams. She relived many of their happiest times.

Slowly the good memories gave in to the more recent ones.

"Eddie didn't drink when I met him but after we'd been married about a year he began drinking everyday."

Jenny listened silently as Windy recalled their second year together.

"It was that night, that Fourth of July, that became the turning point. It marked the difference in Eddie, in our relationship, everything. Funny, I didn't realize it until just now."

"Did something unusual happen that night?"

"He actually hit me." Windy smiled and shook her head. "Up until now I've never really admitted that. You know, acknowledged it for what it was—an intentional blow. He meant to harm me. I remember the look in his eyes, as though he couldn't do enough damage to suit him."

Windy took a deep breath and let it out slowly. "That's frightening, Jenny, to remember something like that."

"I'm sure it is." Jenny reached out and took her friend's hand. They sat in silence for a while, each looking into their own thoughts. "That's an unusual ring." Jenny broke the silence.

"It belongs to Stephan's family. He said I'm the fifth Mrs. Michael's to wear it." She glanced at her hand. "I wonder if they were as emb...delighted to wear it as I am?"

"Emdelighted? Do you like it?"

"It's very valuable."

"It's also very gaudy."

"Jenny! It's an heirloom, a treasure."

"To you? What does it mean to you, Windy? Does it signify Stephan's love or his possession?"

Windy fell silent, searching her mind for an answer.

"Tell me about Stephan. How did you meet?"

"You mean Cora didn't tell you?" Windy asked, relieved to have the subject changed.

"Of course, she did." Jenny laughed. "She gave me the complete romanticized version. I want to hear it from your point of view."

Windy laughed, her eyes sparkled as she remembered their first meeting.

"I said his name wrong, and he corrected me. I was so taken back I couldn't remember what we'd been talking about. Stephan's proud of his heritage, his home, his name. He's very touchy about it. Anyway, I woke up in this hospital bed with a nurse checking my pulse, here," Windy picked up Jenny's hand and found her heart beat in her wrist. "'Umphh. Nothing wrong with you.' she said. Then she left. I had no idea what was going on so I crawled to the end of the bed where I saw her leave my chart and I read it.

"Late that evening this huge guy came into my room. He took up the whole doorway. He wore a white uniform, but didn't look quite like a doctor. He introduced himself and we had a nice talk."

"Stephan?" Jenny asked.

"No. John Garvey, the EMC…"

"The what?"

"Emergency Medical Technician, EMT who took me to the hospital. You may remember his wife, Sally?" Jenny's smile suddenly became fixed, she nodded. "A short time later, this…well…this old guy came in. No mistaking him, The Doctor. He was nice enough but a little nosy. Then I realized he was just checking me because he thought I might have a concussion or something. The next day Dr. Michaels released me and even drove me home. He stayed a short time and we talked. He asked to take me to lunch the next day but I declined. I saw Stephan as an older man, a father-uncle type person. He'd been nice, he appeared concerned, but even if I'd been looking, I wouldn't have considered him 'date' material. The next week I went to his office for a follow up visit. I talked about Eddie, he talked about church. Then I figured out that he was a Christian and as interested in my spiritual health as my physical. Anyway, I found a job right away and kind of forgot about him. But a couple weeks later he called, asking me to join him and the Garvey's for dinner. I really had no idea he was interested in me until halfway through the meal. Suddenly he's making comments and looking at me like, well, like a man looks at a woman. I remember being offended; I'm married, trying to patch up things with my husband and this man appears out of nowhere and lets me know he has intentions."

"And now you're married to him."

"I know." Windy sighed and shook her head. "Isn't life strange? It's been less than a year and my life has changed so completely. Sometimes I feel my head spinning from it all."

"How do you feel about Stephan now?"

"He's my husband, I love him."

"Do you love him because he's your husband, or is he your husband because you love him?"

"I don't think I understand."

"Which came first? Love or marriage?" When Windy didn't answer, Jenny continued, "Windy, do you think the Lord lead you into this union?"

"God?" Jenny nodded. Windy continued in a puzzled voice. "What does He have to do with it?"

"Everything. He cares about all that we do, especially about who we choose as a marriage partner."

"I never thought about it." Windy considered the idea for several minutes. "Yes, I think maybe He did bring us together, if you look at all that's happened. There could have been a different doctor on duty that night.

"Jenny, you're scaring me, asking me such weird questions." Again they fell silent. "I have to tell you…I have to tell you, Stephan doesn't know I'm with you. He knows about Cora's new tenant, but he doesn't know it's you. If he did, he wouldn't approve."

"Like the phone call?"

"So, you do know about that?"

"Yes. Sally also had a heart to heart with me. She's not afraid to speak her mind."

"Sally talked to you? About what?"

"You. She cornered me at church one day, said that the good doctor didn't want us filling your young mind with our radical ideas. I told her I thought your young mind was capable of making its own decisions. Right after that Mary and I visited another church."

Windy consider Jenny's words. Then she shook her head. "I'm more confused now. Stephan and Sally, they're good Christian people. Stephan contributes a lot of money to the church, Sally goes to all the meetings, but they don't talk about God like you do. Stephan doesn't even have a Bible and when I asked for one, he wanted to know why."

"Windy, what's your definition of 'Christian'?"

"Well, you know, people who go to church and do good deeds."

"Ever hear of the Pharisees?"

"No, who are they?"

"They were the religious leaders of Jesus' day. They spent a lot of time at the temple, and did good deeds. Jesus called them hypocrites and vipers. They were responsible for His death."

Windy had never heard this side of the story and her mind filled with questions, which she stumbled over when she tried to ask them.

"Do you have a Bible, Windy?"

"No. I think my folks must have had one because I remember carrying one to my friends youth meetings."

Jenny pushed her chair away from the table and disappeared into the bedroom. She came back a moment later and handed Windy a well used book.

"This is my study Bible. I want you to take it home and read the Gospel of John. Twice. The first time just read it through. The second time, read all the footnotes and comments I've written in it. Okay?"

Windy accepted the book with a nod. "Won't you need it?"

"I have others I can use, so keep it as long as you need."

Windy flipped through the pages, surprised at how Jenny treated what should be an holy book.

"And Windy? You must tell Stephan who I am."

Windy's face clouded over. "I'm going to tomorrow. We'll have the whole day together after church. But why do you say that?"

"If God is in our friendship, and I truly believe He is, He won't want any deception."

Windy smiled at the thought. "You think so?"

"Sure, He frowns on our dishonesty."

"That makes sense, but I meant our friendship. Do you really think He's in it?"

"No doubt in my mind. Look how He's brought us together."

"Kind of like Stephan and I?"

Jenny just smiled, then asked if Windy still attended the ladies missionary meetings. She remembered what Jenny said about God not liking deception. She honestly and openly told Jenny of her dislike of the meetings and the women she met there. She admitted having used Jenny and Mary as an excuse for not going, but now needed to find another. Again, Jenny suggested honesty to Stephan. This time Windy felt a tinge of despair. She remembered telling Stephan about her feelings for Eddie and how he would have to learn to live with them. But that happened before they were married when she could talk more openly to him. If he'd changed his mind about marrying her then, it would have been okay. But now, what would his reaction be? Jenny sensed Windy's hesitation. "Believe me, it's the best course of action. It may cause trouble at first, but you've got to believe the Lord will reward your honesty."

Windy smiled. "Of course. I don't know why I doubted Stephan. I told him I wanted an honest relationship, I'd be very wrong to keep anything from him."

The day passed too quickly for Windy, long before she wanted to, it was time to leave.

Chapter Twenty-Six

Dear Father,
Please be with my children today. Are they living a life that will haunt their memories as I have? The sooner they find You, the less harmful memories they'll have.

"I find your deception hard to swallow." Stephan's stern voice cut to Windy's heart. They sat on the parlor couch, the warming glow of the fireplace filled the room. Windy felt safe cuddled within Stephan's protective arms, safe enough to ask if she could tell him something important. As she began telling him about her excuses for not going to the meetings, she felt his arms tighten around her; she assumed it was his way of comforting her and telling her to continue. Not until he spoke did she realize he gripped her tightly and his own body had gone tense.

"If you disliked the meetings so much you should have told me you did not want to go. Though I can not for the life of me understand what you found so distasteful about them." Suddenly, Windy could hardly remember why she didn't like the meetings, wondered why she'd been so intent on not going.

"But this business over Jenny McCourt, I just do not understand you. You are a grown woman, Elaine, why must you sneak around like a rebellious teenager?"

Windy longed to crawl away from her husband's angry grip. She considered begging his forgiveness on her knees but feared that would anger him more.

"After I explained to you why I did not want you to keep company with her, you seek her out anyway, deliberately disobey my wishes and then come back here and throw it in my face."

A spark lighted in Windy's brain, a spark needing justice. But the timid girl snuffed it out quickly, reminding herself that she'd practically been unfaithful to her husband and anything he said, she deserved.

"I thought you respected me and my concern for you. I only wanted to protect you from this woman. God only knows what she would fill your mind with if given a chance."

'You've got to believe the Lord will reward your honesty.' This is what Jenny filled her head with, Honesty, respect, commitment. But where did it get her? She needed to explain to Stephan that if it weren't for Jenny the deception might be carried further.

"I am surprised at how little regard you have for my opinion and that of Sally, who is probably your only true friend."

Friend? The spark reappeared. *Only true friend? Sally has never called me, never invited me for a visit. The last I heard from her was a Christmas card, minus any personal note at all. Jenny gave me her own personal study Bible.* Again Windy doused the spark with self-condemnation.

"I do not know how to deal with this. I never expected such a thing from you. But then, maybe I should have." With that Stephan pulled away from Windy and left the room, his last comment stung her ears and she tried to understand what he meant by it.

The logs shifted in the fireplace, waking Windy. She lifted her head from the couch pillow and stared into dying flames wondering what time it was and how long she'd been asleep. Swinging her legs to the floor she felt them tingle as the blood began to flow again. She massaged them for a few minutes as she peered into the darkness at the mantle clock, barely able to make out what it said.

"Two-thirty," she sighed. "Stephan must really be mad at me, to let me sleep here this long."

She poked the fire, closing the glass doors over the screen and made her way upstairs. Without turning on the light she undressed and slipped into bed. Stephan rolled over and pulled her into his arms.

"I'm sorry, Stephan. Please forgive me," she whispered.

He kissed her longingly. "Not quite the evening I had in mind," he answered, his voice husky from wanting.

"I know, I'll make it up to you."

Next morning Windy awoke before Stephan. She rolled over and studied his sleeping form. Jenny's question came back. 'Which came first? Love or marriage?'

Looking at her husband's sturdy jaw, the tiny scar on his mouth, the ears topped with graying hair, she tried to remember when she had fallen in love with the 'old guy, the doctor'.

She recalled the night the accident baby died. That must have been it. That was definitely the turning point in their relationship. She remembered wanting to comfort him, to make his hurt go away. Was that love? Or did she just want to pay him back for his kindness when she needed it so.

When had she finally said yes to his proposal? Windy filtered many scenes through her mind, trying to replay that particular one. But it didn't exist. She'd never said yes. She just stopped saying no. Okay. When had she stopped saying no? After the car and her 'thank you.' Windy pushed that memory from her mind. How could she ever explain that to Jenny? But then why did she feel she needed to. Her marriage to Stephan wasn't any of Miss McCourt business. Maybe she should not see Jenny anymore, not if it meant a rift between her and her husband.

Her husband stirred, and for the first time in her short marriage, she felt remorse for a hasty decision. One small tear dropped on her pillow as she gazed at the man beside her.

Think Windy, think! When did you start to love him? When? The word echoed through her mind, bouncing off walls, unable to find an answer.

"If you insist on acting like a child, I can treat you like one."

"Stephan, I hardly think it childish to be able to choose my friends." Windy's resolve not to see Jenny lasted until Stephan informed her she could not. She hadn't even had a chance to tell him of her decision before he came down on her.

"I will not have my wife rubbing shoulders with the dredge of society."

"How can you say that? You've never even met Jenny. She's a wonderful girl. She loves God and she's a far better Christian than anyone I've met at your church.

"Elaine, this issue is not open for discussion. You are not to go to Cora's as long as Jenny McCourt lives there. You are not to call her or associate with her in any way."

"You're punishing Cora for my friendship with Jenny."

"No, Elaine, you are. You knew I disapproved of the young woman. I agree it is not Cora's fault that she accepted her as a tenant, she had no idea of what she was getting into. You did. And as long as she is in Cora's life, you will not be."

"Why do you hate her so? Why have you formed such a terrible opinion of someone you've never met? Meet her Stephan, give her a chance. I know you'll like her."

Stephan turned his back on his wife and walked out of the door. He reached into his pocket, checking to see if both sets of car keys were there, thankful he had never shown Elaine where he kept the extra set of sedan keys. He would have to rely on Elaine's honor concerning the telephone, since he could not keep her from using it.

Honor! He laughed to himself. How good is the honor of a lying woman?

Once inside the garage he noticed the telephone wire, running into the house and considered what he might sever it with.

Remorse overwhelmed him as he realized how far he carried his intentions. He never meant to keep his wife a captive in her own home. Staring at the wire, he jingled the keys in his pocket.

What are you thinking, Stephan Michaels? What's going on in your head?

And so the battle began. For more than twenty minutes he stood in the cold garage, listening to two voices he never knew existed. One chastised him for his behavior toward his wife, the other was appalled at his leniency. He stood silently, listening to the battle as though it took place in front of him rather than within.

He sided with neither voice, not knowing which was right, which represented him. Finally, he stepped into the car, started the engine and turned on the radio, adjusting its dial to the market report. He ignored the voices and by the time the report ended and he arrived at hospital, they were gone.

He went straight to his office where he dialed Cora's number. The number he associated with the pretty little girl who lived upstairs, the one he'd decided would be his wife, share his home, give him the heirs that suddenly became so important to him; the one whom had just admitted deceit.

"Good morning, Cora," his voice sounded normal, nothing like the two he'd imagined in his garage. "I am somewhat in hot water with our precious 'Windy' and I wonder if you could help me out?"

"Jenny's coming here?" Windy closed the oven door as the aroma of roast beef drifted through the kitchen.

"It is what you want isn't it?" Stephan picked up her delicate hand, removed the pot holder and pulled his wife close. "I usually make decisions based on all the facts, and I realized I do not have enough knowledge to form an opinion of Miss McCourt. So I invited her here tonight to get better acquainted. After all, if she is important enough to lie for, there must be something I am missing."

Windy's feelings remained unsure. She delighted in Stephan reconsidering his opinion, relieved that he would relent. Yet, his reasoning, his explanation made her uncomfortable. Why couldn't he admit she was right? Why couldn't he just say 'I'm sorry'? Was he sorry? What would poor Jenny walk into?

Windy, this is Stephan, your kind, gentle husband, she chided herself. He is not the enemy. He deserves your trust.

Windy surrendered to Stephan's embrace, feeling the familiar security it brought.

"Thank you Stephan. This means so much to me. I'm glad I told you about her, even though you were angry for a while. Now that we have it out in the open we can grow closer. They say adversity makes you stronger."

"Who is 'they?'" He whispered, teasing her ear with his breath. "Anybody I know?" He kissed her neck, then her throat.

"Supper now, that later," she pushed him away playfully just as the doorbell rang. "I'll get it."

"No, allow me. I will entertain our guest in the parlor while you put supper on the table."

Windy watched him go, a smile on her lips and tears in her eyes, wondering how she could have doubted him. She'd dealt a blow to his trust, to their relationship and he responded in a kindly act. She didn't deserve him, but she would try.

Chapter Twenty-Seven

Dear Lord,

Today I took flowers to the hospital for Brother Tom. He didn't look well at all. Everyone in the church is praying for him. Between You and them I know he's in good hands. Thank You for my church. If my children don't already have a church will You lead them to a good one?

Windy nestled close to her husband. The intimacy they had just shared completed the wonderful evening.

"Thank you, Stephan for inviting Jenny. Your actions took away any doubts I had."

"Doubts about what?"

"Your love." She whispered hesitantly. She liked the honesty even if it meant a little misunderstanding now and then.

"You doubted my love?" She detected an edge in Stephan's voice.

"Yes. Now that you've put up with me for almost five months I thought you might be getting tired of me and my silly ways."

"I could never tire of you, dear. I know I get impatient, but you must admit I usually have reason. I am working on that area of my life; trying to practice patience with you, just as you a working on not being so silly."

Windy tried to accept his words as a compliment, but somehow they just didn't strike her that way. She kissed his bare chest, rubbing her cheek on the soft fur that adorned it. "What did you think of Jenny?"

Windy had noted Stephan's quick acceptance of Jenny and felt confident asking this question.

"I like her. I believe that she may have given Sally a wrong impression on that original meeting."

Why can't he just admit he was wrong? Windy questioned herself. It's not in his nature, she answered.

"What did you think of her invitation to church?"

"We have a church, Elaine."

"I know, but would it hurt to visit?"

"I am an elder at the Community Church, how would it look if I showed up in some little Evangelical church?"

"A what?"

"Evangelical. I read between the lines, Elaine, I listen to what people tell me about their ailments, it helps me to make an accurate diagnosis. Jenny now belongs to one of those churches on the other side of town that preaches fire and brimstone and claims their members are all 'born again'.

"Is that bad?" Windy couldn't understand Stephan finding fault with Jenny's beliefs. After all, she seemed to know a lot more about God than Stephan did. Windy had looked forward to Jenny sharing some of those beliefs with Stephan, thinking he would quickly embrace them. After all, if Stephan wanted to be a Christian, wouldn't he want to be the best one he could be?

"Unnecessary would be a better word. I fail to understand how people can claim to know God personally. He is God. He is too godly to bother with every human being on the face of this earth. That is why he created us intelligent, self-sufficient and competent; so as not to be bothered with the insignificant details."

"Am I an insignificant detail?"

"No. You are my silly wife, who asks too many questions and tries to find meanings to life that aren't there. And," he said placing his fingers over her mouth to stifle her retort, "you are significant to me and that is sufficient for you."

He kissed her tenderly. "Now go to sleep, my important little detail and stop bothering your poor, tired husband."

Windy smiled and snuggled close. If this marriage were going to work, if she wanted to make Stephan happy she would need to work harder than she did with Eddie. She just couldn't let any doubts spring up. She was glad to be married to Stephan, she had to be glad, and that's that. She was important to

PAMELA GOODRODE SYMONDS

Stephan he needed her and that's all she ever wanted to be. Besides pregnant. The thought sent a jab of pain into her heart but she refused to let it ruin her perfect day. After all maybe this would be THE month.

Her period started three days later.

She called Cora as soon as it started and found herself crying out her misery to the wonderful little lady. Cora's words, meant to comfort, did just the opposite.

"Some folks just aren't meant to have babies, Windy. Look at Clifton and I, married for thirty-eight years and never a child."

After the disheartening talk with Cora, Windy decided to work on the baby blanket she had thrown in the bottom of the closet last month at this time. Instead of being discouraged she became determined. Maybe wanting something so bad could make it happen. If so, she'd be pregnant with twins, or more.

Just as Windy settled into a comfortable position on the parlor couch she heard the familiar grinding of the wood man's truck.

Windy quickly ran to the kitchen window and held up a cup. The man was obviously waiting for the invitation, he smiled and nodded. Windy put the water on to boil and ran upstairs. From the bottom of her closet she pulled out four knit hats with matching mittens. Not knowing how old his children were or whether they were boys or girls she hoped the colors would be suitable.

Running back into the kitchen she pulled the whistling tea kettle from the burner and poured one cup of coffee and a cup of tea, then she went outside.

The wood man had just stacked the last piece of wood when Windy walked around the side of the garage.

"Can you come in for a moment?"

"Is the doctor home?"

Windy shook her head.

"Well, ma'am, then I'd rather not. You understand?"

Windy smiled. "Yes. I just thought you might want to sit down and drink your coffee."

"How's about sittin right here?" He asked as he took off his work gloves and heisted himself onto one end of the rusty tailgate. "Ain't so cold as last week."

Windy agreed, remembering the snowstorm that left several inches of beautiful white snow.

"I'll be right back," she assured the man.

156

Inside, Windy placed the knit items in a grocery bag, hoping the man wouldn't consider her gifts as charity yet not wanting the family to feel they must give her something in return.

Windy placed the steaming cups and the brown bag on the tail gate between her and the wood man.

"Nothin like a good hot cup of coffee to warm the innerds on a cold day." The man took a sucking drink from the cup. "My name's Wilford Packard, Miz Michaels, but most folks just call me Wil." He held out a rough hand and Windy gladly shook it.

"I…I have something for your children, Mr. Pack…er, Wil," she corrected herself, pushing the bag toward him.

He carefully pulled each item out and looked it over, admiring the handiwork. "Make these yerself, did ya?"

"Yes, sir."

"Well, ma'am I just don't know what to say."

"You don't mind, do you?"

"Mind? No, Miz Michaels, I don't mind when the good Lord answers prayer."

His comment took Windy by surprise. Noting the look on her face, he continued. "It's been a mighty lean winter. What money I've earned we needed for food and bills. Just last night my sweet bride showed me the little one's mittens. The end was worn clear through. Missy said they was all that way. So we prayed right then and there for the money to buy new mittens. I knew God would provide, never expected something as wonderful as this though."

This whole idea of asking God for something and actually expecting an answer had never occurred to Windy. She couldn't quite grasp what Wil Packard meant. But she made a mental note to ask Jenny about it.

Their conversation revealed that Wil Packard had been married to his 'sweet bride' for twelve years. They had two boys and two girls who were all two years apart. And Missy was 10 years younger than Wil.

"I depended on the Lord for my good fortune and He gave me a Christian wife and beautiful children."

Windy liked the way Wil explained himself. He gave her facts and didn't make her feel bad for saying silly things. Wil finished his coffee and handed the cup to Windy. "Much obliged, ma'am. God bless you."

Again, he surprised Windy by his use of words. She only remembered being blessed when she sneezed, and nobody bothered to say God anymore. "Good bye, Wil, I look forward to seeing you next week."

Windy placed the cups in the sink and took off her jacket, still mulling Wil's words over in her mind.

The ringing phone pulled her out of her thoughts.

"Hey, lady!" Jenny's voice jumped from the other end. "What are you doing Saturday?"

"Not much, Stephan has to work all week-end."

"How about sitting in a counseling session with me?"

"What kind of counseling session?" Windy wasn't aware that Jenny saw a counselor.

"At the CPC." Windy sighed. CPC. Why did everyone use initials? She had such a hard time with them. CPC.

"Oh, at the Caring Pregnancy Clinic?"

"Center," Jenny corrected. "It's not a clinic it's just an office staffed by volunteers."

"I don't know," Windy answered, remembering her discussion with Stephan. "Are you going to talk about abortion?"

"The subject might come up. I have a couple girls scheduled, I'll give them a pregnancy test and then we'll talk about the results."

It sounded harmless enough to Windy. "OK. I think I might enjoy that. Where is it and what time?"

Chapter Twenty-Eight

Oh Father!
Thank You for letting me go with Margie and be there when Mrs.
Lowden accepted Christ. Margie must have felt this way the day she lead
me in the sinner's prayer. Father, I pray for the person who will lead my
children to You. Give that person strength and wisdom.

Jenny unlocked the front door of the old two-story building and waited for
Windy to enter before turning the closed sign to OPEN.

"This house belongs to an old doctor who used to practice here. This served
as his office as well as his residence. He's since retired to a warmer climate
but allows us to use the office." Jenny explained.

They stood in a dreary hall containing three doors, one on each side and one
at the end. Windy noted the stairway that must have led to the doctor's former
living quarters. "Does any one live here now?" she asked.

"Only the mice." Jenny opened the door on their left, and turned on the lights
as she entered. Windy followed close behind. A desk sat near the back of the
room, two padded chairs were pulled up close to it. A small table appeared to
support double its weight from a large, divided plastic shelf. Hundreds of
pamphlets were stuffed into the cubby holes and the whole thing sagged in the
middle.

A television sat on a small TV table in the near corner, it also had two
padded chairs pulled up to it. A VCR perched on the shelf below the television.

"It's not much, but we like it." Jenny said, walking up behind Windy. "My first appointment is in half an hour that's gives us plenty of time to get ready."

Windy nodded, wondering just what had to be done when giving a pregnancy test.

"First, I'll set up the tapes." Jenny opened the double doors below the VCR and pulled out two tapes. She turned on the TV and VCR and popped the first tape in. As soon as the images came up on the screen, Jenny hit the fast forward button. "We don't have a lot of time with some of these girls and I want them to see the important stuff, not the credits."

She repeated the procedure with the second tape. "For and against." Jenny explained. "If a girl is against abortion I usually show her the ultra-sound video. If she's for it, I show the one that explains just what abortion is."

A video showing what abortion is? Windy didn't know such things existed. She wondered if she'd be allowed to watch it with the girls.

"Okay, now I'll get my paper work ready." Jenny sat down at the desk, opened a drawer and drew out several printed sheets of paper.

"This is a lot more complicated than I thought." Windy finally expressed her growing wonder. "You even have paper work for a pregnancy test?"

"I guess it would all seem a little strange to you. Yes, we keep accurate, confidential records of every one who comes in. We compile statistics on the failure rate of birth control as well as what age group of girls we serve. We find out where our advertising is paying off and can eliminate expensive areas where it isn't."

"All for a pregnancy test."

Jenny laughed. "Well, we do a lot of counseling, too. Unfortunately, we don't often find out the results of our work. And sometimes when we do, it's not very good."

"I thought you'd only been here since August?"

"I have."

"You sound like you run the place."

"I had four years experience at college. Most of these offices are run a lot alike. And, right now our director is sick so I've offered to help with the scheduling and other things for awhile."

"So you do run the place?"

"In a manner of speaking, yes, but only temporarily."

Jenny then took Windy to the far end of the hall and through a wonderful old kitchen. Windy just had to stop and admire the old wood stove that must have cooked many meals in its day. Just off the kitchen was a modern bathroom where the girls were sent to collect a specimen.

"They leave it here and while they're watching the video I come back and do the test."

"How long does it take?"

"The test takes about five minutes; the prayer time usually takes longer." Noting Windy's frown, Jenny smiled. "I pray about the results. If the girl has indicated she'll get an abortion and it's positive, I ask the Lord to speak to her heart through the video and if that doesn't soften her up, I ask Him to give me the right words."

Back in the office Jenny picked up the cordless phone and dialed two numbers. "I'm returning the phone to the office to give Crystal a break. She's answering the help line this month."

Windy decided not to ask any more questions. She would just keep her eyes and ears open.

"There's usually some mail to sort through."

"How much do you charge for the tests?" Windy asked, already breaking her resolve.

"We don't, they're free."

"Then who sends you checks?"

"Mostly churches or other pro-life organizations. We're non-profit and exist solely on donations." Jenny watched her friend for a moment. "Haven't you ever heard of the Red Cross or…oh, I don't know…don't you know what a non-profit organization is?"

Windy raised her eyebrows and shook her head.

"You're mom or dad never did any volunteer work?"

Again Windy shook her head. Her face became warmer. "I know I'm ignorant. But, no, I never knew…never…"

Jenny moved to her friend's side. "I'm sorry Windy, I didn't mean to offend you. I should know better. It's just that I grew up in a volunteer home. My parents are very active in several Christian causes. I just assumed… Windy, I'm the one that's ignorant. Forgive me?" Jenny gave her a loving hug. The act of kindness almost brought tears to Windy's eyes. How could Jenny, this smart, knowledgeable Christian girl be asking her for forgiveness?

The telephone rang, and Jenny pulled away. "Friends?"

"Of course!" Windy smiled.

As Jenny spoke softly into the phone, Windy made a solemn promise to herself. I may not know much now about Christians and what they do, but I'll learn. With your help, God, I'll learn.

Amy shook her long blonde hair. "This is not the most opportune time to visit here." She sat in the padded chair furthest from Jenny, looking impatient. "Will it take long?"

"I need to ask you just a few more questions, Amy. If we come up with a negative test, we'll still need to consider why you've missed a period."

Amy nodded and replied to Jenny's questions with one syllable answers.

"Now if we have a positive on the test, have you thought about what you might do?"

"This is no time to have child. I only have 3 semesters and I've earned my BA. I'll terminate the pregnancy, of course."

"Have you thought at all about adoption?"

"No. I'm not here to 'consider my options', miss, I'm here to find out if I'm pregnant."

"So you're intention is to have an abortion?"

"Yes."

"Amy, calculating from your last period, you're probably about 8 weeks pregnant." Jenny picked up what appeared to be a thin plastic coated book. Windy could see the picture of a baby on the front page. "You're baby would look about like this one." Jenny pointed to one of the pages. Windy couldn't see what Jenny indicated from where she sat but she could see the impact it had on Amy. The girl's face paled, she bit her lip, but said nothing.

"You're baby's heart has been beating since 18 days after conception, brain waves are detected at six weeks. All your baby's organs are formed, and now all he needs, is time to grow."

"Why are you saying 'my baby'?" Amy regained some of her composure. "We don't even know if I'm pregnant, do we?" Sarcasm filled Amy's voice as she again tossed her hair over her shoulder.

"You're right Amy, we don't. I'll show you where the bathroom is and you can get a specimen for me."

As soon as the two women left the room, Windy jumped up from her chair by the television to look at the picture. It lay open on Jenny's desk, where she had left it. Windy stared at the perfectly formed body. It looked just like a real baby. It even had toes, though they were still a little bit webbed. The baby's nose and eyes were clearly visible. She reached out to lay her hand on the picture of this tiny human being.

"Have you never seen these photos?" Jenny's voice startled her.

Windy shook her head, reluctantly pulling her hand back.

"They're actual pictures of babies in the various stages of development," Jenny explained before going over to the VCR where she pushed the second tape into the slot.

Amy appeared in the doorway. "Now what?" she asked.

"I have a video you can watch while you're waiting for the test results. What we do here is more than free testing, Amy, we provide information. We believe you have a right to all information available to you." Jenny turned the appliances on, indicating a chair to Amy. "Be back in a few minutes."

Amy sat and looked at the TV, her displeasure apparent. Windy closed the door behind her and followed Jenny down the hallway. Once in the bathroom Jenny put on a pair of rubber gloves and placed a paper towel on the counter. She took a small foil package out of a drawer and tore it open. It contained a white plastic item and a small eyedropper. Jenny dipped the eyedropper into Amy's specimen cup and placed 5 drops into an opening on the white plastic thing. "Will you pray with me?" she asked.

Windy nodded, unsure of what Jenny expected of her. The only time she had ever prayed with someone was at church and the pastor did the work, she just said amen when Stephan did.

"Father, we lift Amy up to you now. Lord you know her heart, you know her fears. Quiet those fears now, Lord, let her feel your presence. Open her eyes to what she is seeing on the video, help her to realize the personhood of a child in the womb. Father, I ask that Amy not be pregnant, I pray, Lord for a negative result, yet I know you have everything under control. You formed each child at the time of conception. You gave it life and an eternal soul. Father, if Amy is pregnant I pray that she will accept this baby, rather than kill it. And if that is not to be, then I commit this little one into your hands. Amen."

"Amen," Windy repeated. She opened her eyes, surprised to see Jenny crying. Quickly she looked at the test, expecting to find an obvious plus sign on it somewhere. Windy could see a faint blue line slowly traveling up the second opening, but she didn't know what it meant. She looked back at Jenny.

"Can you tell yet?" she whispered.

Jenny shook her head. "It takes a couple minutes for the urine to saturate the paper. See how it's turning blue?" Jenny pointed. "In that window there will either be one line going across, or two. Pray that it's only one, Windy."

Let it be one, please, let it be one. Windy repeated silently, staring at the test, dreading the result.

Chapter Twenty-Nine

Dear Lord,
Thank you for this lovely spring day. Thank you for the early daffodils
and the buds on the trees. Thank you for my church and my friends.
Thank you for my children. Thank you God, for everything!

Jenny sat behind the desk, her head in her hands. Days like this were so hard. All three girls tested positive, all three intended to abort. No amount of explaining or reasoning touched them. One girl admitted it was killing. But in this world, 'you do what you gotta do'. These pretty college girls just didn't have room in their lives for a baby, school and career must come first. They even rejected Jenny's suggestions about reconsidering their lifestyle.

'If you can get pregnant using a condom, think how much easier it is to get a sexually transmitted disease' she had reasoned with Lynn. But the girl insisted her boyfriend was faithful.

'I'm sure he is now, but are you the first girl he's had sex with?'

'Heavens no, he's no home boy.'

Jenny lifted her head, rubbing her open palms down her face. Besides the innocent lives of these three babies, how many other lives would be lost because of this destructive behavior? Again she placed those six precious souls in God's hands.

Windy had been visibly upset by the morning's events. Jenny had seen her staring at the pictures of the babies still the womb. The eight week old seemed to draw the girl's attention. Jenny questioned her own wisdom in bringing her here. Windy's journey toward God hadn't even started yet and already Jenny had given her reason to doubt Him.

She lifted her friend in prayer asking God to make right whatever harm Jenny had caused Windy this day. 'I'm so foolish, Lord, please forgive me.'

Windy had excused herself as soon as the last girl left, saying she'd seen a store on the corner and really needed a cherry cola. Then she'd fled.

Jenny heard the front door open and Windy entered the office. She carried nothing in her hands.

"I thought you were thirsty?" Jenny questioned.

Her friend appeared embarrassed and Jenny quickly changed the subject. "When do you have to be home?"

"Not for awhile, Stephan's working into the evening at the clinic in Dorville today."

"Good. How about lunch and some shopping?"

Again Windy blushed. It suddenly hit Jenny that Windy might not have any money on her. She hadn't even brought a purse.

"My treat," Jenny quickly added. "After a day like today, I have to let loose. Do something drastic. How about pizza and then I'd like to stop at Gray's and check out their sale."

"Gray's?" Windy echoed.

"Yes, to your unspoken question, it is too expensive on my salary. But the other teachers let me in on a secret. This store has a once a year sale taking off 80%. I just can't pass up that kind of bargain."

Windy opened her mouth to take a bite of the delicious thick crusted ham and cheese pizza when her eyes connected with those of a young man sitting across the dining room.

Gray Eyes, the Razor Blade Man.

He was here, apparently alone. Clamping down on the steaming food, Windy tried to look away, visualizing how awkward she must look.

The melted cheese clung to the roof of her mouth and she quickly sucked in some cool air.

"Too hot?" Jenny asked.

"Not really," Windy answered, finally able to pull her eyes away. "I like my food hot, especially pizza." She managed a couple more bites without looking at the forbidden table but when she lifted her cola she lost the battle.

He sat there, looking right at her. She smiled. He smiled and nodded. She remembered the last time she'd seen him at the store, the day she walked home and found the blue convertible parked across the street. The day she stopped saying no.

Now the blue convertible sat in Stephan's garage, the keys in his pocket. Windy frowned. Why had he allowed her to use the car so freely before they were married; and hardly at all now? She and Eddie only had one car and they never asked each other's permission to use it.

Windy considered making small talk with Jenny to take her mind of those disturbing thoughts, but her friend's eyes revealed how tired she was.

Although Windy still had many questions, the events at Jenny's office were really quite clear to her. She had made some decisions and wanted to share them with Jenny. Windy knew she would be pleased.

"Jenny, thanks for today. I learned a lot and I actually enjoyed myself, despite the outcome of the visits." Jenny continued to eat but Windy sensed her attention.

"I agree that abortion is wrong. I mean, who wouldn't after seeing those pictures and videos? I had no idea of what happened during an abortion or what the baby looks like. I see what you're trying to accomplish and I really admire you for it."

Jenny's eyes no longer drooped, they now sparkled. She reached over and grasped Windy's hand.

"I feared just the opposite had happened. Thank you for easing my mind." Jenny closed her eyes. "And thank you, Father," she whispered.

Windy had never heard any one pray as much as Jenny. Every time they ran a test, Jenny prayed. Between appointments, while rewinding the tape, Jenny prayed. Before eating pizza, Jenny prayed, in public! Windy wasn't entirely comfortable with all this communication with God, but she liked it. She wished for Jenny's faith and the ease in which she prayed.

When Jenny opened her eyes, Windy reached for another piece of pizza, surprised at her own hunger. She stole a glance at Gray Eyes. He gazed out the window, chewing his food so she watched him for a few minutes. She noted his handsome features, judging him to be about her age. She wondered if he still shaved with a straight razor and if he were buying his blades at the store.

Her mind wandered for a few minutes, as she thought of where he might live in the area of the store.

Noting the movement of his head she quickly lowered her eyes so as not to be caught staring.

Now Jenny was making the small talk and before long their pizza disappeared. As Windy took the last sip of cola she glanced at Gray Eyes. He stood. Pulling a bill from his wallet he dropped it on the table, then looked directly at Windy. He smiled and spoke a silent good-bye. Windy returned the smile. "Bye," she said, though he couldn't hear her.

"A friend?" Jenny inquired, following Windy's gaze.

"No. He came into the store where I worked last summer."

"Too bad." Jenny said watching him walk to the cash register. "I'd have you introduce me."

Windy grinned at her friend. It suddenly dawned on her that Jenny had never mentioned a boyfriend. Windy just assumed a girl as beautiful as Jenny would be involved with some one. Their conversations always seemed centered on herself. But Windy resolved to change that. She determined to let Jenny know that she was important. That what happened in her life mattered.

Jenny placed a couple dollars on the table.

"Ready for Gray's?" she asked.

Windy hesitated. "Maybe you should take me home before you go. I didn't even bring my purse and I wouldn't want to spoil your afternoon."

"If that's what you want, but honestly, I'd like your company. You can help me decide what really looks good and keep me from buying just because it's a bargain."

Windy wanted to go. She liked shopping even when she bought nothing. She and Eddie rarely had money to buy, but they used to have a lot of fun looking.

"Please?" Jenny prodded, without whining.

"Okay," she agreed with a smile.

Windy was amazed at the beautiful clothes they found at bargain prices. Jenny tried on several outfits and a couple dresses. Some she bought, some, they decided, looked better on the hanger.

When Windy admired a particular dress, Jenny decided to add it to her growing pile, telling Windy she could borrow it anytime.

"It's nice that we're the same size," she commented, "But why don't you try it on just for fun?"

Windy walked out of the dressing room, feeling like Cinderella. The rose colored print dress clung from her shoulders to her hips where it widened into a flowing calf-length skirt.

"I've never worn anything so lovely. Are you sure you'd want it out of your sight?"

"It's looks better on you than it did on me," Jenny complimented.

Windy loved the dress and the way she felt in it, but silently resolved not to take Jenny up on her offer. She never wanted to hinder their friendship by taking it for granted.

On the way home, Jenny chatted about Mary's upcoming wedding.

"Oh, I almost forgot," she said, opening her purse and reaching inside. She pulled out on expensive white envelope and handed it to Windy. "Mary asked me to give this to you." Windy extracted the invitation and read it aloud.

"I'm flattered, but I hardly know Mary."

"She liked you the first day we met. And her opinion was confirmed when you helped me moved. I'm Mary's Maid of Honor, but she's invited Cora, so you two can keep each other company."

"Sounds nice," Windy said, but her thoughts were on her dime store dress, the only nice thing she could wear to a wedding.

"And say," Jenny continued, "you can wear that dress we just got, if you'd like." She pulled up in front of the Michael's Mansion and placed the car in park. "Better take it now, in case I don't see you before Saturday." They stepped from the car and Jenny opened the back door. Windy noticed the dress just happened to be on a separate hanger. Jenny brought the treasured item to Windy's side of the car and handed it to her.

For a moment Windy thought she might cry as she realized that Jenny understood her situation and intended this all along.

Impulsively, she hugged her thoughtful friend.

"Thank you, Jenny, I love you." The words came so easily, so naturally.

"And I love you, Windy." Jenny returned.

Chapter Thirty

Dear Father,
I can't help but to feel this is a very important day for my children. I
lift them up to You, place them in Your hands. May today find them
looking at You in expectation.

Windy knocked on Cora's door and a quick thrill shivered down her back. Stephan had been so good about Windy attending Mary's wedding. Without saying so, he seemed to have had a change of heart, although he disapproved of Windy wearing 'Jenny's' dress and suggested she give it back immediately after the wedding.

Cora opened the door; the sweet little lady appeared flustered.

"I can't find my hand bag," she commented, more to herself than to Windy. "We are going to the reception aren't we? I don't know what to do with my gift if we aren't."

Gift. The word pierced Windy's thoughts and wound it's way into the pit of her stomach. She hadn't thought about a gift for Mary and Andrew. Her excitement suddenly turned to dread. Should she still go to the reception? Should she slip quietly away after the ceremony?

"Oh, here it is, under the sink." Cora lifted her small white hand bag. "Whoever left it down there? My, Windy, you look so beautiful. I've never seen you dressed up like this."

"You've seen me wear a dress before."

"But not one as elegant as this. What a wonderful husband you have to dote on you so. Are we ready?"

"I am, how about you?" Windy answered. She didn't bother to correct Cora's assumption about the dress. Cora saw Stephan as Windy's own white knight and there was no reason to change that. There were still many times when Windy saw him that way.

Windy gathered their purses and the gift so Cora could lock the door. Looking at her key she said, "Oh my, I almost forgot. Jenny wanted us to bring her gift. Would you mind running up to get it?" and handed the keys to Windy.

Windy placed her burden in Cora's arms and moved as quickly up the stairs as her heels would allow. Inside the small familiar apartment Windy found a large box sitting on the table. A note and a card sat beside it.

Windy,
I took the liberty of adding your name to Mary's
gift. I hope you don't mind. I happened to know they
needed a nice bedroom outfit and Mary would feel
awkward knowing I purchased it alone.
Thanks, Jenny

Windy smiled. Jenny had thought of her, even in her own busy week. She wondered if she should refuse Jenny's generous offer, if she should be offended by it. But she wasn't. She knew Jenny's heart and motives were completely sincere and besides, Windy would just give Jenny some of her Christmas money. She quickly signed the card and sealed it in the envelope. In minutes she and Cora were on their way to a beautiful spring wedding.

Windy had seen the little church before but had never been inside. It didn't have the grandeur of Stephan's church, there were no stained glass windows or padded pews. Instead this small church held a warmth and comfort Windy couldn't describe. From the moment she stepped inside she felt at home.

Cora must have felt it too, because she touched Windy's arm and leaned close, "Cozy, isn't it?"

Windy nodded. Two young men stood just inside the doors, each held out an escorting arm.

"We're friends of the bride," Cora whispered to the man at her side. They led the ladies to a pew near the middle of the church. Once seated, Windy took a quick look around, doubtful that she knew anyone.

A familiar face smiled from across the aisle, Wil Packard. Windy smiled brightly at the man and the petite, dark haired woman sitting next to him.

Soon the music started and the procession began. Windy moved back in time, to a small church similar to this one, Aunt Darla's church. Darla Main was Eddie's aunt. She reminded Windy of Cora, sweet, loving, everything the rest of Eddie's family wasn't.

Darla had set up the time and place, even contacted the minister for them. Pastor Reames had insisted on having at least two counseling sessions with the young couple, saying he wouldn't marry them unless they complied. Windy didn't mind, the minister was very nice and made many good suggestions, some of which she and Eddie actually practiced for awhile.

The church had held her mom and dad on one side and Darla's family on the other. Warm June sunlight streamed in on them and Windy's happiness filled her whole being.

"Who gives this bride to this man?" Mary smiled at the proud man standing beside her.

He gently kissed her cheek before saying "I do." Then he placed Mary's hand in Andrew's.

A tear slipped from Windy's eye as she remembered her Dad handing her over to Eddie. He'd expresses his concern before doing so, saying maybe Windy should come east with him and Mom and the next year, if she still wanted to marry Eddie they could all journey back here. But Eddie hadn't wanted to wait, and honestly, neither had she.

Windy listened to the marriage vows, 'till death do us part' echoed through her mind. She and Eddie were both alive. But they had parted. 'What God hath brought together let no man put asunder.' Windy had never really understood that part, though she had agreed to it twice now. She wondered if there were exceptions to the rule. 'That no longer matters' she told herself, there will be no asundering in this marriage. I am Stephan's, now and forever.

As Mary and Andrew exchanged wedding bands, Windy twisted hers on her finger. She remembered the evening her vows echoed in the large Community Church with just the four people in attendance. Shortly afterward they had stepped into the cold October wind. Maybe if the sunshine meant a short marriage for her and Eddie, the cold would mean a long one for her and Stephan. Windy truly hoped so.

The reception followed in the basement of the church. Windy wasn't surprised to see the absence of liquor. Everyone found a place to sit in the small area after filling their plates at the buffet table.

"Miz. Michaels, I'd like you to meet my bride, Melissa," Wil Packard said. Windy extended her hand to the little woman who quickly grasped it.

"My husband has told me what a wonderful lady you are. The children love their winter things, and they were truly an answer to prayer. Thank you, Mrs. Michaels."

"You're very welcome, and please, call me Windy." She returned the woman's grateful smile. "This is my friend, Cora Davis, Cora this is Wil and Melissa Packard. Wil delivers the wood that keeps me cozy in the parlor."

The others exchanged pleasantries.

"So you know our Mary?" Wil asked.

"Not very well, yet. Jenny rents my old apartment from Cora and I must admit, I know her much better."

"They're both fine young women. Hope our daughters grow to be as dedicated Christians as these girls have."

"You know them both, then?"

"Yeah, we attend church here. Missy became my bride right at that alter." His arm tightened around the little woman and the look he showered on her revealed the love in his heart.

"We were so pleased when Mary and Jenny joined our church. They've only been here a short time and already they're active in the ministries." Missy said.

Just then Jenny joined the little group. She hugged them all and thanked them for the comments they made on her beauty.

"Mary is truly radiant. Don't you think?" Jenny's head nodded toward her friend. Windy agreed with a smile. Mary's face glowed with happiness. But the groom caught her attention. He couldn't take his eyes off his new wife. Windy watched people walk up to the head table and congratulate the happy couple and Andrew received them all in a very polite manner. Yet his attention riveted back to Mary as soon as he was free. Windy witnessed a sacred moment between them, feeling embarrassed at first and later realizing they delighted to let the world see their love.

Andrew sat with his right arm around Mary, his fingertips resting gently on her shoulder. Mary's attention was drawn to her mother who sat beside her. Andrew reached with his left hand and gently stroked her cheek. The touch brought Mary's head around and the couple looked at each other. If love had a color it would be blue and Mary and Andrew would be lost in a deep and boundless sky.

Windy felt tears slide down her cheeks but she couldn't tear her eyes away from the couple. An emptiness revealed itself in her heart and she longed to have some one regard her with a look that plainly said there could be no existence without her. Never had she seen or felt that kind of love from either Eddie or Stephan and an indescribable loneliness engulfed her.

"They are truly blessed by God," Jenny whispered to Windy. "There is no doubt that they were meant to be husband and wife."

Windy nodded. "No doubt," she repeated.

Chapter Thirty-One

Dear Father,
Your Word has become so precious to me. I can't imagine my life
without it. May it have the same effect on my children. May they seek You
and desire to know Your Word.

Windy lay in the large comfortable bed listening to the early morning sounds
of Stephan coming home from the midnight shift. Though his room stood across
the open foyer, she found if she left her door open she could see into his room
and even hear his movements. She heard the closet door open and hangers
being pushed gently aside.

In her mind, she watched her husband undress and hang up his clothes,
tossing the soiled items in the hamper. She visualized him lifting his pajamas
from the hook and putting them on. As she imagined his finger on the last button
she heard the closet door slide back into place and she smiled at how well she
know her husband.

Stephan was quiet this morning, trying not to wake her. Windy knew this
meant he had a difficult night and didn't want to be bothered. She contented
herself with listening; hoping not to hear Stephan's soft footsteps in the hall,
hoping her presence wasn't desired in her husband's room. Soon she heard the
settling of the bed as Stephan slipped beneath the covers, followed by a long,
deep sigh.

Windy debated what she wanted to do, relieved that her husband didn't require her, she now looked to the long day ahead. Why not just roll over? What reason did she have for getting up anyway? She checked off an imaginary list: plant flowers, write to the folks, call Cora. Nothing urgent. There was never anything urgent for her to attend to.

Windy groped around under the covers till her searching produced Sachel Page Jr., the stuffed black cat Cora had given her for Christmas. She hugged it. The ache in her heart that she tried to ignore surfaced again. She missed Sachel, the way he used to follow her through the apartment and rub her legs when she stood still. She missed his comforting purr.

She missed having a husband that truly cared for her. Missed strong arms and gentle kisses. She longed for the nearness of a man, his smell of cologne, his warm breath beside her ear.

How can you miss something you never really had? she questioned herself.

Windy hugged the stuffed animal wishing it could hug her back, wishing it had tiny toes and fingers and eyes that could look into hers like Jordan used to do. The memory of the baby aroused a hurt deep within and Windy began to cry. She squeezed the black cat tighter, crying into its velvety softness. She cried with longing, with sorrow. She cried hoping sleep would engulf her and numb the pain in her heart. But still she cried. Windy's mind pulled up the picture of the eight week old baby she'd seen at Jenny's office. The thought of babies like that being killed every day caused her to cry harder.

The hands on the clock hadn't moved far when Windy reached for a tissue. She dried her eyes then blew her nose. Unlike her, Stephan seemed unaware of any noise coming from another room. After dropping the tissue into the waste basket, Windy propped pillows behind her and placed Sachel Jr. beside her. She lifted Jenny's Bible from the night stand and opened it to the first book of Peter. Still unfamiliar with the Bible itself she had decided to read all the shortest books in the New Testament. When she had worked her way up to Peter she found something special in his words. She continued to read the Psalms daily and had long ago finished the gospel of John. Now each morning she began her day with Peter's words of hope and encouragement. This morning she truly needed them.

She skimmed through the first chapter, picking out parts Jenny had underlined, stumbling over the words and phrases. 'Sanctifying work of the Spirit, born again, resurrection, inheritance, redeemed'. Windy turned the page to her favorite verse. First Peter 5:10 and read it aloud.

"And after you have suffered for a little while, the God of all grace, who called you to His eternal glory in Christ, will Himself perfect, confirm, strengthen and establish you." Windy repeated the whole passage, trying to understand it. She couldn't, and she didn't know why it comforted her so. Surely it couldn't be meant for her. After all she was far from suffering, living here in the midst of luxury with a good husband. But the part about being called intrigued her. God, calling her? It seemed quite doubtful.

She read the passage one more time, then turned to Psalm 69, reading the first couple verses. She stopped when she read the third. 'I am weary with my crying; my throat is parched; my eyes fail when I wait for God.' Placing the open book in her lap she looked heavenward. "I am weary from crying, God. I don't think I have any reason to cry. I'm terribly ungrateful. Stephan has done so much for me, yet I'm not happy. Help me be happy, please, and thankful."

Windy pulled on her garden gloves, picked up the tray of flowers and descended the steps into the back yard. Earlier that week, Stephan had surprised her by stopping at a nursery where they picked out several pretty flowering plants, some gardening tools and a pair of bright gloves. Windy rebuked herself for silently questioning Stephan's sudden generosity and tried a new tactic.

"I wonder if I should get a cheap pair of sweats to work outside in?" she had asked.

"You have plenty of old clothes," Stephan replied.

"Yes, I do have old clothes," she agreed, hoping Stephan would realize that was all she had, but her comment didn't phase him.

Windy knelt beside the house and dug the hand rake into the soil. April had started out warm with Mary's wedding but quickly gave in to the last demands of winter. With May came the emergence of daffodils and crocuses. Windy had chosen flowers with names she didn't know and whose blossoms drew her attention.

She looked over her work, proud of what she had accomplished. The flowers all complimented each other. She vaguely remembered her mother's flower garden and wondered why she hadn't paid more attention to it. Wiping sweat from her forehead, she decided it was time to go inside and start lunch as Stephan should be awake soon.

Inside, Windy poured herself a glass of cold water from the fridge. The first big swallow chilled her throat, but she savored the coldness, wishing for a cherry cola, something Stephan had discouraged her from drinking. As she took the eggs out of the fridge the telephone rang. She grabbed it quickly, complimenting herself on her timely return to the house.

"Windy?" Cora's voice tickled her ear and her heart. "How about coming to church with me tomorrow?"

Surprised, Windy asked, "where do you go to church?"

"With Jenny. I've gone a few times since the wedding and enjoyed it. Won't you come?"

"I'll ask Stephan, he's working night shift this week so we're not going to his church." Windy stumbled over the words. She had been a member since November but still it remained her husband's church. She remembered how Will Packard had spoken of Mary and Jenny, saying they had already become 'family'. Windy wondered if she would ever be considered family at the Community Church. As of yet the only people she knew were, John, Sally, Mrs. Dunkirk and Rev. Stockwell.

"Why don't you have him call me when he gets up?" Cora suggested.

Windy agreed and went on to tell her about the new flowers planted outside the house.

Stephan walked into the kitchen, Windy looked up from the counter where she diced onions for his omelet and smiled at her husband. He looked like a little boy, his hair still ruffled from sleep. She stepped over to him and hugged him tight. He grunted softly.

"That is the best sleep I have had in a while," he commented. "What have you been doing today?"

"I planted the flowers," she answered with pride.

"You didn't!" he sighed, shook his head and lowered it all in one motion, a gesture Windy was learning to dread. He walked to the back door and disappeared into the breezeway. A moment later he returned. "I wish you had waited until I could have told you where to plant them."

"I'm sorry, but what's wrong with where they are?"

"Did you check to see which type of soil in which they should be planted? How tall each will grow? How long each will flower? They look fine now, but what will they look like when they drop their blossoms? You are liable to end up with flowers at one end of the line and none at the other. You need to be patient, to plan better. But it's your garden," he shrugged. "If you don't care what it looks like, why should I? I just wish I hadn't wasted the money."

They sat quietly through Stephan's breakfast, his comment having hurt and angered Windy. She visualized herself going outside and tearing up all the flowers, after all, she didn't care what her garden looked like.

As Windy filled the sink with hot sudsy water she told Stephan that Cora called and wanted him to call her back. Stephan smiled and Windy was glad the older woman still held a special place in her husband's heart. She tried not to listen to his side of the conversation but it was impossible since he made it from the kitchen. When he hung up it was apparent Cora had her way.

"That lady is a sly one," Stephan commented with a shake of his head. "I have traded you for dinner tomorrow; I hope you don't mind the sacrifice."

Windy smiled. "What am I in for?" She wiped her hands as Stephan pulled her into his lap and nuzzled her ear. "Mmmm... maybe I should tell you later."

"No, no. Tell me." She didn't want Stephan's intimacy right now, she still smarted from his earlier remarks. 'Let it go, Windy, you're acting like a child,' she told herself as she willed her arms around her husband.

Stephan took a deep breath and let it out slowly. "Tomorrow you are sentenced to joining Cora in Sunday morning services, after which you will go to her house where I will meet you around 2 o'clock for dinner. She promised me homemade crescent rolls, what could I do? You know my weakness."

Yes, and so does Cora, Windy said to herself. She felt a shiver of excitement run down her back at the anticipation of attending Jenny's church tomorrow.

Stephan felt the shiver, too. Kissing her neck he stood and led her upstairs.

Chapter Thirty-Two

Dear Father,
I so enjoyed services this morning. The sermon was just what I needed
after this week. Worshipping You is a privilege. Do my children know
that? Do they worship you?

Jenny watched for Cora from the front door of the small church. Jenny
stood in the warm May sun, wearing a brightly colored, short sleeve dress. She
hoped Stephan wouldn't change his mind at the last minute and refuse to let
Windy come. Jenny had to admire Cora's handling of the situation. She had
'conned' Stephan's approval, but she had done so with no deceit whatsoever
and Jenny was pleased with the outcome.

Soon the little blue car came into view. Jenny watched Windy park it and
hurry to Cora's side to open the door. She noticed Windy wore the dress she
had worn to the wedding. Jenny had found out from Cora that Windy's birthday
was in May so when Windy tried to return the dress Jenny asked if she would
accept a hand-me-down as a birthday present. Her friend hesitated, but Jenny
knew Windy liked the dress and wanted to keep it.

Seeing her token of friendship accepted and enjoyed pleased Jenny.

She descended the steps and hugged her two friends. "I'm so glad you're
here," she said. Linking her arms with theirs she lead them into the building.
Midway through the sanctuary she stopped and they sat down.

Windy looked around, noticing the smiling faces of Wil and Missy Packard. They nodded and lifted their hands in greeting. A moment later Mary and Andrew joined Windy's little group. Windy found herself watching Andrew's face for that familiar look. For the first time she was close enough to notice what he actually looked like. Dark brown hair topped a rather plain face. Nothing about him could be considered handsome. His skin bore the scars of a teenage battle with acne and his eyes were a pale brown. But those eyes... He greeted Windy, shaking her hand when Mary introduced him, his eyes lingering on her face for only a moment. Then he turned to his beloved and Windy felt a tingle. There it was—that look of, how could she describe it, what word fit that gaze that rested on Mary's lovely face? Adoration. Yes, and more. Windy remembered a word, spoken at her own wedding. Cherish. Surely, Andrew must cherish his wife.

"They certainly look happy, don't they?" Cora whispered. Windy nodded; of course it must be as obvious to everyone else as it was to her.

A tall woman with auburn hair stood up at the podium and greeted the congregation warmly. Windy felt as though the welcome was meant especially for her.

"Let's sing number 8 in our hymnals," the woman said.

Windy pulled a red book from the shelf in front of her, found the correct page and handed it to Cora. Then she pulled a second book from the shelf and shared it with Jenny.

"Joyful, joyful, we adore Thee," Windy began. 'Adore, adore,' she repeated to herself. 'Am I, are we, supposed to adore God? And not just adore Him but to do so joyfully?' The whole idea seemed strange to Windy. She shook her head slightly and tried to find the words Jenny sang.

The music moved along faster than what she heard at Stephan's church, she looked around quickly and noted that many of the people weren't reading the words, but appeared to be singing them from memory. And they smiled. A slight movement caught her eye and she noticed Jenny pointing to the second verse.

"All Thy works with joy surround Thee." Windy sang a smile tugging at her own mouth.

After the pastor said the opening prayer, what Windy knew the Community Church called the invocation, the tall lady asked the people to greet one another. Immediately people left their places and began shaking hands or hugging each other. Windy suddenly felt out of place. But only for a moment, until Jenny gave her a firm hug, and then Mary opened her arms to Windy. Andrew shook her hand with both of his, saying how pleased he was to see her there

Wil and Missy crossed the aisle and shook her hand. The dainty Missy smiled and Windy found herself reaching for the woman to embrace her.

Windy listened attentively to the sermon, noting that Jenny sat with pen and notebook, jotting down her thoughts. Windy tried to make a mental note of the pastor's statements that really caught her attention but there were so many she quickly found herself lost in his words.

"The third and final point," the pastor continued. Windy felt disappointment that his sermon would be ending soon then she smiled as she recalled the relief those words brought to her at Stephan's church.

"And if you do not know Jesus as your personal Savior, I invite you to come forward and open your heart to Him during our final song. If you have already placed your life in God's hands, but need to reinforce that decision the altar is open to you, also."

The tall woman joined the pastor and asked the congregation to open their hymnals. Jenny found the page, holding the book open between them.

Windy looked at the words, but felt her eyes drawn to the front as a woman from the other side of the church made her way to the altar. This had never happened in Stephan's church and Windy was curious as to what would happen to the woman. She watched her kneel on a small step and rest her head upon her arms on a railing. A moment later another woman joined her, placing her arm over the shoulders of the praying lady. They talked for a moment and then the second lady prayed out loud, though softly enough not to be heard over the music. Before the song ended the two women returned to their seats and Windy noticed they both were crying. This puzzled her. If giving your life to God was good, why were they crying?

The pastor gave a final blessing and the people sang a chorus while he and his wife walked to the back of the sanctuary.

As Cora and Windy followed the line to the pastor Windy looked around for Jenny. She stood talking to a small group of people but soon came to find Windy.

"Just making some last minute arrangements for a VBS meeting," she explained.

"Oh," Windy nodded, wondering what VBS meant.

"I offered to teach and they ask me to help direct. I had to say no, because of the Caring Pregnancy office. Until our director there is ready to resume her duties, I'm committed."

Again, Windy nodded. Jenny certainly was a busy lady. But at least the school year neared its end and she would have the summer to relax a little. Maybe they would have some leisure time together.

"Thank you for the mittens," came a small voice beside Windy. She looked down to see a rosy cheeked face with big brown eyes peering up at her. The child wore a faded red dress, obviously a well worn hand me down. In her hand the little girl held a cross made from popsicle sticks and beads.

Windy smiled and reached for the child, picking her up. "You must be Wil and Missy's daughter?" she asked.

"I'm Ruthie Packard," the little girl introduced herself. "And I made this for you." Again she held up the cross and Windy accepted it. The child hugged her and Windy set her back on the floor. As soon as her feet touched, she sprinted away.

Windy held the precious cross up for Jenny to see.

"I'm surprised she even thought of me."

"I'm not, our giving has lasting effects on people."

The pastor shook Windy's hand and invited her to visit again. He shook Cora's hand and asked about her nephew. He talked as though he knew Cora quite well. Once outside Windy asked Cora how long she'd been going to Jenny's church.

"Since Mary's wedding," she replied. "Windy, I went to church as a child and I always considered myself a Christian, but I'm finding there's more to that than just being moral and helping people."

"Like what?" Windy asked as she opened Cora's door.

"I'm not sure of all of it yet, but I know it's mostly about placing God first, making Him the most important person in your life, like a husband, but more so."

Windy started the car and headed down the street. For some reason she didn't want to pursue this topic with her friend so she asked about the neighboring family that Cora had taken an interest in.

Stephan arrived at Cora's just as she took the roast from the oven. The threesome sat down and to Windy and Stephan's surprise Cora asked a blessing on the food.

During dinner she chatted happily about the people in 'her' church asking Windy from time to time what she thought about certain things. Windy showed Stephan the gift she'd received and told him about the mittens and hats. He smiled but said very little.

After dinner, they all moved to the back yard to relax in the fresh spring air.

"Where's Jenny today? I thought she might join us." Windy asked.

"I believe she had plans with Mary and Andrew but she said she'd come by and get me for church."

"Church?" Windy and Stephan both echoed.

"Oh, yes, Sunday evening service is such a wonderful time, so informal and friendly. They just talk and share things about their lives. Pastor gives a very short talk, maybe 5 minutes or so, it's a family time."

"So you go twice on Sunday?" Stephan asked.

"Yes and then there's Bible Study on Wednesday night and I've been invited to the ladies prayer meeting on Thursday mornings."

"It sounds as though they are trying to take over your life. Beware, Cora, that you don't get involved too deeply. You never know if this might be a cult of some sort."

Cora smiled. "Oh, Stephan, you're too cautious. This is a reputable church, based solely on the Bible. They have churches throughout the United States and missionaries in other countries."

"Just like your church, Stephan," Windy added.

"Our church," he corrected, looking directly into her eyes. She could almost finish his sentence for him. Just because he allowed her to attend once didn't mean she could form a new alliance.

Windy quickly looked down, sorry for her attitude. Stephan had been good enough to let her go to church with Cora, and she hadn't even thanked him yet. Why did she always repay his goodness with her silent sarcasm?

She reached her hand over to his and smiled at him. "Thank you for letting me go today, I enjoyed my visit."

He raised her hand to his lips, brushing it gently. His smile told her that he knew a way for her to pay back his kindness.

Chapter Thirty-Three

Dear Father,
Irene called today and asked if I would work in the nursery once every
three months. I told her I would be delighted. Lord, do I have any
grandchildren? Will I ever be allowed to hold them? Touch my children
today, please, bless them in a special way.

"How would you like to accompany me to the hospital today?" Stephan
asked. "I happen to know we have a baby who needs some loving arms to hold
her."

Windy sat up in bed and stared at her husband in disbelief. Early morning
sun streamed in through the windows, falling in streaks across the bed. It
caught the light in Windy's eyes and shimmered through her silken hair.

Since the episode over Boy Evans neither Windy nor Stephan had
mentioned Windy visiting the hospital, much less seeing a parentless baby.

"Oh, Stephan, can I really?" The covers slipped down revealing Windy's
soft bare skin. Stephan reached up and caressed her shoulder.

"I think it is time. I believe you can handle yourself with a little more reason
and restraint, can you?"

"Oh, yes, I can, I promise I can!"

Windy tried to contain her excitement as she followed her husband into the
hospital. She had not seen Bernie in months and looked forward to seeing the

friendly nurse again. But what truly made her happy was Stephan's trust. She determined not to let history repeat itself by becoming too attached to this baby. She came here as just a pair of temporary loving arms. What had Jenny said about so many couples wanting to adopt newborns? And now some lucky couple would have just that chance. This baby would be loved and wanted. What more could she hope for?

"I will leave you on your own, you know the way," Stephan said, kissing her on the forehead. Windy nodded.

"Thank you Stephan, you've made me very happy today."

He smiled and pulled a couple dollar bills out of his wallet, "Have lunch in the cafeteria, do not plan on eating with me, I doubt I will be there. And remember, I will come to get you, do not wander the halls looking for me."

"Of course not," she agreed, puzzled by his comment. It wasn't until she reached the nursery that she remembered the day she had watched in the emergency room and he had scolded her. She marveled at his long memory.

Bernie wasn't scheduled until the afternoon shift and Windy had to convince Nurse Payne to let her into the nursery. Once in she checked the rows of tiny patients until she found Girl Roe. Obviously this baby's mother had not cared for herself during her pregnancy. Girl Roe weighed just over five pounds, red blotches checkered her pale skin and her watery blue eyes stared vacantly.

Windy scooped the little bundle into her arms holding it close, breathing in the baby powder scent. She kissed the baby on the cheek and dubbed her Sweet Pea.

"Everyone needs a name, even if it's just temporary," she explained to the quiet baby. "And I remember an old, old song by Tommy Roe called Sweet Pea. So I think it only right that's what I call you."

Sweet Pea looked at Windy but Windy knew she didn't see her. Not yet. "But you will," she assured the baby. "You will see me and you will recognize love."

The paper in the crib slot stated Baby Roe's birth date and blood type. Other than that she had nothing else to give her identity.

Windy spent the morning caring for the baby, feeding her, changing her and just letting her love flow into the child. Shortly after noon Windy laid the sleeping Sweet Pea in her crib and slowly made her way to the cafeteria, using the stairs rather than the elevator.

Her tray bore only a small salad, a dinner roll and glass of milk as she entered the dining area. Suddenly conscience of being alone, she quickly looked around hoping to see a familiar face, though she didn't know who that might be. Across the crowded dining room she saw two heads bent toward each other as though in private conversation. She immediately recognized her husband's brown head next to one full of gray hair. Funny, she thought, how people can see someone from afar off and know who they are, who they belong to.

Windy quietly made her way toward Stephan, deciding that if he were in an important conversation she wouldn't interrupt. A few steps behind her husband she heard his voice.

"...thought maybe it would help in her desire to conceive," he was saying.

"You think holding a baby will help?" came the gritty voice of the older gentlemen, he wore a white coat just like Stephan's.

"Sound superstitious?"

"I would use the word absurd. Women don't conceive in their minds, Stephan, they conceive in their wombs. Do you believe she's resisting motherhood? Might she be preventing it without your knowledge?"

"No, I have no concern in that area. I know she wants children, she would be happy to adopt some little street urchin."

"That wouldn't do for the Michaels name, would it, my boy?"

"Never," came Stephan's deep, determined reply.

Windy's face burned. She backed away slowly, not wanting this man, this strange doctor to know it was she whom Stephan talked about. Shame and anger competed for control of Windy's emotions. She let them rage their silent battle within her as she shied around chairs and avoided incoming diners. She dropped her untouched tray on an empty table and left the dining room, her hunger completely gone.

The physical work of climbing three flights of stairs helped and by the time she entered the nursery Windy had come to her husband's defense. She fought the anger and shame with logic and won. As she reached Sweet Pea's crib she chided herself for being so silly. Stephan certainly had a right to talk with who ever he pleased about whatever he pleased. Didn't she confide some of her personal thoughts to Jenny in conversations she wouldn't want Stephan to hear? She should be ashamed, she concluded. Ashamed that she had eavesdropped and that she had run away with out eating. Now she'd spent Stephan's money with nothing to show for it and she'd certainly be hungry before the day ended.

Windy gently lifted Sweet Pea from her crib and cradled her close. Maybe Stephan was right, maybe being around the babies would help her conceive. The doctor had called that idea absurd but it surely couldn't hurt. And Sweet Pea had someone to love her.

Windy accompanied Stephan to the hospital everyday. They left home early and returned late. She did little cooking that week, Stephan seeing fit to take her to dinner, one night fancy the next night fast.

They laughed almost as much as they did when they were dating and their time at home alone couldn't have been more romantic.

"I know you don't have to work today," Windy said, on Saturday morning. "But the baby's foster parents are supposed to pick her up. I met them a couple days ago and they're really nice people. They hope to be able to adopt her eventually. May I go in by myself?"

Stephan smiled at his wife. "Sure. I've got a few things to catch up on here. I guess I can handle having you out of my sight for a while." Windy thanked him with a kiss and ran upstairs to get ready.

Bernie met Windy at the downstairs desk. "Are you here to say good-bye to the baby?" She questioned placing her arm around the younger woman.

"Am I too late?"

Bernie nodded. "I checked this morning when I came in and she was already gone so I called Martha who worked last night. The case worker had other business today so they came in right after you left. I'm sorry."

Windy smiled. "That's okay, this time I prepared myself for it. They're very nice people, have you met them?"

"Yes, I have and I agree with you."

Windy felt lost, her plans suddenly gone.

"Going back home?" Bernie asked.

"Not right away. Stephan had some things to do anyway. I think I'll stop and see a friend as long as I'm out. If Stephan should happen to call would you tell him I'm going to Cora's?"

"Of course, I will. Enjoy your day." Bernie squeezed her shoulder and turned to answer the question of a confused young nurse.

Windy arrived at Cora's shortly before nine, and found Jenny stepping out of the front door.

"I was just coming to get you," she told Windy.

"Me? Why?"

"Don't you remember you were going to the office with me again today?"

"Oh, I forgot all about it. Jenny I've had such a wonderful week!" Windy grabbed her friend's hand. "Wait till you hear."

"Tell me on the way, our first appointment is at nine-thirty."

The first two girls tested negative, much to Jenny's relief, both said they would keep their baby but she could see they weren't ready for motherhood.

Jenny talked extensively to them about abstinence, the fallacy of 'safe-sex' and the dangers of sexually transmitted diseases, which she referred to as STDs. When Windy heard the initials, she rolled her eyes, making a mental note of them.

The third and fourth appointments were positive; one already had plans for keeping her baby, the second initially considered abortion. After seeing the video and talking to Jenny she changed her mind.

"I didn't know that's what they did," she said.

"That's sick. How can anyone do that? Why don't they tell people?" The girl was obviously upset, more than Jenny expected her to be.

After almost an hour of intense discussion, Angela admitted to already having an abortion the year before.

"No one told me it was a baby; they called it a mass of tissues. I was about eight weeks when I had it done. I can't believe it had a heart and everything. Why didn't they tell me? I wouldn't have done it."

That magic time again, eight weeks. Windy thought of the picture on Jenny's desk, she saw the tiny toes and fingers, the perfectly formed body.

Windy decided Jenny would do better on her own and quietly left the office, glad she only had a couple blocks to walk to Cora's house where she had left her car. This way she reasoned she could spend a few minutes with the older lady and call Stephan to see how he was doing.

Chapter Thirty-Four

Dear Lord,
I hope I never have another summer like this one! I can't even say what
went wrong with it. My relationship with you is growing, my church life
is a blessing. What is it God, that causes me this uneasiness?

Life for the Michaels settled into a fairly quiet routine. Windy tended her flowers and an occasional patient in the nursery. She often shed a few tears when saying good-bye especially if she felt uncertain of the baby's future welfare.

Stephan allowed Windy to visit Cora's church if it didn't interfere with his schedule or plans. She couldn't help but compare the two churches, keenly aware of the differences. One remained distant to her in every way. She wanted to fit in but no one sought her presence, though Mrs. Dunkirk did mention that Dr. Michaels' giving to missions had not yet increased. She invited Windy to the ladies meeting and Windy said she would talk to Stephan about it. She kept her word and the day after the meeting told him of the invitation. No one else made an attempt to be friendly; no one noticed when Windy and Stephan came to church and when they didn't.

The people across town at Jenny's little evangelical church were quite different. Each time Windy attended some one new introduced themselves and some one familiar always remembered the last time she had visited. Windy felt much more like a member in Jenny's church and a visitor at her own.

One Sunday she asked Jenny if she were an official member. When Jenny showed surprise at the question Windy explained how she had become a member of the Community Church. Jenny nodded in understanding and explained that such a ritual wasn't required, that membership in God's Church depended on the condition of a person's soul, not on a signature at the bottom of a doctrinal statement.

Windy decided not to pursue the subject.

Two events took place that summer that caught Windy's attention; Mary's announcement and a simple game of volleyball. Stephan dropped Windy at Cora's one Thursday in the middle of August. He worked afternoons that week and Cora had invited Windy for supper along with Jenny, Mary and Andrew.

Cora actually let Windy help prepare dinner in the little kitchen that always smelled like fresh baked bread. The August heat poured in through the open windows and Cora frequently fanned herself with her oversized apron.

"I expect the children around six-thirty," Cora announced. "I do hope Jenny is back by then." She opened the lid of the crock pot and tasted the goulash for the umpteenth time. "Here Windy have another taste, oh, I hope it's alright."

"Cora, it tastes wonderful, if we keep testing there won't be any left for dinner. I take it we're not having pie for desert." Windy said, looking into the cold oven.

"Too warm to have that thing on. We're having a frozen desert." She opened the freezer and pulled out a dish filled with yummy looking red stuff.

"What is it?" Windy resisted poking it for a taste.

"Oh, I don't know, a mixture of raspberries and whipped cream mostly. It's a recipe I found and changed a little."

Windy knew about Cora's 'changed a little' recipes, they were always great.

"Where is Jenny today?" Windy asked.

"At her office."

"Her office?"

"The Caring Pregnancy office, she's the director for the summer, you know. Sharon had to have surgery and Jenny didn't want her to worry about things while she recuperated.

Windy realized it had been almost a month since she last worked with Jenny at the office. Most of her time had been taken with the newest baby at the hospital. She found that many babies had passed through the nursery over the winter that Stephan had not mentioned to her. At first she was disappointed with him, only to become disappointed with herself. Certainly Stephan had to wait until she could let go of the little ones without a fuss. His conversation in the cafeteria came back to her but she dismissed it immediately. Stephan had allowed her back into the hospital because of his goodness and generosity. If there were any benefits from her visits, that's just what they were, benefits.

The other three guests arrived at the same time and were quickly ushered to their seats around the table. Andrew offered the blessing for the food.

The newlyweds had recently returned from their belated honeymoon and after supper the group moved to the living room where Mary and Andrew brought out the pictures of their adventure.

Windy was surprised to hear they had gone to a small Latin American country for two weeks to work in an impoverished community. They helped build one room houses for families of no less than six; they dug outhouses, helped put in plumbing for a public toilet, mixed cement by hand and poured the foundations of a playground and many other things Windy couldn't remember. Their enthusiasm wore off on Jenny who said she would like to go. Mary encouraged her to do just that.

"The trip is planned through the Christian Fellowship of the college," Mary explained, "I have the coordinator's home phone. You should go Jenny, you'd love it. There are different types of work camps available. We choose one that traveled around rather than staying in one place. It was shorter and worked into our schedule better. Andrew and I were planning to go back next year for the longer trip to help in building a youth camp, but I think we'll have to postpone it." She smiled secretively at her husband.

"What?" Jenny asked. "What is it? Tell me."

Mary returned her smile to her friend. "How does Aunt Jenny sound?"

Jenny nearly flew off her seat and into Mary's arms. "I'm so glad for you!!" she cried. "When did you find out? How far along are you? When are you due?"

"We just confirmed today. And we figure I'm about four weeks along." Laughing at Jenny's wonder she explained. "While we were in Costa Rica we roomed separately most of the time, except for once when Andrew and I stayed in a little beach shack. It was so beautiful, Jenny, watching the sun set in the Pacific Ocean, and so romantic. We were in our own world; the church bus dropped us off and wouldn't be back till morning and well, the timing didn't fit with our natural planning, but we figured the Lord's plans are better anyway and if He thought we should start our family now, that's what we wanted. So we know when we conceived, within a couple days. I calculated my due date as April 8th."

Windy watched the exchange with raging mixed emotions. Initially, she shared the couple's joy, but when she realized they had only been married four months she felt jealousy welling up within. Why had it been so easy for them? Why did God bless them with a baby and not her and Stephan? Did He like them better? Was it because they had gone on a mission trip to serve God? Would she get pregnant if she and Stephan went to a small Latin American country and made love on the beach of the Pacific Ocean?

But seeing their happiness and Jenny's excitement overrode her selfish thoughts. She hugged both Mary and Andrew, telling them how fortunate they were. Jenny took the lead and briefly explained to the couple how much Windy looked forward to making that announcement herself someday.

"And the sooner the better," Windy added.

Mary took Windy's hand, "I hope this doesn't sound like a pat answer, Windy, but God has a wonderful plan for everyone, including you and Stephan. He'll know when the time is right for you to start your family. Have you given this to Him?" Windy frowned. "I mean, have you asked for a child? And then placed your request in His hands and left it there?"

"No, I guess not. I didn't know I was supposed to. I thought those things just happen."

"We don't think so," Mary looked at her husband who shook his head, in agreement. "Windy there's many scripture verses that tell us to ask God for the things we want. They don't promise the answer will always be yes, but it will be what God determines is best for your life. I suggest you tell Him tonight or in the morning, whenever you have your personal prayer time, and then relax and let Him decide the next step."

"Would you…" Windy began, remembering how the pastor at Jenny's church asked for prayer requests, "would you pray about it too?"

"Of course, we all will," Mary replied, Jenny and Andrew nodded their agreement.

"Thank you, I guess if good people like you are praying for me to have a baby, it ought to happen right away!"

"Well, the Bible says 'the prayers of a righteous man availeth much' and we'll remind God of your desire, but mostly we'll ask for His will in your life."

"Thank you," Windy said, believing that God should want them to have a baby as much as they did.

The next week Stephan surprised Windy by accepting Jenny's invitation to a church picnic and volleyball game hosted by Wil Packard and his family.

Windy looked grudgingly at the volleyball net recalling the few games she'd played in High School Phys. Ed. The taunts and discouraging comments of the other girls came back to her. She simply wasn't athletic. If she even managed to hit the ball it never went where she intended. She usually wound up costing her team a point if not the entire game.

"It's been a long time," she told Jenny. "I'm not a good player."

"Don't worry—we just play for fun."

After teams were determined Windy found herself on Jenny's team along with Stephan, thankful that those two people would be most forgiving. But as the game progressed, Windy could do little right in Stephan's eyes. She had never been in a situation where his competitiveness showed as it did on that day. Every time the ball came near Windy she resolved to make her husband proud of her, to redeem herself in his eyes. But each time she messed up. Stephan's remarks, though not as mean as the girls in school, cut far deeper. He constantly gave her 'tips' on how to hit, where to stand, how to hold her hands. Each time she tried so hard to follow his advice the attempt ended in disaster.

"Elaine, if you can not play properly, just step aside and let some one who knows how to play hit the ball. We may not win, but it would be nice to at least score a point."

Jenny, on the other hand, continued to call encouragement to her friend, reminding her it was just a game and they were there to have fun. When Windy managed a perfect serve Jenny clapped her hands and praised Windy. She managed to repeat the accomplishment and the team actually scored points.

A black pick-up pulled into Wil's driveway as the third point scored. Jenny threw the ball to Windy. "Maybe we have another player," she commented. Windy placed the ball in her left hand as she watched Wil greet the young man who stepped from the truck. She drew her right hand back and released her energy as the men looked her way, the gray eyes of the newcomer connected with hers. Her hand hit the right side of the ball sending it sideways into the face of the player on her left, Stephan.

Chapter Thirty-Five

Dear Lord,
Here it is fall again. It's a beautiful season but for such a short time.
I don't look forward to another winter but I feel better about this one than
the last. Maybe it's because I understand prayer better now. Do my
children pray? Do they find peace in their prayers? When, oh when, will
I know what's happening in their lives?

Autumn made its appearance, when the trees dropped their leaves, life
looked barren and empty for Windy. She and Stephan sat before their parlor
fire, he read a text book, she hand sewed a little sleeper for Mary's baby.
Windy had mentioned the prayer request to her husband shortly after she made
it. His response silenced her and widened the growing gap between them.

"Elaine, babies are conceived through a physical act between a man and
woman, not through the prayers of religious fanatics."

"You've met Jenny; you know she's not a fanatic."

"I tend to wonder when you bring home reports like this."

"Don't you believe in prayer?"

"Of course, I do. But I do not believe in miracles."

Miracles, Windy repeated to herself, would it take a miracle for her to have
a baby? Wasn't Jesus' birth a miracle? "What about Jesus?" she asked out
loud.

"What about him?

"He was born to a virgin."

"So the story goes."

"You don't believe that?"

"I am a doctor who has studied the human body for the last twenty years. Virgin births don't occur."

"Then you don't believe what the Bible says about Him?"

"Jesus was a good man, a prophet, and a teacher…"

"The Son of God," Windy interrupted.

"We are all children of God, according to the Bible. Read it if you question me." Windy determined to find where the Bible said Jesus was no different from Stephan or herself. She thought of asking Jenny but suddenly realized she'd like to find the answer herself.

On this cold November night as Windy's fingers pushed the needle through the soft flannel material she remembered her search and frustration. She finally turned to Jenny who gave her a list a verses and told her to come to her own conclusions. Windy did. She believed Jesus to be the only Son of God and that only through His death could Stephan call himself God's child. But she didn't have the courage to tell her husband of her findings.

Now she wished for the bygone days when she and Stephan sat in her apartment over pork chops and fried potatoes and Windy could tell him just about anything without fear of being reproved. Just as she tied off an arm seam the telephone rang. Windy picked it up and heard Cora's excited voice at the other end.

"Windy, I just accepted Jesus as my Savior!" she said bypassing any greeting.

Windy quickly glanced at her husband, wondering if Cora would now join his list of fanatics.

"That's nice," she responded. Stephan looked at her and she mouthed Cora's name. He nodded and went back to his book.

"It's more than nice, it's wonderful! Oh, Windy, all these wasted years I thought I knew God and I didn't know Him at all."

Windy heard the excitement in Cora's voice, but the confusion in her own heart sounded louder.

"I can't wait to tell you all about it. Can you come over tomorrow, dear?"

"I'll ask Stephan."

196

"Tell him I have an extra blueberry pie I could send home with you."

"Where did you find blueberries this time of year?" Windy watched her husband. She received the reaction she hoped for when his head jerk upward.

"Blueberry what?" he whispered.

"Pie," she whispered back.

"...had them in the freezer." Windy heard from the phone. "If you let them thaw completely the pie's not runny. Is he interested?"

Windy placed her hand over the mouthpiece. "Cora says she'll send one home for you if I visit tomorrow."

Stephan grinned. "Done," he said, wetting his lips. Windy could see him already savoring that pie.

"Can you take me over to CFTA? I have a couple pies for them too," Cora asked.

With her hand still over the phone Windy relayed Cora's question. Her husband nodded.

"Yes," Windy answered her friend. "I'll drive the little blue car," Stephan again nodded his approval. "And I'll see you about nine. Is that okay?"

"Just fine, dear. See you then."

"Bye." Windy replaced the phone and sat next to Stephan. "Thank you." She nestled close.

"You're welcome," he mumbled not looking up.

"Aren't you tired of reading?" She rubbed his shoulder and kissed his neck.

"No."

"Do you want to be tired of reading?"

"Elaine, this is important."

"And I'm not?" she said in a teasing voice.

Stephan sighed. "Of course you are. But I must finish this chapter. I have a consultation tomorrow and a man's life depends on what we decide. I must be as informed as I possible can be."

"Oh, I'm sorry." She looked at the clock, though still early, it had been dark for some time. She gave her husband a quick kiss on the cheek and stood up. Retrieving her sewing she stuffed it back into the plastic bag and quietly went upstairs to her room.

After putting the bag in the closet she filled her tub with steaming water and lots of bubble bath. Windy laid her night clothes out on the bed and pulled a towel and washcloth from the linen cabinet in the bathroom. She lined up her toothpaste, facial wash, deodorant and body lotion on the counter then returned to the bedroom for her Bible.

She no longer used Jenny's Bible but a new one, a gift from Jenny. Windy's new Bible didn't bear the marks as Jenny's did, but was well on its way.

Back in the bathroom, Windy draped her clothing on the hooks on the back of the door and stepped into the hot water. She eased herself in carefully and finally settled back, her head on the small air pillow she kept there just for this reason. Windy opened her Bible and turned to Exodus.

She had long ago finished the New Testament and found the Old Testament fascinating. Different than Jenny's Bible, this version was written with new Christians in mind and had many comments and explanations. Windy loved it.

Stephan looked over at his wife to find her gone. He frowned trying to remember when she had left the room. He looked at the clock surprised to see the late hour. He knew he should have stopped after that one chapter but the next two were so interesting he could hardly stop.

He placed the book on the end table, stood and stretched. He checked the front door, finding it locked, he continued throughout the house, turning off lights and checking doors. With the downstairs secure he made his way up to the bedroom.

His bathroom door stood slightly open with the light on inside. Elaine always left it so when she retired before him. It gave sufficient light for him to change by without turning on the lamp. His slipped his clothes off, hanging them in the closet, and reached for his pajamas which Elaine had placed on the bed. His eyes were now accustomed to the semi-darkness. The faint light from the bathroom cast a soft glow on his wife's young face. Her hair spread out on the pillow framing the innocent picture.

Stephan ignored the pajamas and pulled the covers back. He slipped in next to his wife, drawing in her lovely fragrance.

His heart raced as he pulled her close and despite her sleepy state she responded immediately.

Chapter Thirty-Six

Dear Father,
Help me accept Your wisdom and understanding. Sometimes I'm so
impatient. I know You have control over all things, You see the big picture
while I can only view one scene at a time. I know You love my kids far more
than I do, help me relax in that knowledge.

Windy knocked once on Cora's door then opened it, knowing Cora
expected her. She took a deep breath, drawing in the familiar odors of the
friendly little kitchen. She thought of the many good times spent in this room,
drinking tea with her substitute grandmother.

"Come in, come in," Cora invited. She placed two of her best cups on the
table and turned to pull the tea bags from the old ceramic canister that had stood
guard on her counter for years too many to count.

The moment Windy sat down Sachel jumped onto her lap and made himself
comfortable. She scratched his ears, realizing how much she missed this
familiar setting.

"Ever since I started going to Jenny's church I knew I'd been missing
something all these years." Cora began as she placed tea bags in the delicate
china cups. She attempted no small talk, obviously thinking only of the reason
she had called Windy over.

"Clifton and I talked about a religious up bringing for our children," Cora continued. "We intended to find a church as soon as we started our family. Well, you know that never happened." She sat down opposite Windy but didn't remain seated very long. Her excitement kept her moving. "Mind you, Clifton was a good man, a very good man. We believed in the Almighty, knew that we needed Jesus as Savior, but never experienced a real relationship with Him. To us God lived in Heaven, ruling over the important things on earth. We were good, moral citizens, even supported some missionary work. Just didn't know He wanted to be included in every part of our lives."

The teapot whistled and Cora jumped to the stove, turned off the burner and lifted the kettle in one swift motion. "At Jenny's church I heard sermons that helped me recognize what was missing in my life. I thought it was Clifton, you see, with him being gone these years."

Cora poured the boiling water into the cups and returned the kettle to the stove.

"But the emptiness inside had been there long before I lost my precious husband. I needed Jesus all the time and just didn't know." She sat down again and Windy looked into the robust woman's eyes. The ever present merriment remained, but something new had been added, a sparkle that outshone the sun streaming in the kitchen window.

"Yesterday, during the pastor's sermon, a light slowly dawned in my mind and grew steadily brighter. By the time the pastor gave the alter call I knew I was ready but I just couldn't make myself stand."

Windy grew uncomfortable with Cora's recitation. She wasn't sure what Cora's light meant and she knew nothing about alter calls. She tried to place herself back in Jenny's church to see if she remembered any such thing. The memory of the crying woman came back to her.

Cora lifted the tea bag from the steaming water and mashed it against her spoon with her stubby thumb.

"When I got home I was so disappointed with myself for not responding," Windy watched her drop the tea bag on the table and open the honey jar. "I spent the afternoon looking at scripture and suddenly…" Cora spooned the sweet, heavy liquid into her cup and stirred it vigorously, Windy sat mesmerized by her actions. "…I knew what I needed to do. I got down on my knees and admitted that I am a sinner…"

Windy's eyes jumped from the cup to her friends face. Cora a sinner? This sweet little lady who baked bread for anyone less fortunate than her? Who went to the old people's home and made them feel loved and needed? A sinner? Never! Who would dare call her such a thing? Then Windy remembered the phone call so long ago, telling her boss that Windy had the flu. Did Cora still bear the guilt for that? Windy's eyes filled with tears. How could she have let Cora lie for her? If only she had known, she could have comforted Cora.

"...that I wanted Jesus to be my Savior and my Lord. I admitted I wanted to live a pure life and hadn't done so. Oh, Windy, such terrific peace flooded over me! I have never felt so good in my life. I read a bit longer, seeing things in the Bible I never knew were there, promises and such. I told Jenny at church last night. She sounded as happy as I felt and suggested I call you. So I did." Cora lifted the cup to her lips and took a sip. She looked at Windy and smiled.

The younger woman quickly looked away, making herself busy with her tea. But not before Cora saw the tears in her eyes.

Cora felt a chill of excitement run down her spine. She silently pleaded to her Lord that she be the one to lead Windy to Him. She thanked Him for the break through already made by her relating her story to the girl.

Windy took a sip of tea and placed the cup back in front of her. "I'm very happy for you, Cora. It's great to see you so...so happy," she stumbled over her words and quickly took another drink of tea.

"Don't you want some honey?" Cora asked, pushing the jar towards her.

"What?"

"Honey, you always put honey in your tea. Or you changing your habits?" Windy shook her head and accepted the jar. Cora studied her friend for a moment.

Maybe Windy was just reacting as she herself had the previous morning, knowing what she wanted to do, but not yet having the strength to do so. Cora made a mental note to place Windy's salvation at the top of her prayer list. "Didn't you want to go to CT...CAF...oh, you know."

"CFTA? Why yes, I do have some baked goods to take over there today."

"Well, I drove and I'm ready when you are."

"Don't you want to finish your tea?" Cora said taking a quick gulp of the still hot liquid.

"Oh, of course." She stared at the cup she held in her hands. Cora mistook the younger woman's nervousness for a hesitant heart. She patted Windy's hand and smiled a knowing smile at her. They finished their tea in silence.

The trip to the CFTA ended too soon for Cora. She had hoped that Windy might even accept Christ before their visit ended.

For Windy, the afternoon lasted an agonizingly long time. When she finally settled back into her car and headed for home, the tension broke and her tears ran freely. She didn't want to go back to Stephan's house, nor did she feel comfortable with her friend. She dared not drive around, lest Stephan should call Cora and learn when she had left.

She entered through the back door and immediately busied herself with preparing Stephan's supper. When he popped in some time later and inquired about her visit she shrugged and said it went well.

"Where's my blueberry pie?" he asked sniffing.

Windy stopped dead in her tracks. She slowly turned to face her husband. "Do not tell me you forgot."

She didn't have to, her look told it all.

"How could you possibly have forgotten the pie? I do not understand what goes on in that head of yours, Elaine."

"Do you want me to run over and get it?"

"No, you are liable to forget why you returned there. I'll just drive over while you finish supper."

Windy tensed, wondering if Cora would repeat her story to Stephan. As soon as she saw him leave the driveway she called Cora.

"Do you believe I forgot the pie?" she tried to sound lighthearted, even managing a choked laugh.

"Well, so did I!" came the voice from the other end of the line.

"Stephan's on his way over, he must have been thinking about it all day. Cora?" she continued before the woman had a chance to speak. "You might not want to mention what we talked about today. Um, Stephan is still a little uncomfortable with me going to your church and..."

"I understand," she assured Windy. "He's pulling up now. I'll call you tomorrow. Bye."

Windy hung up, relieved.

Chapter Thirty-Seven

Dear Father,

I'm finding a new emotion. Anger. Somewhere during my life I learned anger was wrong and I never allowed it. Now it's surfacing in strange ways. Like when I couldn't get the flashlight to work and wound up throwing it across the room. It scares me, Lord, I don't understand. Sometimes I get angry when I think of my son. Please help me deal with this.

Fall blended into winter and Windy found herself looking forward to Wil's weekly deliveries. Despite his full time job, he still maintained his wood customers. Windy enjoyed hearing the delightful stories that only a loving father can tell about his children.

They reminded Windy of her own dad and for the first time since their move over three years ago, she truly missed her parents.

She called them at Thanksgiving and, without intending to, developed the habit of calling them every week.

When December's phone bill arrived, Stephan called her into the parlor. She wiped her hands on the dish towel and quickly followed his summons.

"What is this?" he queried.

"The phone bill?" she asked hesitantly.

"Yes, Elaine, it is the phone bill. What I want to know it why there are four more calls out east. I thought you talked to your parents at Thanksgiving."

"I did."

"Then why these other calls?"

"I miss them," Windy explained, her hands wringing the towel she still held.

"You miss them? How could you miss them after these conversations? Look at this one, 15 minutes! What can a person possible talk about for 15 minutes?"

"They're my parents, Stephan." She felt an unfamiliar rise of anger.

"Yes? Elaine you can say much more in a letter and it is certainly cheaper."

"I only called in the evening or on Saturday when the rates were down."

"It's a good thing. I can not imagine what they would be at full price. Elaine this instrument," he picked up the phone, "is not for entertainment. It is in this house to keep me connected with my work."

"Why do you begrudge my a few phone calls?"

"I do not begrudge you the calls; I am just not willing to put up with wasteful spending."

"Talking to my parents isn't wasteful!" The anger she tried to suppress came spurting out. "I haven't asked much from you in the last year, Stephan. I don't think calling my folks is so terrible."

"Elaine, I will not have you speak to me in that tone of voice."

"And I'll not hold my tongue any longer! What is wrong with you Stephan? What has happened to you since we married? Where's the man who paid my bills, took me to movies and dinner and paid for my divorce? Who are you? Where's the Stephan who couldn't wait to marry me? Do you realize that two Christmas' and one anniversary have passed unnoticed by you? You haven't even bought me a Christmas present. I'd still be wearing the same Buy-Mart dress if it weren't for Jenny's generosity."

"So that's it?" he interrupted. "That religious fanatic has really gotten to you, has she? Filling your head with woman's liberation garbage?"

"Jenny?" Windy asked, not believing her ears.

"Yes, your precious Jenny. She buys you a pretty dress so she can lure you away from your own church. She lies to you about political issues you have no business dealing with and now she has influenced you to the point of being disrespectful to your husband."

Windy stared at him, wide eyed and opened mouth, unable to believe what she was hearing. "How did this conversation turn to Jenny?"

"You brought her up, threw her in my face."

"No, I didn't."

"Elaine, I have put up with your lies before, because you have never lied to my face. Now you stand here and look me in the eyes and lie. I suddenly find looking at you distasteful." With that he left the room.

Windy watched him go, wondering what had just taken place. She lifted the phone bill from the desk and searched for the phone calls that started this whole scene. There were four, the longest one 15 minutes. It cost $3.16 the others were even less. All four totaled under ten dollars. She stared long and hard at the paper in her hand. Eddie hadn't even reacted this way when she called her folks and they had far less money to spend than Stephan.

But, she reasoned, I rarely made such calls back then. She looked at the dates of the calls and saw a pattern emerging, one for every week in December. Maybe Stephan was just concerned that she would start a bad habit.

She dropped the bill on the desk and went back to the kitchen where she finished the supper dishes. She scrubbed the stove, swept the floor and then decided to mop. When she finished the clock read 9:06. Stephan would probably still be reading. Windy filled the small pail kept under the sink with hot soapy water. She opened the fridge and began placing it's contents on the table.

With that task accomplished she slowly looked around the kitchen for something else she might do to please her husband. She placed fresh grounds in the coffee pot and plugged it in. Then she checked the doors and turned off all the downstairs lights.

She climbed the stairs quietly and slipped into her room, noting that Stephan's light shone under his door. She showered quickly and sprayed on some enticing perfume. She pulled on her robe and headed back downstairs.

Windy poured the steamy dark liquid into Stephan's favorite mug, unplugged the pot and switched off the light. Once upstairs she peeked into the bedroom she sometimes shared with her husband. He sat under the covers, a large textbook in his hand. The lamp beside him highlighted the graying temples, and cast a shadow on his chest from his chin. He appeared older than his forty-two years and Windy stared for a moment. This man, this old man with the gray hair and drooping chin, was her husband.

Trembling, she spilled hot coffee over her fingers then steadied the cup with her other hand.

Stephan noticed the movement. He looked at her and frowned.

"Would you like a cup of fresh coffee?" she asked in a timid voice.

"Is it decaffeinated?"

She shook her head.

"How do you expect me to sleep tonight, then?"

Windy placed the cup on the closest dresser. She walked over to the bed and dropped her robe revealing her soft naked body.

"I was hoping to keep you awake for a while."

Stephan let his book fall to his lap and gazed at his wife's delicate curves for a moment then looked up at her face. "When is your next period?"

"Pardon?"

"Your next period, when is it due?"

In her confusion Windy tried to count. She visualized the calendar hanging in the next bedroom. "In about three days."

"There's no reason for lovemaking, then. Right now you are either pregnant or infertile." He looked at her slender belly. "And I doubt that you are pregnant." He picked up the book and resumed reading.

A feeling of vulnerability washed over Windy and she quickly retrieved her robe, covering her nakedness. She willed herself to calmly turn and leave the room taking the cup of coffee with her.

Slowly she descending the dark stairs and entered the kitchen. It smelled of scouring powder. She dumped the coffee into the sink, rinsing both out. Still dazed from Stephan's rejection she went back upstairs to the pink room. She flipped on the light and looked around. Every where she looked she saw herself. Her clothes lay on the bed and hung in the closet. Her toiletries decorated the bathroom counter. Her handiwork sat beside the bed and her Bible lay on the night table. She realized she was in her room and Stephan was in his. She may have married Stephan 14 months ago, but she had never become his wife. Not like she had been Eddie's wife. Not like Mom was Dad's wife.

Windy opened a drawer and pulled out a worn t-shirt and undies. She dropped her robe where she stood and slipped on her night clothes. Once under the covers of her bed she pulled Sachel Jr. close and poured her tears into his velvety fur.

Chapter Thirty-Eight

Dear Lord,

I'll be so glad to see spring. Sometimes I think I've lost touch with You. Margie says that happens and I shouldn't worry. That we all have to digest after a big meal and I had been devouring Your Word a lot last fall. Do my kids read Your Word? Will You lay it upon their hearts to do so?

Windy awoke to Stephan's tender caress and opened her eyes to the pre-dawn darkness.

"Does your offer still stand?" he whispered in her ear.

"I dumped the coffee down the sink," she murmured.

"Then maybe we should go on to the second suggestion."

"Maybe." She waited silently as Stephan slipped under the covers beside her. She waited for his apology but heard only his anticipation.

"I'm sorry about the phone bills," she opened the door. "I won't let it happen again."

"I know you won't," he pulled her close.

"I'm sorry about yelling at you," she opened the door wider.

"I know," he answered, his need heavy in his voice.

"Do you want to say something to me?" The door stood as wide as it would go. But Stephan refused to walk through it.

"Shhh…" his mouth silenced her question and the door slammed shut.

Windy endured her husband's lovemaking while she replayed the cutting remark he made the night before. Silently she asked why he bothered with her now if she couldn't conceive that all important baby. She wanted to scream her questions at him, but bit her lip instead.

When Stephan's energy was spent he kissed her forehead and left her bed. She watched him leave the room and soon heard his shower running.

Memories of her last night with Eddie came flooding back. This time she lay in an expensive bed with fashionable covers in an old mansion. This time her husband had been sober and hadn't disappeared in the middle of the night. This time she had not been forced or slapped. But this time she felt just as dirty.

This is different she scolded herself. Stephan used no force; he would have stopped if I told him to. I can't expect to enjoy lovemaking every time.

Her arguments continued until she had no reasoning left and then the tears returned, silent this time.

Stephan's movements as he readied himself for work were audible to Windy. She heard his footsteps in the hallway and watched him through her open door. He didn't come in to say good-bye, didn't even glance toward her room.

She told herself he assumed she was sleeping as she heard the car pull out of the driveway.

Windy sat up and lifted her Bible from the night stand. She opened to the Psalms as she did every morning. But the words of praise only served to feed the hurt in her heart.

"I'm sorry, Lord," she said. "I can't seem to praise You today."

She turned to the New Testament, flipping the pages, not knowing what she looked for. She stopped at an underlined passage in Philippians and read it aloud. "For to you it has been granted for Christ's sake, not only to believe in Him, but also to suffer for His sake."

"Well, I believe in You," she commented. "And I guess I could consider Stephan's words and actions as causing me to suffer, but is it for your sake? If it were, it might be easier to handle."

She closed the book and returned it to the stand then slid back underneath the covers, pulling them over her head. Her first breath reminded her Stephan had been there. The sheets smelled of that combination of cologne and antiseptic she associated with him when they first met. Throwing back the covers, Windy jumped out of bed and quickly stripped it of all it's linen. She separated the sheets from the rest of the bedding and threw them in a pile. She pulled on the sweat pants and shirt that lay discarded on the floor from yesterday. Gathering the offending sheets in her arms she headed downstairs.

She quickly laid a fire in the parlor fireplace and watched as the wood began to burn hot. Opening a desk drawer she found a pair of scissors and cut the sheets into pieces that burned brightly when thrown on the fire. She counted them, 14 pieces, one for each month of marriage. As she watched the fire die, her anger subsided. Where had it come from? This anger that was usually so foreign to her? Where would it lead her?

Windy's Bible lay untouched on the night stand for several weeks. Once in awhile she entered the room and stared at the book as though expecting it to speak to her. But the ears of her heart were closed and could not hear the Book's silent pleadings.

The young woman continued to function in a reasonable manner. Every day she performed her duties around the house. Each night she lit the fire in the parlor and cooked her husband's supper. She visited her friends at the cozy little house on Maple street and when they inquired about her she always assured them she was just fine.

Stephan surprised Windy one morning in February by handing her a fifty dollar bill.

"This is your allowance. You may spend it as you please, on phone calls to your parents, gas for the car, whatever personal items we do not normally purchase at the grocery store."

Windy's eyes brightened for the first time in weeks.

"Thank you, Stephan," she could hardly believe her good fortune. What can I do with fifty dollars a week? Windy thought. Call my parents, drive Cora to the CTFA or CAFT or whatever, maybe make a donation to the Help office and I should even be able to save some of it towards Christmas, next year.

Windy hugged her husband, kissing him in gratitude. She didn't know why this sudden generosity on his part, but knew better that to question it.

Stephan returned Windy's kiss. "Spend it wisely, Elaine, it has to last all month."

"All month?"

"Yes, of course. Fifty dollars a month is certainly more than you'll ever need."

Winter left reluctantly and spring made its way into the world around Windy. She planted her flowers, again without consulting her husband.

Occasionally she accompanied Cora to the CFTA or Jenny to the office but without energy or enthusiasm.

Stephan didn't notice the change in his wife. He didn't see the dull look in her eyes or the lack of enthusiasm in her voice. When she accompanied him to the hospital to care for the newest orphan, they parted at the front door and later met at the pre-arranged spot.

Each month Stephan made a single inquiry about her 'health' and each month she assured him everything was normal. Though Windy's periods had never been regular they were consistent. Two days late meant nothing nor did three days early.

On April 7th Jenny called to tell Windy about the birth of Hannah Mary Catherine. She weighed 7 pounds, 3 ounces and had lots of soft black hair. Through unshed tears Windy asked about Mary.

"She's just fine. The doctor said her delivery went smoothly. I'm going up tomorrow to see them. Want to join me?"

Windy agreed, saying she would ride in with Stephan who was working days.

Windy held little Hannah in her arms. To keep from crying she silently told herself it didn't matter if she ever held her own baby.

In mid May Jenny called again.

"How about a morning at the office?"

"Why not?" Windy answered. "This Saturday?"

"No, next. The college students have exams all next week then they're finished for the year. We've found that many of them put off a visit to the office till the last minute hoping they'll start. When they don't they all come in the same day. We just man the office and let them walk in. I could probably use some help."

"Sure, be glad to." Windy decided a day with Jenny sounded pretty good.

They arrived at the stately house at the same time but Windy reached the door before Jenny. She waited impatiently, hoping Jenny wouldn't see the excitement in her eyes. They walked in together and Jenny entered the office while Windy excused herself to the rear of the house. Sensing the urgency in Windy's voice, Jenny followed. She stopped outside the bathroom and called out.

"You'd better let me in on this." She heard the toilet flush and a moment later the door opened. A nervous Windy looked at her. "It may be nothing," she said.

"It may be," Jenny shrugged. She had never seen Windy like this before. She stepped in beside her friend and watched her pull a test from the drawer.

Jenny took a deep breath and said a silent prayer, asking God for His will to be done.

Windy smiled at Jenny and dropped the sample into the small opening on the test.

"How long?" Jenny asked.

"A week. It's never been this long before, a couple days, maybe even three, but never a week.

Jenny took her friend's hands in hers, closed her eyes and began to pray. Windy willed herself to keep calm, resisting the temptation to look at the test until Jenny had finished praying.

When Jenny ended the petition she looked into Windy's eyes. Windy didn't move. Jenny tilted her head forward.

"Well?" Windy stood staring at her friend. "C'mon, we'll look together." Both heads turned, both eyes saw the result.

"Think it could be wrong?" Windy asked.

"Not likely. But we could do another if you want."

"No. Why waste it." She stared at the test as though willing a second line to show itself. Then she dropped it into the basket and poured the contents of the cup into the toilet before she sent it to join the offensive test.

Together, they walked back to the office where they were met by a young woman. "The door was unlocked…" she began.

Jenny resumed her duties and guided the girl to the chair by her desk. Windy pulled a tape from the cabinet and quickly forwarded it to the appropriate number on the counter. She then went back into the bathroom and placed a clean cup by the sink. She returned to the hall and entered the door opposite the room where Jenny sat with her client.

This large room held everything from brochures to baby beds and worked as a second counseling room in the warm months. The unused rooms of the big old house were not heated. In here, Windy found a bag of newly donated baby clothes; she pulled out several and checked them for cleanliness. They looked as though they should be washed so Windy didn't bother to sort them.

Windy heard the front door open and knew it must be another client. She stepped into the hall and led the newcomer back into the room. Here they sat while Windy took down her initial information on a client form. When Jenny finished Windy would turn this young lady over to her.

Chapter Thirty-Nine

Dear wonderful Father,
Thank You! Thank You for sunshine and beautiful days. Thank You
for Margie and Pastor. Thank You for my son and who ever You've
chosen for him. And thank You that You know about his life even if I don't.

Stephan covered the distance to his car in record time. He couldn't wait to get home and tell Elaine that Mr. Graves would live. Stephan had proved himself to be the best doctor in this entire hospital. When every other diagnosis claimed no hope, he, Stephan Michaels didn't give up, and now a man owed him his very life.

The great doctor opened his car door and slipped behind the wheel. He would take his wife out to dinner tonight, to celebrate his victory. He realized his thoughts had been completely on his patient these last couple months and knew he owed his wife that much. She had been patient with him.

The short drive home seemed longer than usual. Soon Stephan pulled into his driveway, but not into the garage.

Elaine kneeled before her flower bed, slowly pulling out weeds and tossing them into the yard. Stephan stopped short. "Elaine, I have told you not to throw the weeds onto the lawn, remember?"

He walked toward his wife as he reprimanded her but she appeared not to have heard. Her face remained bent toward the earth and her hands continued to disobey him.

"Elaine!" He called again and again until he finally stood over her.

She slowly lifted her face. Tears fell from her cheeks and her red, puffy eyes told him she'd been crying for some time.

Stephan reached his hand out to his wife and helped her to her feet. He pulled her into his arms but felt no response from her.

"Do you want to tell me why you are crying?"

Elaine barely shook her head against his chest.

Stephan sighed, his perfect day suddenly ruined. He had just experienced a miracle; he helped return a man from the dead. And now Elaine stood here weeping. What could she possible have to cry about? A broken fingernail?

'No,' he chastised himself. 'If Elaine did not cry over bruised ribs and a battered body she would not cry over something simple.'

"I have some wonderful news. Go in and clean up and I will take you out to dinner."

His wife nodded and allowed him to lead her into the house.

By the time she descended the stairs she was her normal self again. The puffiness around her eyes remained but at least they weren't red and wouldn't draw attention in the restaurant.

"You are dining with the best doctor in this city tonight, Mrs. Michaels, possibly the entire state." He informed her over prime rib and Chablis. "How does that make you feel?"

"Proud." She smiled at her husband.

"Of course, you are proud, who wouldn't be?"

Stephan felt so generous he even ordered desert. "So what if it is a terribly overpriced piece of chocolate cake? We are celebrating tonight!"

"Stephan, you're living so dangerously!" Elaine teased.

He gazed thoughtfully at his wife. She never quite fit in this type of setting. Even in that expensive dress Jenny McCourt gave her, his little Elaine was still 'Windy' and he could never change that. She might be cute and witty at times but she would never be elegant. Stephan looked away. He had never given much thought to what his wife should be like, but had always assumed she would be of equal class with him. He thought he had covered all bases when it came to checking out Windy Jordan Bilmon. With a contractor for a father and her brother in the Secret Service her family and quality of upbringing seemed assured. The fact that she had received a scholarship to an eastern university spoke of the girl's intelligence. Now he believed he may have acted hastily and the result smiled at him from across the table.

And why should she not smile? After all, had he not taken her right out of the gutter and placed her in his own mansion? Rather like Henry Higgins and Eliza Doolittle in My Fair Lady. Yes, he had given this little waif everything, even the revered Michaels name. And what had she given in return? She could not even present him with the one thing that had become most important to him. A child. An heir. What was so difficult about that? Women had babies every day. Why not Elaine?

A thought occurred to him. He reached across the table and took her slender hand in his.

"We will wait another month or two, then you shall undergo some testing."

"What kind of testing?" Her hand trembled.

"Nothing difficult, I promise. Remember Dr. Sells, he performs your annual pap and pelvic exam in the fall?"

Elaine nodded.

"There are many tests to determine why a woman is not conceiving. We will see him and find out what he would recommend."

Elaine looked away, but nodded her consent.

"I'm going! I'm really going!!" Jenny gripped Windy's hands as soon as she stepped through the door.

"Going where?" she smiled at her friend.

"Costa Rica, of course." Jenny dropped Windy's hands and pulled her into a bear hug. "I'm so excited! It took all year to save for this, but I sent in my money and got my confirmation today." She released Windy and picked a paper off the table. "See, there it is, in black and white."

Windy had almost forgotten about the trip Mary and Andrew took on their honeymoon last summer; the trip in which they conceived little Hannah.

"When do you go?" Windy asked, making her way to the Jenny's refrigerator.

"I leave July 1st. Not much time to get ready, huh?"

"How long will you be gone?" Windy pulled out a can of cherry cola and popped the top.

"Three weeks, I'm going on the longer trip where I'll be at a camp on the Pacific Ocean and gee, Windy, try not to be so excited, okay?"

"I'm sorry," the girl smiled, placing the can on the counter. "I am happy for you; I just haven't been excited about much of anything lately." She crossed the room and gave Jenny a quick hug. "I will miss you though."

"It's only three weeks, and besides you went longer this spring without seeing me. It shouldn't bother you too much." Windy's smile disappeared. "Oh, get your pop and come sit down."

Windy obeyed, joining Jenny at the small table. She told Jenny of her dinner date two nights ago, the night of her negative test and of Stephan's success with his hopeless patient.

"He said that's why he's been so preoccupied the last couple months, but now he would have more time for me."

"That's great, Win. I'm sure you two need some time just for each other. Are you going away?"

"No." Windy looked at the can she held, rubbing the condensation off its sides. "He said we're going to do some testing."

"What kind of testing?"

"To see what's wrong with me."

"I'm sorry Windy, I don't follow you."

"To see why I'm not pregnant."

"Oh." Jenny looked at her friend and detected the fear in her eyes. "So you started your period?"

Windy nodded. "Yesterday"

"Look Win, there's nothing to be afraid of. These tests, it's all routine stuff, you know."

"Probably, but what if the doctor says I'm...barren. I don't know how Stephan will take it."

"There's always adoption. We have numbers at the office you can call for information."

Windy shook her head. "Stephan would never adopt. His name is too good to give to some little orphan."

"Maybe you underestimate your husband."

"He's as much as said so. No, I think he'd divorce me."

"Oh, Windy, Stephan isn't the type of person to just toss some one aside if they don't suit his purposes." *'Or is he?'* she wondered.

Windy smiled. "You're right. He's a good man. I guess I'm just depressed because you're going so far away."

Windy's explanation lacked sincerity and Jenny saw it. She took her friends hand. "Everything will be okay."

Windy's eyes filled with tears. "Please pray that I get pregnant. Soon."

Chapter Forty

Dear Father,
It's interesting how one person can have such an impact on our lives.
Just one person can change our whole future. What kind of people are
effecting my children, Lord? Are their lives being changed for the better?

"Windy, I have a favor to ask." Jenny's voice came from the other end of the telephone line.

"Sure."

"We have a girl coming in and no one to cover the appointment. She can only come tomorrow and I'll be at school. Darla is sick and Angie's on vacation. Would you go in?"

"By myself?"

"Yes. Win, you've been going with me for almost a year. You know all the facts, you often counsel as much as I do."

"But, never by myself."

"It's not that hard, I know you can do it."

Windy took a deep breath. "All right, I'll try. What if she's a real hard case?"

"I've already talked to her on the phone, and she sounds like an easy one. I think she just needs confirmation."

"Promise?"

"Windy, I've not met her, so I can't promise, but I'm quite sure, otherwise I wouldn't ask you."

"I'm sorry, I trust you judgment."

Windy arrived half an hour before the scheduled appointment. She slipped the video into the machine and stopped it at just the right point. She took the client information and test release sheets from the drawer, checked the last client number and wrote accordingly in the upper right corner of the form. Then she went into the bathroom and placed a clean cup on the counter.

Back in the office she opened the log book and recorded her name, the date and hour. Windy debated changing the phone over to the office. She really didn't want any interruptions during the counseling session, and once she was finished she would just leave. She looked at the paper she'd brought from home with the girls name and phone number on it. Diana. 6691. If Diana didn't show up, Windy would call her to find out why. She knew many girls didn't bother to keep an appointment if they started their period. Maybe Diana had started and wouldn't come.

Windy preferred that solution.

The sound of the front door opening caught Windy off-guard. She still wasn't sure if she was ready to solo.

Windy felt intimidated at first glance. Diana wore the latest in women's fashions. Her frosted blonde hair stood windblown in the recent popular style. Make up accented her face as it disappeared into her natural beauty.

Still sitting behind the desk, Windy touched her own cheek thinking of the powder she had quickly applied before coming. That one little compact represented her complete line of beauty products.

"I'm Diana," the woman said. "I have an appointment for a pregnancy test."

Windy found her voice and stood. "Please, come in and have a seat. My name is Windy." She held her hand out, smiling into Diana's piercing blue eyes. Diana placed her own hand in Windy's removing it as soon as their skin touched. She sat in the chair Windy indicated.

"First Diana, I'll need to ask you some questions." Windy retreated to the chair behind the desk. "They're routine and will simply help me determine how I can best serve you." Windy picked up a pen and placed her initials at the top of the client form along with the date.

"All of these questions are confidential and the information you give will stay in the office." Diana nodded her understanding. "Would you spell your name for me? First and last." Windy willed her hand to be steady.

"D-i-a-n-a W-e-s-t-f-i-e-l-d."

"Address?"

"411 Crest View Court." Windy wrote down the information, picturing the small subdivision of new, expensive condominiums.

"How old are you, Diana?"

"26."

"Are you a student at the University?"

Diana smiled for the first time. "No. I am a Registered Nurse at Community Hospital."

"Oh?" Windy perked up. "Do you know…" As quickly as it appeared the smile had been replaced with a look of impatience. Windy decided to stick to the routine; she glanced at Diana's left hand. "Are you married?"

"No."

"How did you hear about our services?"

"I looked in the yellow pages."

"Do you have a church affiliation?"

"No."

"If we have a positive result, will you to keep your baby?"

"No."

Windy hesitated for a moment, "Are you considering adoption?"

"No."

Windy's hand poised over the paper. "I'm sorry, I must have misunderstood. You talked with Jenny on the phone didn't you?"

"Yes."

"She had the impression that you were going to keep your baby."

The woman shrugged. "I didn't want a sermon on the phone. Look, I came here for a pregnancy test. Are you going to do one or not?"

"Yes, of course." Windy took a slow deep breath, wishing Jenny were there, wishing she herself were home. "But I still have a couple more questions. What was the date of your last period?"

"The last week of January."

Windy's head bobbed up. "You've missed three periods already?"

"I don't have periods on the shot," Diana answered without hesitation.

"So why are you wanting a test?"

"There are other indications. It's time for the next shot but I thought I'd better check first and have it taken care of."

"Do you believe that's your only option?"

"It's my choice." The cold blue eyes dared Windy to question her statement.

"Well, let's determine if you are pregnant before we discuss your choices. Have you had any of the following symptoms?" Windy read off the list of questions which normally indicate pregnancy. Diana answered all of them with a yes. With each affirmative Windy's heart sank a little more.

With the form completed, Windy led Diana down the hallway into the bathroom, where she explained what Diana needed to do. Back in the office she stood by the VCR, knowing Jenny would ask God to use the information on the tape to soften the woman's heart.

Diana appeared in the doorway and Windy directed her to a chair. She started the video then excused herself to perform Diana's test.

Windy placed the drops into the proper opening, then closed her eyes. She listened for the familiar words Jenny always repeated at this time and found the words coming from her own mouth.

"Please, God, let this test be negative. You know Diana and you know her heart. You know her situation, God, and why she doesn't want a baby in her life right now. I know I have no right coming to you now. It's been months since I really sought Your presence and now I do so out of selfishness, requesting instead of praising. But, God, I'm not asking for me, I'm asking for Diana. And if she is pregnant, then I…I…" Windy tried to remember Jenny's words. "…I claim this baby as Your's and I ask for your protection for it. In Jesus name, Amen."

Windy opened her eyes and stared at the two lines in the result window.

Chapter Forty-One

Dear Father,
How limited our understanding really is. Just when we think we've had a little victory it can be turned into a major defeat. Are my children turning their defeats over to You? Are they praising You for their victories?

Windy stood outside the office door, trying to remember how Jenny broke the news. Each time was different, depending on the woman. Windy wished this was one of the times she could present a smile and a handmade baby blanket as the result. She loved seeing a woman's eyes when Jenny came in carrying one.

Mustering up her courage, Windy stepped through the doorway catching Diana off guard. The woman quickly drew her manicured fingers across her cheek. Sniffing slightly she raised her head, readying herself for Windy's news.

"I suppose it's positive," she stated, the reserve in her voice appeared strained.

Windy nodded. "The test registered a positive result, but I can't confirm a pregnancy, only your doctor can do that."

Diana looked away, blinking her eyes. Her chin quivered. "Well, give me the address of the nearest abortion clinic."

"I can't do that, Diana. We…we don't refer for abortions."

"What are you here for then?" A shrillness crept into the woman's voice and she looked accusingly at Windy.

"To provide you with free tests and information."

"I need to get this done as quickly as possible. Should already have taken care of it, I suppose." She murmured the last sentence to herself as her eyes reverted back to the television screen. It showed a picture of a four month old aborted baby.

"That's what your baby looks like, Diana. You must be close to four months now." The words spilled out, Windy unaware of their origin. "You're already feeling the baby move, aren't you?"

"Don't start," came the soft warning.

But Windy could not stop. She had no control over the words that came from her lips. "Diana, you have within you the greatest gift a woman could have. A baby. A brand new life. What ever your reasons for killing this baby, they couldn't possible be as strong as the ones for letting it live."

Diana's cold blue eyes turned on Windy, a smudge of mascara sat on the rosy cheek, defying Diana's every word. "You know nothing of my reasons. You have no idea of what I'm faced with. I just received my certificate. I am now a Registered Nurse, something I have worked very hard for. I live with the man I love. My life is perfect just the way it is. A child doesn't fit in."

"Is that your decision or your boyfriend's?"

"It's our decision. This baby had no business being conceived. It isn't planned or wanted. It isn't going to be, do you understand? I'm not giving up everything for a baby I don't want."

"You don't have to give up anything. You can release your baby to adoption. Let her bring joy to another couple. You've already completed almost four months of your pregnancy. Five more months could be the price tag of three happy, fulfilled lives. In just five months, Diana, you can give a lifetime, to your baby and a couple who can not have one of their own."

Diana shook her head furiously. "You have no idea of what you're talking about. You don't know my situation."

Windy crossed the room and pulled up a chair beside the distraught woman.

"I know you have access to pregnancy tests at the hospital. Why did you come here? Was it because you want help with this decision? You wanted someone to tell you it's okay to keep your baby?"

Diana looked at Windy her eyes revealing the truth of Windy's words.

"It's true that I don't know anything about you or what you're going through. I do know that your baby is a small human being who has received life from you. She's a complete person already. Everything about her is determined, her hair color, the way she'll walk, even the foods she may like. All she needs is time to complete her growth and she's counting on you to give her that. You're her mom, you know."

Then Diana cried. She forget about the mascara, the blush. She forgot about the reserve that was supposed to carry her through the process of eliminating her baby. And she cried.

Windy handed Diana a tissue, glad that a box was always kept on the desk.

"Diana, whatever you're facing will not be as hard as what you'll have to face in the future if take your own child's life. If you feel this way now, think how you'll feel in five years. We see it more all the time. The long term affects of abortion are far worse than the fear and confusion you feel right now."

Windy tapped the off button on the remote.

"Don't do this to yourself, don't do it to her."

Windy pulled her chair closer to Diana's. "Let's just talk this out, okay? Let's look at all the obstacles and determine the best way to deal with them. I want to help you."

"You just want to say you've saved a baby."

The remark hurt Windy, because of the truth in the statement. Until now, she had never really considered what the woman was going through; she had concentrated on the horrors of the abortion itself.

"You're right, to an extent. But Diana, I want to care about you, too. I want to see you through this."

"Why?" The blue eyes peered into hers. They had lost the hardness, but remained untrusting.

Windy shrugged. "I don't know," she whispered. "I just know I do."

Windy let herself into the Michaels mansion. She heard Gretchen's soft humming from the front of the house. Not wanting to confront the unfriendly woman, Windy quickly ascended the back stairs and slipped into her bedroom. She had just enough time for a quick shower before Stephan came home. She hoped she could perk her face up enough so he wouldn't realize she'd been crying. As she drew a cold cloth over her eyes, she wondered why she should worry about that. He rarely noticed her at all, anymore.

Windy let the hot water pelt her skin as she relived the conversation between herself and Diana. The young woman revealed her desire to have her baby while the father insisted she abort it. His ultimatum left no room for compromise. Diana either kept him or the baby.

Windy found herself telling this stranger about her own desire and inability to conceive. They had cried together and departed friends. Diana promised to see a doctor to confirm the pregnancy and said she would call Windy with the results. She also promised not to make any other plans until talking with Windy again.

Windy found it hard not to pick up the phone and call Jenny. But she kept hearing Diana's accusation. Windy knew Jenny would call her asking how things went, it would be okay then to recount the visit.

Chapter Forty-Two

Father, how many people have asked You that age old question—why am I here? What is my purpose in life? What is life itself? Forgive me, Father, it must be the heat that making me ramble like this. How are the kids, Lord? What kind of summer are they having?

Stephan asked the hospital operator to connect him with Dr. Sells office. When the receptionist informed Stephan that Dr. Sells was in radiology, Stephan decided to hunt him down. He had told Elaine they would wait a couple months for testing but he found himself impatient. He didn't like not knowing what he was dealing with. He didn't like not being in control.

"Come in, Stephan, this might be of interest to you." said Dr. Sells when Stephan poked his head in the door. "You know Nurse Westfield, don't you?"

Stephan nodded to the figure laying on the examining table. He knew the face if not the name. It appeared tense beneath the white nurses' cap. She nodded in return.

Dr. Sells directed Stephan's attention to the monitor that displayed the nurse's womb. Stephan was immediately captivated by the amount of activity.

He saw the child bouncing wildly as though on a hidden trampoline. When the baby stopped and turned his face toward his audience, his features became clear and visible. Big round eyes stared at Stephan, his month opened in a yawn after which a tiny tongue popped out and back in again.

A smile slid across Stephan's face. He leaned closer to the monitor, enthralled by what he saw. Suddenly the baby's hand shot up beside his head, fluttered a couple times then returned to his side. Stephan stepped back his face alive with pleasure.

"He waved at me!" he announced, his eyes still affixed on the tiny creature.

"She," a soft voice corrected.

Stephan turned his attention to the woman laying on the table. "You have seen that too?"

"No, I just know it."

'*Nonsense*', thought Stephan, '*those things are not simply known.*' "What's the gestation?" he directed his question to Dr. Sells but the woman answered.

"Almost four months. I've just started feeling life, but look how active she is."

All eyes returned to the monitor where the baby had resumed her exercise routine.

Stephan smiled at the woman then pulled his attention back to the task at hand. "Robert, I need to speak to you when you have finished here."

"Why not wait in my office, I won't be long."

Stephan nodded his agreement, his attention back on the monitor.

"How does Elaine feel about all this?" the fatherly doctor asked when he joined Stephan a short time later.

"What do her feelings have to do with the tests?"

"Stephan, if she's uptight, if she's trying too hard to conceive, that in itself can create problems. How often do the two of speak about this?"

"Every month," replied Stephan with disgust.

"And how often do you make references to her not being pregnant, subtle hints of your displeasure?"

This question caused Stephan to stop and think. "I don't know, maybe too often," he replied.

"Woman are complex creatures, my friend, they are built completely different from men. Not just physically either. If she's picking up on your disapproval, that stress alone may be the reason why she's not conceiving."

"You are kidding!"

The graying doctor shook his head in obvious wisdom.

"Allow her to relax. Don't make her feel as though she has to perform for you. Let her know she's important because of who she is, not what she can do. Give her a couple months, then maybe, we'll do some testing, on both of you."

"What do you mean both of us?"

"Unless you already have proof to the contrary, you're as much a candidate as your wife."

Stephan stood and shook his friend's hand, covering the resentment he felt. How dare this man question a Michaels ability to produce fruit. Yet at the same time he admired the fatherly gentleman for his honesty. As Stephan left the office, he decided there had really been no harm done. He would allow Elaine her relaxation, maybe that was all she needed. And if not, he would submit to the tests, to settle that issue.

Windy noticed a sudden change in Stephan but was too pleased with his actions to question them.

May turned into June and Windy felt as though they had returned to the early days of their marriage. She found herself doing special little things to show Stephan her gratitude. She even dug the cookbook given her as part of the cooking lessons out of the bottom of the kitchen junk drawer.

With the warmer emotions came the summer climate.

When Stephan suggested they travel an hour to Lake Michigan and spend a couple days on the beach, Windy felt as giddy as a new bride. She listened as Stephan made phone calls to a quaint little Bed and Breakfast. When Windy commented on the cost of the resort, Stephan shrugged. "It's only money," he said.

Windy wondered why it was only money when it came to something he wanted, but when handing Windy her allotted fifty dollars per month, it equaled gold.

"Did you order this special?" Windy asked her husband as they sat in the sand looking at the moon glistening off the still blue water.

"It did not just happen you know. When I spoke to the moon and told him about my beautiful wife and how I wanted this to be a night for her to remember he gladly cooperated." Stephan thought of all the planning that had actually gone into this one rendezvous. He had kept very careful watch on his wife's monthly activity and after consulting with Dr. Sells knew that these couple days could be the most important in her cycle. He planned to spend at least two nights here, calling the hospital each morning to check on his patients through another doctor. As luck had it, Stephan had no patients with serious problems just then.

Rather than get Elaine's hopes up for extending their stay, Stephan would just add to her joy each morning when he would tell her he had decided to wait another day before going home.

After Stephan had fallen asleep Windy moved to the window and returned her gaze to the moonlit beach. She recalled Mary's account of the romantic Costa Rican beach. She hoped the prayers of her righteous friends were being answered. She just knew she would conceive this night and finally bring joy to her husband. She had charted her monthly cycle closely and knew Stephan must also know this was the time when their chances were highest.

Three days later the Michaels' loaded up the sedan and headed back home. Both felt a new awareness of each other. Windy assured herself that even if she hadn't conceived at least their marriage had been refreshed and she would not allow it to fall back into the despair she'd felt over the last year. Stephan's outlook appeared more positive, but the narrowness of it spelled doom. He allowed for Windy's conception with no compromise.

Windy called Jenny as soon as Stephan left for the hospital that evening. She couldn't wait to tell her friend about the romantic get-a-way. Jenny expressed her happiness for Windy, then relayed a message.

"Diana called. She left a number and wants you to call her as soon as possible."

Windy wrote the number on a piece of paper and Jenny graciously cut their conversation short.

"I didn't know of any other way to contact you," Diana explained. "I called the office but the lady didn't have your phone number. She finally asked Jenny to call me. I guess there's a policy that you don't give out any numbers over the phone."

"That's right," Windy responded. "I'm sorry Diana. Usually Jenny gives the girl a card with her home phone on it. You were my very first solo client and I forgot to do that."

Besides, she had never told Stephan she spent time at the office and dared not get a phone call here anyway.

"It's alright. I just wanted you to know I saw the baby on ultrasound."

"When?" Windy tried unsuccessfully to hide the excitement in her voice.

"Shortly after we talked. Oh, Windy, she's beautiful!"

"Have you told Mark?"

"He knows, he thinks I'm still going through with an abortion. But I think if he gives it a little time, he'll get used to the idea and will accept it."

"And if he doesn't?"

"I'll worry about that when it happens. But if he's really that set against a baby, well, maybe he's not the man I want."

Windy didn't know if she should cheer or cry. She didn't want to see Diana's relationship break up, but at the same time she didn't believe that couples should just live together anyway. Besides, Diana's baby would be born and Diana wouldn't have to live with the memory of killing her own child.

"Diana, it's hard for me to give you my home phone, but you can contact me through Jenny anytime. Is that okay? I have your number here now and I'll be certain to keep track of you. Maybe we can meet again at the office sometime."

Diana quickly agreed and Windy marveled that the woman who had so intimidated her in the office could actually become her friend. As she replaced the phone, Cora's long ago words echoed through her mind. 'Jenny says everything happens for a reason.'

Windy crawled into Stephan's bed that night, promising herself a long overdue call to the sweet little lady first thing in the morning.

Stephan walked toward the front entrance of the hospital, squinting at the morning sun that pored through the glass doors. He had paid dearly for his romp at the beach. His patients had fared well in his absence but his paper work had not. Now all the good doctor wanted to do was slip into his bed and rest his tired body. Sleeping in a strange bed might be fine for a younger man, but three nights on a poor quality mattress had taken its toll.

Stephan opened the door just as a young nurse trotted up the sidewalk. Her face stirred his memory but it was her slightly protruding stomach that brought recognition. He stopped and held the door for her.

"Good morning, Dr. Michaels, long night?" she smiled at him.

"Yes, Nurse…"

"Westfield. My little girl waved at you, remember?" she patted her belly.

"I will never forget. Have a good day."

"Thanks," she slipped through the door and glided down the hallway. Stephan stood watching for a moment suddenly aware of the glow about this woman. Was it this one in particular, or did all expectant mothers appear more beautiful?

He hoped to soon find the answer through his own wife.

Chapter Forty-Three

Good morning, Father!

Vacation Bible School starts today. I've been looking forward to this, although I admit I'm a little scared. I've never taught a class by myself. I've read this material enough to almost know it by heart, but what I really need is Your guidance. Are my kids involved in any summer programs? Please bless them in whatever they're doing. "Windy, can you come over? I need to talk to you about something."

Windy hardly recognized Jenny's voice. She sounded tired or discouraged, something completely foreign to her friend.

"Sure, I can't stay long though; Stephan will be home in a couple hours."

In the short drive to her friend's house, Windy imagined all the bad things one person can think of in five minutes. When she opened Jenny's apartment door, she was greeted by a young woman who looked about to cry.

"Are you all right?"

Jenny nodded, and took a deep breath, obviously fighting to keep control of her emotions. The girls sat at the table and Jenny reached over to take Windy's hand.

"My mom called, Dad has to have surgery."

Windy's shoulders relaxed and she breathed a sigh of relief. People had surgery every day; at least it wasn't anything too serious.

"What kind?" she asked.

"Bypass," Jenny whispered the word.

"Oh," Windy acknowledged quietly. She wanted to ask what they had to bypass, but somehow knew that wasn't a good question.

"Mom says they've already talked to the heart specialist and feel very good about his ability. It's just so sudden, you know? I mean, he went in for some routine tests yesterday and they kept him. The surgery is set for Friday. I've already called the airlines and have a reservation for tomorrow morning."

"Where do your parents live?"

"Florida, they moved down there a couple years ago to be close to Gramma."

Windy felt confused. She tried to piece together what Jenny was telling her. Then she remembered Jenny's long awaited trip which began in just over a week.

"Are you flying to Costa Rica from there?" she asked.

"No, Windy! I'm not going to Costa Rica. How can I fly off to a missions camp when my dad's having open heart surgery?"

Jenny had never raised her voice to Windy before and at first the girl was startled. Then the seriousness of what Jenny told her sunk in. Jenny must be afraid of losing her dad. That's why she called Windy over, for encouragement, and she offered dumb questions.

"Oh, Jenny, I'm so sorry. I guess...I didn't... realize what bypass meant. Is your dad going to be okay?" another dumb question, she wanted to kick herself.

"Mom says this is the best doctor around and he says the success rate for this kind of surgery is 95%. So I'd say, yes, he'll be okay, but it'll take awhile. Mom needs me right now, and when Dad gets home. She won't be able to take care of him by herself, I don't know how long I'll be gone, maybe a month."

Windy pictured her own dad and put herself in her friends place. Understanding replaced confusion.

"What can I do to help you? Do you need me to cover at the office? See that Cora gets to the store and the CT...CF...you know?"

"Well, actually, I have something a lot more difficult in mind."

Windy frowned, she didn't want to disappoint her friend in her obvious need, but she almost feared what Jenny might ask.

"You brought it up just a few minutes ago." Jenny looked expectantly at her. Windy slowly shook her head.

"Costa Rica," Jenny said quietly.

Windy waited.

"I've already paid the entire fare, and now I'm not going. It would be a shame to waste all that money."

Windy smiled in understanding. "You want me to call and see about your refund? Well, sure, it would be too hard for you to do it from Florida. I can do that; don't worry about it, okay?"

Now Jenny smiled. "No, Windy, I want you to go."

"Go where?"

This time the other young woman laughed. "To Costa Rica."

Windy stood quickly almost knocking the chair down.

"Me? Oh come on, I can't go!"

"Why not?"

"Jenny, this isn't a pregnancy test we're talking about here, this is big stuff, high adventure, I couldn't do that!"

"You couldn't do what?"

"Fly in an airplane to some little country where I don't know the language or any of the people. I don't know how to do missions work."

"This missions work is easy, it's all manual labor."

Windy walked away in disbelief, then turned and grinned at her friend. "You're kidding, right?"

Jenny just shook her head.

"Do you want to go?" Jenny asked.

Windy paced back toward the table and shrugged. "I don't know. I never thought about it."

"Well, think about it."

Windy retreated again, half way across the small room she turned on Jenny. "Why are you doing this to me?"

"I'm giving you the opportunity to be a part of something really wonderful, three weeks in the presence of committed Christians, at no cost to you and you act of though I asked you walk through fire."

"You might as well; one would be as easy as the other."

"Do you want to go?" Jenny repeated.

"Why me? Why not offer this to Mary?"

"She has a two month old baby."

"What about someone at school, or church?"

"Because this is very important to me, I'm missing out on something I desperately want to do. So I thought I'd offer it to some one who means a lot to me. In some strange way it'll still be as though I were going myself."

Jenny's explanation stunned Windy. She knew how much this meant to Jenny. Jenny didn't just offer a free trip, she offered her dream.

"Stephan would never let me," Windy stated, nearing her friend again.

"Maybe not, but you don't know till you ask him."

"I'm not asking him, you ask him!"

Jenny's eyes widen. "I'm not asking him, he's your husband!"

"It's your idea!"

They stared at each other, each working out the problem in their own silent way.

"Girls, girls, what's the shouting for?" Cora's voice drifted up the stairway and through Jenny's open door. The two young women smiled at each other.

"Cora!" they said, the same idea formulating in their minds.

"Have another piece of blueberry pie, Stephan," Cora lifted a hearty slice from the round pan and placed it on Stephan's plate.

Stephan had readily accepted Cora's invitation to dinner that evening. Now he and Windy, Cora and Jenny sat around Cora's table, their bellies full of Cora's newest recipe.

"Cora, I will burst!"

"Nonsense, you have plenty of room on those bones for a little meat. You're much too thin Stephan."

"I work hard to stay in shape. I happen to have some inside information on heart disease and stroke."

At the mention of heart disease, Jenny spoke up. "Have you ever heard of a Dr. Zenka?"

"The heart specialist from Florida?"

"Then you have heard of him? Is he a good doctor?"

"One of the best, is he your Father's doctor?"

"Yes, Dad's regular doctor called him in after Dad's tests. I guess his heart's in pretty bad shape."

"If they scheduled him that quickly, there is a good reason for it. How are you doing?"

"I don't know yet. I fly down tomorrow and I plan to be there for awhile to help during Dad's recuperation."

"Well, I wish you and your parents my best."

"Thank you, Stephan." Jenny's eyes began to water and Windy knew she'd forgotten about the task at hand.

"It's a good thing your parents have you," Windy interjected. "And it's actually happening at a fairly good time, I mean, being summer, you don't have to worry about taking a leave from school."

Jenny looked at her friend and nodded. "That's true, but I was supposed to go to Costa Rica next week. Of course, this is certainly more important."

"Yes, Elaine mentioned your trip," Stephan said, finally biting into his pie. "You have nothing tied up in this do you?"

"You mean financially?" she asked. Stephan nodded. "Yes, the entire trip is paid for." Stephan winced.

"But your money will be refunded?"

Jenny shook her head. "No, it's too late. I don't mind the money; really, I just wish that since it's already paid some one else could enjoy it."

"Have you spoken to any of your friends?"

"Most of the people I know couldn't get away on such short notice. Teachers often find summer jobs or even leave for a couple months."

"Tell me a little about this…what is it, a missions project?"

"Yes," Jenny started, seeing the conversation going in just the manner she hoped it would. She explained the basics of the work program. "Mostly I just hoped to get away, do something completely different. There's a certain kind of relaxation in leaving your world behind, temporarily, of course. I know that when I come back everything will be just as it always is, but the break in routine would change my outlook. It did for Mary and Andrew. I suppose that doesn't make much sense, does it?"

"On the contrary you have a very good point. I work in a clinic once a month. When I leave there and walk back into the hospital I have a new appreciation for my work, the technology and equipment that I take so for granted."

Windy caught Jenny's eyes, silently asking if this were the time, but Jenny seemed to sense some thing Windy didn't and shook her head slightly.

"How long is the trip?" Stephan asked, placing the last bite of delicious pie in his mouth.

"Three weeks, at a camp right on the Pacific. But a short time will be spent in one of the larger cities. It's a chance to see a different culture. In some of the poverty areas people live in tin shacks."

"Tin shacks," Stephan dabbed at his mouth with a paper napkin. "That is a side of poverty few people ever see." Jenny nodded in agreement.

"It would certainly make a person take notice of how good they have it back here."

"I intended to use my experiences in my classroom. That's why I'd hoped to find someone to take my place, so they could bring back the knowledge I'll miss."

"Hmmm…" Stephan nodded his head. "How much did your trip cost?"

"A thousand dollars, sure is a shame to see that money wasted."

Again Stephan nodded, his eyes focused on the napkin he held, intense concentration lined his face.

"When do you leave for Florida?" he asked.

"Tomorrow morning."

"Ummm…" Stephan continued to nod. "So you need to resolve this dilemma tonight?"

"It would be nice."

A long silent moment passed. "Elaine?"

"Yes, Stephan?"

"Do your friend a courtesy and bring back a very detailed report on Costa Rica."

Chapter Forty-Four

Oh Lord, help me through this, please. I'm enjoying the little ones, but they require so much energy. After working all day and Bible School in the evening, I'm just very tired. Please give me the energy to make it through the week. And be with my kids, too.

Stephan watched his wife board the DC 10 that would take her to Chicago's O'Hare Airport. There, her group would switch to a 747 which would take them to Miami. Again they must change planes to the Costa Rican airline for the third leg of their journey, ending in San Jose, Costa Rica.

Stephan felt a number of misgivings. Elaine appeared to want to go, but he almost felt as though he had pushed her into taking Jenny's place. All he heard that night at Cora's were Dr. Sells words, sounding over and over in his mind. Relaxation could make the difference.

Stephan didn't wait until the plane left the terminal, he saw no reason to watch the outside of the plane while Elaine busied herself inside. Chances of her having a window seat on the side where he stood were minimal. He turned and walked down the concourse, deep in thought.

Their lake excursion had proved unsuccessful and he had allowed his frustration to show when Elaine told him. His words hurt Elaine, he could see the wounded look on her face, but he'd been unable to control his outburst. Maybe if Elaine could get away from everyday pressures for a while she could physically and mentally relax. Three weeks of hard physical labor ought to create changes in anyone's attitude.

Stephan knew his motives were selfish. He was enough of a man to admit that. He even felt a little ashamed. When Jenny mentioned the poverty that would confront an American traveler he pictured Elaine as he first saw her, living in the dredges of life. She had it so good now, but she seemed to have already lost sight of all Stephan had done for her. Maybe a walk through the seamy side of life would revive her memory. Maybe she could once again appreciate what had been handed her along with the Michaels name.

The good doctor reached the sedan, unlocked the door and seated himself inside. As he exited the parking lot he noticed the plane taxiing down the runway. Stopping before he entered the street, he waited for the plane to take flight. Moments later it disappeared into the clouds. Stephan felt a quiver of elation. He smiled. A small laugh escaped his lips. He was free. Free for three weeks. He entered the street and drove home faster than usual. By the time Stephan arrived home he had chastised himself several times for the feeling of relief that flooded over him. How could he feel this way? he asked himself. A good husband would feel alone, abandoned. A good husband would be counting the days until his wife's return. But as Stephan walked through his front door, he looked around the empty house and smiled.

He walked slowly through the house, looking into every room, reveling in the quiet he found. He considered going out to dinner but hesitated to leave his new found solitude. He turned on the evening news, picked up his phone and ordered a pizza, to be delivered to his door.

Stephan sat in his chair, placed his feet on his coffee table and listened to his television. For three weeks life would return to the serenity he had known before his marriage. His home would again become his refuge, his sanctuary.

Stephan pushed aside the feelings of guilt that accompanied his sense of pleasure. After all, he had lived here for twenty years by himself. Adjusting to another person in the house had not come easy, if at all.

The doctor ignored his inside information on heart disease that night. He ate the entire pizza, skipped the nightly exercise and failed to brush his teeth before bed.

The next morning he called the hospital, inquiring about his patients and telling the head nurse he could be reached at home if needed. The doctor didn't shower or shave that day. He lounged around his home, thoroughly enjoying the silence.

During the evening news program his telephone rang.

"Is Windy home?" a soft voice inquired. Though he didn't recognize the voice it sounded vaguely familiar.

"No, she is not. May I ask who is calling?"

"This is Diana. When do you expect her home?"

"In about three weeks, Elaine has left on a missionary trip to Costa Rica."

"Elaine?"

"That is Win-dee's proper name. How do you know my wife?" Stephan determined to keep the voice talking until he recognized it.

"I met her at the Caring Pregnancy Office. She's the one who told me about my little girl."

"Nurse Westfield?" The lilt in her voice as she said those last two words finally gave her away.

"Yes. Now it's my turn to ask who I am speaking to."

"Dr. Michaels. Your 'little girl' waved at me. Do you remember?"

"I will never forget." He listened to her laugh, thinking how pleasant it sounded. "I certainly didn't realize you were Windy's husband. She didn't mention it when I told her I worked at Community General."

"Don't feel left out, Elaine did not tell me she was working at that office either." Stephan chalked up one more deceit from his innocent little wife.

"Oh, I'm sorry; I hope there's no problem. I really wanted to talk to Windy and Jenny wasn't answering her phone, so I called the PREGNANCY number. The volunteer gave me her home phone so I assumed it was okay to call her."

"No harm done," he assured her. "How are you doing?"

"Fine, that's why I wanted to talk to Wi…your wife. I wanted to thank her for her help. She really does an important work there. I assume she didn't tell you she kept me from having an abortion?"

"You assume correctly. What did she say that made you change your mind?"

"Just the truth. She told me the facts about my baby's development. Then we talked. I owe her a lot. Where did you say she went?"

"Costa Rica, on a missions trip. She is helping out a friend who was unable to go."

"Sounds exciting. I'll be sure to call her when she returns."

"She would like that."

"Good-bye, Dr. Michaels."

"Good-bye, Nurse Westfield." Stephan placed the phone back in its cradle and stared at for several minutes trying to recall the young woman's face. All he could see was the tiny person on the monitor waving at him.

Windy looked around the airplane seeing not one familiar face and felt very alone. She quickly found her seat, placed her bag on the overhead shelf, and slipped into the window seat. She scanned the windows looking for Stephan and caught a movement of blue turn from the tall window in the building. She knew it was her husband. She knew he would see no sense in watching her plane leave the runway. Her insecurity increased.

"Hi," came a voice from her right. "I'm Lana."

"Hi," returned Windy, glad some else had started the conversation. She knew she would never have the courage to do so. "I'm Wi…"

"Elaine, right? I overheard your husband saying good-bye."

Windy hesitated, looking at the group of travelers. Many were college students who talked to each other as they found their seats and stored their luggage. She wasn't much older than them, yet she felt older. All these young people were probably single, and she was already into her second marriage.

"Right, Elaine," she finished, hoping the name added a maturity to her. She shook the hand Lana offered.

"Glad to meet you. I take it you're going to Costa Rica?"

"Yes, I am, how did you know?"

"You look as scared as I feel." Both girls laughed and an instant friendship formed. By the time the plane landed in Chicago they had exchanged pertinent information plus a little conversation just for fun. Windy felt emotionally better, having left out parts of her life she wasn't ready to talk about to a stranger, her marriage to Eddie in particular.

Physically, Windy wasn't doing well. She handled the take off by concentrating on Lana's words, but the landing demanded her attention.

"Elaine, you're green!" Lana reached into the pocket on the seat in front of her. "Here use this."

Windy looked at the little paper bag with pink tulips on it. "For what?" her voice cracked.

"You know, in case you need to, um…"

Windy's eyes grew large and her head drooped to one side.

"Oh, my, well, if the plane stops quickly enough, maybe you can make it the bathroom before…"

Windy's head glided down and around, resting almost on her opposite shoulder. "Ohhhh…" she moaned.

The plane taxied toward the building, Lana pushing it with her prayers. "Just hold on Elaine, I'll tell everyone to stay in their seats until you get past." She took a look at Windy's pasty green face, "I don't think they'll need convincing."

As soon as the plane stopped, Lana whipped off hers and Windy's seatbelts, and tugged Windy down the aisle. Once inside the steel cubicle, Windy tried to sit on the floor, but there just wasn't room. The toilet had no lid, and she didn't want to sit on it. Finally, she turned on the cold water in the sink, pulled a paper towel from the holder and soaked her face in the soothing liquid.

She emerged to an almost empty plane. Lana stood nearby loaded down with her own bag as well as Windy's.

"I have your purse, too, you just work on getting off the plane." Windy silently obeyed.

Inside the terminal chaos reigned. The plane destined for Miami waited on the other end of the airport. The group rushed past other harried travelers, all determined to find the correct boarding gate in the time allotted.

Windy kept pace with the others, having relieved Lana of her double burden. She feared she would be left behind. Being on that airplane with a group of strangers was far better than being in this crazy building.

The group reached their assigned gate and fell exhausted into the chairs. A young man stood, counting heads.

"That's Tyler, I guess he's in charge of getting all of us on the planes." Lana explained to Windy who nodded. "How do you feel? You look much better."

"I feel better, but I dread getting back on another plane."

"Oh, this won't be as bad, DC 10's are smaller. You hardly feel the movement on a 747."

"How often do you fly?"

"I've flown home a couple times. I'm from out west, remember?"

"Oh, yes." Windy did remember that part of their conversation, but only because of Lana's reminder. "I don't think I'm going to make a very good traveling companion. I'm sorry, Lana."

"Don't be. Listen," Lana looked around, finally spying an empty row of seats in the corner of the waiting room. "I think we have a few minutes, why don't you lie down over there."

Windy didn't resist Lana's assistance and was soon almost comfortable. "Let me know when it's T minus 10, will you?"

"We won't leave without you, I promise."

Lana found Tyler, checked their departure time, then enlisted one of the other young men to carry Windy's bag.

The remainder of the flight Windy spent trying to sleep in a chair that couldn't replace her bed, no matter how far it reclined. The continual doses of 7-up helped but Windy longed to be off the plane. Changing planes in Miami was just as hectic as Chicago had been. Without Lana's help, Windy knew she would never have made it.

When they finally left the airport in San Jose, they boarded an old rickety bus that promised to try to take them through the mountains to the Pacific Coast.

The roads proved to be far bumpier than any air pocket and Windy would have gladly traded the bus ride for the airplane.

Halfway across the small country the bus stopped, a young woman disembarked and left behind the clear soda and crackers she had been fed on the last flight.

Chapter Forty-Five

Dear Lord, only two days left. I'm so tired, please forgive me if I fall asleep... Father, my kids... I love them...

Martin Garien surveyed the group as they emerged from the gasping vehicle. They were a good looking lot; Martin liked to see as many men as possible in the group though he knew well that some women worked as hard if not harder than some of the men. Martin could also spot the ones who would get the easier jobs. Gigglers were given a consistent job, one they could perform without having to ask for directions all the time. Small women he liked to put at the wheel of the cement mixer. They could keep track of proper amounts of sand, gravel and cement and call out orders to the handlers.

As Martin sized up his workers for the next couple weeks, the last member of the group stumbled down the steps. Damp brown hair surrounded her green face. Martin shook his head. He wouldn't be able to count on this one for at least two days.

"Okay folks, my name is Martin, I'm the camp director. Ladies, your cabin is to my left, guys, to my right. You'll want to get your gear inside, find your bunk and meet me in the cafeteria in half an hour. That's the farthest building on my right. We eat dinner at 5:30, after which time we'll have early devotions and you'll become acquainted with each other. We start work promptly at 5:45 AM tomorrow morning and since it gets dark by six here you'll want to hit the sack right away."

One girl raised her hand.

"We're not in school, miss. Speak your piece."

"Can we shower?"

"Before or after supper?"

"Whenever."

"Outside shower is behind the cafeteria, that's for when you come off the work site or out of the ocean. There is a shower in each of the cabins. I suggest you not be late for your meal." With that Martin turned to leave. He didn't like being so gruff with his new workers but he found they respected him more if he laid down the law the minute they arrived. He would have time to get to know each one of them and enjoy their company before they left.

Lana felt rebuffed. She wasn't thinking so much of herself as she was of Elaine. The poor girl needed rest and a relaxing shower more than she needed something crawling around in her stomach. She picked up a suitcase with one hand and supported Elaine with the other. "Come on, kiddo, we'll get you settled in."

Inside the cabin, Lana looked around. The main room held four beds, three smaller rooms held two beds each. She entered the nearest room, placed the suitcase on one bed and her patient on the other.

"You rest; I'll bring in your things."

"Lana?"

"Yes?" she bent close straining to hear the whisper.

"Thank you."

Lana smiled and patted the clammy skin of her friends arm. "Get some sleep and when you're rested, take a nice shower. Elaine?" The girl opened her eyes. "We'll be gone to the cafeteria, so don't be alarmed if you wake up and no one's here. Okay?" Elaine nodded. Lana opened the two small windows, hoping to give Elaine some fresh air. She pulled her blouse away from her skin and fanned it. Walking back into the main room she saw Christy coming through another doorway.

"I wonder how hot it is here."

"Too hot." Christy pulled her long curly blonde hair into a low pony tail and secured it with a thick cloth band. "Didn't someone say we're not far from the equator?"

"Tyler." Lana confirmed. "He seems to know a lot about this little country. Find your room?" she indicated where Christy had just exited.

"Yes, Julia and I thought we'd share. There's a table in there. It should hold all our make-up." She smiled a slight apology. "Unless some one else needs it."

"No, I'm sure that's just fine. Then Carrie, are you and Beth bunking together?" She addressed the quiet girl with short auburn hair.

"It appears so."

"Will that be a problem?" Lana grew concerned; since they'd be spending three weeks together she wanted to make sure all the pieces would fit well.

"Oh, no, no, it's just, well, I am rather quiet and she's so…" Carrie looked almost fearful of her next words.

"Not quiet?" Lana offered.

"Yes," Carrie accepted with a smile. As if on cue Beth danced out of the third room.

"Can you believe this? No closets, no dressers, why we'll have to literally live out of our suitcases. All my clothes are going to wrinkle, why there isn't even a decent window sill to put my toiletries on." Beth danced back into her room without waiting for a response.

"Maybe, you'll rub off on each other, Carrie," Lana suggested. And for the first time, Carrie almost laughed. "Well, c'mon ladies. If we're late for supper we'll be in trouble before we even get started."

Beth bounced out of her room, carrying several hangers full of clothing. "What am I supposed to do with these?" she asked looking at Lana.

"Lay them out on one of these beds for now. When we come back we'll rig up a make-shift closet. Okay?"

"Thanks, Lana; I knew you'd think of something. I sure am glad you're here, I have a feeling we're going to be relying on you a lot…" Beth continued her one sided conversation as she swung out of the main door.

Lana looked at Carrie and smiled. "Christy, Julia? Are you coming?"

"Be there in a sec, we have to freshen our faces," came a reply from the other room. Lana couldn't resist a peek and saw the girls had already rearranged their beds to become vanity chairs on either side of their table. Mirrors, small cases of make-up, bottles of hairspray and perfume covered the table top. Lana shook her head, wondering how their make-up would stand up to the heat and humidity they would experience tomorrow at the work site.

"We're leaving, don't be late."

"What about the other girl, Elaine, is it?" Carrie asked.

"She'll be fine, but she needs rest, more than food." Together they exited the small building, with the other two close behind them.

"Let's start with you," Martin indicated the talkative girl with short, curly dark hair who sat on his right. The short devotion and singing had gone well and Martin was anxious to find out about his new workers.

"My name is Beth Hardister. I came because I wanted to see another country and have a little vacation. I'm probably going to be a teacher, elementary maybe. Dad says he's sending me to college to find a husband." She turned and smiled at the good looking young man on her right noting his strong build and unruly blonde hair.

"Scott James. I like a challenge and wanted to come before I graduate and find a job. I'm a Phys. Ed. major. I hope to coach and teach P.E." He nodded to Carrie.

"I'm Carrie Beaumont, from Canada. I want to serve God in every way and I hope to go into missions, probably Africa, I'm intrigued by the native dialects." She passed the silent baton to the tall, brown eyed fellow next to her.

"David Walker. I wanted to serve God with other Christians in a unique setting. I plan to be a youth pastor. I'm also from Canada, and no, Carrie and I don't even know each other, yet." He smiled at her before indicating the next person's turn to speak.

"My name is Julia Armstrong," she tossed her mane of long red curls over her shoulder and her face lit up. "Adventure! Excitement! Activity! Christian fellowship and stories to tell my future students! That's why I'm here." She turned her twinkling eyes on Lana.

"I'm Lana. My friends came two years ago and were so excited they encouraged me to come. I'm in Nursing and once I get established I may consider a couple weeks each year volunteering in a country where medical help is scarce." She looked at the young man sitting next to her.

"What's your last name, Lana?" Martin interrupted.

"Turner."

"Lana Turner?" he grinned.

Lana nodded with a smile and a shrug, but it appeared only she and Martin knew the significance of her name.

"My name is Scott Bradley," stated a young man with close-cropped blonde hair and a day's growth of dark beard. "At the last camp we also had 2 Scotts and I'm often called Brad, so that's who I'll be this week. I'm spending the summer here. I intend to go into the ministry either in the states or on the mission field, wherever I'm called." He nodded to the large young man sitting on his right.

"Mike—Um, I'm Michael Scott Reames, Jr." he said slowly. "My dad's name is Michael so at home I'm Scott but at school they usually call me Mike so that would be okay. Um, I'm here cause I never been here or anywhere like here. Um, I like computers, I'm pretty good with them." He seemed to look at Martin for approval and found it in the nod of Martin's head.

"My name is Tyler Wellborn. I'll graduate next term at which time I'll join my dad's insurance business. I wanted to do something before that happens." He motioned to Christy.

"I'm Christy Colson. My brother came 2 years ago and I wanted to come then but I couldn't. His name is Andy, you might remember him?" She looked at Martin who was already concentrating."Have a picture?" he asked.

"Yes, I do. Anyway, I want to travel and serve God." She looked at the two identical young men who sat between her and Martin.

"I'm Sam, he's Eric, don't worry if you can't tell us apart, most people can't," stated the one nearest her.

The other one picked up the introduction. "The only person who always knows who we are is Mom. She named us."

"She read a weird book once that had twins named Sam and Eric," explained Sam. "She says it was a great book—we saw the updated movie version and thought it was pretty weird, even for mom."

"We wanted to join the Air Force and become fighter pilots but dad said college first. We want to go everywhere and do everything. Good of course." Eric finished.

"I am Martin Garian. I intended to be a teacher but found my calling in God's mission field. I strongly believe in international cooperation, that's why I joined Builder's Ministry. I have helped build seven camps in the last four years. This year I'm working on two sites here in Costa Rica." He turned his attention to Lana. "I saw a green lady get off the bus. I'm not surprised to see her absent tonight and expect her to be for couple days. Can anyone tell us a little about her?"

Lana started to raise her hand, only to remember her earlier rebuff.

"Her name is Elaine, um, Michaels, I believe. We met on the plane. She's married, to a doctor. She came here in place of a friend who couldn't make it. That's all I know."

"Thank you Lana. Now I might suggest you all turn in. As I said 5:30 comes awfully early."

Martin groaned inside. His first assessment of the group would appear to have been too optimistic. After listening to the reasons why these young people were here, he wasn't sure how many would actually buckle down and work. To top it off he had not only a sick girl, but a sick substitute. He hid his disappointment as he bid the group good night.

"Brad, just a minute," he spoke to his friend. "We need to discuss a few details about tomorrow's work schedule."

Chapter Forty-Six

Is it morning already, Lord? Oh, thank You, I still have time before the alarm goes off, please help me go back to sleep. Please be with my kids, let them be sleeping soundly now.

Windy opened her eyes to a shadowy darkness and tried to remember where she was. She lay quietly repeating her journey until she realized she had actually made it safely to Costa Rica. She then recalled Lana's last words to her and assumed the others were still eating supper.

"I wonder what time it is?" she asked herself aloud. Swinging her feet over the side of the bed she stood slowly and groped her way around the room until she found a door handle. Opening it gave her a little more light and she located a switch on the wall. Blinking, she surveyed the small barren room, glad to see Lana's suitcase next to hers. She entered the larger room and found the main light switch. A moment later she located the bathroom and, remembering Lana's suggestion of a shower, she returned to her belongings, finding all the necessary items.

Windy reached into the shower stall and turned on what she hoped was the hot water; she held her hand under the tap and waited. The water felt warm to her touch, but never hot. Deciding she must have turned the wrong faucet she tried the other and received the exact same result.

After a couple minutes waiting she climbed into the stall and let the refreshing water pour over her.

Back in her room she pulled on a large t-shirt and a pair of shorts, pulling her hair into a loose ponytail. As she slipped her feet into a pair of flip-flops she heard the door open.

"Elaine?" Windy chided herself for not telling Lana to call her Windy, she certainly preferred it.

"In here," she called back. Lana walked through the door.

"You look good! How do you feel?"

"Hungry," Windy laughed.

"Well, Martin and Brad were still in the dining room when we left, if you hurry, they might feed you."

"Who?"

Lana flopped on the other bed. "Martin, he's the boss, and Brad, I guess he's the foreman. Anyway you'll meet them." She lifted up on her elbow. "Are your sheets in your suitcase? I'll make the beds while you eat."

"Oh, Lana, you've done so much for me already."

"Don't worry, you'll have plenty of time to repay me."

"Thanks, again," Windy said as she slipped out the door. Two curly headed beauties walked into the cabin as Windy started out. She knew they'd been introduced at some time during the journey, but still didn't know their names.

The redhead smiled at Windy, her tired eyes twinkled. "Glad to see you upright, Elaine. I'm Julia and this is Christy. Beth and Carrie are right behind us." Windy nodded, connecting names to faces. "Lana said I might be able to get something to eat?"

Julia pointed to the furthest building, "The lights are still on, Master Martin is probably in there." Both girls giggled at Julia's remark as Windy headed towards the lighted building. She nodded to the other two girls, one of which talked non-stop as she passed while the other nodded and smiled at her.

Windy walked through the open door into a small deserted dining hall filled with tables and benches.

"Hello? Martin?"

"He's already left, can I help you?" came a male voice from the kitchen as the light went out. "Ah, you must be the green lady. Elaine, right? How are you feeling?" Windy nodded at the shadowy figure emerging from the darkened room. She sighed, resigning herself to being Elaine for the next three weeks.

"I'm Brad," the figure stepped into light, looking down at Windy. "What can I do for you?"

"Well, I slept through dinner and I'm a bit hungry."

"So the lady seeks food, uh? I'm not much of a cook but I can probably whip you up a roll and butter, maybe even a banana. Sound okay?"

"Sounds great."

Brad returned to the kitchen and flipped the light back on. "Have a seat," he called. A moment later he returned with the promised items.

"Fresh pineapple, my favorite, a banana and a warm roll with red jam, I don't know what kind." Brad sat a small tray on the table and took the seat opposite her. He picked up the slice of fruit and held it out to her.

"I never cared much for pineapple," Windy said.

"This is fresh, cut open at supper, that canned stuff isn't real, you know. But if you don't like it." His hand lifted toward his opening mouth. Windy grabbed his arm just in time.

"I'll try it," she laughed as Brad guided his hand toward her mouth. She took a bite of the pineapple, her eyes opening in surprise. "It's delicious!"

Brad shrugged with a smile, "Guess I'll have to share now." A puzzled look fell across his face. "I thought Lana said you were married."

Windy followed his gaze to her unadorned left hand that still grasped his arm. She quickly loosened her grip.

"I am. The rings are a valuable family heirloom. My husband thought I might lose them, so they're home, on his dresser."

"THE rings? Not YOUR rings."

"They're not really mine, just on loan from...my husband's dead ancestors." Windy quickly changed the subject. "So, tell me what I'm in for."

As Windy finished her meal Brad explained a little about the camp and the work to be done. He brought her a cold cola to wash her food down and told her pop was the only cold drink she would have while at camp.

"Everyone gets one pop a day, part of your meal package. If you want another it costs 25 cents."

"That's a good deal," Windy swallowed the cold liquid. "Oh, by the way, there's something wrong with the shower in the women's cabin. Who do I tell?"

"What's wrong?"

"It's just warm, no hot no cold. Really strange."

"What's strange in the States, isn't strange in Costa Rica. That's the temperature of the water as it is comes out of the ground. No hot water heaters here and no such thing as a cold glass of water."

"What about at meals? There is milk isn't there?"

Brad shook his head. "The powdered milk they have in this country is not very good and it's mixed with tap water. We usually have hot chocolate in the morning before work and juice or lemonade with the meals. This is a different country, a different culture. But it doesn't take long to get used to and besides it's only for three weeks, enjoy it!"

A few minutes later Brad looked at his watch and declared it to be far past his bedtime.

"I know you didn't get to hear Martin's pep talk but we go to bed early and get up about 5 AM. We have to get in as much work as we can before the heat of the day."

"Oh," Windy looked around the quiet dining room. "I'm not at all tired. I slept all day, between trips to the…well, I was pretty sick."

"I know," Brad grinned. "I saw you get off the bus. Look, let's take a quick stroll on the beach, it's really pleasant and maybe you'll relax enough to sleep."

They talked little. There seem to be no need for words. A sliver of the moon gave them just enough light to keep them from stepping on the busy crabs that scurried from their path. The ocean lapped gently at the wet shore. Brad explained how the tide went out at night and the beach extended out further than during the day. Windy commented on the lack of stars though there were no clouds either. Brad had noticed the same thing when he came in the beginning of the summer but didn't know why the stars weren't visible. Soon Windy grew tired and they returned to the camp, Brad walked her to the door of her cabin where they whispered a goodnight.

Chapter Forty-Seven

Thank You, Father for a wonderful night's sleep! Why I believe I can face the boss and a roomful of six year olds today. Please help my kids face whatever they must.

Windy had barely closed her eyes when someone tapped on the window. "5 o'clock ladies, time to get up." An unfamiliar voice followed the tapping. She groaned and rolled over. After sleeping so much on the plane and then when she first arrived, Windy found last night that she just wasn't sleepy, combined with the excitement and expectation of this entire adventure, it spelled a fitful night for her.

Lana's bed creaked and Windy heard her new friend sigh. "Elaine? Are you awake?"

"Yes, I have been most of the night."

"I'm sorry; want me to tell Martin you can't make it?"

"No." Windy pulled back her sheet and swung her feet from the bed. "I came here to be a part of this. Besides if I sleep now, I may not be able to again tonight."

"Okay, but I'm sure Martin will understand, well, maybe he will."

Windy reached for the light switch, "Close your eyes" she warned Lana before flipping it on. The two dressed quickly then entered the main room to see if all the others were awake.

Carrie stood by the open front door. "It's still dark out." She told the girls. "I know." Lana replied. "Is Beth up?"

"She's in the bathroom but I still don't see a light under Christy and Julia's door. I've already knocked a couple times."

Lana rapped softly on the door then opened it. "You girls have 30 seconds before I turn the light on. One. Two. Three…"

Windy heard much unhappy mumbling from the darkness. Then a voice interrupted Lana as she started the twenties. "Go ahead and turn it on."

Lana obeyed, greeted the girls good morning and closed the door. The other three took turns using the bathroom after Beth came out. When they were all ready Lana opened the girls' door again. "You two ready?"

"Ready?!?" came the irritated answer. "I've got to shower and everything. What time is it anyway?"

Lana glanced at her watch. "5:20. You have 10 minutes to get to the dining hall."

"You gotta be kidding," answered the second voice. "I can't shower in ten minutes."

"Then I suggest you get dressed first and shower during free time. We shouldn't be late, especially on the first morning."

"What's he going to do? Fire us?"

"Look girls," Lana reasoned, "You came here of your own free will. I'm not going to plead with you or yell at you. But while you're here, I think you should be considerate of everyone on the team and not just your own needs. We're leaving. See you in the dining hall." With that, Lana closed the door and looked hesitantly at the others for approval. They all silently applauded. Stepping outside Lana turned to Beth. "Why so quiet?"

Carrie patted her friend's shoulders. "Beth hasn't woke up yet. She warned me last night that she's not too sociable in the morning. I told her we'd wait patiently." Lana and Carrie laughed lightly while Beth moaned and rolled her eyes in reply.

Windy followed the small group across the already familiar lawn.

The smell of hot chocolate greeted Windy as they entered the quiet room. She noticed Lana poured herself a cup of coffee which she drank black. The girls found a table and sat down together savoring their warm drinks. A noise outside disturbed them. Three young men came into the room, Windy recognized Tyler but not the other two. The guys all poured coffee then joined the girls.

"Hi. You must be the green lady, I'm Eric," one of the strangers said as he sat across from her. Windy looked over the table into deep, dark, puppy dog eyes, surrounded by tanned skin and wavy black hair.

"Edd…" she whispered as she felt her cup sliding from her hand and color drain from her face.

"Careful!" The boy reached across the table and grabbed the cup before any of the hot chocolate spilled on Windy. "You okay?"

Windy closed her eyes and shook her head slightly. When she opened them again the face was still there, looking concerned.

"Yeah, I guess I'm… still a… a little jittery. I'm sorry, thank you. I'm really sorry." She retrieved her cup and set it securely on the table. As she did so another replica of Eddie sat down beside the first.

"Hi. I'm Sam, you must be the green lady." Windy could only nod, staring at the brothers.

The rest of the group trickled in as the sun's rays slowly lightened the morning. With the whole group present Martin asked for their attention.

"This is Katarina, she's the camp clown," he looked at the little dark haired lady with a big grin and sparkling eyes. "She's the cook and a very good one as you found out last night. She and her husband, Manuel, live here. He's the caretaker."

Katarina smiled brightly and returned to the kitchen. Martin went on to explain some of the work they would do that day. He called out names and job assignments, but hesitated when he saw Windy.

"I'm sorry, I forgot your name."

"Just call me the green lady. It got started somewhere and seems to have stuck." Windy heard Lana draw her breath in quickly.

"I believe I'm at fault there," Martin confessed in a stiff tone. "Are you up to this…?"

"Elaine, and I'm fine."

"Okay, you're on the cement mixer. You'll call for the ingredients and see that they are added in the right amounts. The mudders will let you know if your mixture needs thinning or thickening. I'll show you where everything is and how it's done." He looked over the whole group. "Any questions?" There were no takers. "Okay, lets' go."

Windy watched as the others stood and walked to the door, cups in hand. Outside, a table held two pans of hot water, one with suds, and a dish drainer. Each person washed their own cup, rinsed it and placed it to dry. Windy imitated their actions.

"How'd you sleep?" Windy turned to see Brad standing beside her.

"Good morning," she greeted him. "Not well." She admitted. "How about you?"

"Not well," he repeated and smiled. "Are you ready for this?"

"Sure. I now do adventures."

Windy caught right on, enjoying her job from the start. Scott and Mike shoveled sand and gravel into her mixture as she counted out the shovelfuls. Ten to start with. Then while Scott sprayed water in the tub Mike broke open a bag of cement and dumped half of it on top of the mixture. All the while Windy kept the machine turning, watching the texture, listening for the moment the slushing gave way to swishing.

Sam and Eric manned the wheelbarrows that took Windy's finished product to the workers. The first few times they came to the mixer they would identify themselves with a simple, hi, I'm Sam or hi, I'm Eric.

Then Windy surprised Eric by repeating his name before he could. "How do you know who I am?"

"Aren't I supposed to?"

"Nobody can tell us apart except mom."

"Well, I know you're Eric. You have on the blue shirt."

Eric grinned in understanding. A few minutes later he returned with an empty barrel and a brown shirt. "Hi, I'm Sam," he announced.

"No you're not, you're Eric."

"No, I'm Sam. See—brown shirt."

"Silly, you obviously changed with Sam."

"No, really, I AM Sam."

"No, really, you're not."

"Do we have dissension among the workers on the first day?" Martin inquired as he appeared beside the twin in question.

"No, dissension here," Windy assured him. "I really don't think Eric has any real problems either, do you?"

"No," he answered roughly as he moved away with his load.

"You're doing a fine job, Elaine. You must have mixed cement before."

"Not a drop," she confessed. "Actually Scott and Mike know exactly what they're doing, they're just letting me think I do."

Martin nodded but Windy noticed he hadn't heard. His eyes were on Lana and Carrie who stood on the two by four rafters of the nearest cabin. Scott and

Mike had already started loading the mixer with sand so she turned her attention back to her job. Martin walked away, never acknowledging her comment, his eyes watching the progress on the roof.

At 8:30 Martin halted the work and everyone returned to the dining hall for scrambled eggs and toast, served by the ever smiling Katarina. They resumed work by 9 and accomplished much in the next three hours. Hot dogs, and a fruit salad of pineapple, watermelon and bananas made up their lunch. As Windy raised a chunk of pineapple to her lips she noticed Brad watching from across the room. A smile spread across his face. Windy smiled and toasted him with her fork.

The afternoon sun made work impossible after lunch so the group enjoyed a little free time. Windy took a short nap, but felt more exhausted when she awoke an hour later. She walked to the shore and watched many of the others swimming. She noticed Eric on a surfboard. He hadn't yet mastered the skill but his determination was paying off.

At 2:30 Martin summoned the group back and they worked until 6 pm when he dismissed them for showers before dinner. Windy could smell the spaghetti before she could even see the dining hall.

After everyone had washed their dishes and wiped off the tables, Martin and Brad moved the chairs into a circle for the service. Since Windy had missed the get acquainted time the night before Martin asked her to tell a little about herself and why she came.

"I'm subbing for a friend," she confessed. "But I'm almost glad she was unable to come, now."

"Even after your green experience?" Martin smiled for the first time.

"Even so, but I warn you. I hope you have other transportation lined up for the trip home, cause I'm not getting back on that bus!" A couple of the others laughed.

"No problem," Martin said without hesitation. "The family across the road have a donkey we could borrow. You'll just have to start a couple days earlier than the rest of us." Windy smiled, glad to see Martin relax a little.

"I thought I'd just have Eric teach me to surf. I'd probably beat all of you home." She looked at Eric. "What do you think?"

"I'm Sam," he tried.

"No you're not."

"How do you do that?" Sam asked. "Only mom can do that."

"Shut up, dummy, you just admitted she was right."

"Oh," Sam frowned.

Martin's fears were never realized. Though the group wasn't quite what he expected, they worked better together and accomplished more than any of the other groups he had worked with for some time. He marveled that even the gigglers, and there were two, worked consistently and never complained.

Windy kept her promise to Jenny and wrote down every sight, smell and action in her journal. She took pictures of everything and made a note of all the pictures she took. She detailed accounts of the country, the camp and the workers.

Stephan looked at the long cafeteria line. He had hoped to grab a quick bite. As he was about to turn away a young nurse who had just picked up a tray motioned to him.

"Dr. Michaels, are you in a hurry?"

He nodded, trying to place her. "Doctors are always in a hurry."

"How well I know. Come, you can take my place."

"Only if you'll join me, Nurse Westfield." he said as he slipped into line behind her.

"Thank you, I'd like that. But please, call me Diana."

"As in Lady Diana?"

She smiled and nodded, a slight blush accenting her natural beauty.

Stephan's quick bite turned into a leisurely half hour as he and Diana talked of her upcoming event. The young woman's excitement was contagious and when Stephan finally excused himself, his desire to experience the anticipation of his own child grew stronger, as did his displeasure with his wife for her inability to grant his longing.

Chapter Forty-Eight

Lord, I've learned so much this week. I feel as though I've been the student and my little ones have been the teachers. I've explained the plan of salvation to six year olds and Lord, they understood. May my kids understand that easily and accept that readily.

Windy's days were filled with working, eating and sleeping. No one knew the actual temperature because Martin allowed no thermometer on the camp, saying he didn't want to know how hot it was. But Windy thought it was really for their benefit, knowing would just make them more uncomfortable.

Two days after arriving she sat on the beach recording her observations when Eric came dripping up to her, one of the camp surfboards under his arm.

"Do you want to learn to surf?"

"Why?"

"You said you were going to surf home so you wouldn't have to take the bus, now's your chance to learn."

Windy remembered the comment well and almost wished it were a possibility. She dreaded the trip back.

In just two days Eric had improved drastically at the sport. Windy had noted his progress in her journal.

"Sure, why not!" she finally answered. "I need another adventure."

That afternoon, Windy swallowed gallons of salt water, landed on her face too many times to count and collided with Eric or the board on a regular basis.

But her will power paid off and at the end of an hour when she drug her exhausted body out of the water Eric gave her a quick hug.

"You surprised me. I kept expecting you to give up. I've never seen any one take so much abuse before." He ran off to lean the board against the stone fence then turned to Windy. "Same time tomorrow?"

Windy barely found the energy to nod, wondering how she would get through the last three hours of work.

Once she showered in the outdoor shower and put dry clothes on, Windy was amazed at how good she felt. That night she slept soundly, waking up in the same position she had fallen asleep in.

During the morning work sessions she found herself looking forward to the hot afternoon, hoping Eric was serious about another lesson. She had given up the idea of surfboarding home but found herself fascinated with the idea of learning this unusual sport.

At lunch Windy sat beside Eric. "Are you ready to play teacher again?" she asked.

"There's a price for my services today," he informed her.

"You want my free coke?" she asked, aware of how precious those cold bottles were in this climate.

"No, I want information."

Windy listened then tilted her head when he didn't answer. "Yes? What kind of information do you want? If it's free medical advise Lana appears to be our resident nurse."

"I want to know how you can tell us apart."

"Oh. Is that still bothering you?"

Eric nodded. "No lessons til you tell me."

Windy considered from a moment. No one here knew about Eddie, no one knew she was only 22 and on her second marriage. Did she really want to reveal it? Was learning to surf worth being vulnerable? And did she want to tell Eric? Lana maybe, or even Brad they were both older, a little more understanding. Eric was just a kid, fresh out of high school.

Eric downed his warm lemonade. "Take it or leave it," he said.

"You set me up, didn't you?" Windy asked. "You knew I'd be hooked on surfing and at your mercy."

Eric grinned. "That's what I hoped for. I figured if you could be caught as hard as I was, I had it made."

"You're a rascal, Eric." She hesitated. "Let me think about it."

"Sure, you know where to find me. On the board," he said enticingly, his eyes beckoning her just as Eddie's had. "In the water," his eyes brows lifted and his chin started to dimple as his smile grew, just as Eddie's did. "Enjoying myself…"

"Oh, get out of here." Windy grabbed his plate and cup adding them to her own dishes. "I'll think while I wash."

He winked his right eye, just like Eddie did and headed for the beach. Windy didn't decide. Her mind kept replaying scenes of life as it used to be. Eddie in the apartment sitting at the table, lifting his fork just like Eric did. Eddie's stance, so similar to Eric's she could recognize the boy from across the camp. Yes, the same similarities could be seen in Sam. No doubt they were identical twins. But Eric held himself like Eddie, he moved and walked like Eddie. She could not ignore what she saw. And Eric loved life like Eddie. Sam may look exactly like his brother, but he didn't have Eric's enthusiasm for simple everyday living. These two strangers, Eddie and Eric, shared a spirit that thrived on life itself. How could she explain all that to an 18 year old? More importantly, did she want to?

Still reviewing those scenes Windy returned to her cabin and changed into her bathing suit. She walked toward the beach, but realized little of what she did. Her heart and mind were in a small apartment, sharing moments with the man who still shared her heart.

"Lesson first," She informed Eric after he came in from a near perfect ride.

"How do I know you'll pay up?"

"I'm trustworthy, you have my word."

"You'll be too tired to talk."

"Maybe, but if you don't agree, I'll tell everyone but you."

"You wouldn't. Would you?"

She shrugged, giving him a wry smile. He bargained like Eddie, too, and she knew how to handle that.

"Half a lesson," he began dealing. "Say half an hour. Then you tell, then we finish the lesson."

"Half a lesson, half an explanation."

He tossed his head to one side, his frustration showing. She knew just what to do next. "Take it or leave it." She repeated his earlier words knowing she had him.

"All right," he agreed, and his smile returned, just like she knew it would. His spirit simply couldn't be dampened.

A short time later, they agreed to end this half of the lesson. Windy made no progress anyway, her mind on what she would say to the boy.

They grabbed their towels and sat down on the surfboard avoiding what Martin called the black sand that covered the Pacific coast.

Windy took a deep breath. "You must promise me this is between us. Not a word to anyone, even Sam. OK?"

"Sure," Eric readily agreed as she thought he would.

"You remind me of my husband." There she said it, she couldn't back out.

"I look like a doctor, huh? My dad will be glad. What is it, my handsome face, my amazing intelligence?"

"No," she said quietly. "Not the doctor, my,... well, my first husband."

"You mean you're on your second?"

The words made the girl wince. Why am I doing this? she asked herself as she nodded a reply. "Yes," she hoped she could sum this up neatly and be done with it. "I got married right out of high school, it didn't work. You act a lot like him. It's that simple. Ready to surf?"

"So you were like too young and just made this big mistake?"

"No," Windy pulled her knees close and hugged them. "We were young, but that wasn't why we split." She thought for a moment. "I'm not sure I'd call it a mistake."

"You still love him?"

Do you? she asked herself. Again she thought of Eddie as he had been while they dated and in that first year of marriage. She remembered watching him in a crowded room and the emotion that surged through her being.

"I still love the man I married. But he changed."

"And you didn't, right?"

"No, Eric, I didn't."

"Who left, who got the divorce?"

"He left. I got the divorce."

"But you still love him. Maybe he would have come back; you should have given him a chance."

Windy's eyes suddenly filled with tears, they spilled down her quivering chin. Her mind replayed that horrible scene when Eddie returned on their second anniversary. She'd only spoke of it once before, to Stephan; hadn't allowed herself to think of it, because reliving it was so painful.

261

"He did come back," she managed to whisper. She swallowed hard, forcing herself to concentrate on the movement of the waves, pushing those hurtful memories back into storage. She sniffed, rubbing the tears from her face. "But he…he left again. And that's that. Ready to surf?"

"How long were you married?" Eric ignored her question, pushing her back into her memories.

"Two years."

"How long you been married to the doctor?"

"Almost as long."

"Why'd you marry him if you still loved the first guy?"

Windy couldn't answer that one. She didn't know. She now realized she didn't love Stephan though she thought she did at the time. No, it was his idea, his insistence, his planning. She really had little to do with the whole ordeal. Stephan just took control and she went along with it, believing it to be the best thing.

"How am I like the first guy?"

Again the girl winced. First guy, second guy, it sounded so immoral. "His name is Eddie," she paused. "You look like him, in almost every way, hair, skin, build, you have the same sad puppy dog eyes. You walk alike, move alike, hold your fork the same way." She smiled. "You even think alike. Life is important to you; fun and adventure are what you want."

"But you knew it the first day, the first time you even looked at me, before you had a chance to see those things."

Windy nodded. "There's just that something about you, I don't know, but it's there."

"Is Eddie a Christian, too?"

Windy caught herself before she laughed out loud. "No, he's not."

"Does it bother you to see me? Do you sometimes think I'm him?"

This time Windy did laugh. "Too many times. Sometimes it just seems that I should walk over to you and touch you, hold you. Eddie and I touched a lot. I miss that."

Eric grinned. "Sounds good to me." He sat quietly for a moment. "Were you mad when he left?"

"Hurt," Windy nodded. "Very hurt." She began to cry again, this time the tears wouldn't be held back. She pressed her face against her knees tightening her muscles against the sobs.

Eric waited for her crying to pass. He offered nothing, just waited. When she looked up again and wiped her face with her hands he asked, "Ready to surf?"

"I can't believe how well you're learning," Eric complimented Windy two nights later. It was Saturday and since they could actually sleep in the next morning the group decided to hold services on the beach. After the closing prayer Windy noticed Brad looking in her direction, he stood and walked toward her. A second later Eric sat at her side.

"That's not what you were saying today," she reminded him.

"I was just frustrated. Every time you stand up it's like you think, oh I can't do this and you just topple over. You gotta have more faith in yourself."

Windy shook her head. "I have no reason to have faith in myself. I seem to botch up most everything I do."

Several of the others were leaving the fire; Windy noticed Martin and Lana slowly walking down the beach and realized they were often in each others company. Brad stood by the fire, staring into the dying flames.

"I find that hard to believe."

"You sound like Stephan! Why not just say you think I'm lying?" She tried to hold the contempt from her voice.

"Because I don't. I'm just surprised you would think so little of yourself. I mean, you're really a neat lady."

"A neat lady, huh? You of all people should know better than that."

"Why?"

Windy looked around. She and Eric were the only ones still seated by the fire. "You know why."

Eric remained quiet for a moment. "Cause you told me about Eddie?" Windy nodded. "I don't see it that way. I figure he had a good thing and didn't realize it."

"A good thing would have been more important than a beer can."

"So you think the blame lies with you rather than Eddie's drinking problem?"

They sat silently for a while, watching the last embers of the fire die off. Windy's mind began replaying memories, good and bad, of her life with Eddie. She felt the tears swelling in her eyes and the lump growing in her throat and knew she must think of something else.

"Do you have a girlfriend, Eric?"

She felt rather than saw his smile. "Yeah. Angie. We've been going together for two years. This is the first time we've been separated."

"Do you miss her?"

"So much, I try not to think about it. You remind me a little of her. Guess that's why I decided to teach you to surf. I don't feel so lonely with you around."

"Do you have future plans?"

"Oh, yes! I'm gonna marry that girl. She's a senior in high school this year. We've talked about waiting til I'm out of college, but I don't want to wait four years."

"What's the alternative; can you support her and go to school? Will you let her support you?"

"I don't know and honestly, I'm not worried about it. I know God wants us together and I know He has a plan far better than any I can come up with."

"Is she going to go to college?"

"She doesn't want to. She says the best profession is womanhood, being a wife and mother. That's all she's ever dreamed about being."

Silence reigned again as each fell into their own thoughts.

"Did he hurt you? I mean, more than just your heart?"

"Yes, he did."

"Do you think of him when you see me?"

Windy nodded. "Sometimes I want you to hold me. I guess I really want Eddie to hold me again. I felt good in his arms. And in some ways I miss him, a lot. Stephan is a good man, he takes care of me, but there's something missing. Eddie gave me life. He gave me a reason for getting up in the morning, a reason to look forward to the end of the day. Well, for a while anyway, before things went bad."

"Before he started drinking you mean."

"Yes."

The logs shifted again and the last ember disappeared from their sight.

"Thanks for trusting me," Eric said quietly. "I assure you everything you've said is between us."

"Thanks. I'm glad I told you. I rather feel like I'm not being honest with the others."

"You haven't lied. Your past is no one's business but God's. It's not something to be ashamed of."

"Married for the second time at 22 is nothing to be ashamed of?"

"No. It isn't. If you really tried to make it work like you said, then you did all that could be expected. I'm gonna keep you in my prayers. I know God had me listen for a reason, if He tells me anything, Elaine, I'll let you know."

"One other thing? My name is Windy. Windy Elaine. Lana overheard Stephan calling me Elaine at the airport and it just became too awkward to try to correct it. But, when it's just you and I, would you call me Windy?"

Eric laughed. "I knew it. I knew you weren't an 'Elaine' it just doesn't fit you. But Windy,...yeah! That makes much more sense.

Chapter Forty-Nine

What a wonderful service this morning, Father! My little ones made me so proud when they recited their memory verses without hesitation. I pray, Father, that my kids have learned them too. Oh that I might have taught them myself. But I gave up that privilege, didn't I, Lord?

Sunday morning Martin made his morning window knocking rounds at 8 am instead of 5. A breakfast of pancakes and delicious homemade syrup awaited the group. They were given time to shower and dress for morning service in the dining hall. They sang several songs and choruses, none of which Windy knew by heart as the others seemed to, though she had heard many of them nightly. Martin talked for 10 or 15 minutes and hard as she tried, Windy couldn't concentrate on his words.

A delicious dinner of chicken and rice followed then some one decided to play volleyball. Remembering the last disaster Windy quietly slipped from the group. She retrieved her camera and note book from the cabin and took pictures of the crew at play while jotting down her thoughts for Jenny.

Later that afternoon the group settled into relax mode. Mike challenged the guys to a game of football and several of them accepted the challenge. Christy and Julia caked their faces with mud packs hoping to ward off the aging effects of the sun.

Brad found Windy sitting on the beach, her brown hair glistened from the long periods in the sun. Her complexion had deepened and her eyes held a healthy glow.

"You're not playing football?" she asked when he sat next to her on the black sand.

"Not my game. I'm too fragile."

She looked at his muscled arms and broad shoulders and smiled. "I doubt that."

"What's on your agenda today?"

"Nothing. Absolutely nothing. Here I am in a beautiful Latin American country, a once in a lifetime venture, and when I'm not working all I can think about is sleeping. In a couple weeks I'll be home, with all the same routines, and obligations and all I'll remember is that I wanted to sleep on my only day off."

"You've done some surfing, I've noticed."

"Oh, yes, I counted that. It comes under 'work'."

"You don't enjoy it?"

"I love it. And it's certainly a highlight of my time here, but I can't just sit back and enjoy the fact of where I am when I'm surfing. I'd drown!"

"I see your point. I've been here all summer and I have days off between teams so I hadn't thought about how you guys must feel."

"The friend I came for asked me to keep an account of my experiences for her. So I'm always thinking of how I can express this and describe that. But after photographing one volleyball game I decided not today. Today is mine. The journal's back in my room and it's staying there!"

They listened to the sounds of the waves against the shore, disturbed by the far-a-way sounds of the football players. Windy chuckled.

"It's hard to believe just a couple days ago I questioned you about the lack of stars in the sky. Since then I haven't even looked at the night sky."

"Until last night," he reminded her.

"Yes," she nodded. "But last night I watched the faces of my new friends, committing to memory their looks, their voices. I am awed by the security I see here.

"Security?"

"In God. Everyone here, even Christy and Julia, knows just who they are and pretty much where they're going. It must be nice to be so certain."

"It is Elaine, and there's no reason why you can't have that security. We've given our hearts to Christ. That's the key."

"Hey, you two, how's the sand?" Martin asked. He and Lana stood so near the couple Windy wondered how she had missed seeing them arrive.

"It's beautiful, come on down," Brad invited.

"We're going for a walk," Lana explained. "I'm determined to find a sand dollar, come along."

Windy could feel Brad hesitate. She admitted to herself she would enjoy just talking to him, continuing the discussion they had started and yet not sure she was ready for it.

"I'm game," she volunteered. "How about you?"

"Sure," Brad replied with slightly less enthusiasm.

Windy watched Martin's actions toward Lana as they walked along the shore. He listened to every remark she made and tried hard to answer all her questions about the ocean, Costa Rica and the camp. Windy remembered Lana saying she felt intimidated by Martin when they arrived and wondered if this was truly the same man. Even Windy had seen the obvious improvement in his attitude.

When the walkers returned, a light meal of cold sandwiches and fruit awaited them. The four entered the dining area where most of the others had already gathered so they sat together, Brad and Windy sharing a large bowl of fresh pineapple.

After the meal had been cleared Brad retrieved his guitar from the corner and began playing a chorus he had taught them in Spanish. This one Windy knew since they all learned it together. She enjoyed the group singing, but found tears in her eyes as Carrie and David sang a song common to the churches in Canada. Brad accompanied everyone on the guitar; it seemed he only needed to hear the melody and he could pick out the notes. Though he knew many songs and choruses by heart he simply couldn't carry a tune. Yet Windy marveled at his ability and determination. Julia also sang a song that touched Windy's heart and the tears that formed during the first song spilled during the second. She brushed quickly at her eyes, hoping no one had noticed until she heard Brad miss a note. When she looked she realized he, too, had to wipe away drops from his cheeks.

Martin asked for prayer requests then suggested people pray as led. Windy wasn't sure what that meant but since he didn't ask her personally she intended to remain quiet. Several people prayed, Lana being one of them. Windy listened to her talk to God, she sounded just like Jenny. Windy hoped that some day she would too.

Martin talked for a short time, encouraging each of the group to recognize their own God given abilities. He affirmed the need for each job and each worker comparing them to the body of Christ. Windy didn't exactly follow his words but marked the scripture in her Bible intending to read it later. Then Martin opened the floor for testimonies. Windy remembered this term from Jenny's church so she wasn't caught completely off guard.

Brad stood quickly. "This is the third camp I've worked in this summer beside spending a couple weeks in the city with a door to door outreach. I've made many new friends and grown much closer to God because of my time here. I know all of you know God in some way or other. It's my prayer that none of you leave here without knowing Him not only as your personal Savior but also as the Lord of your life." He looked at Windy before sitting down.

Lana stood. "My family didn't go to church during my childhood except a couple times on Easter. But we had a Bible and I remember wanting to read it. I would start at the front, like all books, but never made it past Genesis, which is probably for the best. I'm sure I would not have liked God if I had read Leviticus at age 9. But I knew I wanted God. As a teenager I met kids who went to church and invited me. After attending a few different churches one really clicked. I knew I'd found a home and I asked Christ into my life. For years I thought there was something different, something special about me because I wanted God and no one else in my family really took an interest. I thought He must have some wonderful purpose for my life. One day I read Romans 8:28. You all know it. At least the first part. 'For we know that God causes all things to work together for good…' But the second part caught me off-guard. '…to those who love Him, to those HE CALLED according to His purpose.' It about knocked me over. I thought wanting God made me special, then I realized I was special because HE wanted me. He is, as Brad said, my Savior, but He's also Lord of my life. I simply can't imagine life without Him. God does have some special purpose in my life, just as He does for yours. If you haven't turned your life over to Him, completely, you just don't know what you're missing." Lana sat down but all eyes were still on her except Beth's, who looked out the window.

Several others shared bits of their life, some told how they came to Christ, others shared an unusual situation where God intervened.

At 9 o'clock Martin had to stop the testimonies, promising to allow time each night for this type of sharing. They sang one last song about loving each other. When the final note ended Brad offered a short prayer for restful sleep for everyone. Putting down his guitar he walked over to Lana and told her how much he appreciated her testimony. Then he hugged her, an action Windy found reassuring. She had received many hugs in Jenny's church and always looked forward to visiting there if for no other reason. Stephan's hugs had grown less frequent and when he did honor her with one, it was only a prelude.

Brad's hug seemed to create a chain reaction and suddenly everyone was hugging. The walls of uncertainty people automatically build around them for protection were no longer needed by this group. And with the hugs came the whispered words I love you. Windy smiled, remembering when Jenny had first said those words to her. Windy had felt uncomfortable yet comforted, because she knew Jenny's love was pure.

As Windy looked around her she realized she stood alone. No one had yet offered her the hug that she knew she desperately needed. Did they exclude her because she had remained silent during testimony time? She really had nothing to share. Brad's prayer hit her right in the heart. She still didn't know just what it meant to accept Christ as Savior. And she certainly didn't know Him as Lord. No, right now Stephan was her lord, the one she lived for.

As these thoughts began to undermine the good she'd been sensing all evening she felt a touch on her shoulder and turned into it. Brad stood beside her. She caught her breath, hoping beyond hope that he would actually hug her. Hug her tight and deep. Lana had offered a hug now and then, and Jenny's were always welcome. But the desire to feel a man's strong arms around her overwhelmed Windy almost to the point of pushing herself into his arms.

"Can I walk you back to your cabin?" he asked quietly. Windy nodded her consent.

They walked slowly, noticing that a few of the others headed in the same direction. None of them were ready to arrive at their destination, but knew a walk on the beach would be forbidden by Martin at this hour.

"Elaine, have you accepted Christ as your Savior?" Brad asked as they stopped to sit under a tall palm tree. Windy hesitated. She thought of the times she'd spent in church, the books of the Bible she had read. She believed in that Book, even looked for answers to some of her questions there. But she had never taken the steps that had allowed Cora to call herself a new creature, unsure of what it all meant.

"I…I don't think so," came her weak reply.

"Do you want to now?"

"I...I'm not sure. I'm not sure what it's all about."

"Do you love God?"

Windy nodded hesitantly.

"Have you read about Jesus' birth and death?"

Again she nodded. "Do you have any questions? Something in particular that just puzzles you?"

"I don't know," Windy admitted. Then she smiled at Brad. "I'm sorry, I must sound really confused to you. And maybe I am. Right now I'm experiencing two different types of religious people. They both believe they're right and have Bible verses to support their views. I know the truth is there somewhere and I know if God wants me, He'll lead me to it, and to Him." Windy surprised herself with these words that had yet to show themselves as thoughts. But now she knew they had been there all along. "Brad, you said you prayed that everyone would know God before they leave. Would you mind, saying a little extra one for me?"

"I welcome the opportunity." Brad stood and pulled Windy to her feet, naturally slipping his arms around her. Windy felt her arms encircle his slender waist and she leaned her head against his chest. She felt him inhale and knew he wanted to speak. Would he whisper the words she heard in the dining hall? What did they really mean? Was it right for him to say such a thing to a married woman?

"God bless you, Elaine," he said.

Windy almost cried with disappointed relief. She wanted Brad to say he loved her. She wanted to be a part of that inner circle of believers, sharing the most precious feeling in the world, without fear or conditions. She wondered if he had said those words to Lana. Were they reserved only for the special elite, those who claimed Christ as Savior? But no, Jenny had stated her love for Windy even knowing that Windy hadn't yet taken that all important step.

As these thoughts swirled around Windy's mind, Brad's arms remained strong and protective. She knew she should pull away. Knew if she stayed here any longer she would never want to leave. It wasn't just Brad, though she couldn't imagine holding on to Martin or any of the other men like this, even Eric; no, she didn't seek the person, she sought the security. A security not found in Jenny's soft, sweet hugs, or in Stephan's demanding ones. This felt more like the arms of Jesus Himself. Strong, comforting, assuring. What would

271

it be like to be held by Jesus? She would never know until she proclaimed Him as Savior.

Brad moved slightly, shifting his weight and Windy realized just how tightly she clung to him. Suddenly embarrassed, she pulled away.

"Thank you, Brad, for…for being such a good friend." The words sounded hollow to her and she wondered what Brad must think of this crazy married woman who clung to him. "And for saying you'll pray for me," she added hoping that sounded more sincere.

"Prayer is always a pleasure. Thank you for the opportunity." He patted her shoulder then turned toward the beach. "At least you're not the last one in," he nodded toward a couple who stood gazing into the ocean, their identity a mystery without the moonlight.

Chapter Fifty

Father, tonight in Bible study we talked about handing control over to You. About not worrying and trying to make things be okay. So tonight I'm handing it all over to You; my life, my job, especially my kids. I'll still pray for them, of course, but I'll no longer worry about them. They belong to You and I place them in Your capable hands.

Windy avoided Brad the next couple days. She felt so guilty for enjoying his company, his words, and especially his arms around her. She threw all her energy into her surfing lessons and stuck close to Eric. Their relationship was growing but it had safe boundaries. Windy knew Eric looked at her as a sister, an older married sister. Since first confiding in Windy how much he missed Angie he now talked freely about the girl.

As much as Windy avoided Brad, he seemed to seek her out. He would often appear beside her at the dining table. When time for evening worship came Windy lingered in the cabin until she knew Brad would already be seated. During work she felt secure behind her cement mixer, knowing Brad kept busy in other parts of the work area. But one day Martin came to her.

"We're caught up on the cement and need a sidewalk dug and framed around the newest cabin. When you finish this bag, go see Brad."

She spent that afternoon working beside the man she'd been trying so hard to avoid.

Her experience in handling a shovel was limited to her flower bed. She never knew digging a simple six-inch trench could be so much work. Brad sensed her inability to keep up with him and several times found little things for her to do that would allow her a few minutes rest.

By the end of the day it was apparent Brad's reaction to last Sunday night was nothing like hers. She realized he spoke to her much like Eric did, as a sister or a friend. She began to understand what being in the family of God really meant.

At supper that night she welcomed Brad's presence beside her, the tension she'd been feeling had disappeared. She found she could appreciate Brad as a Christian not just a man.

Diana placed her clip board on the counter and picked up her purse. Her hand brushed against her protruding belly. At six months her baby kept an active schedule. Now the little one kicked against her mama's hand. Diana instantly felt for the next kick smiling when it came.

"See you tomorrow," she said to Bernie Laswell.

"Okay, dear. Are you feeling okay? You look a little peaked."

"I'm fine." Diana smiled at the motherly nurse. In truth she wasn't fine. She dreaded going home to an empty apartment. Mark had left the day before. He'd been waiting for her yesterday when she arrived home and delivered an ultimatum—him or the 'kid'. Diana had made her choice two months earlier, and waited for Mark to notice. Within hours he packed his things and left with a warning not to expect any support from him for a kid he didn't want.

Though Diana had prepared herself for this time and had even accepted it before it happened, she still disliked the idea of being alone. She wished the next three months would fly by so she wouldn't have to be.

She stepped into the elevator and looked into Dr. Michaels' smiling eyes. She thought how lucky his wife was to have such a gentle, caring husband.

"Difficult day, Diana?"

"Yes," she replied quietly.

"Not having any problems, are you?"

She touched her belly in an affectionate gesture. "Not a one. Dr. Sells says we're both fine and healthy."

"That is good to hear. Are you eating properly?"

She smiled at his concern. "Oh, yes, this little girl is too important to me, not to take care of her."

The doors opened and the couple walked through the main lobby.

"You still insist the baby is female? Have you had confirmation yet?"

"The only confirmation I need is here." She placed her hand over her heart. "Win…your wife was the first person to identify my baby as a girl. It just seems right."

"My wife has no knowledge by which to make such a judgment. You would do better to place your trust in medical technology. Does the father wish for a girl also?"

Dr. Michaels held the door open for her and they passed into the late afternoon sun.

"The father is gone." Diana said, shielding her eyes. "He's not ready for a family."

"I am sorry to hear that. Is that the reason for your difficult day?"

She nodded. "Empty apartment syndrome."

"I understand. I admit my house is a little on the quiet side these days." They stood beside her small black sports car and Stephan reached for the door handle.

"Been eating out a lot lately?" she asked.

"As a matter of fact, yes. It never bothered me before I married but I have grown accustomed to home cooked meals."

"Listen, uh," she hesitated. "I really don't want to sit in that lonely apartment tonight. How about coming over and I'll cook you a meal no restaurant can match?"

"I'd be a fool to pass up that offer. What time?"

Diana suggested 6:30 then gave the good doctor directions to her house. An uneasy feeling accompanied her home. She tried to silence it by saying she was just paying back a kindness to the woman who helped her. Surely Dr. Michaels would not interpret this as anything but a friendly gesture. She convinced herself the feeling had no basis.

That evening Diana Westfield fell under the charm of the gentle doctor. She found herself wishing her baby could have such a loving father. When she closed the door after her guest she determined to avoid him from that point on. No need to make life any more confusing.

Days drifted by and Windy began to ask herself if she had ever lived anywhere else. She liked waking up in the morning knowing just what was expected of her. Standing in the doorway and gazing out at the ocean calmed her deep inside. Evenings of Christian fellowship and worship came so natural she simply couldn't imagine life any other way. Slowly a change took place in her, a change so deep and natural she hardly knew it was happening. Her first thoughts in the morning were of God usually in the form of a chorus that had been sung the night before. Her last thoughts at night lingered on Him. His presence permeated her inmost being. She spent much of her time reading the Bible, and would start conversations with anyone working within hearing distance. Her thirst for the Word grew daily and her new friends praised God for the change they witnessed.

Eric watched and listened to his friend and when the time seemed right, he decided to share his thoughts with her.

Windy had graduated from student to surfing buddy in a short time. One afternoon they finished an hour of pure enjoyment and as they emerged from the water Eric sat her down on the beach.

"I've been thinking and praying about you," he announced, noticing Windy's surprised look. "Well, I told you I would."

The girl smiled and nodded. "I guess you did." Eric noted that even her voice had changed; it no longer held a hint of fear or apprehension.

"Well, I want to talk about you and your first husband."

"Okay." Her quiet acceptance encouraged Eric to continue.

"What if he had died instead of leaving? What would you have done?"

Windy looked startled but rather than question him, he could see her considering an answer.

"I would have mourned. I'm sure I would have found his death quite hard to accept."

"Why?"

"Why?! Because he's young and because a part of me would have died with him."

"Would you go on living?"

Windy shrugged. "I guess I'd have to."

"How long would you mourn?"

"I don't know."

"Would you mourn forever?"

"I doubt it."

"How about just a couple months?"

"Probably longer than that." Eric could see she wanted to ask her own questions and he had more to say before he would let her.

"Would you marry again?" he asked quickly.

"Probably."

"How soon? A month? A year?"

"I don't know. Not soon, not after what Eddie and I had. I would want to let it all sink in first. Where are you taking this?" she finally asked.

"The way I see it, you don't just lose someone you love through death. You can lose them in lots of ways, to another person, or to a lifestyle. Either way, you lose. When they die, you know they're gone, you go through a period of mourning and you get on with your life. But if you lose them to something besides death, you don't usually mourn because it's doesn't seem so final. Do you think you'll ever get back with Eddie?"

Windy shook her head. "No, of course not."

"Did you enjoy the time you had with him?" Windy nodded as he continued. "Do you cherish the memories you made together?" Again she nodded.

"Well he's gone. Maybe he's not dead, but you can't have him anymore. You lost someone very important to you. It was taken away and because he didn't die, because it was a bad situation you think you're not supposed to mourn. But your husband is gone. You'll never have him or that part of your life back. You began another part of your life so quickly, you didn't give yourself a chance to mourn, Windy, and I think you should have. Let him go."

They sat for several minutes, both reviewing Eric's words. Finally he slipped his arm around her and gave her a little hug. He kissed her temple and patted her shoulder. "Okay?"

"Okay." She whispered.

Eric stood and retrieved his surfboard. He walked away slowly, knowing Windy needed time with her Lord now.

The waves continued to touch the sand one after another as they always had. The sun moved ever so slightly on its westward course. The breeze tickled the palms overhead causing them to rustle with quiet laughter. Nature took no notice of the girl who sat on its beach, her life in the process of changing for ever.

Windy brought memory after memory to surface, she explored each one, good and bad. She laughed as she remembered the good times, and allowed the tears to flow unhindered as the bad ones replayed in her mind. Slowly, action by action, event by event, Windy let Eddie leave her life. She watched him go just as she watched the waves retreat into the unknown and be swallowed up by the ocean, losing their identity to become part of the greater whole.

Windy saw her life now, just as she viewed that ocean, made up of a thousand little pieces. Whether they be events or people, victories or defeats, they disappeared. The important wave became the next one to surface. Yet Windy knew that without each anonymous wave the ocean wouldn't exist, so she needed each event to make up her life. And just as the tide controlled the length and timing of the waves, so God controlled each situation in her life, drawing her closer to where she belonged as the ocean drew the breaking surf home.

Afternoon break ended and the last work period began; without Windy. She sat on the beach, sifting through a short lifetime, communicating with the only One she need be in touch with. Eric went to Martin and asked that the girl not be disturbed. The workers continued to make an impact on the camp while God made an impact on one girl's life.

Lana summoned her friend in time to change clothes for supper and afterwards they walked on the quiet beach, the sounds of evening worship in the background. They spoke little. Mostly they just walked, content to be together.

Chapter Fifty-One

Father I have such a longing in my heart tonight. I left my kids to You. Where are they, what are they doing? I know they are safe in Your hands, but I hurt so much inside when I think they may never come to know You. Please, Lord, please speak to their hearts, tell them how much You love them. Convict them of their need for You.

During lunch the next day Martin made a surprising announcement. "We have completed our work. You folks have used up all my materials and I won't be getting any in until Thursday. You've dug every hole and trench we'll ever need, you've clean up every downed pineapple and palm leaf. I want to thank all of you for your hard work. We leave tomorrow morning around nine so you'll want to get your belongings packed and your cabins cleaned up, but there will be no afternoon work period."

A cheer rose from the group and Martin smiled as he sat down, looking from one excited face to another. He heard talk of a football game from the guys while the girls mentioned relaxing. Eric jumped up on a bench and pretended to surf. "You know where I'll be," he said to no one in particular.

After lunch clean up the group returned to their cabins to begin cleaning and packing. Soon they spread out over the camp engaging in their last day activities.

Windy strolled through the grounds that had served as her home for almost three weeks. Each spot, whether it represented work or leisure, held a special memory for the girl. *'Christy sat here mixing cement in her little bucket;'* Windy thought as she stood next to what was left of the gravel pile. *'This is where Ty lost his footing and almost landed on Mike,'* Windy looked up at the finished roof. The cement mixer looked bare without the twins beside it waiting for the next load of gray sludge.

These were the buildings her team had finished. This roof they framed, making it ready for the next group to tile. And there was the sidewalk she and Brad had dug; it's long dried cement already showed signs of use. She pictured Lana and Carrie sitting on two by two boards twelve feet off the ground, waiting for Beth to bring more roofing tiles. And beautiful Julia; probably the hardest worker of them all. She was always in motion, never needed to ask what to do next, she just seem to know.

At the beach Windy thought of the dark sky, adorned with very few stars and a bright, huge moon. She listened as the ocean played back the songs Brad strummed on his guitar and the wind repeated David and Lana's clear voices.

Julia interrupted her reverie, calling her to supper. The dining room was surprisingly quiet. Everyone began to realize they had spent their last day in this remote section of land on the coast of a small country called Costa Rica. In many ways they knew they would never be the same again.

Windy left the group beside the bon fire and slowly made her way down the beach. The moonlight reflected off the silvery water mirroring her thoughts. Tomorrow she would leave this heavenly place, this temporary refuge. She would soon board a plane and fly back to her waiting husband, a husband who expected her to conceive that long desired child. She remembered his parting words; I think this is just the change you need. When you return you should be relaxed and refreshed, more susceptible to conceiving.

Crabs scurried to their homes beneath the wet sand, watching her with cautious eyes. A life and death struggle took place at Windy's feet known only to those engaged in battle. The receding tide continued to wash snails of all kinds to the end of the oceans reach. With a lap of a silent wave another snail lay victim to its aggressive cousin as the larger snail slowly began to engulf the smaller. Nature was cruel on this beautiful night. If the tide had placed it's rider an inch in any direction it would have been safe. Now it struggled in vain to free itself from one who might in another movement of the ocean become a victim too. As the captive lost it's final battle, a sea gull cried, a crab scurried and a woman brushed past on bare feet, the wet ocean sand squishing between her toes.

Ahead, Windy saw a log partially buried in the sand. She sat on it sifting her toes in the wet grains. Brad's song filtered through her mind and she pictured him sitting near the fire, light reflecting off his blonde hair, his voice capturing the words if not the notes.

She visualized her circle of friends as they sat before her every night these past three weeks. She committed them to her memory; each voice, each talent, each special characteristic which set them apart and made them unique.

Windy silently thanked God for Jenny's love. The faith and trust of this one person had sent her here to experience the Christian fellowship she so desperately needed. She heard Jenny's parting words, the same ones that held such meaning for Lana.

"And we know that God causes all things to work together for good to those who love God, to those who are called according to His purpose."

When Jenny should have been saddened by her inability to go on this long anticipated trip she had expressed joy instead. She had thanked God for providing Windy with the means to go, even at her own sacrifice.

Windy looked up to the clear sky and again wondered where all the stars were. "Jesus," she said. "I still know so little about you. I've read your story according to your friends, I have you in my head, but I desire you in my heart. I can't say I'm no longer confused but I do know I want you. You have become most important to me; I want nothing between us, especially myself. Thank you for giving your life for me, please, be my Savior. I'm sorry for my sins and my sinfulness. I want to be like Jenny and Lana and Brad, whole and complete. I see their dedication, their commitment and I desire that for myself. I hope that's not a selfish request. I want a new life with you, one that's free from the hurt and pain that's been a part of me for so long. Please, Jesus, make me new, be my Lord, and my God."

As the words of longing fell from her lips so the burden of life fell from her shoulders. Her arms lifted skyward as though released from shackles and dammed up tears flowed from eyes ready to look upon her Savior.

Peace washed over her being as surely as the ocean washed over her toes and Windy became a new creature. Her confessed sins were tossed into that vast ocean and the tide of God's love drew them away from her and deep into the recesses of the cleansing water.

This new creature, worm turned butterfly, sat revealing in her new found peace, arms clasped tightly around her knees. She would have remained there with her precious Lord until dawn if Brad hadn't noticed her leaving the fire. He watched her walk away, noting the sadness on her face, sensing she needed time alone.

Only low embers remained of the fire and all the others had headed for their beds in anticipation of the long day the dawn would bring. Brad's watchful eye stayed on Windy as he slowly made his way down the beach. He stopped several yards from where she sat, wanting to announce his presence without disturbing her. When he saw no response he moved closer, a few steps at a time.

"Does this night have to end? Can't I just stay here and become part of this beautiful setting?" she whispered, without looking up.

"Too many people would miss the blessings you bring if that happened."

"Your prayers have been answered."

Brad's heart quickened at her words, he sat beside her on the wet sand. "Will you tell me about it?"

"I know him as Savior now and suddenly life is beginning to make sense. I believe I can even go back home and look to my future with some hope."

"Then my prayers have been answered. You're too young and lovely to look as sad as you do."

She turned her head at last and smiled at the young man who had made such an impression on her.

"May I tell you?" she asked.

He nodded.

In a few brief moments Windy completely and accurately guided Brad through the dark passages of her life. Without dwelling on any scene, with no words or pleas that might draw his pity, she opened the doors to her inner hurts and fears only to let him see the marvelous work God had accomplished in her heart that night.

When she finished they stared into the ocean depths, each one thanking God in their own way for the miracle that had taken place.

Then Brad stood and reached his hand out to his sister, gently helping her to her feet. He held her in his strong embrace, allowing himself to be used of Christ to love and comfort this precious new born babe.

"I love you," Brad whispered.

Windy had heard these words before, in a passionate embrace or a savage encounter with Eddie; on her living room floor from a helpless doctor; in her own husband's bedroom where she had never felt welcome. They were words that she longed to have true meaning. For the first time, they did. She lay her head against Brad's chest and stood safe within his love. How good it felt to be loved freely, not for what she could give in return. How wonderful to feel arms around her that held no strings, contained no demands. They were the arms of Christ Himself, come to strengthen her with His love. Brad moved to her side, still holding her under the shelter of his arm and together they walked down the beach, heading back to the harsh reality of life. But the Savior walked before them, making clear their paths. Brad gave her another tender hug as they stood at the door of her cabin. All lights had been extinguished in the silent camp. This time Windy returned his embrace noting the difference in what she was used to. Stephan's hugs were now only a prelude, used sparingly, Eddie's had been fun and exciting until they turned vicious. Brad's hugs made her feel secure and safe.

"Thank you," she whispered.

"Thank you, Elaine," he returned. As he released her and they stepped apart Windy suddenly felt lonely and vulnerable. Tears slid down her cheeks and she quickly looked away.

"See you in the morning," she could barely hear Brad's voice, Windy nodded, not trusting her own. She looked at her door then out toward the ocean not wanting to leave this moment. Brad remained too, though Windy assumed he waited for her to step safely inside.

God's healing of her wounded heart had begun but completion would take a long time. She reached for the door handle but her grasp fell short.

"Elaine?" Her name fell almost inaudibly from his lips. She looked at him, forgetting the tears. "Come here," he whispered. She wanted to rush to him but she held back, the security she felt on the beach suddenly left her. Was it wrong to want to feel his strong arms around her? Why was that desire so powerful? She never wanted to trade Christ's arms for man's again. In fear she asked herself if it was Brad she wanted or just the security she felt in his embrace? Was hugging another man, a Christian brother, a sin?

She stood looking at his outline in the full moon, aware that the light shone on her glistening tears. He lifted his hand and she placed hers in it.

"Always remember that you are God's special creature and He loves you dearly," Brad's gentle voice touched her. "You are His child; never feel inadequate or inferior to anyone. To allow those feelings is an insult to Him. It's just like saying He can not take care of you, see to your needs. It's telling Him, His grace and power are ineffective on you."

He reached for her other hand which she gladly provided. "You are a bright, beautiful creature. I'll be praying that your husband will recognize that and cherish this precious gift God has given him. I'll pray for his salvation and the growth of your marriage."

He gave her a little tug and she gladly stepped into his circle of love. With her head resting on his shoulder she thanked him again.

"I love you," the words tasted sweet on her tongue.

Brad closed his eyes tightly, kissed the top of her head and gave her a little squeeze before he released her.

"Goodnight," he whispered, catching her falling hand in his. "See you in the morning."

Windy turned and entered her cabin, closing the door quietly behind her. "I am God's special creature," she repeated Brad's words committing them to heart and memory. The moonlight still streamed in the windows and she found her bunk without turning on the light. Believing she couldn't sleep a wink, Windy fell asleep instantly.

Brad walked slowly to the men's cabin, praise still falling silently from his lips. And though he cheered God with one voice, he cursed Him with another. Brad's arms stung with the closeness of the delicate creature called Elaine. Her fragrance lingered in the air he breathed and her words caressed the lonely chambers of his heart.

How could he pray for the very man he envied? How could he petition God for blessings on a union he wished had never begun? How could he feel so strongly about a woman he just met, when he believed God intended him for another? The questions battered the young man. He cried out to His Lord for release from emotions that might separate him from the One he loved most.

"Oh, God, take this hurt from me, replace this love I feel with Your love and allow me look upon her with Your eyes," he prayed. He finally fell asleep with his desperate plea still on his lips.

Chapter Fifty-Two

Father, I'm looking forward to Bible study tonight. Margie said a friend of hers has finally agreed to come and we should pray for her today. So I lift Valerie to You and ask that tonight she might open her heart to Your word and Your Son. I pray, too, that my kids are opening Your word.

The sun had not yet risen on the little camp when it's occupants forced themselves out of bed, complaining every moment. Their day held a long bus ride to San Jose where they would check into a hotel. They'd be allowed an afternoon of shopping before turning in early in preparation for the flight home the next day.

Some of the group had long lists of friends and family who expected souvenirs from this little Latin American country. Windy easily checked off her list in her mind; Stephan, Cora, Jenny, Mom and Dad.

The aroma of breakfast wafted through the air. Windy put two pieces of French toast and three strips of bacon on her plate, generously poured syrup over it all and sat beside Brad.

"Here," Beth plopped down beside her and held out a little white pill. "I think you'll ride more comfortably if you take this." Windy hesitated. "It's for motion sickness. It might make your throat a bit dry, but I think it's worth it."

Windy accepted the pill and washed it down with some warm water. "Thanks."

"You might get a little sleepy, too."

"Anything else I might get?"

"You won't get sick," Beth promised as she moved back to her table.

"We'll have to say our good-byes this morning," Brad lifted a chunk of fresh pineapple from his plate.

"You're not going to San Jose with us?" Windy knew her disappointed showed, but she didn't care.

"No, I stay here and wait for Martin to return with the next bus load of prisoners."

"How long will that be?"

"Friday. Your group flies out tomorrow, the next one comes right in the next day."

"Isn't it a little eerie being here by yourself?"

Brad nodded and smiled. "Sure is. Manuel and Katarina usually visit relatives between camps. After weeks of activity this place seems a little unreal when it's empty. I think the most unusual part is when the next group comes and takes over the jobs of the previous group."

"You mean my cement mixer will now belong to someone else?"

Brad nodded. "Some other fragile little lady who's afraid to climb up on the roof," he teased.

"I went up there one time," Windy corrected.

"I know. Martin watched you carefully; he didn't want to ruin his perfect record of no casualties."

Windy spied Martin sitting next to Lana. She knew there were at least two casualties in this camp, though it wasn't a roof they had fallen off of.

Windy suddenly lost her appetite. Her dream world was ending and all too soon she'd be back in Stephan's home. At that moment the girl made a decision. She didn't see how she could give her life to Christ and accept His will without accepting her husband and the life they shared. She remembered Jenny saying it may not have been God's will that she and Stephan marry but it was His will that she do everything she could to make the marriage work. She resolved to do just that.

"Brad, you said you would pray for my husband's salvation and for our marriage."

"Yes, I did. That's okay with you isn't it?'

"I would like that. Stephan's a very strong person; he won't give up control of his life to Christ easily." She willed herself to finish the food on her plate hoping Beth's pill would work. When they finished, she and Brad took their plates outside to wash them, then he walked her back to the cabin. They stood for several minutes just holding each other then he kissed the top of her forehead and walked away without a word.

Soon all the luggage and 20 reluctant bodies were crammed into the small bus. Martin turned the ignition causing the engine to grumble. He pumped the gas peddle several times and tried again. This time the engine whined and coughed. So began a conversation between driver and vehicle; one coaxing, the other responding more angrily each time. The engine cursed in its own foreign language, but Martin remained calm, more than could be said for some of his passengers. When it appeared the engine was winning the battle, Eric jumped off the bus and opened the hood. Minutes later he yelled for Martin to try again. This time the engine turned over without a complaint. "I didn't know you were a mechanic." Martin said.

"I'm not." He admitted as he sat down.

"How'd you get it to start?" Martin asked.

"I laid hands on it and asked the Master Mechanic."

A cheer went up and Martin shifted gears, ready to start the journey. Windy looked for Brad who stood leaning against the dining hall, she rose her hand in a farewell greeting. He smiled and waved in return. She watched him as the bus pulled onto the bumpy road blocking her view.

David sat across the aisle from Windy, she noticed his head lower and his lips begin to move. She silently followed his example. Almost as one the others quieted and when the bus became silent David spoke aloud, echoing the thoughts of each person on the bus. He asked for a safe trip and good weather. He thanked God for the time they had shared together and the work accomplished in His name. He asked the Lord to go with each of them back into their homes and families; that their experiences here would have a lasting effect on them and those they loved. Each person repeated his amen.

Windy's mouth soon turned to cotton and she knew Beth's magic pill was beginning to work. Glad she had heeded Beth's advise to bring some water, Windy tipped the coke bottle to her lips and let the liquid rest in her mouth a few moments before swallowing it.

Beth's warning about the drowsiness proved right, too. The seats on the rickety old bus were never intended for comfort. Windy wadded up her jacket and stuffed it behind her head, which only made her more uncomfortable. Her eyes drooped and her mouth grew dryer with each breath. Windy seriously wondered if this was better than being sick.

Lana sat next to the window and watched her friend's efforts with amusement. Finally she spoke.

"You can put your head in my lap, if you want to," she offered.

With half closed eyes Windy smiled her appreciation, placed her jacket on Lana's lap and was out in a minute.

She couldn't call her drowsy state sleep. She was constantly aware of her surroundings, the bumps in the road, the hard seat and the kink in her back. Her mind drifted in and out of dreams that made no sense.

Lana placed her hand on her friend's shoulder and shooed the flies from her face. The bus came to a screeching halt and Windy's head flew up, her eyes wide open. A family with several children stood by the roadside. Martin opened the door and conversed with the father. Soon the family piled into the bus. The few empty seats were quickly filled and some of the camp workers pulled a child up into their laps.

A little boy of about 3 stared with huge dark eyes at Windy. She reached out to him and a grin spread over his face. He settled into her lap, his head resting on her shoulder.

"Do you want me to take him?" Lana offered.

Windy shook her head. "No, I feel some better, thanks to my nap." She pulled the little fellow close and kissed the top of his head.

The bus continued to bounce down the road as Windy imagined what it would be like to hold her own child in her lap. The boy fell asleep, his even breathing brought great comfort to the young woman. She leaned her head against the back of her seat and found herself dozing again.

When they neared the capitol city of San Jose, Martin called the father up for directions. They began winding through narrow streets that served as market places for booths that sold everything from fresh pineapples to hand made jewelry. Windy found if she tried to peer out the window her head began to spin and she feared her stomach would retaliate.

They soon came to a stop and the little family began to file off the bus. Windy reluctantly woke her passenger. He smiled with sleepy eyes then gave Windy a quick hug before jumping down and joining his family.

Martin continued through the streets making sudden stops to avoid

THE HOLLOW OF HIS HAND

pedestrians. Each turn caused Windy to feel worse. She looked questioning at
Lana who smiled and nodded. Windy lowered her head to Lana's lap where
her jacket still remained.

Soon the tired group quickly unloaded their belongings unto the street in
front of a shoe shop. Beside the shop a single glass door sported the letters.
JOHNSON HOTEL. Martin opened the door and Christie moaned as she
looked up a flight of stairs.

"Hurry up, we don't want to leave our luggage out here too long," Martin
commanded. Windy gathered up her bags and climbed the crowded stair case
beside Eric.

"The green lady returns!" he laughed.

Windy growled in reply. She still felt groggy, her throat had long since seized
up on her. All she wanted was a cold drink, a hot shower and a soft bed. Was
that really too much to ask?

At the main desk Martin received their room numbers and he and Lana
quickly assigned rooms. The girls had two rooms containing three beds each,
Carrie volunteered to bunk with Lana and Windy. Before Martin allowed the
group to climb the next flight of stairs to their rooms he informed them of the
day's schedule. They had one hour to freshen up, then the whole group would
have lunch and begin their shopping spree.

Windy shook her head as she made her way toward Martin. "Can't do it,"
she informed him. "I just can't. I'm not hungry, I couldn't eat if I wanted to.
I have very little shopping to do and if I don't get some rest I'll never make the
trip home tomorrow. Can I meet you somewhere in a couple hours?"

This time Martin shook his head. "I can't have you wondering unfamiliar
streets by yourself. We go in groups of at least three when we shop."

Windy sighed knowing she couldn't hold up the whole group but also
knowing she'd never last an hour.

"Couldn't someone come back and get her in a couple hours?" Lana
suggested.

Martin thought for a moment then shrugged. "I suppose. Are you
volunteering?"

Lana smiled, "Only if I have an escort who knows his way around."

"I believe that can be arranged." He returned the smile. "Well, time's a
wasting." He herded the group upstairs where Windy fell onto her not so soft
bed while the other two girls showered. Before Lana left she woke her friend.

289

"Don't sleep too much longer. Martin and I will be back to get you in a while."

Windy nodded her appreciation. When the room emptied Windy listened to the noise of the street below her for a short time. She got up and went to the window, taking in the strange sights and sounds of this bustling city. Yawning, she opened her suitcase and pulled out the necessary items. In the bathroom she turned on the hot water and stepped into the stream.

San Jose is located in the mountains of central Costa Rica. Though still very warm, the temperature is considerably cooler than on the coast. Windy savored the hot water on her aching muscles. She leisurely shampooed her hair and worked up a good soap lather over her entire body. By the time she finished, the effects of Beth's magic pill were wearing off and Windy actually felt human again.

She chose a skirt and short sleeve blouse, having been warned by Martin that woman in this country did not wear shorts in public. At the main desk Windy found a pop machine and used her newly acquired 'colones' to buy a Fanta Root Beer, the next best thing to Cherry Cola.

She returned to her room and began recording the trip in her journal. She looked out the third story window, and took several pictures. From her vantage point she saw Lana and Martin round a corner, Lana's hand held securely in his. Windy quickly snapped a picture.

Chapter Fifty-Three

Father, Valerie's a nice lady, about ten years older than me, but You already know that, don't You? She seemed to enjoy the study, but said very little except that she would come next week. Please be with my kids today.

Martin led the girls to a huge steal building where dozens of small booths lined the dirt walkways. Windy found she could buy anything here from fresh vegetables to fine jewelry. She chose a hammock for Stephan, some delicate silver earrings for Jenny and a wooden teapot for Cora.

Back outside they walked past vendors who had set up booths along the street. Pedestrians paid little attention to cars, often using the street as a sidewalk. Lana stopped to admire some leather wrist bands and soon made a deal with the seller. She purchased one dozen for the price of ten.

"I know you have this idea you're supposed to dicker for bargains in foreign countries," Martin explained. "But that isn't the norm here. You may get them to come down a little, but basically what they ask for is what they need to make."

Windy noticed a variety of necklaces at that booth. One type in particular caught her eye. Crosses made with twisted leather hung on leather strings. They were so simple they were attractive to the girl. She purchased two, and counted her remaining colones, thankful for the extra fifty dollars Stephan had given her.

Next they entered a brick building sectioned off into small shops. Here Windy chose a wooden handmade bank with 'Costa Rica' painted on it for her mom and a miniature wooden chess set for her dad. She tucked the last of her colones into her purse intending to give Jenny one of each coin plus a 'dollar' bill for use in her class.

Soon they headed back to the hotel where the rest of the troop waited for them. All the girls gathered in Windy's room where newly purchased items were dumped on beds and shown to admiring eyes.

Martin knocked on the open door and asked the girls to meet in the small upstairs lobby.

"We're going out to dinner," he announced. "Since this is our last night together I have something nice planned for us. You have one hour to nap, shower, shave, whatever, then we'll meet back here."

Windy used the time to record in her journal and take a couple pictures of the hotel. She also went from room to room getting addresses. Though her intentions were good she wasn't sure if she would actually write to anyone.

Each person she asked liked the idea and Windy was quickly appointed secretary, promising to send everyone a copy of the roster. After getting Martin's address at the camp she asked about Brad's.

"Well," he replied. "I'm not sure what his plans are and I don't know where his folks live, but if you give me your address, I'll see he sends his to you."

"What's his last name?" Windy asked, her hand poised over the journal ready to record. But Martin's eyes had settled on something behind her and when she turned, she saw Lana float toward them in a dark green dress. Windy smiled, knowing all contact with Martin was lost for a while.

The group walked several blocks to an upstairs restaurant where they enjoyed a delicious meal of steak, potatoes, rice, salad and chocolate ice cream for desert. Three musicians serenaded them throughout the evening.

Windy sat between Lana and Eric alternately sharing memories which each of them. But she found plenty of time to just sit and listen as the others around the table shared their memories too. She wished Brad were there as he was as much a part of their adventure as anyone else.

The evening ended too quickly and they all walked back to the hotel in silence. Not wanting to part company just yet the group stood in the small upstairs lobby. They shared hugs and wiped away tears until Martin reminded them of their early departure time the next morning. He walked the girls to their rooms where five of them quickly stepped inside, leaving Lana and Martin to say their good-byes.

Though she didn't want to, Windy accepted another of Beth's little pills the next morning. She dreaded getting back on an airplane and hoped she would sleep better on it than on the bus. Martin rushed the group through all the necessary preliminaries at the airport and they quickly settled into their seats.

The trip took all day as they were now traveling backward in time losing hours instead of picking them up. Darkness had descended on the airport when they reached their final destination.

Windy and Lana walked into the terminal and Lana's eyes lit up. "My parents," she explained to Windy before hurrying to the couple that waved at them.

As the others disembarked, relatives snatched them up, except for Carrie and David who now must catch a flight back to Canada. Windy searched the waiting room for Stephan but found no trace. She slowly made her way through the terminal to the baggage claim where she picked up her luggage with no problem. Again she searched for her husband to no avail. Lana appeared with her parents.

"Elaine, this is my mom and dad." Windy shook their hands and told them of their merciful daughter and the attention she'd lavished on Windy. With a long hug, a few tears and the promise of letters the two girls parted company. After Lana left Windy found a pay phone and called home. The machine answered.

Windy hung up and glanced at the clock. 11:15 PM. She quickly reviewed his schedule in her mind and determined him to be on midnights. Knowing he wouldn't be able to leave the hospital, she dialed the phone again, this time calling Jenny, wondering if she was even back from Florida yet. When she heard her friends muffled voice she quickly apologized. Jenny was immediately awake and excited about seeing Windy, she promised to be right down.

"How's your dad?" Wendy asked as the two friends embraced.

"Everything is wonderful. Dad is recuperating very well, Mom is a lot stronger than I thought. She's the one who held everything together, comforting and encouraging us all."

"That's great, gee, you could probably have gone on the trip after all."

"No, I needed to be with my family and you needed to be in Costa Rica. I know God had it all planned!"

"I have about 4 rolls of pictures for you," Windy changed the subject as she threw a suitcase in Jenny's trunk.

"I can't wait to see every one of them. Did you have a good time? What was it like? Did you make some new friends? Did you swim in the Pacific?"

"Yes, yes, yes and yes. And I'll tell you all about it. I recorded everything in the journal you gave me. You know, I'd like to make a copy of it before I give it to you. I went intending to make memories for you, but I sure made a lot for myself."

"What I can do is take the journal to school and use the copy machine there. I want you to keep the journal."

"Are you sure?"

"Of course. The journal itself is part of your memories isn't it?"

"Yes, how did you know?"

"It would be for me if I'd kept all my thoughts in it."

'All my thoughts,' repeated Windy. *'Except those of Brad.'* Windy silently reviewed the many personal thoughts she'd left out. Remembering Jenny's reaction to her lunch with Stephan right after Eddie left, how could she possibly explain to her friend how she felt in Brad's arms?

They soon entered Windy's driveway and Jenny helped her carry the luggage into the house. "I'd like to stay, but—school tomorrow."

"I know, thanks so much for picking me up. Jenny I have so much to tell you. We just have to take a whole day to talk."

"Saturday. I've been keeping it open for you."

After Jenny left, Windy took her suitcase and duffle bag upstairs to her room. She unpacked only the bag of dirty laundry then slipped her clothes off, pulling on a t-shirt to sleep in. Although Jenny claimed the July temperature to be the hottest this year, Windy found it almost cool compared to what she'd become used to.

She crawled into her bed, a shiver of excitement slipped down her back. My own soft bed, she whispered. No more sagging lumpy mattress for me. Windy sighed deeply and looked at the clock, it read 12:10. She closed her eyes in anticipation of a good nights sleep. The worksite appeared in her mind. The cement mixer stood waiting for her. The sound of the ocean pounded in her ears and Eric beckoned her to join him in the surf. Windy tried to clear all the images out of her mind but they refused to leave. Events, important and insignificant, replayed themselves. She listened to voices she knew she would never hear again, looked into eyes she would never see again and held hands she'd never touch again. She listened as Eric talked to her about losing someone she loved and she knew a grieving process was just beginning that would take her a long time to work through. Tears dripped onto her pillow and she reached out, searching for her stuffed black cat. He lay on top of the other pillow just waiting to be pulled close to his master who let her sadness rush from her in sobs heard only by an empty house.

Stephan stopped by the nurses' lounge and checked the schedule, noting with disgust that Diana's name had been erased from days next week and added to afternoons. He frowned. He'd been looking forward to working with the young woman and checking on her progress. But, he reasoned, nothing prevented him from working late one day next week. He quickly exited the building, looking forward to the comfort of his bed. Once in the car he suddenly remembered the date. Elaine should have arrived last night. He wondered if she'd managed to get a ride home, knowing she would have spent all her money and wouldn't have enough for a taxi. Within minutes he pulled into his drive. Not bothering to put the car in the garage he quickly entered his house and made for his room. Finding it empty he turned toward Elaine's open door at the other end of the long hall. His heart skipped a beat at the thought of seeing his young wife again. He didn't realize how much he missed her until now.

"Welcome home," he whispered to the sleeping form. Elaine rolled over, looked at him and smiled. "I missed you," he said. He hurried out of his clothing and into his wife's waiting arms.

Chapter Fifty-Four

Valerie called, Father, just to chat she said, but she asked lots of questions. I didn't have many answers and suggested she talk to Margie. But Lord, she stirred my desire to find those answers. Thank You for Valerie and thank You for my kids.

Jenny insisted Windy allow her to have all the films developed and though Windy wanted to refuse she knew she couldn't afford to pay for them herself. The Saturday following her return Windy rushed over to Jenny's to see them.

"Who is this?" Jenny asked Windy as they sat at her kitchen table.

"Brad. He works at the camp, spending the summer there I believe."

"What's his last name? Do you have any closer pictures of him?"

"I don't know his last name," Windy answered, not yet ready to tell Jenny about Brad. "Say, can I use the typewriter at the office? I have to send out the addresses and I'd rather type than write them 20 times." Windy started a quick search through the piles of photos.

"Sure. He looks so familiar. What do you know about him?" Jenny asked still looking at the picture.

"He's a committed Christian man who cares a lot about people." Windy answered, picking up another envelope. "He's a hard worker. That's about it."

"No background?"

Windy shrugged. "I missed the first night introductions—motion sickness.

I learned a little about Lana on the plane, and I know Eric fairly well. Sorry. No close ups. I'm surprised. I thought I had good pictures of everyone."

"Oh, no big deal," Jenny assured her, setting the picture down and picking up the next one. "Who's this?"

"Eric, my surfing buddy. Jenny," Windy decided the time had come to share her news with her friend. "I want to tell you about something wonderful that happened right here on this beach." She held up a picture of a perfect sunset over the Pacific.

Jenny cried when Windy relayed the story of her prayer of acceptance. She hugged Windy tightly, finding no words that expressed her feelings.

The girls spent the rest of the day looking at pictures while Windy relived her time on the Pacific coast.

August turned into September and the Michaels life resumed as though Windy had never left. Several times she tried to tell Stephan about her new life in Christ but he always interrupted, asking if she's seen enough of the poverty during her trip to realized how fortunate she was. When she explained that she spent all her time on the ocean he accused her and Jenny of misleading him, tricking him into letting her go.

For Windy, life would never be the same. Some mornings she woke up at 5:30 listening for Martin's voice outside the window. Often she would step out the back door and expect to see the ocean greeting her. In the evening she would wonder where the others were and what they were doing at that moment. She waited for Martin to answer her letter, giving her Brad's address. She had typed the roster soon after coming home but didn't want to send it out incomplete.

Stephan confronted Windy about working in the Pregnancy office, telling her of his chance meeting with Diana. When she tried to explain that she didn't work there on a regular basis, he refused to listen to any more of her 'half-truths'. He simply forbid her to set foot in the office again.

"We'll wait till next month, and then begin the tests." Stephan stated as they sat in the back yard, she in the fading September sun and Stephan in the shade. He briefly described the tests stating they were painless, but awkward.

"What will they determine?" she asked.

"Why you can not conceive."

"But I can conceive."

"Pardon?"

"I said I can conceive, I think."

"After trying for two years with no results, it is obvious that you can not."

"But I might have."

"Windy," he jumped from his chair and pulled her to her feet, hope twinkled in his eyes. "Do you mean you are…"

"No, I'm not. But I might have been, once."

"Might have been?"

She nodded.

An ominous look crept over Stephan's face as he nudged Windy to her chair. "Explain," he said.

Sorry for her words, she quietly began. "We'd been married about a year, Eddie and I, I missed a couple periods. That's all."

"That can not be all. Did you miscarry?"

"I don't know, maybe."

"Elaine, you are not that stupid. You would know if you miscarried. Did you have a lot of stomach cramps and excessive bleeding?"

"When my period finally came, yes. I thought I just had stomach flu." Stephan's face turned white, he stared at his wife.

"Did you see a doctor or go to the hospital?"

"No, Eddie's insurance didn't cover doctor visits and the pain and fever went away after a couple days."

"Fever?" his voice held an ominous tone.

"Yes, I thought I was just sick and that's why I skipped those periods and then with flu, I thought a fever was normal."

Stephan flushed red. "Fever is normal with infection Elaine. You obviously miscarried and since you had no D&C what you did not expel became infected. No wonder you can not conceive now. Heaven knows what happened to your insides. The test schedule begins right away. It is more important now that ever."

Stephan looked at the test results one more time. They all confirmed his suspicions; Elaine would never conceive his child. He plunked his elbows on the desk and rested his face in his hands. The memory of his grandfather loomed before him. The old man's short white hair and neatly trimmed white beard were just as Stephan remembered.

"My commission to you, son, is to carry on the proud name of Michaels. This house will be yours one day, I hope I live to see it filled with my descendants." But Grandfather had not lived that long, nor had Stephan's father.

Children. The idea had recently become an obsession with Stephan. Five years ago he had not given them a passing thought. Now all he could think of was fulfilling his grandfather's desire.

He had placed all his hopes in Elaine and she let him down. She had stolen grandfather's dream, robbed Stephan of his manhood.

"You are as much to blame, old boy," he chided himself. "You did not ask enough questions. After all, the girl had been married for two years; you should have inquired more about her health history. You should have insisted on these tests before you became so enamored with her. But she knew. She knew she could count on your generosity. She set the bait and just waited for you to take it.

"Now what will you do? Will you submit to a life of fruitlessness with a deceiving woman? Will you accept the demise of your future?"

Stephan rubbed his temples and sighed deeply. "You have never been one to accept defeat without a fight, Stephan Michaels. You fought for your home, you forfeited for your schooling, will you now lie down like a wounded dog and see the rest of your life drained from you?"

Windy sat on the couch staring at the cold fireplace. Stephan had instructed her to come right home and rest. He said he'd bring supper home so she needn't cook. His voice had been calm and doctorly, as though she were just another patient. With a tug at her heart she realized his voice had sounded that way for some time; even before she told him about the miscarriage. Yes, that's what it was. She knew all along, deep inside. She and Eddie just never had the courage to admit it. She shivered in the cool parlor, silently cursing the central air that cooled the warm autumn days.

A miscarriage. A baby. How far along had she been? At least eight weeks. She rehearsed the words she used at the office. 'At eighteen days the heart is beating', her baby's heart had been beating for over a month. 'At six weeks brain waves are detected', her and Eddie's baby had been capable of thinking in it's limited way. 'At eight weeks all the organs are formed and functioning', her baby was a real person who just needed to grow.

She recalled the night she told Eddie about her suspicions. 'A baby? No foolin? So I'm gonna be a Daddy.' His grin spread over his face then suddenly disappeared. 'Me—a daddy. I don't how Windy.' He shook his head. She assured him it would all come naturally, something they would learn together. But as the evening passed he became more upset, eventually leaving the apartment and not returning until the next morning. When he returned he smelled of beer, a smell completely foreign to him. For the next couple days Eddie acted strange, refusing to touch or even look at her. Then one night they left the apartment and went.

"Where did we go?" Windy asked herself. She closed her eyes and took a deep breath, willing herself to remember. Fireworks exploded in front of her and her eyes popped open. Fourth of July, Fireworks, Eddie drinking a six pack of beer and afterwards… Windy's mind fought her but she insisted, "Remember!" she commanded it. Eddie yelling, telling her he couldn't be a daddy. He didn't know how. "What if I turn out like my ole man—mean and hateful. I ain't gonna do that to a kid, I can't." Windy tried to calm him, assure him that he'd be a wonderful dad, but he refused to listen. He grabbed her and threw her against the car. She fell, then stood. He knocked her against the car again and again until she could barely stand, then he pushed her into the back of the car and drove home, taking his remaining fury out on the car. She'd crawled onto the back seat and vomited. Her stomach heaved and cramped, then she felt something warm and sticky on her bare legs.

Windy lay her head against the back of the couch and breathed deeply, her eyes closed. That had been the beginning of the end for her and Eddie, the beginning and the end of her motherhood—her womanhood.

"Okay Lord," she whispered. "I've refused to face this for years. I've pretended it didn't happen, but it did. I need Your strength now, Father. I need Your healing."

The ringing telephone pulled her out of the thoughts.

"Windy, it's Jenny. You need to sit down if you're not already."

"I am. What's wrong?" Windy heard the hesitancy in her friends voice. "Is it Cora?"

"Yes, I just called the ambulance and they've taken her to Community. I…I think she may have had a stroke. We were talking one minute and the next, well, I can't explain it. But she was conscience when they left. I've already called the pastor and the prayer chain has been started. I'm going to the hospital; I thought you might want to come."

"Of course. I'll be right there." She hung up, grabbed the purse she had dropped on the couch and returned to the car, fear mounting with each step. *'Poor Cora'*, she thought. *'Poor Jenny after just having to go through this with her dad!'*

When the hospital staff wouldn't allow the girls in to see Cora they set out to find Stephan, easily locating him. He sent them to the waiting room saying he would meet them there as soon as he knew something. A short time later he appeared.

"Cora is doing quite well," he informed them. "She evidently suffered a light stroke but she seems to be recovering as we speak. It must have been your quick reactions, Jenny."

"I'm so glad to hear that," Jenny's eyes began to release to tears she'd been holding back. "I called the prayer chain and I know people were praying even before the ambulance arrived."

Stephan threw the young woman an irritated look, but did not respond to her statement. "The attending physician has admitted Cora for some tests and will keep her over night for observation. I fully expect her to go home tomorrow." Windy noticed Stephan's comments were directed toward Jenny. He had not even acknowledged her presence until now. He looked at his wife. "I have a patient on the critical list. He may need emergency surgery during the night so I'll be staying here." With that he turned and started to walk away.

"Dr. Michaels?" Jenny called to him. He turned. "Will you call if there's any change in Cora."

"Certainly, leave your number at the desk." Then he disappeared. Jenny looked at her friend.

"Trouble?" she asked.

Windy shrugged. "Probably. Mind if I spend the evening with you?"

"I'd love it. Have you had supper?"

When Windy shook her head Jenny continued. "We'll stop and get pizza to take home, that way we won't miss Stephan's call."

However, Stephan did not call Jenny, Cora did.

"I won't stay here, I want to sleep in my own bed," the woman insisted.

"If your doctor calls and tells me I can come and get you I will. Not until." Jenny informed her. Within minutes Dr. Craun called giving Jenny permission to take the lively woman home only if some one stayed with for the next 48 hours. Windy volunteered since Jenny would have to be at school.

Two days later an exhausted Windy drove slowly home. All of Cora's tests came back indicating nothing seriously wrong. The doctor prescribed some blood pressure medication and gave Cora a list of foods to stay away from. She promptly marked off several of the items saying she wasn't about to give up her favorite foods for a couple years of a temporary life.

Windy entered the breezeway and had to step around several large boxes all secured with packing tape. Stephan met her at the back door.

"Come," he told her. She obediently followed him to the parlor were she sat on the couch and looked up at him.

"Yes, Win-dee the boxes belong to you." He informed her. "I would like the keys to the car please; you will not be using them. A van is coming to take you and your possessions wherever you want to go." He held his hand out and Windy dropped the cars keys into it.

"I'd like to go to bed, if you don't mind." Windy answered trying to understand what Stephan was saying.

"I do mind, Win-dee. I find I can no longer tolerate your deceptions. I have tried to provide you with a home and a future and all I have received in return is lies."

The exhausted girl looked at her husband.

"You're kicking me out?" she asked, still confused.

"I am righting a wrong. I should never have allowed this marriage to take place. I still marvel at how you maneuvered your way into becoming Mrs. Stephan Michaels!"

"Maneuvered? I was… I was…" she started to say trapped but the words wouldn't come. "This was all your idea, not mine."

"And I forced you into saying I do?"

"No more than I forced you." Her confusion turned to anger as she realized what was happening. "I assume the test results came in?"

"Yes, they did. They proved what you must have already known. You can not bare children, Win-dee. You did have a miscarriage. Your insides are so scarred up, you will never produce a child."

"I thought you wanted me as a wife and companion not for breeding purposes." Windy stated, her tired mind suddenly alert.

"One of a wife's jobs is to bear fruit in the marriage," he informed her, his doctor voice remained calm. "I want a family. I thought you were going to give me one."

302

"And if I can't I'm no use to you, is that it? You can just kick me out as though I'm nothing to you?"

"After your marriage to Eddie would you have consciously married another alcoholic? You made a decision in your life, to omit something you didn't want. I made a decision to include something I did. Why do you consider one decision right while the other is wrong?"

"I choose to have a family too, only I can't produce my own child," she desperately reached out to her husband. He drew away from her. "In our position, Stephan, we could adopt much easier than many other couples."

"I will not give my family heritage to someone's bastard son!" His raged poured from him as he attempted to control himself. "And now I find I no longer desire to give my name to the child of a liar."

Windy stood, looking up into his face. "Stephan, too many times you have accused me of lying to you and I never have. At times I keep things from you, for a while, but I always tried to be honest." She raised her voice over his protest. "You tell me when I actually lied to you."

"You first lied about your father. You said he was a contractor. Later I found out he is a simple carpenter." This time he raised his voice over her objections. "You said your brother was in the Secret Service. But he is a mere embassy guard in some little god-forsaken country."

Outraged, Windy shook her head. "Never... Never did I tell you those things nor do I know where you got such ideas."

"You've plotted behind my back with your lying friend who sent you on a vacation to a beach in the Pacific. Where were the one room tin homes you were supposed to sleep in; the desolation and squalor you were supposed to experience?"

"I don't understand what you're saying, Stephan."

"Enough!" Stephan commanded. "I have had enough. I will not let you rob me of my manhood! I want you out of here. Now." He grabbed her arm and escorted her through the house. At first she attempted to fight against him then realized her actions were futile. She allowed herself to be pushed into the breezeway.

"My lawyer will be in touch with you." With that he closed the door and locked it. Windy listened in disbelief to his retreating steps.

Moments later a horn sounded in the driveway and a man stepped from a delivery van. He knocked on the screen door. "Michaels residence?" he asked.

Windy nodded. She stepped to the inside door and knocked. When Stephan didn't answer she knocked again and continued knocking as the driver loaded all the boxes.

"Ma'am," he interrupted. "Are you going too?"

Windy looked at him, then looked away. "Yes," she whispered. Inside the van she gave him Cora's address.

Chapter Fifty-Five

Father, it's autumn again. My summer was busy enough that I forgot about the approaching winter and how my heart becomes so lonely. But today I feel at peace. I know You're in control, and I really like it that way. Valerie and I have talked several time. I've invited her over but I guess she's not ready for a closer friendship. In Your time, Lord. Father, thank You for this peace and please pass it on to my kids.

Windy told Cora she had come to take care of her for a while, deciding to wait until Cora was strong enough to hear the truth. Jenny helped Windy store her things in the basement, sifting through and finding the items she needed right away, including the stuffed Sachel.

Windy tried to think of ways to tell Cora that she had been kicked out of Stephan's house. She didn't have to.

Cora answered the phone the next day. After hanging up she located Windy outside, pinning clothes on the line. The older lady sat down in a lawn chair on the porch and called to Windy.

"Stephan called," she stated, her voice almost a whisper. "What's happened, honey?"

Windy took one look at Cora's face and felt the pent-up tears coming. "What did he say?" she asked.

"He said he would send his lawyer over with papers and you were to give him the ring." Windy looked at the ugly green gem on her finger, surprised Stephan had let her walk out of his house without it. She would gladly return it to him, it meant nothing but heartache to her. She left the laundry basket in the yard and sat next to her friend, her surrogate grandmother. She took a deep breath and stated from the beginning. By the time she ended the story of her and Stephan's short marriage, both women were in tears, holding each other. Cora continued to whisper how sorry she was, until Windy pulled back.

"I don't understand it all, Cora, but I know it'll be okay. Remember how Jenny said everything happens for a reason? Well, when I was in Costa Rica, I gave my life completely to Christ, I accepted Him as my Lord and Savior. I may not understand everything, but I know I'm in God's hands now."

The older woman burst forth with a new set of tears, claiming these to be of joy.

"Windy, you know you're welcome here as long as you like, I just wish this little house had another bedroom so you didn't have to sleep on the couch."

Soon Windy helped her friend back into the house and settled her in the living room where she could watch Windy prepare their lunch. That afternoon Windy called the grocery store and talked to Don King, the owner. He was pleased to hear from her and told her to come in the next day.

The following morning Windy left Stephan's ring with Cora, asking her to accept the papers Stephan's lawyer would leave.

"Do you need help paying for a lawyer yourself dear?"

"No, I'm not going to fight Stephan on this. I wonder if the marriage should have ever taken place."

"Do you think Stephan will treat you fairly in a settlement after the way he kicked you out?"

"I want no settlement, I wouldn't accept anything if he offered, not that he will."

Cora then offered to let Windy use her car to drive to work but Windy declined, saying the walk would do her good.

The warm days of September faded and winter sprung harsh in early November. Windy settled into a fairly happy life. She enjoyed being with her two best friends. Windy moved upstairs with Jenny. They purchased a twin bed and a small dresser, turning the living room into a second bedroom. Together, with much laughter, skinned knuckles and sore muscles, they moved the couch into Cora's basement. Windy tried to share expenses with Jenny but her friend wouldn't hear of it.

"I have a teacher's salary, you have a grocery store job," she said.

"'To him who is given much, much is required.' That's found in Luke. I have all I need, Windy, let me help you."

Finally they agreed Windy would buy the groceries and pay her own phone bills. Each week Windy set aside a little money in her savings account.

She mentioned to Jenny that she would like to pay Stephan back for her hospital bill and divorce.

Jenny's eyes lit up. "Don't you dare!" was all she would say.

Both girls worked days allowing them to spend their evenings with Cora who appeared to have never been sick. After supper, the three would sit in Cora's warm living room, hearing tales of Jenny's young students or watching a movie. All three loved needlework and kept a sewing basket beside their favorite seat.

They attended church together and Windy was welcomed into the family with no questions asked. Only Wil looked at her with doubt in her eyes, though he still shook her hand and smiled. She wanted to explain, but didn't know how.

Jenny continued her Saturdays in the Caring Pregnancy Office, sometimes accompanied by Windy. But on her days off from the store, Windy began counseling on her own. She discovered a true desire to help the young women who came into the office. She began reading all the literature available from abortion to sexually transmitted diseases and birth control. She quickly learned she couldn't make decisions for the girls, but she could help them see the risks they were taking because of their lifestyles.

An official envelope arrived for Windy one cold, gray day. It held her second set of divorce papers. She was surprised a week later when a letter arrived from the Community Church informing her that her membership had been revoked.

Windy kept busy. She kept her mind on work, the office and her growing understanding of the Bible. Not a day went by that she didn't spend at least an hour reading and studying the scriptures. She knew a time would come when she had to face the reality of another failed marriage, of her lost child and her inability to have another. She knew she wasn't ready to deal with any of the issues, but planned to be as strong in the Lord as possible when the time came.

Jenny decided to visit her parents at Thanksgiving, asking Windy if she'd like to join her, but the girl declined, preferring to stay with Cora.

When Jenny returned she bubbled with excitement. A young man she'd grown up with was attending seminary in the city where her folks lived. He'd spent the Holiday with them. Windy could see by the look in Jenny's eyes something serious was afoot.

"He was my best friend when we were kids. We were in the same class every year up to the seventh grade. We both gave our lives to Christ the same night at youth camp that summer, then his folks went into the missionary field and I haven't seen him since. But I've prayed for him everyday. I have to admit in the back of my mind, I've been waiting for him. I've always believed we were meant to be together, but I knew God had to come first and if the Lord willed it, we'd meet again some day."

"What's his name?" Windy asked, excited for her friend.

"Scott, Scott Bradley."

"Where's he been since seventh grade?"

"His parents were sent to South America, he finished high school there, went to college in Washington State and then went back to South America for a couple years. Now his dad isn't well, the family's tried to talk Mr. Bradley into coming home, but he says he is home. He insisted Scott go back to school, knowing he really wanted to; so Scott chose Florida to be as close as possible to his parents."

"Did you spend much time with him at your parents?"

"Not as much as I wanted. He was only there for the one day, and my parents kept us pretty busy. But he promised to come up here for Christmas."

"Then he feels the same way you do?"

"I think so. He was certainly glad to see me." Jenny smiled, but her chin quivered and eyes looked into the past. "All these years of waiting and trusting." She shook her head and shrugged. "I can only put it in God's hands."

"He'll love you, Jenny," Windy gave her friend a hug. "How could he not?"

Several days later the girls returned from taking Cora Christmas shopping, the older lady felt tired so the girls took their loot upstairs and dumped it on Jenny's bed.

Jenny held up the sweater she'd bought for Scott, then hugged it to her breast. "I know he doesn't need this in Florida, but you never know what his future plans are, I just hope they include me!"

"What if he decided to become a missionary? Are you ready for that?"

"Teachers are needed everywhere," Jenny smiled.

"But is it what you want to do?"

Jenny sighed, her eyes swelled with unshed tears. "I want God's will in my life, but I admit I want His will to include Scott, where ever that might be."

"You really love him, don't you?"

Jenny's tears spilled and she wiped them away. "I always have."

They quickly wrapped Cora's presents then headed for the kitchen and a cherry cola. Sitting at the table Jenny asked Windy how she felt about the upcoming holiday.

"Funny you should ask, sitting here in this apartment, at this table. It's my first Christmas alone, besides you and Cora of course. The last two were spent with Stephan, though they weren't much like Christmas. Before that was Eddie and before him my parents."

"How are you handling this business with Stephan?"

Windy shook her head. "I don't know," she sat her glass on the table and drew a line in the moisture with her finger. "Losing Eddie was hard. I guess because marriage to him was real and it started out good. Sometimes, being here in this apartment I walk through a doorway and expect to see him. I look out a window and turn around, thinking Eddie should be standing there, as though the last two years never happened. Stephan seems like a fairy tale, complete with Ogres, something I read rather than lived. He never really became a part of me, like Eddie did. Now I almost feel like I was a...well a prostitute," she almost laughed at her friends' expression. "I was being given room and board in exchange for my body. I believed we had a marriage because that's what I wanted to believe." Windy rubbed her fingers against her temples and looked at her friend.

"Sometimes, Jenny, I wake up and I don't know where I am, or who I am. I've lost more than a couple husbands, I've lost years of my life, they're just gone and for what purpose? Sometimes I believe I've even lost me."

Again she smiled at her friends' reaction. "Oh I know, I'm there somewhere. I'm a person, a child of God now. But I've always been a part of someone else I looked for love in other people. Eddie was an adventure, he appealed to my youth. Stephan appealed to my womanhood, the me that wanted to be secure, married, raising a family. What I really want is someone who appeals to the most important part of me; my spirit, my relationship with God. A man who touches my being, who is not just my husband but my soul. I no longer miss Eddie but I miss the fun we had. I don't miss Stephan but I do miss the security, however false it was. Jenny, I want a man that I miss with my heart. When he's not around, I want to be incomplete."

Her mind returned to Costa Rica and a man who held her, in whose arms she felt whole. But she pushed the man out of her mind believing it wasn't Brad she longed for but the type of person he was. And yet, if he appeared today, she knew the potential for a relationship was there, on her part anyway. Certainly not for Brad, whose last promise to her was his prayers for her husband and her marriage.

Chapter Fifty-Six

Valerie finally visited. She admitted she's drawn to me but doesn't know why. We talked for a long time and I found out she has two daughters and a son, whom they adopted at birth. Father, he has the same birth date as my son. I was so afraid when she began looking for a picture and relieved when she couldn't find one. I'm being silly, aren't I? Please be with my kids, I hope they have a wonderful Christmas. I didn't ask if Valerie's son is married.

"You and Cora go ahead," Windy told Jenny on the phone. "I'll get there as soon as I can." As she hung up, she made a mental note to stop at the mailbox, feeling guilty that her Christmas cards were not yet mailed. She'd put it off until the last minute hoping to hear from Martin. But she hadn't and the long overdue addresses were inside the Christmas cards.

She hadn't anticipated working late today but couldn't refuse when her boss asked her to. *Tonight of all nights,* she thought. The children's Christmas program started at 6 PM and since Jenny helped direct it, she had to be there early. Cora was working with the ladies, setting up the fellowship snacks for afterward.

Business at the store had picked up as Christmas neared, and shoppers arrived later every night.

"Paper or plastic?" she asked as the groceries came down the counter toward her.

The cashier picked up a product, looking for the price. "This isn't scanning and it doesn't have a price on it, could you go look, Windy?" she asked. Windy took the item and headed down the aisle, she stopped in front of the shampoo, looking for the correct brand.

"They moved the razor blades while you were gone," a soft, husky voice sounded behind her.

Windy's head jerked up and she found herself looking at Gray Eyes.

"Welcome back, Windy," he said confidently.

"Thanks." They stared at each other. She noted his mustache, a new feature since she saw him last. "Did you need some?" she finally asked.

"Some what?"

"Razor blades."

"No..." his confidence wavered. Then he smiled.

"Actually I came in for some cherry cola." He held up a 2 liter.

"Good choice," she smiled back.

"Windy!? You find that price?" came a shout from the front of the store.

"Excuse me," Windy said backing away. "Have a Merry Christmas."

"You too," he fell in step beside her and they walked in silence to the check-out.

Windy finished bagging the order on the counter then watched as Gray Eyes counted out the change for his cherry cola. His hands looked clean but not soft. She liked the way he moved them, steady and sure. She smiled. He had changed. She no longer saw the embarrassed man who had difficulty speaking to her. "Paper or plastic?" she asked him.

"Neither, I'll just carry it." He took the bottle from her, looking directly at her left hand then into her eyes.

"Spending the Holidays alone this year?" he asked.

Windy shook her head, puzzled. "With friends. How about you?"

"With my folks."

"Oh," she nodded. "Well, have a Merry Christmas."

"Thanks, you too." He turned and walked out of the store as Windy looked at the next customer.

"Paper or plastic?" she asked before glancing out the window. As she placed the order into bags she watched Gray Eyes open the door of a black pick-up and jump inside. She recalled the last time she'd seen him in the store, hoping he would invite her to a movie or something, anything. She smiled and shook her head. That was over two years ago. She wondered if he'd wasted the last two years the way she had.

Scott Bradley stared at the dark house. "You're sure this is the right address?" he asked the taxi driver.

"This is it. Looks like you ain't expected."

"I'm expected, she just didn't know when." He drew a couple bills out of his wallet and handed them to the man.

"You want me ta wait?" the driver asked.

"No, I noticed a station on the corner, I'll go down there and use the phone if need be. Are there any hotels near by?"

"There's one a couple blocks away, nothin fancy."

"It'll do. Thank you and Merry Christmas." Scott climbed out of the taxi, pulling his suitcase with him. He looked at his watch, 5:15, a little early for church he reasoned, unless there was a special program going on. He shook his head, *'of course there's a special program the week before Christmas,* he reminded himself.

"Well, I'll see if the front door's open and leave her a note," he mumbled, pulling his scarf up around his face. December in South America is a summer month, Scott wasn't ready for the cold and snow of Michigan.

He trudged up the snow covered steps and pushed on the outside door, thankful to find it unlocked. Inside he sat his suitcase on the floor and looked for a light switch. A car pulled into the driveway, and Scott looked up into it's lights. A young woman jumped out of the car and bounded up the steps, swinging the door open.

"Jenny?" he asked, startling the woman.

She reached to her left and switched on the light.

"No," she answered. "Who are you?"

He recognized the voice, but it didn't belong here, in the snow, in Jenny's house.

"Elaine?" he asked hesitantly. "No, couldn't be," he laughed. "I'm sorry to startle you, I'm looking for Jenny McCourt, she does live her, doesn't she?"

The woman reached up and pulled her knit hat off, letting her hair fall around her face.

"Elaine, it is you. Heavens, I never expected to find you here!" He pulled the scarf down revealing the face, then scooped her up in his arms, laughing.

"Brad," she whispered. "Oh, Brad!" she laughed with him. "What are you doing here?" She pulled back and looked at him. "How do you know Jenny?"

"I could ask you the same thing."

She stared at him for a moment, then began fumbling with her keys. "Come on up," she said, and he followed her up the stairs. Once inside the apartment she pulled her coat off and hung it on the back of a chair, then she took Scott's from him and did the same thing. He couldn't take his eyes from her, still unable to believe what he saw.

"You look the same," she said. "Just colder." She managed a weak smile. "Have a seat and tell me the story."

"Not much of a story, Jenny and I grew up together, met again at her parents at Thanksgiving and I promised her a visit at Christmas. Your turn."

"She's why I was in Costa Rica; she's the friend I was subbing for." Her brow furrowed. "Jenny told me about a boy from her childhood named Scott."

"Scott Bradley. That's me." They looked at each other for a moment. "You were sick that night," he said more to himself than to her. "You never knew my name."

"No," she shook her head and turned away. "And Martin never sent me your address."

"He couldn't, I didn't have one," he took a deep breath. "I had to leave the next camp, my Mom took ill."

Memories flooded into the young man's mind, memories he had refused to allow an audience for the past five months. Once again he stood on the sand in Costa Rica listening to a young woman who had just given her heart to Christ, he felt her in his arms once more, her gentle scent mingling with the night air.

"How…how have you been?" he asked, pulling himself away from the past.

She turned back to face him, arms folded in front of her. Scott sensed of wall of protection around her. She smiled an empty smile.

"Lots of changes since I saw you last. Stephan divorced me in September," she stated as casually as one would give their recipe for sugar cookies. "I live here now, with Jenny. I work at a grocery store and volunteer at a Crisis Pregnancy Office. I attend church, also with Jenny. And Cora. My walk with the Lord is growing stronger," she bobbed her head. "Guess that sums it up." She started to turn away again. "Oh, my, the program! Jenny and Cora are there already, we've got to hurry. It'll just take me a minute to change. You will come with won't you?"

"Sure," Scott nodded to Elaine's retreating back. He watched her disappear through a doorway to his left. *'Elaine'* he thought, *'here of all places, here with Jenny. And just when I thought I had her cleared from my mind.'*

Windy grabbed a clean pair of pants, a turtleneck and a sweater from her little dresser. She took a deep breath and walked back into the kitchen.

"Be just a minute," she promised her guest. Without looking at him, she ducked into the bathroom and turned on the cold water, splashing it over her hot face. She couldn't believe it was Brad standing in the next room. Her Brad, Jenny's Scott. She closed her eyes and saw his short blonde hair, and the day's growth of beard on the face she believed she would only see again in her dreams. She heard his voice and the strumming of his guitar.

"What is this, God, some kind of joke?" she whispered, "I thought You loved me, I thought You even liked me. Why this, God, why?"

She turned off the water and clamped a towel over her face.

'You're not in control here, Windy, keep trusting, just keep trusting.'

She peered at herself in the mirror. "You can do it," she nodded. "You can do this for Jenny."

Windy slipped into her clean clothes, ran a comb through her hair and joined her guest, smiling.

"We'll be late, but I'm sure as soon as Jenny sees you she'll forgive us." Windy picked up her coat and Brad took it from her, holding it while she poked her arms into the sleeves. "Oh, yes, my name's Windy," she noted his confused look. "Windy Elaine Jordan. It's a long story." She assured him.

"So I should call you Windy?" she nodded. "Guess you should call me Scott then." Again she nodded, *'Jenny's Scott,'* she added.

Windy pulled up outside the church and drove through the parking lot, finding an empty space in the back. She turned off the ignition, becoming more aware of the silence that had accompanied them thus far.

"Brad," she turned toward him. "Scott, I mean, Scott." She shook her head. "No, in my heart, you're Brad. You don't even look like a Scott. Can I still call you Brad, sometimes?"

"It would seem strange if you didn't."

"Good, that's settled, I'm glad we got that settled" she nodded her head and looked away. "Brad," she began again. "Before…" *'before I turn you over to Jenny,'* "we go inside, well, I guess there are some things I'd like to say, and I may never have another chance."

She hesitated, looking at the young man sitting beside her, refusing to believe it was really Brad. If she allowed herself that luxury she'd want him to pull her into his arms and hold her the way he did last summer. An image of him appeared in her mind. He stood, arms crossed, against a brick building, the hot Costa Rican sun shining on his blonde hair and tanned face staring at her from outside a bus window. She shook the image from her mind, concentrating on the young man who sat beside her, Jenny's young man, Scott, the one Jenny had waited so long for.

"You made a difference in my life," she started haltingly. "Your friendship and your prayers supported me at camp. Having the memory of that friendship helped me through the last few months. When I seemed to have lost everything, I realized I had something no one could take away, my relationship with God and His children, my brothers and sisters. Thanks, brother." She held out her hand, glad he couldn't see her eyes in the dark car. He slipped his glove off and grasped her little hand in his big one.

"You're welcome, sister…" Before he could say more, Windy quickly opened her door.

"We'd better hurry, if we want to see any of this program." She jumped out of the car and waited for him to come from his side. He surprised her by putting his arms around her and pulling her into a hug. Windy forbid her arms to encircle him, but she leaned against him, savoring the moment, knowing it would be the last. She lifted her head slightly so he could hear her. "Jenny loves you, you know," she whispered.

He kissed her forehead. "I know," he whispered back.

Chapter Fifty-Seven

He's Jimmy all over again, but with my gray eyes and he lives here. We've lived in the same city all this time and I've never seen him. Why now God? I'm trusting You. I am trusting You. Please, be with him. He's not married, not even dating so maybe he hasn't met her yet. But she's still my girl.

Scott Bradley took a room at the motel a couple blocks away, but spent all his time with Jenny. It was easy to see how they felt about each other. Windy rejoiced for them, but decided not to punish herself by being around them too much. She never again called him Brad, finding it easier to disassociate Jenny's young man from the one she had known in what seemed a lifetime ago.

Windy volunteered for all the over time available the next few days. She even managed to work part of Christmas Day, staying around the apartment just long enough to open presents that morning and returning in time for supper that evening.

"I think I can speak for everyone, Mary," Jenny said into the phone receiver. "We'd love to come. About 8 PM? Sounds good to me." She hung up and looked at the others who sat in Cora's living room. A brightly decorated tree stood near the window, the evidence of the morning's excitement cleared away.

"Mary and Andrew are having a New Year's Eve party and we're all invited," Jenny announced.

"Goodness sakes, I haven't been to a New Years Eve party in years," Cora laughed. "I don't think I can stay up that late. But you young folks go and have a wonderful time."

"A wonderful time?" Scott exclaimed. "How could we enjoy ourselves if you're not there?"

Cora blushed. "Oh, you do go on so. Jenny, I don't know about your young man. He's much too charming, you know."

"Don't I know it!" Jenny laughed, and reached over to take Scott's hand.

Windy forced herself to watch the couple, to acknowledge the look that passed between them. She recognized that look, remembering it vividly from Mary's wedding day. Her heart tore within her, in happiness for Jenny and pity for herself. Would anyone ever look at her that way?

"You night owls will have to excuse me," she said, standing. "I help open tomorrow morning, so I'm going to call it a night."

"Goodnight, Windy," Jenny said. She touched the sweater she wore. "And thank you for this beautiful gift. You sure surprised me, I never knew you were making it."

Windy studied her friend whose thick blonde hair fell over her shoulders and unto the white angora sweater. Her hazel eyes smiled into Windy's brown ones.

"You look like an angel sitting there," she smiled at her friend. "I guess because you really are one." She bent over Cora and placed a kiss on top of her head. "Merry Christmas to all and to all a goodnight," she said, slipping out of the room.

Once upstairs she climbed into bed and pulled the real Sachel close. "I love you," she whispered to the purring cat. The tears came unexpected, and she let them.

When Windy arrived home from work the next afternoon, she drug herself upstairs and into her bedroom. She'd hardly slept the night before and her eyes hurt terribly from all the crying. She just wanted to sleep.

She heard laughter and peered out the window. Scott Bradley and Jenny were involved in an aggressive snowball fight. Jenny hid behind the big tree, while Scott tried to fit his large frame behind a bush. Deciding his shelter wasn't preventing him from being pelted he moved out into the open, closing the distance to his opponent in about five steps and as many snowballs. Jenny laughed with delight every time her round white missiles hit their target. Soon

Scott reached the tree and chased Jenny from her cover. He wrestled her to the ground where he promptly washed her face with snow. Time stood still for the two players and their secret audience. Then Scott Bradley lowered his head and kissed the angel in the snow. Windy pulled back, ashamed for having spied on them. She sat on her bed and found herself wondering what Brad's kisses taste like.

"If only I hadn't been married when I met him," she mused. *If you hadn't been married, you wouldn't have met hi*m, a little voice informed her.

"And why not?" she asked.

If you hadn't been married, you wouldn't have gone to Stephan's church. If you hadn't gone to Stephan's church, you wouldn't have met Jenny. If you hadn't met Jenny, you wouldn't have gone to Costa Rica.

"Oh, shut up, who asked you anyway?" The girl kicked her shoes off striking wall. Sachel looked at his master, then curled up beside her, purring. Windy slowly moved back to the window, peeking around the curtain. Jenny and Scott Bradley stood facing each other, their hands entwined in front of them.

"I love Jenny," she told the black cat. "I love her enough to want the best for her," she moved away from the window. "And Brad's the best," she reasoned, sitting on the bed. "I also love Brad enough to want the best for him." She scratched Sachel behind the ear. "And Jenny's the best."

She sat quietly for a moment, rubbing the cat's soft fur and pondering her last words. "Why, Sachel, it makes so much sense. If you could pick one person, just one person, to love and care for Jenny, who would it be?" Sachel purred his answer. "Of course! Brad, my Brad. And if you could pick just one person to love Brad, we wouldn't settle for anyone other than Jenny, would we?" Sachel rolled over in agreement as Windy's hand rubbed his belly.

"You're right, Sachel Page," her brow furrowed as she continued to think. "When I moved into Stephan's house and left you here with Cora it wasn't because I didn't love you enough to take you with, it was because I loved you too much to sentence you to a cold garage. I would never want Jenny or Brad to settle for a cold garage, when they can share each other's warmth." The cat continued to purr his approval, allowing Windy to believe she actually made sense. The girl slipped into her nightshirt and crawled into bed where she slept soundly for the first time in months.

Although Jenny and Scott were very much in love, they weren't so engrossed with each other they didn't notice the difference that came over Windy. They both noticed a sparkle about her they had never seen before. Jenny believed her friend was coming to terms with the end of her marriage and the knowledge that she couldn't have children. But Scott believed something else had taken place.

One morning he showed up at the store. "If you have a break coming, I'd like to talk to you for a few minutes," he said.

Windy checked the clock on the front wall. "Sure," she answered. "Let's go in the break room." She led him into the deli department, through double doors, down a hall and into a small room. She pulled a couple chairs away from a cluttered table and motioned him to sit down.

Scott looked around. "Not exactly the setting I had in mind," he said as he positioned the chairs to face each other. "I'd prefer something in sand and sunshine."

Windy laughed. "So would I."

They sat and Scott held Windy's hands in his. He took a deep breath, once more questioning his judgment.

But something told him Windy needed to hear what he was about to tell her.

"Windy, for years, I dreamed of going back to my home town, knocking on Jenny's door, and asking her to be my wife. I always thought it would happen, but I had to be sure it was God's will and so I waited." He looked down at the hands he held, rubbing their softness with his thumbs.

"Something happened this past summer that caused me to doubt that dream, to seriously question where God might be leading me." He looked up into Windy's eyes and smiled, then looked down again. "You see, I met a woman. A beautiful, loving, searching woman and she became very important to me. I pulled her into my heart and found my thoughts turned upside down by her. But this woman already belonged to someone else." He looked at her again, searching her face for permission to continue. She nodded.

"When we said good-bye, I thought she was out of my life forever. But she still lived in my heart. I was relieved to get away from the camp and the memories I'd just formed there. My folks needed me, and I needed them, too. I talked for days to my dad, and found peace in his words."

He stopped and stared at the hands he held. "At least I thought I had, until last week, when I saw her again, then all the doubts came back. And the situation had changed," he laughed and shook his head. "Talk about confusing! But the words you spoke to me that first night I arrived, were a release, weren't they?"

Windy nodded slowly.

"I needed that release to bring me back on the right track, to remind me of the reason I came here." He struggled for the next words, knowing how very important they were.

"Windy, I love Jenny with all my heart, and I'm going to ask her to be my wife. I do this with no hesitation. But you need to know that you are a beautiful young woman, a woman worthy of a decent man. I don't know why your marriage ended, I don't need to. But I know if my heart didn't belong to Jenny, it would belong to you," he said those words with hesitation, not wanting to lead Windy down a road of false hopes, but needing her to understand how much he valued her. The words were true, no doubt in his mind, if he didn't have Jenny, he would give his heart to Windy. Yet, he knew the path he would take and he knew it was God's path for his life.

"I've questioned God's wisdom in bringing you to Costa Rica instead of Jenny. Seems very ironic doesn't it? But I thank Him for those weeks that belong to you and I. That special time that God gave us. He knew exactly what He was doing, just like a writer who sees the end of the story. My life is richer, fuller for having those weeks and I will treasure them just as I treasure you." He didn't really know what she had been through the last few months, what those events had done to her perception of herself.

They sat quietly for a moment, knowing words weren't always necessary to communicate, then Scott looked deep into her eyes.

"Never think less of yourself…"

"I am God's special creature," Windy interrupted. "He loves me dearly, I'm His child and I should never feel inadequate or inferior to anyone," she recited. "To allow those feelings is an insult to Him, it's like saying He can't take care of me and see to my needs. It's telling Him His grace and power are ineffective on me." Windy smiled. "A very wise and wonderful man spoke those words to me as we stood in the moonlight. I've never forgotten them, they've helped me through so much."

Scott gazed at the young woman before him, silently asking the Lord to touch her and bless her. He stood and pulled Windy into his arms, she felt so small and helpless, he wanted to keep her there and take care of her, but he knew she was safe within arms far stronger than his own.

Chapter Fifty-Eight

Mary and Andrew invited me to a New Year's Eve party tonight. Valerie and her husband will be there. Should I tell her, Father?

"Windy, I'd like you to meet Doug and Valerie," Mary introduced her to a couple slightly older than Windy's own parents. "Doug and Andrew work together." She motioned to two other ladies. "This is Connie and Margie. You know them, you've seen them at church before."

"Of course," although Windy still didn't know many people very well, Margie was the ladies Bible study leader and well-known throughout the church. She had seen the other lady several times, but didn't know her name.

"Glad to meet you," she addressed them all. Looking at the couple she continued. "I'm still fairly new in church, I'm sorry I don't remember seeing you before.

"Oh, we don't come, although I have attended a couple studies at Margie's home," Valerie explained. They spoke politely for a few minutes then Windy noticed Missy and Wil coming in. She excused herself and went to greet the couple.

"Wil," she said. "I'd really like to talk to you and Missy for a few minutes, if I could."

"Of course, Miz Mi...Windy," Wil agreed.

They found a quiet corner in Mary's living room, Wil and Missy sat on the couch while Windy pulled up a chair.

"I don't know where to start," she began. "I just know I treasure your friendship and I fear I may have lost your respect."

"Oh, now, you don't have to do any explainin to us," Wil said. "We don't poke our noses in other people's business."

"But as Christians we are accountable to each other. Wil, I can't explain everything just yet. But I need you and Missy to understand a few things. Most importantly is that I accepted Christ this past summer in Costa Rica." This brought a big smile and a "Praise the Lord" from both of her listeners.

"I'm now a new creature in Christ, the old is passed away as Paul says and I claim that promise. I wasn't seeking God's will when I met Dr. Michaels," Windy paused for a moment, surprised at how natural the formality came to her. "He attended a church then and still does, but I know that he wasn't seeking God's will either. I don't believe in divorce, I never have and yet… well, let's just say, if the doctor had wanted me to stay, I would have. I…I didn't leave, I was told to. I…" she could hardly speak; this wasn't going the way she intended.

"It's alright," Missy reached out and took her hand. "We're not judging anyone. Some things happen in life that we have no control over. Most folks look at them as good or bad, but we believers have to trust that the Good Lord is the only One who truly knows the difference."

"Thank you," Windy nodded. "Thank you." She grasped the little woman's hand and smiled into her eyes.

"There's plenty of food in the dining room," Mary stated as she passed the threesome. "Missy that homemade bread looks delicious and Windy I can't wait to taste the frozen raspberry desert you brought."

Windy held up her hands. "Cora's recipe, I just stirred it together as she was saying, 'oh, a little of this and a little of that'."

Some one began playing the piano at the other end of the room and a clear soprano voice filled in the words to the well known hymn. Soon most of the people in the house gathered round and joined in. Windy heard the door open and Jenny and Scott entered, she quickly helped them with their coats.

"Where's Hannah?" Jenny asked immediately.

"She's supposed to be sleeping, but I wonder how long she'll be able to."

"Not long, now that Aunt Jenny's here." Jenny quickly ascended the steps, leaving Scott and Windy to look after her.

"I hope you like children," Windy told him. "I think you're going to have quite a few."

Scott nodded. "One of the many things Jenny and I agree on. When you consider all the things that are important to both of us, it's obvious God really does have a plan, a wonderful plan as far as I'm concerned."

He placed his arm around Windy and they joined the crowd at the piano. Windy had to chuckle as Scott's off key voice pulled her back in time. She slipped her arm around him and gave him a little hug, sighing with contentment. She looked at the small group and felt a sense of being with family, people she shared the most wonderful common bond with, their love for Jesus Christ.

Doug and Valerie stood back, not joining in the singing. Windy guessed they were facing decisions but not quite ready to make them. She understood and knew that when the time was right they too would understand and God alone knew when that would be. She made a point of speaking to the couple and found herself quite drawn to them. She learned that Doug had taught high school economics for thirty years but enjoyed his job so much he had no intention of retiring just yet. Valerie appeared to want to talk more openly with Windy, but seemed reserved around her husband. Windy made a mental note to contact the older lady in the near future.

Windy enjoyed the evening and wished Cora had joined them. She certainly would have delighted in little Hannah's antics.

About 9:30 Windy found Mary and Andrew. She thanked them for their hospitality and admitted she had to leave.

"I have to help open again tomorrow and 6 AM sure comes early," she explained.

As she left the house she marveled at the still beauty of the night. Out here in the country, away from the noise and lights, Windy felt as though she were in a different world. The stars twinkled brightly and the moon glistened on the gently falling snow.

She easily dusted the layer of white fluff from Cora's car. It started without complaint and she pulled from the driveway onto the deserted road.

Ten minutes later, she thumped to a familiar stop.

Getting out of the car she looked at the left rear tire, tempted to laugh. She pulled the keys out of the ignition, opened the trunk and pulled out the jack.

Standing in the moonlight she remembered a night so very long ago when faced with the same situation. But tonight she wore gloves, a present from Scott Bradley, and boots, Cora's gift, and a warm winter coat, from Jenny, of course. The girl laughed and kicked at the fluffy snow.

"But best of all, Father, I have You. I have Your love and the love of Your children." She stood for several minutes enjoying the solitude, knowing she was far from alone.

Necessity soon took over and Windy managed to jack up the car without a problem. She found the tire iron and struggled with the lug nuts which came off with just enough resistance. But when she looked in the trunk again, she realized it was empty. Shaking her head, she wondered why she hadn't already noticed that.

"Well, I'm at least 5 miles from Mary's and more than that from the nearest station which would be closed anyway," she reasoned. "But, Jenny has to come along this way eventually. I might as well settle in." She returned to the running car and checked the time. 10:00. Next she checked the gas gauge and found that very encouraging. She cracked the window slightly and turned on the radio which remained on a Christian station. She listened to the soft evening music for a few minutes, but soon turned it off, enjoying the silence.

"Father, I'm about to enter a new year," she whispered. "I don't want to do that yet. I need to leave some things behind in this old one before going on. Lord, here I am, twenty-two years old. I've been divorced twice, and I've already lost my womanhood. This year, this year's been the hardest. Meeting Brad, losing Stephan, acknowledging the baby, letting go of Eddie, facing my future. Then Brad all over again."

Windy reached over and flicked the switch to the radio, unwilling to face the emotions within her.

A quiet male voice came into the car and she leaned back allowing it to sooth her.

"…with me in Isaiah 40:12. 'Who has measured the waters in the hollow of His hand, And marked off the heavens by the span…'" Windy bolted and reached for the radio wanting to hit rewind and hear that line over.

"Measured the waters in the hollow of His hand," she repeated. The enormity of that statement hit her. If God, the same God who loved and cared for her, could measure the water of this earth in His hand, He could do, why, He could do everything, anything.

"Oh, Father," the girl cried out. "I am a drop of water in the vast oceans of this earth, and You can measure them in Your hand. How very insignificant I am. My little life, with all its troubles and hurts could very well mean nothing to You. Yet, You do care. You do care. All along You've held me in the hollow of Your hand, haven't You? You've known everything about me, who I am, what I need. You've cared for and protected me all this time."

Peace flooded over the girl's heart, she finally knew the security she had sensed in her friends in Costa Rica.

"Lord, I want to be Yours and Yours alone. I want no one but you. I want nothing and no one to come between us, no one, Father. You are all I need, all I desire. There isn't a person in this world I would chose over You, no matter how secure and comforting his arms may be. I don't want those arms, Lord, I don't want them in my life, if it means losing You."

Tears streamed down her face and Windy felt the need to move, to be free to communicate with her Lord. She opened the door and stepped out into the moonlight. She walked round and round the car, still talking with her Father, the pent-up anger and frustration she'd been ignoring for months poured out of her and she lifted each thought, each burden and praise to heaven.

As Windy rounded the rear of the car, lights slowly moved around a curve behind her. She stopped, unsure whether she should flag them down for help, or hide in the car for safety. She quickly chose the latter and looked at the clock. 10:25, too early for Jenny or anyone else from Mary's party to be coming. She huddled down in the seat after locking the doors and watched her rear view mirror.

The lights pulled in behind her and the large form suggested the vehicle was a truck. Windy tried to swallow her fear, wondering what to do. *I can say my husband if off getting help, but that's lying. I'm a Christian now. Is it okay to lie under these circumstances?*

She chanced another peek in the mirror and saw a man walking toward the car, inspecting the jack. He wore a police jacket. A moment later he tapped on her window. Hesitantly, she rolled it down. "Yes, sir?" she asked.

The officer bent toward the open window. "Windy?"

"Yes," she answered. "How do you know my name?"

His face appeared in the light from his headlights.

"We've been in this situation before," he smiled beneath his mustache, gray eyes shining.

"We have?" Windy's heart raced.

"Yes, about three years ago. I changed your tire and then we arrested your husband."

"That was you?" she asked, shaking her head. "No, no, it couldn't have been, he was older…"

"My partner talked to you, I just changed the tire."

They looked at each other for a moment before the officer broke the silence. "Looks as if I have the honor again tonight, but I see you managed to get the tire off this time, where's the spare?"

Windy laughed, the awkwardness of the moment gone.

"There is none. I didn't notice til I had the other tire off." She took the key from the ignition and handed it to him then left the car to follow him to the trunk.

They looked inside and the officer pulled the lining of the trunk away to reveal an empty round hole just the size of a tire.

Windy laughed. "I didn't even know that was there."

"Guess it didn't matter," he laughed too. "Why don't you lock her up and I'll take you into town. I can't leave you sitting here." He gave the keys back to her, picked up the flat tire and threw it in his truck bed.

"I know where we can get this fixed tomorrow."

Windy started around the car and stopped. She looked at him, then at the truck. "Where's your police car?" she asked, suspiciously.

"At the station, I'm on my way in now."

Windy lingered a moment, thinking.

"Working midnights?" He nodded. She smiled and quickly locked up the car. On the way into town, Windy recounted the events of the night three years before. She told the officer about her visit to the bearded stranger's house and though he laughed, the officer looked at her with open concern. "You could have been in danger," he said, sobering.

"Believe me, I know," she smiled, remembering how God measured the waters. "But I was in good hands."

The officer pulled up in front of Cora's house and shut off his lights. "Would you like me to walk up with you?" he offered.

She glanced at the dash looking for a clock but saw none. "No, you must be late already," she reached for the door handle. "Do you need a note for being tardy?"

"Not necessary. Listen, I get off at seven, I'll get your tire fixed then swing by and pick you up."

"I work tomorrow, starting at seven."

"How will you get there?"

"My friend will take me."

"What time do you get off?"

327

"Noon, it's a short shift because of the holidays."

"Yeah, that's why I'm working midnights tonight. I usually work afternoons. I'll pick you up at twelve at the store, then."

"It's not too much of a bother?"

"Not at all."

"Thanks." Windy pushed the door open and placed a boot in the snow. She stopped. "How did you know where I live?"

"I have a good memory."

She thought for a minute, recalling that other night. "Oh, yes, you did follow me home didn't you?"

He nodded. "Yes, we did."

Windy moved away and closed the door but quickly reopened it. "Just one more thing?"

"Just one?" he smiled and in the light of the truck Windy took a moment to study his features, lingering on his gray eyes.

"What is your name?"

He laughed and reached out a strong hand to her.

"Rick Notts."

She accepted the hand, "Glad to meet you, Rick Notts, I'm Windy Jordan."

"I know." His hand squeezed hers ever so gently before letting go. "Goodnight, Windy Jordan. I hope you have a wonderful new year."